HIDDEN HUMANITY

A Trafficking Rescue Novel

Book One of the *Never Lost Series*

D.I. Telbat

In Season Publications
USA

Publisher's Note: This is a work of fiction. Names, characters, places, and incidents are a product of the author's imagination. Locales and public names are sometimes used for atmospheric purposes. Any resemblance to actual people, living or dead, or to ministries, businesses, companies, events, institutions, or locales is completely coincidental.

Printed in the United States of America

HIDDEN HUMANITY: A Trafficking Rescue Novel
/ D.I. Telbat -- 1st ed.
Categories: Christian Suspense;
Contemporary Christian Fiction

D.I. Telbat / In Season Publications
https://ditelbat.com
https://books2read.com/DITelbat

ISBN 978-1-7371777-2-2

Cover Design by 100Covers

DEDICATION

For those who are taken captive
but are never lost from God's sight.

ACKNOWLEDGEMENTS

This book wasn't in my sights until Patrick Klein of Vision Beyond Borders (VBB website) suggested I write a book (or series) with a fresh voice exposing human trafficking to the Christian church. I thank him for his initial shared intel and experience, which set me to task. Thanks also to Dee for her willingness to tackle yet another series that encourages God's people to live like Christ. And thanks to our local proofreader, Sharon, and several helpful Beta Readers who have given invaluable time and help proofreading and advising in the final stages of this project. We are humbled by your willing assistance to make this the best book possible.

CHARACTER SKETCH

Aidan Nevins – At the age of 8, he was sold by his parents to human traffickers. His sister is Marcy.

Binsa – After losing her six-year-old daughter to human traffickers, she came to Christ and joined TROAS to minister to women and children recovered from traffickers.

Brody Sladrick – As one of COIL's most experienced agents, and now as a trafficking retrieval expert, he recovers trafficked children from anywhere in the world. His TROAS headquarters are in Tampa, Florida, where he has teamed up with Greg Rotz and Binsa.

Cole Nevins – This father of Marcy and Aidan sold his children for drug money and to break into the GLOW trafficking ring. His wife is Emma.

Elliot Madison – This mouthy New York senator hides in a bunker while employing Sladrick to make him look good for his constituents.

Emma Nevins – This mother of Marcy and Aidan sold her children for her drug addiction. Her husband is Cole.

Jerome Wessel – As an agent for Homeland Security, this zealous ex-Marine hunts human traffickers from his office in Davenport, Iowa.

Marcy Nevins – At the age of 13, she was sold by her parents to human traffickers. Her brother is Aidan.

Preeda and Arthit Somdet – This husband-and-wife team exploit children in Bangkok, Thailand.

Pug "PJ" Johnson – This sizeable, cruel man runs security for the trafficking ring in Davenport, Iowa.

Tory and Trey Dosier – This husband-&-wife team traffic young children all over the world for GLOW from their mansion headquarters in Davenport, IA. Tory's brother is Pug Johnson.

Zayed Aziz – Once a physician in Saudi Arabia, his connection to the royal family was severed by scandal, then he became a human trafficker of Middle Eastern families, based in the Carolinas.

GLOSSARY

COIL: Commission of International Laborers, a Christian rescue organization; first appeared in *Dark Liaison: A Christian Suspense Novel,* Book One of *The COIL Series.*

GLOW: Abbreviation for "Global Wares," this fictional network of human traffickers boasts in its secure smuggling rings in every community around the world. Its leader is called the Executive.

TROAS: This fictional recovery and assistance ministry stands for "Trafficking Recovery Operative Assistance Services." Its leader is Brody Sladrick, assisted extensively by Binsa and Greg Rotz.

"When the world has gone crazy and is only concerned about themselves and their causes, the weak and vulnerable suffer the most, and these are the ones Jesus sent us to minister to."
Patrick Klein, Founder & Director of Vision Beyond Borders
~

*"But go and learn what this means:
'I desire compassion, and not sacrifice,'
for I did not come to call the righteous,
but sinners."* Matthew 9:13 (NASB)

OTHER BOOKS BY D.I. TELBAT

The COIL Series: Christian Suspense

The COIL Legacy Series: Christian Suspense

COIL Legacy Collection: 3 Books in 1 Volume

The Resolution Series: America's Last Days

The STEADFAST Series: America's Last Days

STEADFAST Collection: 6 Novellas in 1 Volume

Last Dawn Series: America's Last Days

Leeward Set: Where Christians Dare

Never Lost Series: Trafficking Rescue Novels

~

Arabian Variable

Called To Gobi

God's Colonel

Soldier of Hope

Short Story Collections

~

Coming Soon

Shadow Slave: Never Lost Series; Book 2

Visions of Hope: A Short Story Collection; Book 3

A NOTE FROM THE AUTHOR

Dear Friends,

This novel with human trafficking as the backdrop has been one of the more challenging books I have written. It was challenging for one specific reason, and I wish to explain that reason as a warning to the reader. Human trafficking is a graphic subject by its very nature. As a Christian writer, I have prayed daily about portraying the source of the problem while also revealing the solution for God's people to offer their love, compassion, and grace to those trafficked as well as to the traffickers.

This book contains graphic subjects in fictional form to inform readers, beginning with the first chapter, but we have endeavored to limit graphic content and details. Within all of my novels, we have sought to hold a high standard of "clean Christian fiction" in regard to violence, vulgarity, and sexual content.

All of mankind's sinful indulgences are involved in human trafficking, yet it's not normally confronted by the Body of Christ in a confident and caring way. We hope this book gives both insight and encouragement for God's people to respond in a Christlike manner.

Within this novel, **I have chosen six sample locations to reveal the human trafficking trade**— three cities in the U.S. and three foreign cities. I could have chosen any town in America since there is actually no town, city, state, or country free from human trafficking these days.

Human trafficking is now everywhere. I believe we would be hard-pressed to find a single neighborhood in the U.S. that isn't plagued by the indulgence in some form of trafficking and exploitation—including the viewing of pornography that exploits trafficked women and/or underage children.

Survivors who emerge from trafficking may require much time and attention to recover. Everyone is different and the church must exercise love and Bible-based care to address a variety of needs. I am aware that some individuals need medication for existing psychological conditions, yet I have intentionally presented in this book the sufficiency of God's Word to lift up the believer in life and godliness through any circumstance (2 Peter 1:3).

My sources for writing this book varied from UN programs, secular U.S. watch groups, international ministries, and U.S. Christian outreaches. Through my work with inmates in state prisons, I have spoken with men who had trafficked women and children, as well as with young men who were trafficked in their youth. Their candid conversations have influenced some of what is contained in this book.

A few of the following organizations provided statistics or other information on human trafficking, either for domestic workers or the sex industry, or both:

Vision Beyond Borders (visionbeyondborders.org) is a U.S.-based ministry that supports teams who deliver Bibles and supplies to many restricted countries, as well as supports efforts to bring trafficked women and children into safe environments. Their regular reports of courage for Christ around the world have been the main inspiration behind the writing of this book. Specifically, their work with women and children in Nepal inspired an entire chapter within *Hidden Humanity*.

Restoring Hope Nepal (restoringhopenepal.org) is a U.S.-based ministry that focuses on meeting the needs of families in Nepal to protect women and girls from traffickers.

Voice of the Martyrs (persecution.com) is a worldwide ministry that delivers Bibles to closed countries, supports believers in hostile areas, and reports on persecuted and trafficked people wherever they are found.

Polaris (polarisproject.org) has exceptional material and resources to help fight domestic trafficking. They assist civilians with awareness information to report trafficking as they travel cross country.

Truckers Against Trafficking works to disrupt trafficking and assist law enforcement nationwide (truckersagainsttrafficking.org).

The U.S. Department of Homeland Security employs agents around the world to fight human trafficking, often using **ICE** offices and foreign law enforcement partners to target traffickers.

In my research, I also came upon several Special Forces groups that take it upon themselves to use their contacts and experience to infiltrate countries and organizations to recover children and bring traffickers to justice. One of these is **Phantom Rescue** (phantomrescue.org) who describe themselves as "an elite group of former Law Enforcement, FBI, State Department, U.S. Special Operations, and Business Professionals who have united with one clear objective—to eradicate child trafficking through education, outreach and by assisting authorities with identifying the Global Sex Trafficking Industry Network."

Global Wares, or GLOW, is a **fictional trafficking network** I designed for this book. Although GLOW is fictional, its activities, practices, and agendas embody actual smuggling rings and trafficking networks worldwide. As this book portrays from chapter one, trafficking children is carefully scripted from the purchase of children, to the transportation of the abducted, to the exploitation of them.

Trafficking Recovery Operative Assistance Services, or TROAS, is another **fictional organization** I developed for this novel to embody a Christian recovery and assistance ministry. Their gospel-minded approach to confront traffickers and assist in the mental and emotional recovery of survivors leaves **a biblical example for us to follow**.

For those who have read my *COIL* novels, this ***Never Lost Series* can be read independently** from those and other D.I. Telbat books, but this book **does indeed fit into the *COIL* timeline**. This series features Brody Sladrick, the retrieval expert, and takes place three years after the *****Believers' Boot Camp* novella** (where we first meet Brody), and immediately follows the three ***COIL Legacy* novels**, specifically *Distant Harm*, and **precedes** the *Last Dawn Series* by twenty years.

Although some trafficking statistics are sprinkled throughout this novel, one of the above organizations (Phantom Rescue), which works closely with U.S. Justice Dept. offers following numbers for awareness purposes:

- Human trafficking is a $32 billion a year industry
- 27 mil. people are affected by human trafficking
- One million children are exploited by the international sex trade
- There are more than 300 thousand underage girls being sold for sex in America
- One out of 5 pornographic images is of a child
- Over 100K websites offer child pornography
- The average age of entry into coerced prostitution is 12-14 years old
- 70% of female victims are trafficked into sex trade
- On average, sex trafficking victims are sold 10-15 times a day

At the back of this book, we've included ideas for you to pray and intercede personally for those harmed by human trafficking. And remember: ***God never loses those who are His!***

David Telbat

*****Believers' Boot Camp*—one of the three novellas offered for **FREE in the *Three For Free*** gift to all who subscribe to the biweekly D.I. Telbat Newsletter.

PROLOGUE

Wendy Oliver stood in the doorway of the nursery that she'd decorated herself. The walls were blue, and a dozen stuffed kangaroos sat in the corner. The stuffed animals would be enjoyed by any toddler.

But there was no baby—no crying infant to wake her and Jax in the middle of the night, no squealing child to cause them to rejoice in the family God had given them.

It had been a month since their baby boy had been stolen from the Tennessee hospital maternity ward. Wendy had cried for days. Now, she just stared at the empty nursery and wondered if she'd ever feel anything again.

Though Jax was only twenty-four, a year older than she, he'd been a pillar of faith and comfort for her. She almost felt guilty admitting that the kidnapping had actually brought the young couple closer together.

The detectives had no leads, but Jax reminded her constantly that God was with their little baby. In the evenings, Jax imagined aloud how God would still guide their stolen child as he grew into boyhood and then became a man in another land. They'd done their own research on black-market babies. Their little Joey was long gone by now, probably overseas.

Jax was a manager in the plant at the edge of the city. As a supervisor, he'd had the authority to race home occasionally when Wendy had called him, her voice too broken to speak. But she'd stopped begging him to come home from work, finally resigning herself to the loss. Somehow, God had purposed this terrible act by sinful people for something good someday, but she couldn't yet imagine what that something could be.

There was a knock on the front door. Or maybe it was just Jax doing yard work out front. It had been weeks since she'd cleaned the house or he'd worked on the yard. But today was that day, like a passage from their valley-of-despair to the road-of-repair. And it would be a long road.

Sighing, Wendy turned from the nursery. She couldn't pack up the things in Joey's room yet. Maybe tomorrow. Or maybe Jax would do it for her. He had wept as much as she had, but he was stronger.

In the kitchen, she leaned over the sink to see outside. Jax was raking the side yard next to the neighbor's fence. Then who had knocked on the front door? She tapped on the window and he looked up.

"Front door," she called through the glass, pointing toward the front of the house. "Someone's here."

He leaned the rake against the side of the house, and Wendy walked across the living room carpet to meet him at the front door. She peeked through the peep hole but saw no one. When she opened the door, she found Jax kneeling over a baby car seat.

Wendy nearly fainted at the sight of a tiny sleeping baby swaddled in blankets, tucked into the car seat on their doorstep. She knelt with Jax to draw the baby blankets away from the infant's chin.

"Jax?" Wendy trembled. "*Jax?*"

Standing, Jax walked up the yard path and searched the street left and right. There was no traffic and no sign of any visitors. He returned, his hands on his hips.

"It's somebody's idea to console us," Jax said. "Wendy, this is someone's baby. We can't take someone else's baby just because ours was taken."

"Jax, *it's Joey!* Look!"

He knelt again and glanced from the baby to her face.

"I don't . . . know. I know we want it to be him. But I don't see how it could be. We need to call the police."

"No, it's Joey! I know it is. A mother knows."

"Oh, Wendy . . ." Covering his mouth with his hand, he shook his head at her. "He's about the same age as Joey would be, but I think . . . Joey's gone, sweetie. This is just so . . ."

Wendy was about to answer when Jax plucked at the corner of a piece of paper at the foot of the car seat. He felt under the baby's feet and lifted him a little to draw out a small envelope. On the front were three words: *"Wendy and Jax"*.

"Open it!" Wendy gasped. "Read it."

His fingers fumbled as he opened the envelope.

"It says, 'Found Joey outside Wenzhou, China. Had to check his DNA to confirm his identity. That took a few days, but we took good care of him. Joey's been on an adventure, but he seems healthy. Praise God. Your servant, *S*.'"

"*S*?" Wendy accepted the letter from Jax. "That's all it says? It's Joey, for real?"

"Whoever *S* is." Jax slid his hand under the baby to pick him up. The baby grunted, his eyes wide at being startled from his sleep. "Hey, little Joey. Here's your mama."

"Jax, *is this real?*" Wendy took the baby and held him close. "Has God really brought our baby back to us? *Jax?*"

Her husband staggered onto the lawn where he collapsed to his knees. His shoulders shook as he wept silently, his hands clasped in front of him and his face turned to the heavens.

Wendy closed her eyes. *China?* Joey was already a world traveler. *Their baby was back!* She felt sure they'd never meet this *S* person. He or she obviously didn't want to be known. But like them, this *S* seemed to understand that God alone was to be thanked for all things.

"Thank You, Lord, for this gift," Wendy whispered over her son as her tears wet his face. "You've given me Joey twice. Protect this *S*, whoever or wherever he or she is. They are obviously Your servant. *Thank You, Lord.*"

CHAPTER ONE

Marcy Nevins remembered the night her parents sold her. It had been a cold night in Davenport, Iowa, midway through her second year of junior high school. She'd been looking forward to starting high school the next year, her outlook on life full of anticipation, regardless of the chaos within her family home.

"Get your shoes on," her father said as he tossed her coat onto her bed. "We're going out. Leave your phone."

She looked up from her tablet screen. He reminded her more of the junkies behind the school gym than a father of two growing kids. Under his sleeves, he hid the sores from infected needle marks. For as long as Marcy could remember, he'd had sores on his arms, some of them healing on one arm while he used the other for his injections.

"Dad, I can't go anywhere." She spoke with the patient pity of an adult rather than as a child of thirteen. "I have homework."

"I said we're going out!" He wiped his runny nose on his sleeve, dragging strands of his long hair across his cheek where it stuck. "Your brother's already in the car."

He turned and left her room before she could argue. It wasn't really her bedroom. A couple years earlier, she'd taken it upon herself to nail up a pair of green army blankets to separate her bed from her brother's bed. Aidan had objected at first, since he felt cut off from his childhood playmate, but as Marcy matured, he'd found comfort in his video games in the noisy living room where he now spent most of his time.

"Going out?" Marcy set her tablet aside and tugged on her tennis shoes. "Going where?"

It was almost nine o'clock at night and freezing outside. There was nowhere to go. Her parents never took her or Aidan to their drug connections in the city. They never went out to eat anymore as a family, either. Marcy could remember only one occasion when they'd gone out bowling, though Aidan was too young to remember that night.

Using a cracked mirror with a plastic frame, Marcy bound her dark hair in a ponytail and widened her eyes to stretch the skin above her cheeks. The shadowy circles under her eyes never seemed to go away. Aidan had them, too, so she guessed they were hereditary. But she wasn't about to wear makeup, not like the tramps at school—and definitely not like her mother. Of course, her mother wore makeup to cover up the bruises most days, but it was still too much.

"It's so late," Marcy complained as she approached the front door, held open by her father.

"Don't talk back." He slapped her on the back of the head, not hard enough to make her stumble outside, but it still hurt.

She was just glad he never punched her like he did their mother, but half the time, she knew he beat her because the woman wouldn't stop screaming or breaking things. Again, Marcy felt pity when she thought of her mother. Her health had deteriorated the past year. Marcy guessed it was something in the drugs, or maybe it was because the poor woman rarely ate a real meal.

Outside, her mother stomped her feet and wrapped her coat around her slim midsection. The porch light had been fixed, so Marcy saw her mother try to smile.

"Ready for some fun?" The woman moved aside and pulled the front seat forward.

"Where are we going?" Marcy climbed into the back seat where eight-year-old Aidan immediately grasped her hand. "Isn't it kind of late?"

"Just do what you're told, Mars."

Her parents climbed into the front seat and started the car. Snowflakes floated across the windshield.

"I'm freezing, Dad." Marcy felt Aidan's small frame quiver next to her. "Can you turn on the heat? Addy's hands are freezing. How long has he been out here?"

No one answered her as the car crept down the dark street. Her father drifted into the opposite lane. Marcy expected her mother to criticize him, but instead, she only stared silently out her own window.

In fact, Marcy couldn't remember such silence, not from her family. Crying or yelling, loud music, and Aidan's video games usually defined the atmosphere of the Nevin household. Marcy's escape from harassment at school and the noise at home came only on Sunday mornings when she walked Aidan to the small chapel at the end of the street. The church lady who taught the older kids offered some distraction with her stories, but usually, Marcy's mind was consumed by what she would return to at home.

Resting her head on the back of the seat, Marcy appreciated the silence for however long it lasted. The next day was Thursday. Math test on Friday. Sunday school on Sunday. She still needed to read that online paper about Alexander the Great and type up her five-page report for history class. Tomorrow, after school, she needed to get groceries for her and Aidan. They couldn't afford milk, but Aidan didn't mind eating dry cereal for breakfast and bagels with strawberry jam for dinners. The school provided lunches, though they'd warned that next year that would cease due to lack of funding. Sometimes, the discount store on the corner had lunch meat packages in Marcy's price range. On those nights, she cooked Ramen soups with bits of meat sliced up—a real banquet!

Aidan shifted next to her, dragging his backpack onto her lap since the thing was wrapped over one arm.

"Why do you have your backpack?" She felt the exterior of the pack. "You have clothes in here?"

"Dad said to get pants and shirts for a trip."

Marcy noticed her dad glance at her mother, communicating without speaking. No, this was all wrong. Everything was off.

"Where are we going?"

Leaning forward over the front seat, Marcy heard the demand and accusation in her voice, so she wasn't surprised when her mother threw her arm back at her. But in the darkness, Marcy didn't immediately flinch away. Her mother's elbow smashed solidly against Marcy's front teeth, mashing her upper lip into an instant bleeder.

"It's your own fault!" her mother yelled, half-turned. "How many times have I told you I hate it when you breathe down my neck like that?"

Marcy scrambled to control the bleeding. *No, no, no—* her mind screamed. Not this blouse! She had only three outfits for school. With blood staining this one, she was down to two. From the car floor, she found fast-food trash and held it against her lip. Tears streamed. Her gums hurt more than her swelling lip. Gingerly, she used her tongue to feel her front teeth, expecting to find jagged breaks. However, only the left front tooth was loose. Loose was tolerable, as long as it didn't fall out. Her school photo would look atrocious if she was missing a front tooth!

"You okay, Marcy?" Aidan patted her shoulder.

"Hmm," she responded, not trusting her lip to speak with blood in her mouth. Of course, she wasn't okay. Nothing about the night was right. If they were going on a trip, why hadn't she been told to pack a bag, too? She'd only been told to leave her phone behind.

The car pulled up to a curb in front of a tall house with bright lights. Marcy didn't recall ever being there before. Maybe a drug connection?

"Come on." Her father climbed out, then leaned back in to glare at his wife. "I said get out!"

"I'm not going!" her mother spat. "You take them. Make sure you get it all."

Hesitating, her father then forced his seat forward.

"Come on, kids. Out."

Aidan dragged his backpack with him as he exited, and Marcy squeezed through the gap. She'd always been thin, a fortunate characteristic in her family since she didn't need much to eat.

"Come on." Her father slammed the car door.

He led the way up a walkway to the house. With the hand not holding her mouth, Marcy touched some sort of bushes near the porch. But they didn't smell real. Surely, only rich people could afford such plastic yard ornaments!

Her father knocked on the front door. In the porch lights, Marcy noticed the house was made of red brick—a mansion! It had white window frames and stood three stories tall. They must've really been wealthy to keep all their lights on this late at night.

The front door opened. Marcy had never seen a larger man. He was dark-skinned with short-trimmed hair. His brown eyes revealed boredom, and it was hard to tell if his lips were curled in a smile or a snarl.

"Here they are, PJ." Marcy's father grabbed her shoulder and forced her through the door, crowding into Aidan and the big man. "You got it all?"

Marcy darted to the left inside the foyer and backed up against the wall with Aidan in one arm. Her other hand still held her lip.

A Hispanic woman with beautiful flowing hair and a flowery skirt approached the door. Strolling close behind her was a light-skinned man, his shoulders wide in a silk shirt. Marcy noticed gold rings on both his hands.

"Let's have a look at your little creatures," said the rich man as he pinched Aidan's cheek, forcing his chin up. "You said they were both young, Cole. He's young enough, but she's no nine-year-old!"

"How old are you, sweetie?" the woman asked.

"Firteen," Marcy mumbled carefully through her mangled mouth, afraid to lose her front tooth altogether if she spoke too much.

"She's small for her age." Marcy's father scratched at his sleeved arms. "Dress her up right, nobody'll care. So, are we in or what?"

"Thirteen's too old, Cole!" The rich man's voice raised with authority, and with it, the big door man looked over Marcy's father. "I've told you before: there's a window of opportunity in every child's life. She's no child. What'd you do to her face, beat her?"

"Let me see, sweetie." The woman gently took Marcy's hand and inspected her mouth. "Trey, look. He messed up her mouth. She's a tragedy."

"Cole, this isn't what we agreed to." The man called Trey crossed his arms. "The boy—fine. The girl—messed up mouth or not, the people we work with aren't going to want her. She's maturing. She's not even . . . cute. What's with the black eyes? No, our clients won't be into this. I can't sell ugly. If you're going to work with us, you need to learn these things."

"We need ten for each," her father pressed. He didn't seem too confident in the shadow of the big man. "Trey, please. They're our kids. Ten apiece. There's no paper trail. We'll do better with the others, I promise."

The rich man looked to his wife.

"She's skinny. Won't eat much." The woman studied Marcy's figure. "GLOW might have someone in Asia looking for a young white wife, if we want to bother with a transport, but it'll cost us."

"It'll have to be someone who doesn't care about her looks." The rich man nodded his head at his door man. "Give it to him—if it gets his sniveling carcass off my doorstep."

Suddenly, another figure skulked up to the door. It was Marcy's mother. Marcy recognized the craving in the woman's face. She was hurting and wouldn't even look at her own children.

The big man offered a debit card to her father. He

snatched it away and turned, his shoulders curled like a vulture's wings.

"Is it all there?" her mother asked him as they hustled away on the walkway. "Did we get it?"

The door slammed, cutting off Marcy's view of her departing parents. Her eyes shifted to stare back at the three adults.

"Do you like to be hit?" the rich man asked. "Either of you?"

Marcy and Aidan both shook their heads.

"Then you do exactly as you're told. Otherwise, PJ here will introduce you to pain and misery you can't imagine. Understand?"

Both children nodded while eyeing the big man at the door. He glared at Marcy. It seemed like hatred, like the girls at school who laughed at her clothes. But how could this man hate her so much if they'd never met before?

"PJ, take her to the side room," the woman said, then caressed Aidan's arm. "I want to get this precious one in front of a camera before midnight."

"No, my brother and I stay—" Marcy began, even forgetting her mouth.

But PJ's enormous hand suddenly clenched around her throat. An instant later, the back of her head slammed against the foyer wall. Her feet dangled off the ground from where he held her. She couldn't breathe! Her vision faded.

PJ released her and she fell to the floor, gasping.

"She bled on me!" PJ cursed and wiped his hand on his pants.

"Probably won't be the last time," the woman said, then guided Aidan toward a hallway. "Come on, sweet boy. I have some outfits I'd like you to try on. Have you eaten? Do you like pizza? How about chocolate milk?"

Marcy panted and drew her knees under her. Fury boiled inside. It wasn't wrath aimed at her new hosts, not entirely, but at her situation. She couldn't protest. There was nowhere else to go. *Her parents had sold them!*

"This one's going to be trouble, Trey," PJ said, his feet planted wide apart. "You can see it in her eyes."

"Yeah." Trey waved his gold-covered fingers. "Just put her away and clean up this blood. I'll make some calls tomorrow. See if we can ship her out right away."

PJ reached for her. Marcy scrambled aside and swatted at his hand. But his fingers found her hair where her ponytail had loosened. Her mouth opened to scream, but no noise escaped as he dragged her clawing into another room. As she saw carpet and expensive furniture, she reached for a desk leg, a chair, a doorknob—anything to halt this monster. She needed to go get Aidan, then go and scream some sense into her parents!

Down a long hallway, PJ stopped at a wooden door and threw back a heavy latch. He hurled her inside like she was a toy. She landed on the floor, bruising her shoulder, and rolled over to charge him, determined to overcome his brute strength by her nails and teeth if she had to. But he slammed the door, leaving her alone under an orangish ceiling light.

Holding her mouth and limping, she inspected the room. The room had a wooden bureau, a bed with a bare mattress, and a bathroom with a tub, sink, and toilet. The door to the bathroom was a blanket nailed up high, not unlike the one she'd fashioned to separate her side of the room from Aidan's.

In the bathroom, she found no mirror under another orangish light high on the ceiling. She washed her lip and chin in cold water and inspected her stained blouse front. It was a total loss. Now, she was down to only two outfits. No, wait. *No* outfits. She had nothing else. What would her parents do with her room now? What about her report due on Friday?

She cried against the sink, then wandered into the bedroom and crawled onto the bare mattress. It smelled bad, but all she wanted to do was sleep, to vanish from this nightmare.

In the morning, she woke to light pouring in through a fogged plastic window. Sunlight came in, but she couldn't see out. She tied her hair up into a ponytail and straightened her clothes. It was Thursday. Yesterday was past. Today had to be better.

The door latch clanged loudly. PJ opened the door only a foot, his frame filling the gap. His bored eyes glared at her a moment, then he set a microwave meal on the floor. When he closed the door, Marcy waited a few seconds. That was it? No instructions? Weren't they taking her somewhere else? Aidan was probably scared. All he knew in life was his video games. He hardly paid attention in school. All of this was probably terrifying to him.

Marcy retrieved the tray, which included a plastic fork and a triangle of sausage, eggs, and hashbrowns.

"Whoa!" Marcy hadn't seen such a feast except on TV. She tore off the plastic cover, feeling the hot meal on her lap, realizing the household must've had a microwave that actually worked. Starting with the eggs, she ate slowly, careful with her front tooth. Maybe this place wasn't so bad, if Aidan was getting fed well, too.

No, she caught herself. These were bad people. At school, she'd seen videos about those who sold other people, even cutting some individuals into pieces to sell their organs to the rich. She didn't want to be cut into pieces. But maybe she was too ugly for anything else. The man named Trey hadn't seemed to know what to do with her, but they obviously had plans for Aidan. Sick plans. *Perverts.*

After licking her tray clean, Marcy set it by the door. PJ was the worst person she'd ever met, though she'd only seen him twice. But whatever she could do to keep him from being violent, she had to do it. She had to survive.

For Aidan. Poor Addy. A big sister was supposed to protect her baby brother better than this!

She slurped water from the bathroom faucet and wandered around her small room, lost in thoughts of possibilities and nightmares. Aidan was being mistreated somehow, and she might become someone's wife? It didn't seem like she was old enough, but maybe in strange parts of the world, that was allowed.

Around noon, PJ brought another tray. Marcy stood politely by the window as he retrieved the last tray, studied her a moment, then left.

Lasagna this time, and vegetables Marcy had never seen before. A biscuit that needed no butter since it was already sweet. At least the food was better than the dry cereal and Ramen noodles with bagels. Maybe Addy was enjoying that part, too, even with whatever else was happening. She refused to imagine what that could be.

The microwave dinner that night was meatballs and rice with more vegetables. Marcy stood across the room again as PJ set it on the floor.

"Excuse me," Marcy said in her most grown-up voice, the way she spoke to store clerks or school administrators. "May I have some sheets and a toothbrush?"

He surveyed the room, the mattress, even the walls, then closed the door. A few moments later, after Marcy started on her meal, PJ returned. He dumped a pillow, sheets, and toiletries on the floor.

"I've asked Trey," he said, his voice husky. "If they can't find anyone to take you, I get you."

"What?" Marcy's jaw trembled, her fat lip throbbing.

"You don't want anyone else. Ol' PJ'll treat you real nice." As he laughed, he closed the door. "Real nice!"

Marcy felt sick. The rich food suddenly didn't appeal to her that night. She set it aside and sat in the bathroom on the edge of the tub. At least she could be alone in there. Please, not PJ! It seemed so wrong. There were boys at school that Marcy had once had crushes on, but they were just junior high school students. PJ was forty or fifty!

Maybe she wasn't ugly enough. Could she make herself uglier, so no one, not even PJ, would want her? She contemplated using the plastic fork to hurt herself, maybe gouge at her face, create sores on her arms. That would be gross. No one would want to touch her then.

The days slipped by. With every meal he brought, PJ left her gifts—a blanket, a book about dirty things adults did, and a coloring book—though she was far past the age for coloring books. With every visit, however brief, PJ told her crude things he wanted to do to her. He never did them, but he kept talking about them, then laughed and left. Marcy decided if he ever did try those things, she'd fight back. Maybe he'd beat her. Maybe starve her. But she wasn't going to allow him to gratify himself. Though she feared him, her helplessness made her brave. At night, she practiced punching her pillow and digging her fingernails into the mattress. If necessary, she'd do the same to PJ.

The day came, about two weeks later, when PJ slipped inside the room and brought no food tray or gift at all. The look on his face was pure craze. Marcy darted from her mattress toward the bathroom, but he intercepted her and carried her kicking and fighting back to the mattress.

"You're mine," he said over and over. "Nobody wants you."

Marcy fought just like she'd practiced. She kicked and spit and punched until he threw her against the wall, cracking even the window. On the edge of consciousness, she watched him strip her bed bare, then take everything he'd brought her—even the toothbrush and toilet paper.

Lying there on the floor, sore and bleeding, yet finally alone, she wondered if she'd won or lost. Something hurt so bad in her chest that it pained her to breathe. Her lip had healed from her mother's elbow, but now it bled again, and her skull had a lump on it from hitting the window.

"Nobody wants me." She closed her eyes, drifting in

and out of sleep, celebrating, and smiling. "Nobody wants me."

Days and weeks passed. PJ tried the same routine of gifts mixed with wicked threats. Marcy knew what was coming. She accepted the gifts to accommodate her life, but secretly rehearsed ways to defend herself. She wouldn't win, but she also knew she couldn't give in. For herself, for Addy, maybe even for her parents, she couldn't give up.

PJ's advances continued, which ended each time with Marcy unconscious, or nearly unconscious, on the floor, bleeding, battered, and bruised, but not broken. Once, she'd clawed his face so badly that he'd fled the room screaming. The next day, she'd seen him with bandages, but he seemed no less determined to make her a willing participant as much as she was determined to resist.

During the aftermath of one attack, after he'd swept her room bare of everything again, Marcy ran herself a hot bath and let her wounds soak in the warm water.

Water . . . Water . . . She remembered a story about water. And people being rescued in a boat. Rescue. Yes, the first time the smiling people from down the street had invited her and Aidan to Sunday school years earlier, there'd been a story about water. "A flood came," the lady teacher had explained, "and swish—washed away all the wicked and violent people. But God saved the faithful, good people in the ark. See the picture of the boat here? God rescued this man and his family. His name was—"

Marcy couldn't remember the man's name. She couldn't exactly remember the drawing of the boat, either, but it seemed like it was a box with a roof. And hadn't there been a cross on top of the roof? A boat with a cross. God rescues. A flood was coming. Or maybe the flood already happened, Marcy considered. Either way, she needed one of those boats—an ark. Maybe God would save her from just one wicked man since He'd saved that man and his whole family from a lot of wicked men. It was reasonable. Though she'd never prayed before, it seemed like something to pray about. She saw nothing else to bring change to her situation with PJ.

The next time PJ gave her the crayons for the coloring book, she instead selected a patch of wall behind the door where she drew the blue surface of water. Then, from what she remembered from the church lady's story, she drew a big, box-shaped boat. On top of the roof of the boat, she drew an enormous cross. The only crosses Marcy had seen had been on the roof of churches, but this cross seemed to belong on this boat, like the two were connected somehow.

Weeks and months passed of attacks, fighting, and beatings. Sometimes, PJ starved her for a week after she fought him off, and all she had to take in was water from the bathroom. Fear gripped her during those days—afraid that she'd ask PJ for food and succumb to his advances. Of course, he could overpower her without even using both hands, but it seemed he wanted more than her body. He wanted her mind, her spirit. Through the hardest days, sometimes she would lay hungry and battered on the bare mattress, staring at the boat and its cross. Whatever it meant about God, she knew it was important. God had rescued people once from the water. He could rescue her before she drowned. God was good like that, she hoped.

Then one day, PJ didn't bring her the cardboard food tray. Instead, it was the woman in the flowery skirt. Her nose was a little big, but with her dark, flowing curls, and full, red lips—she seemed beautiful to Marcy.

"Are you tired of PJ?" she asked, the tray of food in her hand.

"What?" Marcy stood against the cracked window. She hadn't eaten in two days. He'd taken even her toothbrush again.

"I asked, are you tired of PJ? Have you had enough?"

"Yeah, I don't want . . ." She cleared her throat. "I don't want him coming in here anymore."

"Don't worry. He's got himself a new toy now. Eat, then come find me. I'll get you started on your chores. You hear me, sweetie?"

"Chores?"

"Yeah, living here isn't free, honey. If you're not earning your keep one way, you'll earn it another."

"Where's my brother?"

"Oh, he's long gone, sweetie. Months ago. To someplace exotic, better than Iowa, I promise you that!"

She guffawed. Marcy accepted the tray, and the lady walked down the hall, leaving the door open. *Unlocked!* Marcy tore open the plastic on the dinner tray and started shoveling food into her mouth—chicken, potatoes, peas. If she were going to escape, she'd need food in her belly.

Walking as she ate, she retraced the way PJ had dragged her that first night. Up the hallway, across the carpeted room with fancy furniture, and then to the foyer. The front door was padlocked, but Marcy wasn't daunted. At least she'd found the front door. They couldn't keep it locked all the time. God had rescued her from PJ. He would rescue her from the rest of the horrors in this terrible house.

On her way back to her room, she came upon a box against the wall. It contained all the things PJ had ever given her and taken away over and over again. She checked both ends of the hallway, set her tray on the items, and picked up the box. In her room she closed the door softly, certain that the outside latch needed to be manually placed and couldn't lock automatically. Then she emptied the box of everything she wanted, leaving behind only the crude toys and books PJ had used to try to draw her in.

The house was monstrous, but she found the kitchen at the end of the next hallway toward the back. The woman stood against the counter, her phone in her hand.

"I'm here," Marcy announced.

"Stack all those TV dinners in the freezer before they thaw out."

Marcy adjusted her stained blouse. It'd been torn several times by PJ, but she had nothing else to wear.

She pulled open a walk-in freezer and shivered from the cold temperature.

"Hurry up," the woman said, not looking up from her phone. "Don't stand around wasting energy."

In just a few minutes, Marcy had carried all the meals into the freezer and stacked them next to other pallets of bulk purchases. She swung closed the freezer door.

"What should I call you?" Marcy asked. "Ma'am?"

"My name's Tory." Still, she didn't look up. "I'm not your mother, your nurse, or your psychiatrist. I'm your employer. Got it?"

"Yes."

"My husband and I paid good money for you and your brother. You work off that money and someday you'll be free. You ever seen twenty thousand dollars?"

"No."

"Well, it's a lot of money."

"How long will it take me to work for it?"

"You got somewhere to go?" Tory glanced up. "Got a hot date? Cinderella's got a ball to go to or something?"

"No, I just—"

"Just work. I'll tell you when we're even. Now, go upstairs one floor and clean all the rooms that aren't locked. Get all the bedding. You know how to run a washing machine?"

"If it's like the ones at the laundromat."

"They're all the same."

"What about . . .?" She heard someone in the house. Was that . . . him?

"Your brother? Forget about him. He's gone. Don't bring him up again."

"I was going to ask about PJ."

"Well, I don't know how you did it, but he's tired of

you." She cursed. "Or maybe he just found someone prettier. Sorry, sweetie, but evolution took a step backwards with you."

"What if PJ bothers me?"

"I said he moved on, didn't I? You work for me now. The only way PJ'll do anything to you now is if you don't do what I tell you. Then I'll send him into your room in the middle of the night. You want that to happen again?"

"No."

"Then get upstairs and clean those rooms. We're supposed to get some more guests in a couple days. You do the laundry and heat meals for the others three times a day. If I have to tell you again, PJ will make your life more miserable than it already is."

"Okay."

Marcy set about in search of the staircase. On the second story, she found eight rooms, some sort of activity room, and several bathrooms and closets. All but two of the bedrooms were unlocked, a latch on each door like her own downstairs. She tapped lightly on the locked doors and imagined throwing up each latch. They weren't padlocked, but the front door downstairs was. Whoever was imprisoned inside couldn't be rescued by helping them out of their bedrooms, since they couldn't leave the house.

In the empty rooms, she stripped the beds of bloody or soiled sheets, gasping at the disgusting conditions of each room. But at least she was out of her own locked room. She worked for Tory now. The God of the boat and cross had rescued her that far. The fact that nobody wanted her was turning out to be in her favor!

Three industrial washers and dryers stood in the basement, which doubled as a warehouse for additional nonperishable food and other products for mass amounts of people. Even clothes! Once a load of laundry was started, Marcy searched racks, boxes, and shelves of clothes for her own size. In no time, she had an armful of outfits. Without asking Tory, she carried them upstairs to her room and set them against the wall behind the door— at the base of the boat-cross. If the clothes were discovered, what would happen? Someone would beat her, maybe PJ. She needed clothes. Maybe Tory would add it all to her debt, which Marcy doubted she'd ever be able to pay off. Twenty thousand dollars seemed like an enormous amount of money.

Though Marcy didn't mind the new routine, she couldn't imagine it was permanent, not with escape on her mind. The moment the front door wasn't padlocked, she wouldn't wait to ask for anyone's permission. In PE class, she'd proven to be a fast runner for her age.

Three times a day, she used the kitchen oven to heat up TV dinners from the freezer. PJ or Tory took the meals to the locked-up guests upstairs, and Marcy was free to eat what she wanted. The beds were changed, the rooms cleaned, and everyone was fed. Anything else that was laying around the house, if Marcy thought it wouldn't be missed, she took it. Books were a given. Magazines as well, though she took those back to the den when she finished them. Once, she even found a chair in the basement that seemed forgotten. It fit nicely into one corner of her bedroom. At night, after she was locked inside her room, she wedged the chair against the inside door handle, like she'd seen done in the movies. PJ nor anyone else could attack her at night.

But true to Tory's word, PJ left her alone. He actually ignored her, like she didn't exist. He never spoke to her, which didn't bother her, but she still steered clear of him. Before entering a hallway, she'd ensure he wasn't there. When he was, she'd use another hallway or wait until he'd come and gone.

She found a handheld mirror in the basement and brought it up to her bathroom. Through the mirror she found her left front tooth had darkened or died. That hadn't been PJ. The discolored tooth was from her mother's elbow. That fateful, confusing night, another lifetime long ago.

Tory's husband Trey seemed to be on business trips most of the time. If he left alone, he returned with a child. Or if he left with a child, he returned alone. Marcy guessed these were kidnapped kids, or children whose parents no longer wanted them, either.

As long as the kids were in the house, Marcy kept their stomachs full and their beds clean. She didn't see them unless she was upstairs cleaning and PJ or Trey were moving the kids in or out of a room. But she heard them. Some screamed. All of them cried. And that made Marcy cry. She hid her tears by crying in her bathroom at night, the door sufficiently barricaded. Addy was gone, somewhere out there. And she was a prisoner.

Then she would dry her eyes, bathe, sleep, and begin the next day the instant the latch was lifted on her door. Nightly, she thanked the God of the boat-cross that He'd made her ugly. Otherwise, she would've become like all the other children bought and sold, attacked by PJ or smuggled to somewhere across the world. Even her blackened tooth became a part of her cherished features. It helped her to be less desirable. Nobody wanted her. Many things were very wrong in her life, but she clung to the things that were okay.

Between loads of laundry and meals, she read like she'd never read while free. The huge basement had boxes of old, mildewy cheap novels—romances, westerns, and mysteries she'd never imagined reading while attending school. Tory and Trey didn't have a TV except in their own rooms on the third floor, where PJ also lived. Marcy wasn't allowed up there, ever. They never left their phones lying around, nor the front door unlocked, but Marcy escaped into her books—sometimes passing whole days without speaking to anyone.

One day, while Tory was delivering breakfast to the children on the second story, Tory started to curse PJ and argue with him. Trey was gone on a business trip, so Marcy feared that PJ might hurt Tory during their dispute. Marcy picked up an umbrella with a sturdy handle from a peg by the front door and crept up the stairs. Whatever the consequences, if she got a chance to wallop PJ, she wouldn't hesitate.

"He's dead!" Tory shouted at PJ. "Trey is going to go crazy on you for this one. There's no excuse, you idiot!"

"It was an accident! What do you want me to say?"

"I want you to say you'll clean this up."

"I'm not cleaning it up. Make your little house mouse clean it up."

PJ stomped away and up to his room. Tory came around the corner at that instant and saw Marcy crouching in the stairway.

"What were you going to do with this?" Tory snatched the umbrella from her and held it up threateningly.

"I wasn't going to let him hurt you." Marcy cowered, only because she guessed that was the expected reaction, not because she was afraid of being hit. "I had your back, Tory."

"Oh." The woman lowered the umbrella. "Well, you heard? One of the kids died in the night. Good thing he's small. Get a box of garbage bags and that roll of duct tape from the drawer by the fridge."

Marcy fetched the items, then returned upstairs to an open bedroom door where Tory stood waiting.

"We'll have to throw the mattress out, too," the woman said, shaking her head. "Trey will be back tonight with three more guests. We'll need the room. Okay, put five trash bags inside one another. Hold this. Good."

"You've done this before?" Marcy asked.

"Enough to know how to do it right. Hold up the bag!"

The scene made Marcy wretch. She helped carry the oddly-shaped garbage bag downstairs and out to the back porch where Marcy had never been allowed to go before. The direct sunlight was reviving. Tory stood there panting as Marcy admired the sparse clouds for the first time in a long time.

"Come on." Tory nudged her shoulder. "Let's change out that mattress."

"You should make PJ do it. This was his fault."

"Don't talk like that. Never speak of this again. Family covers for each other, no matter how ugly the secrets get."

"Family?" Marcy winced. "I'm not . . . family."

"I am." Tory led the way inside, though not before mumbling her expression of shame. "PJ's my brother."

Several months passed, though Marcy couldn't keep track as she cleaned, cooked, and read. Trey came and went with children, and the household seemed plentiful with food for the residents and new clothes and shoes for Tory, though she rarely left the house. Marcy was left alone, but she didn't stop pitying the children upstairs. They stayed only for a week or two in most cases, then Marcy changed out their bedding. The boat-cross faded, so Marcy traced it with a bolder, more permanent marker, and prayed to God for her brother and parents.

Then one day Tory got sick. Trey was home, so he took her out the front door to drive her to the hospital. Suddenly, with both Trey and Tory gone, the front door wasn't padlocked! Marcy stared at it. All this time—years, maybe? And here it was—her escape. But where could she run? She knew no one. What had become of her parents? Maybe all she needed to do was walk outside, and then—

"Don't even think about it." It was PJ. He was leaning against the foyer wall by the hallway behind her. He'd gained weight and lost hair since Marcy had first arrived at the house. But his eyes were the same—bored. No . . . *dead.* "With Tory gone and all, I have a bit of a craving to pick up with you where we left off."

Marcy tensed and let her gaze drift to the left, where the sturdy umbrella hung. But really, she tensed to dart to the right. If she could reach her room first, she could block the door with the chair. The doors were heavily constructed so they couldn't be broken through. Even PJ wouldn't get through a barricaded door except with an ax or electric saw.

She went for it. Out of the foyer, across the carpet, and— Her foot caught a table leg. She tripped and dove headfirst into the hall entry. Dazed, she didn't realize that PJ had her until she felt his mouth on hers. Then she fought like a wounded cat—nails and teeth and fists.

He smashed her into furniture, and she smashed furniture over him. Twice, he threw her off him only to find that she came back with renewed fury. Finally, he stomped on her and she went still, conscious, but still and breathless. She felt crippling pain as she became aware of her wounds through the fog of adrenaline. *Where was the boat-cross God to save her from this?*

PJ was bleeding from the head and neck, but he still had strength left. He dragged her by one leg down the hall into her room and into the bathroom. She lay immobile and in shock on the floor as he ran the tub water.

"You know how to fight," he said, spitting blood into the water, "but you don't know how to be broke. I'm going to teach you."

Marcy's eyes opened wider. *He was going to drown her!* He'd killed kids before. It meant nothing to him.

She hurt all over, but she couldn't let him win. He'd broken her body, but she'd kept her will, her spirit, her mind.

In a final burst of energy, she rolled to her knees and reached for her hand-held mirror. He grasped at the back of her shirt, but she was already spinning toward him. The mirror glanced off his brow, shattering glass across the floor. Stunned, he fell against the door frame, then crawled out of the bathroom. The tub water lapped at the edge, on the verge of flooding.

Marcy picked up a shard of glass with her bare hand, then wrapped it in a towel. She dove at PJ and fell upon his legs, stabbing his feet and ankles. He screamed, cried, and kicked. Then she was on his back.

She held the glass against his neck, knowing exactly where his carotid artery was. Medical thrillers had been one of her favorite genres of books. Now, she would exercise lethal justice. PJ the pervert would be no more.

But PJ didn't move. He hardly breathed.

In that moment, Marcy realized she couldn't kill him—not even PJ. She hated herself for such weakness—or was it strength? Sobbing, she clung to him, prohibiting him from moving a muscle, but restraining herself from murder.

"If you ever touch me again . . ." she hissed in his ear but didn't finish. She didn't need to. Instead, she stood and screamed incoherently at him until he crawled out of the TV room into the hall. When he was gone, she slammed the door and braced the chair against it.

The water spilled out of the tub, so she quickly turned off the faucet. After draining some of the water, she slipped under the surface to soak her scrapes and cuts and welts. She was safe now. Until Tory came back. The boat-cross God had saved her again. And yes, she realized it had been strength indeed that had kept her from killing PJ. He was the killer, not her. She was a junior high student, just a kid in school. Sure, she was behind in her classes, but she'd learned so much about life and the world from the hundred books she'd read.

Late that night, Marcy finally released the chair from the door and eased warily into the hallway. Her stomach rumbled with hunger. If she was hungry, then the kids upstairs were hungry, too. With Tory and Trey still gone, there was no one to feed them. Judging by his blood loss on the hallway floor, PJ was in no condition to care for anyone else. The blood needed to be cleaned up, but the kids came first.

As she'd done a thousand times before, she heated the TV dinners in the kitchen oven. But this time, she took them upstairs herself. There was a little blood on the stairs, so she knew PJ was somewhere above, hopefully hiding in his room. Or maybe he'd died from his wounds after all. Marcy didn't want to think about that.

All but one of the eight rooms were locked. She set the trays down and quietly lifted the latch on the first door. It was impossible to know what she'd find inside. The only times she'd been inside the rooms were to clean them—or that time she'd helped Tory collect the dead child's body. Otherwise, they remained locked with each latch in place.

She pushed open the door a few inches. The bed was there, but it wasn't made as she'd left it last. The sheets were strewn across the floor and the blanket was missing altogether. Wider, she opened the door to find the room empty. Why lock an empty room? Then she noticed the doorless bathroom. Like her, this person may have found the isolation of the bathroom comforting. When she peeked past the door threshold, she saw a young girl sitting in the space between the tub and toilet, her shoulders wrapped in the blanket. She couldn't have been older than five.

"I brought you some food," Marcy whispered, showing her the tray. "Are you hungry?"

The girl only stared back with big, frightened eyes.

"Come on." Marcy forced a smile. "I'll peel the wrapper off for you. You need to eat to keep up your strength. You can't have courage without strength. Don't worry. The bad people are gone right now."

Sitting on the edge of the tub, Marcy set the tray on her lap and peeled off the plastic cover. The aroma of chicken breast and pineapple sauce made her mouth water, reminding her that she hadn't eaten yet herself.

The child emerged from her hole an inch at a time. Marcy studied what she could see of the child—her brown skin and wrinkled clothes. Trey and Tory didn't seem to abuse the kids they bought so they would retain their sale value, but there was no telling what PJ might do when no one was watching.

"It's chicken." Marcy walked into the bedroom. "Sit here."

The little girl sat next to her on the bed, and once she accepted the plastic fork, she went to gobbling the food. Unable to cut the chicken breast herself, she picked it up with her fingers.

"That's how I eat it, too." Marcy giggled. "There's no way to cut chicken with a plastic fork!"

She combed the child's greasy hair with her fingers. Kids this young didn't often know how to keep themselves clean, even with running water in the bathroom. Marcy wondered if she had time to give the girl a bath—before she was discovered inside the rooms of the kidnapped children.

"You finish eating." She gave the girl a one-armed squeeze. "I'll come back in a little while."

She rose and started away, but the child took hold of Marcy's hand and hung on tightly, dread revealed on the little girl's face.

"I'll be right back." Marcy peeling off the girl's strong grip, finger by finger. "I have to feed the other kids."

The children in the adjacent rooms were also young and no less terrified. Marcy spoke little encouragements to them and left their trays on their beds, then collected their empty trays as PJ had done with her months earlier. Or, no—had it been *years* now? Then she locked their rooms and hurried back to the first room.

The girl had returned to her hiding place next to the tub.

"I'm not going to make you come out from there," Marcy said, kneeling over the tub, "but I'm going to run you some water. It's up to you if you want to climb in. A hot bath always helps me feel better."

After getting the water running, she checked the sink for toiletries. She found only a toothbrush, still sealed in its original package, and a bar of unused soap. Marcy had shampoo in her own room. A little shampoo would do wonders for this little girl's hair!

Marcy darted into the hallway, leaving the bedroom door unlocked, and descended the stairs—careful to avoid the drying blood. In the foyer, she froze. There was no padlock on the front door! *Now was her moment!* She could escape! Never again would PJ hit her, assault her, or speak wickedly to her. Never again would she be locked in her bedroom and given chores to do all day. Never again would Tory remind her she was too old and ugly to be sold—though she knew now that had been providential!

Outside that door, there were houses and families and . . . policemen! But could she find help in time? As soon as she was discovered to be gone, PJ might move—or worse— the children upstairs . . . She'd already seen how he'd killed the boy, and Tory and Trey didn't seem bothered about throwing away evidence in the trash.

With a sad sigh, Marcy doubted she could effectively escape, anyway. She was just a kid herself. Tory, Trey, and PJ were adults. Who would the police listen to? A junior high student?

Then, she pressed her lips firmly together. She hadn't been re-sold. God had kept her alive through everything— to be there now. For the kids. Leaving the house without a plan wasn't right unless she could leave with all the children. There had to be a way!

At the door, Marcy touched the padlock where it lay on a small tray with car keys, a comb, and a pack of gum. Tory and Trey could return any minute. They'd see she hadn't escaped. What could that earn her? Their trust? Perhaps. The more privileges they gave her, the closer she could get to escaping for good—and helping the kids leave forever.

From her own bathroom, she took her shampoo bottle and returned upstairs. There, she found the girl had climbed into the tub. Kneeling, Marcy turned off the water, and playfully splashed the little girl. She tried to forget about the unlocked front door.

"See? Not so bad. When I was your age, I hated baths. My brother Aidan was even worse, though! He only bathed when Mom chased him in with a broom. Staying clean is important, you hear? No matter . . . what happens to you, you keep yourself clean. Wash all over. Otherwise, you'll get sores and stuff."

The girl never said a word, so Marcy did all the talking. Later, she dressed the child in her wrinkled clothes, but promised to find her some clean clothes in the basement. With a heavy heart, she left the girl in her room and locked the door outside. She thought about helping the other boys and girls as well, but it was too risky. She wasn't even supposed to be doing what she'd done!

Downstairs, she ate two meals of her own choosing, then went about the house cleaning up PJ's blood. She didn't regret cutting him with the broken mirror glass, but she didn't really want him to die. Before he died, he needed to be arrested. Marcy had read enough novels to understand the authorities wouldn't hesitate to put this wicked family in jail. However, she'd also read enough books to know that this family couldn't function so well without relying on a corrupt system or crooked cops. Some in authority had to know what was happening there. Maybe they were clients of Tory and Trey. What if she escaped and spoke to the wrong police officer? When she was returned, PJ would beat her senseless.

For two days, Marcy fed the children upstairs without seeing PJ. She learned a couple of the children's names when they finally spoke a little, but most hid from her or refused to speak—as if they thought she was one of the bad people.

On the third day, Tory and Trey returned, and Marcy was there to welcome them home in the foyer.

"Appendicitis," Trey reported, his arm around a pale Tory. Then the man, who hadn't removed his gold rings even while gone on a medical emergency, glanced at the padlock in the tray. "Where's PJ? Why wasn't this door locked?"

"PJ's up in his room. He attacked me, so I cut him real bad. I've been feeding everyone myself."

"Good, uh, good girl." Trey continued toward the stairs with his wife.

"PJ's such an idiot!" Tory gasped, one hand holding her side. "He could've blown everything."

"I know." Trey supported her. "Up you go. Come on. I can't carry you."

"Trey?" Marcy called when they were halfway up. "You want me to put the lock on?"

He and his wife shared a look.

"Yeah, do that, would you?" Then he continued up.

Marcy picked up the heavy padlock and slid it through the metal holes. She didn't want to lock it, but she realized this was a process. PJ had tried to groom her to be a willing participant in his wickedness. Now, she would groom her captors to trust her—until she could locate the padlock keys and figure out which authorities to go to. If only she had a phone!

She was in the kitchen cleaning up when Trey came in.

"You did good while we were gone. I talked to PJ. You messed him up bad, but I know how he gets. Without you stepping up, we might've lost a couple kids upstairs. You're finally earning your keep around here."

"It's my house, too," she said, not looking at him. She put several metal forks in the drawer, since she'd been allowed for some time to use them instead of the plastic tray forks. "It's my home."

He stood there watching her work. Marcy wondered if he could read her mind—that she wasn't really complying. She was *planning*.

"Tory won't be moving around downstairs for several

days still. I want you looking in on her. Starting tomorrow morning."

"Up to her room?" Marcy tried to hide her surprise.

"Yeah. PJ can't walk right yet. He said you sliced his Achilles' tendon pretty bad. That means you'll have to keep feeding the kids while I'm gone, too."

"I don't mind. I gave some of them baths and clean clothes from the basement and washed their old clothes."

"You did?" His voice sounded angry, but Marcy opened the fridge and acted preoccupied with counting out the next day's meals. "Well, I guess it can't hurt. Tory used to do that. She stopped when she realized it never mattered. They come and go, filthy or not. Nobody cares."

"It does matter," Marcy said meekly, wiping her hands on a towel. "And I care. If they're clean and healthy, it helps everything. And everyone."

"Yeah. You've got a point. Just don't get too attached. By the way, I'm hitting the road tomorrow."

He returned upstairs. For the first time since she'd been in the house, Marcy felt like she had some control, some dignity. Helping the kids—it had to be God's idea all along! Just like her bad tooth had made her less appealing to buyers, everything seemed to have a purpose.

The next morning, she climbed the stairs to the third story. Trey had left on a business trip, and Tory was half-dressed when Marcy knocked on the door and entered.

"Good. Get over here." Tory waved, beads of sweat on her forehead. "I'm all stiff and sore. Get me into the bathroom."

Marcy helped her walk, then helped her dress in sweats. Finally, Tory relaxed on the bed, exhausted.

"I don't want to have to call for you," Tory said. "I don't have the energy. So, check on me every couple of hours, and I'll tell you what I want."

"I don't have a watch, and there aren't any clocks downstairs."

"There, on my dresser. The silver box. The one with

the pink band—you can have it. That's a girl's watch. You can keep it."

Fitting the watch around her slender wrist, Marcy left and closed the door. She turned in the hallway and bumped into PJ. Afraid he'd attack her, she yelped and bounded backwards. He hadn't shaved or showered in days—and smelled like it.

"PJ!" Tory yelled from her room. "You leave that girl alone! We need her!"

"I'm not touching her!" he shouted back, then snarled at Marcy. "You messed me up good, you little slut. But I'm patient. I'll hurt you so bad, you'll wish you'd never—"

"PJ!" Tory called. "Let her do her chores! Thanks to you, no one else is doing them."

Marcy darted past him and leaped down the stairs three steps at a time. She believed him. He would get revenge. It was just a matter of time.

But things were changing in the house, and Marcy focused on that. Every morning and every night, she prayed to God, sensing that He was watching, aware, and guiding events. A rescue was being orchestrated, somehow. Trey came and left with more kids, one at a time, and Marcy prayed for each one, but something was changing in the wind. Some nights, Marcy fell asleep with a smile, barely containing her excitement to see what would happen next.

PJ remained upstairs, ordering her to bring food when she was up checking on Tory's little needs. Otherwise, Marcy had the run of the house. She fed the kids three times a day and began to spend more time with them in their rooms. Even if they were too traumatized to speak, she spoke to them and for them. She'd been rescued by the boat-cross God, so she told each child about Him. He'd become real to her, even though He was just a memory from stories in Sunday school long ago.

"You don't look rescued," a boy of seven criticized her

one day. He had shaggy, red hair. "You're locked up like me."

"I know, but . . ." She thought for a moment, then placed her hand over the boy's heart. "God rescues you in here. Somehow. He knows all about us. He . . . wants to help us. The world is bad. I've read a lot about it. But He is good. He rescues us from the flooding water of evil things."

The boy hadn't seemed convinced that day, but Marcy was doubly convinced of God's ambition for them the more she told the children of her experiences and prayed for them.

No one locked her in her room any longer, so Marcy took the opportunity to go into each of the children's rooms and tuck them in, even late at night. From some movie or TV show in her own youth, Marcy recalled people kneeling and praying over their beds. Whatever children were in the locked rooms, Marcy prayed with them and tucked them in. Sometimes one or more left with Trey the very next day, but Marcy hoped they would remember God and her vague explanations of who He was.

In an effort to locate kids' clothing apart from the adult clothes in the basement, Marcy set about organizing the dimly-lit expanse. In the process, she uncovered two more boxes of books, even an old set of fifty-year-old encyclopedias. Under *Volume G* she found the subject of God and hungrily read about a variety of gods that humanity had revered throughout history. A couple of the gods sounded like they might be her God, but she wasn't certain until she looked up Cross in *Volume C*.

Numb and wide-eyed, she read of Jesus who had died on the cross as a sacrifice for sinners. These things were spoken of in a book called the Bible. The Christian belief was, the book said, that Jesus rose from the dead, defeating sin and death, and prepared a way for all to be resurrected. Jesus Christ was her God, Marcy decided. He had to be. No one else had such compassion for children, for the lost and poor and lonely. But she needed to know more. She needed a Bible. How else could she convince the kids upstairs that God was real?

She scoured the basement, even checking previously located stacks of books for a Bible. There wasn't one, and she was hesitant to bring up the subject with Tory, since she was certain Tory would frown on her growing awareness of an Almighty God out there somewhere watching all the good and bad people.

Occasionally, PJ limped down to the kitchen, or he left in his vehicle to pick up groceries that Tory ordered by phone. But Tory stayed in her room watching TV, even long after she'd healed from her appendectomy. Marcy still checked on the woman, though less frequently, and never saw an opportunity to use her phone. However, Marcy was given the key to unlock the front padlock when Trey came home every few days, though she had to return it to Tory immediately.

These moments of trust built into more solid plans in Marcy's mind. If she unlatched the children's doors ahead of time, then unlocked the front door when she was given the key, she might have a few minutes to lead all the children outside. But where would they go?

Without a Bible, Marcy searched the encyclopedias for hints of any record of people God had spoken to in the past. Subject by subject, she studied about God, shocked that she'd never heard of Him in school or at home or on the TV. She didn't even remember anyone on social media talking about Him when she'd had her own phone.

Finally, she found in *Volume N* that which completed her memory of the water, the boat, and the rescue from the flood. Noah was the man's name who'd been rescued! The ark really was like the cross of Jesus, she realized, but she had incorrectly thought the cross was on the ark. Slowly, more of the truth came out, and she connected the major characters in the Bible and what it all meant to her and other sinners. The gospel, the Romans, the Jews,

Jerusalem, and the Garden of Gethsemane—each topic answered questions as quickly as she read about them.

Every night and every morning, her own private prayers intensified, yearning for Jesus to be with her and thanking Him for dying for her and the children—even for PJ, Trey, and Tory. She became even more convinced by learning these truths that God had sent her to that horrible household so she would learn about Him and explain Him to the children as they passed through the locked rooms upstairs.

One night, many months later, Marcy was organizing TV dinners in the walk-in freezer when the door slammed shut. Panicked, she dropped the trays and ran to the door, but there was no interior handle.

"PJ!" She slapped on the door. "Let me out! This isn't funny!"

Silence was the only response, and she began to doubt that PJ had closed the door at all. Maybe groceries had fallen against the door and knocked it closed.

She clutched her midsection and rocked on her feet. It was pointless to call for Tory; she was two stories upstairs. Trey was gone on a trip. PJ had to be the culprit, but knowing that didn't get her out any quicker. Tory would miss her first, but not before the children went unfed and unloved for several hours!

The cold pierced her skin and made her bones ache. According to her watch, ten minutes passed before she decided to continue making noise. She would die from cold within an hour. For five minutes straight, she pounded on the door, bruising both hands and growing hoarse from shouting.

After another five minutes, she dropped to her knees, shivering uncontrollably. This had to be PJ. This was his revenge. She huddled between the racks of TV dinners, reminding herself of the little girl so many months earlier she'd found hiding between the toilet and tub. But here, there was no escape from the cold. It had been this cold in her parents' car on the way to this house, but she'd had a coat that night.

"Please, God . . ." she mumbled, her eyes drifting closed. "Help the kids to . . ."

The door clicked open. With groggy awareness, Marcy lifted her eyes to see PJ glaring down at her. His face was full of triumph. He grabbed her by the hair and drew her out of the freezer, then slammed the door.

"This is for my foot, you slut!" he said, standing over her where she lay curled up on the kitchen floor. Then he gave her the worst beating she'd ever had. In the past, she'd been able to fight back and defend herself a little, but she was half frozen this time, her mind slow and her limbs stiff. His heels and the toe of his boot found every soft spot on her body and bruised every bony area. Expectedly, he avoided her head and face, and even as she whimpered through the blows, she knew he meant to leave no marks on her that his sister Tory would discover.

When he was finished, he dragged her, limping in his permanent way, back to her room. He left her on the floor, saying nothing, and locked her door for the first time in many months.

Marcy couldn't manage to get herself to the bathroom that first night. She rested on the floor, drifting in and out of consciousness, swimming in pain, pleading with God for relief, help, or saving. Or death.

The next day, she reached the bathroom, where she passed blood and vomited painfully. She spent that whole day on the bathroom floor, not certain that if she went to her bed, that she'd make it back.

The following morning, her door latch sounded loudly, waking her in a frenzy of fear. *He was back!* Now, he would finish her off. Maybe God was tired of rescuing her, and now she was going to be with Jesus in heaven.

Instead, Tory walked into her room and leaned against the bathroom door frame.

"So, you actually tried to escape, huh?" Tory clicked

her tongue. "PJ said he caught you. I wondered if we'd given you too much liberty."

"He's . . . lying," Marcy said with effort. She hadn't drunk much except what handfuls she'd palmed from the tub faucet. "He's mad."

"Oh, he's definitely mad. You crippled him for life. What'd you expect? Maybe he caught you trying to escape and maybe he didn't. Either way, vacation time is over. No more going into the rooms while the kids are in them. Do your chores and we lock you back in here like we used to. You're not trustworthy for anything else. I don't want you making things worse for us. PJ got even. That's all. Now get up. There's laundry to do."

Tory left and Marcy wept. Where was God? This wasn't better. This was worse. So much worse. What about the kids? Who would pray with them at night and tell them about Jesus?

It took several minutes to climb up the sink to her feet. There, she swayed and practiced breathing, which hurt terribly. She figured several ribs were broken, and her insides felt knotted. Her arms and legs were bruised in dozens of places, and her muscles trembled, but she was still alive.

"They beat You, too," she said, steeling herself, thinking of Jesus' mistreatment. "You know what I'm going through."

After changing her clothes, she climbed the stairs to the empty rooms and began to clean—far from her healthy pace. If she had no more access to the kids, then what further purpose could God have for her there? It seemed time to leave before PJ beat her so badly that she never recovered.

CHAPTER TWO

"Nobody wants me." Marcy's eyes opened slowly as the words swam in her mind. Sore all over, she sat up and slipped her feet into tennis shoes she'd found in the basement. "But God cares for me."

The latch being lifted on her door had woken her, and she knew she was expected to present herself immediately. She'd overslept, her body in agony, and it still hurt to breathe.

"Look at you!" Trey laughed and pointed at her when she walked into the kitchen. He shook his head. "You look like you fell down the stairs."

"She crossed PJ," Tory said from the corner where she stood in her nightgown sipping coffee. "Get moving. The kids are hungry."

"Serves her right after what she did to his foot." Trey kissed his wife. "Okay, I'm off. I've got two coming home tonight. Have two rooms ready."

"Oh, she will," Tory said, "or I'll give her to PJ again."

They both chuckled as Marcy moved from the freezer to the oven with breakfast trays. She heard their mockery, but it didn't bother her. Her mind was on the front door, the padlock, and getting far enough down the street before PJ could catch her ever again. Even as sore as she was, she'd force herself to run, even if it killed her.

She carried the trays upstairs and Tory took the food into the kids' rooms. Marcy checked the empty rooms for readiness for the new arrivals. Everything seemed to be in order. Now she could focus on herself for a few minutes—eat, wash up, and read a little from the encyclopedias. PJ was still in his room and Tory had gone back upstairs.

Marcy descended the stairs and froze on the bottom

step. *No one had replaced the padlock on the front door after Trey had left!* Of course, Tory had been upstairs with her, and PJ was probably still sleeping.

"Don't think!" Marcy told herself and walked briskly to her room. She knew exactly what to take and threw her things into a pillowcase. Although she'd arrived at the house with nothing, she was leaving with more than just her wounds. The last item she packed was the *Volume C* encyclopedia. Wherever she ended up, she didn't want to be without that. It contained the topics of Cain, Capernaum, Christ, Christianity, Church, Corinth, Cross, and Crucifixion—more Bible topics than any of the other volumes.

No time for anything else! She emerged from her room and bumped into PJ. He groped at her, howling, his breath smelling like sour milk. When she swung her pillowcase at him, he limped backwards, dodging it easily. Marcy retreated into her room and slammed the door, then wedged the chair into place. His footsteps continued down the hallway to the kitchen.

She tossed the pillowcase onto her bed. That was close. He probably had no idea what she had in her case, or why. The opportunity had passed. Next time, she needed to move faster—maybe have her pillowcase ready ahead of time. And she'd need a coat. She hadn't thought to fetch a coat from the basement. If she'd been wearing one right then, PJ would've known her exact intentions.

That afternoon, she found a small coat that fit her frame perfectly and hid it in the pile of clothes she kept in her room for herself. The padlock was again on the front door. Everything was still okay, she comforted herself in a new handheld mirror. She needed to heal up a little more, anyway.

After the dinner trays had been served and before Marcy was locked in her room, she lounged on her bed, reading in the last light through the cracked window. A tiny draft of cold air whispered in through the crack. She'd never patched it with tape. It was her only connection to the outside world. If only she could see outside, that would be—

Suddenly, she heard a loud noise toward the front of the house—*the front door!* It had bounced off the wall in the foyer.

"*Sladrick!*" Trey yelled from the foyer. "Tory, it's Sladrick! It's got to be. PJ, where are you?"

"What?" Tory called. She sounded like she was at the top of the stairs, descending. "Oh, no! What do we do? Lock the door, Trey!"

Marcy dropped her book on the bed and moved to the chair against the door. What was a Sladrick?

"What do we do?" PJ repeated, his voice from the hallway near the kitchen. Marcy had never before heard fear in the big man's voice. "You must've been followed!"

"But I was careful!" Trey yelled back. "I didn't even get on the train. He was at the depot. I've been running and hiding all day!"

"I'm not ready!" Tory shrieked. "Trey, the car isn't packed. Do we have time to leave?"

PJ's limping footfalls scurried up the hall to the front door, then returned back to the kitchen. No, he didn't stop at the kitchen. The back door slammed as he left the house. Then there was a loud crash at the front door, like the door had been forced open. She heard a man's voice she didn't recognize, low and threatening. Tory screamed. Trey cursed at someone, then there was a struggle.

As quickly as the panic had begun, it was over. The house was now silent, except for Marcy's heartbeat in her ears. Someone in heavy boots walked up the hallway. They weren't loud footsteps, but Marcy had learned to distinguish every tiny sound in the house, always aware of who was moving about and where. Someone rattled her doorknob, and Marcy nearly screamed, but she kept quiet, glad to see the chair was holding the door shut.

The boots continued to the kitchen, then returned,

checking all the locked doors again. It didn't sound like a police raid. Maybe a competitor. *Sladrick?* Marcy had never heard such fear in Trey or Tory's voices, and now she couldn't hear them at all. Maybe they'd been killed. But she hadn't heard gunshots.

The boots went past her door, then mounted the stairs. She heard him upstairs. The children would be found! Or stolen and moved again.

Marcy dug out her coat and slipped it on. No time to zip up. She grabbed the pillowcase and shifted the chair away from the door.

In the hallway, she listened for the person in the house. It had to be a man with heavy boots like that. He was unlatching the kids' doors, talking to them, or trying to get them to talk. Yes, a man's voice, muffled but definitely upstairs with the kids.

She walked hastily through the carpeted room and reached the foyer. The front door was wide open. The padlock was still locked, but its flange lay torn from the door frame. Tory and Trey lay unconscious on the floor, maybe even dead, at the foot of the stairs. There was no blood, but Marcy didn't want to check for a pulse.

Seconds later, she leaped off the porch and ran up the side of the street. She felt tears in her eyes. The pain from her injuries was bad, but she had to get away. While crossing an intersection, a car honked at her, alerting her to the fact that she was in the street. Moving to the sidewalk, she kept running. The cold air bit her lungs. Oh, it felt good to run, but it had been so long.

Blocks later, she stumbled to a stop, then collapsed to her hands and knees on dead grass—someone's lawn. It was early spring or fall, maybe. At least there was no snow. She lifted her head, trying to remember more of Davenport. The tall building ahead didn't look familiar. Nothing did. The ride in her parents' car that final night was so vague and distant in her memory.

"Hey!" yelled a uniformed woman from an office

building doorstep. "Get off there. Keep moving or I'll call the police!"

Marcy forced herself to her feet and ran away, toward the tall buildings.

"Excuse me!" she asked a man who was walking on the sidewalk with a gym bag over his shoulder. "Can I borrow your phone? It's an emergency."

"Not a chance." He scoffed and kept moving.

She wandered across a grocery store parking lot, asking others, but everyone hustled away from her or told her to move along. Sobbing for the children, she stopped on the next street corner and looked back at the way she'd come. On which street was Trey's house? Was she still on it? With disappointment, she realized she hadn't looked back at the house to see the number on the front.

A police car chirped as it pulled against the curb. The policeman climbed out of his car, his mouth cupped over his radio as he spoke to the dispatcher.

"Excuse me, young lady. How are you doing today?"

"Please, you have to help me!" She trudged toward the car and tripped. "There are kids locked up in a house, a brick house. I ran away from—"

"Whoa, whoa, whoa. Slow down." He took her wrists and forced her arms down. "It's okay now. We got a call that you were bothering people along the sidewalk. Having money problems, huh? Looking for food? Maybe you just need a warm place to sleep."

"No, listen!" She broke her hands free like she'd done a hundred times from PJ, but this man was skilled at submission holds. "Ow! Please!"

He forced her to turn as he twisted one arm and cuffed one wrist at a time. She dropped the pillowcase.

"Don't resist, ma'am. We'll get it all figured out at the station. This is for your safety as much as it is for mine. Just relax, ma'am."

"*Ma'am?* I'm in junior high!"

"Of course, you are. Come on, ma'am. Into the car. Watch your head."

"My stuff! My clothes!"

He nudged her into the back seat, then slammed the door. Marcy recovered in time to see him pick up her pillowcase and sort through it. Finally, he brought her belongings with him into the cab and set them on the passenger seat.

"Excuse me?" Marcy couldn't control her tears. The cuffs cut into her bony wrists. "I was locked up in a house for a long time. There are kids still there. You've got to save them before they're moved! There's a man who got away. PJ has killed before. Listen! Excuse me? Aren't you listening?"

She tried and tried to get his attention through the thick partition, but he didn't respond. Finally, he pulled into a car lot full of other police cars.

"My stuff!" she pleaded as he led her from the car toward an unmarked metal door. "My encyclopedia . . ."

"It'll all be inventoried and signed for," he said. "Just relax. We'll get you to a safe place for the weekend."

She was led through several clacking doors, then set free in a large cage that smelled like urine. Her cuffs were taken off, then the police officer left her there.

"Please!" Marcy reached through the bars. "He didn't bring me my stuff. My clothes and book!"

"Relax, darling." A female officer moved past her. "You'll get processed at the speed of growing corn with everyone else."

Marcy paced for a few minutes, then sat on a metal bench against the wall. Only then did she notice three others in the cage with her, lying on other benches on the opposite wall. They were older women, so why was she in there with them? She was just a junior high school student.

Hours passed, and Marcy fought sleep and bouts of

weeping. The kids in the rooms—they must've been killed or moved by now.

The jail cage door opened and Marcy jumped to her feet. She looked into the familiar face of Tory. *It was her!* A police officer uncuffed her wrists, then Tory sauntered across the cage, eyeing Marcy suspiciously. As Tory approached her, Marcy expected the grown woman to attack her. Backing away, Marcy tripped and sat down roughly on the bench. Tory sat down close enough to take Marcy's elbow tightly in her claw-like fingers and pull her close.

"You keep your mouth shut," Tory whispered, "and we might get out of this."

"I'm not in anything!" Marcy argued. "You guys—"

"No, you and I are in this together. You're in it as deep as I am. You've kept those kids locked up with us. Remember the boy? You want to go away for murder? They'll probably put you in prison for life unless you do what I say. I'm your only chance, sweetie. We just keep silent."

"I didn't kill anyone! That was PJ!"

"PJ. Right. He got away. He might be our only hope now. He'll be waiting for us somewhere, if we can get out on bail. Or better yet, you and I can say that Trey kept us locked in there. We're victims. We've finally been found, rescued."

"I'm telling them the truth." Marcy pushed away, but Tory slid closer, her breath in Marcy's face.

"You listen to me! I'm not going down like this, so you stick to our story. If you get out without me, I'll make sure PJ hurts you bad, you hear? All those years, I kept you safe from him. You know I can still keep you safe from him. As soon as we get out, we can start over somewhere fresh. One big happy family again."

"You're insane." Marcy elbowed Tory, forcing the woman away. She stood and looked down at her former captor. "You did nothing for me in that house. I'm not afraid of PJ!"

"Yes, you are." Tory cackled. "I can see it in your eyes. He'll kill you if you don't do what I say. There're phones in jail. I'll call him. You'll see. You won't be safe without me."

Marcy sat across the cage on another bench next to a prostitute who was using her leopard skin jacket as a pillow. Nothing had gone right. This wasn't how kidnapped kids were supposed to be treated. Where was God? But Marcy wondered if there was some truth to Tory's claims about her being guilty of helping her dispose of the dead boy's body. Could she get in trouble for that? Should she keep her mouth shut or risk going to jail? If she went to jail, she wouldn't be able to find Aidan or her parents. Oh, there was so much to fix! God would need to guide her forward.

"You!" A policewoman waved her to the door.

Rising, Marcy glanced at Tory who held up a threatening finger, warning her.

"Come with me." The policewoman unlocked the cage door. "Walk on the yellow line. Turn right. Stay on the line. Hands behind your back."

The next hour was spent explaining her story time and again to a growing audience of police officers and plainclothes detectives. Some took notes. Some just stared. Several times, Marcy asked for her belongings, but they responded with more questions for her.

Finally, she was offered food and a soda, then a muscled black man in a tie and shoulder holster knelt in front of her. His skin was darker than PJ's, his cologne was strong, but his eyes were kind.

"You've been through a lot." He held out his hand. "My name is Agent Jerome Wessel. My friends used to call me Germs, maybe short for Jerome, I guess, but I promise you I have very few germs. You can call me Jerome."

Marcy breathed with relief and smiled, accepting his hand. Finally, someone nice!

"I'm Marcy Nevins."

"That's what they told me. Can you walk with me? I have an office up the corridor here. You can see what the locals think of us Homeland Security boys by the way they gave me the smallest office with the least ventilation, but it'll give us some privacy."

He led her into a cramped office. In the chair in front of his desk was her pillowcase. She clutched it and sat down.

"Homeland Security?" she asked.

"That's me." He flipped through several forms and studied his laptop screen. "You'd be surprised how much human trafficking Davenport sees. Interstates and bus routes all over the place. Yeah, we're real popular here. You'd be surprised."

"No, I wouldn't be."

He looked up.

"Yeah. I guess you wouldn't be. Did they really have you in the drunk tank downstairs with Dosier? Geniuses— could've gotten you killed."

"Dosier?"

"Tory Dosier." He turned his laptop screen toward her, showing her an arrest photo. "The woman who held you for eight years."

"*What?*" Marcy blinked rapidly. "No . . . not eight years. I'm just . . . thirteen. I mean, I was. My brother Aidan was sold with me the same night. It was . . . a long time ago. But not *that* long!"

"Captivity can distort our perception of time. It's weird like that. I have your file here. We found you as soon as the boys up the hall plugged in your name. Turns out your junior high world history teacher filed a police report on your parents eight years ago when you suddenly stopped coming to school. A remarkable student suddenly disappears? Unfortunately, there were a dozen others in Davenport who'd vanished that same month.

Disappearances. Nobody looked for you like they should have."

"Eight years . . ." Marcy shook her head. "That means . . . I'm . . . *twenty-one?*"

"Uh, yeah. So, I have a million questions for you. I mean, we've been hunting this GLOW ring for years—the Dosiers—but you're here in front of me. How are you doing? Are you, you know, catching up mentally?"

"I don't know. What's a GLOW ring?"

"GLOW. Uh, yeah. It stands for Global Wares. That's their full name. They're a human smuggling network that spans the globe. The Dosiers were just a small, local part of it. There's hardly anyone in the trade not linked in with GLOW nowadays. They have resources and offer protection, even countersurveillance. Dangerous people. Efficient. And they make billions each year moving people around—mostly kids. Tory and her husband were almost caught in Seattle ten years ago, but they slipped through our fingers. They're not kind to their victims. We think they recruited your parents but required them to sell you and your brother first. I don't know how you survived for eight years with the Dosiers. It's . . . amazing."

"They said no one wanted me." Marcy smiled shyly, but not too broadly, remembering her dead tooth. "I was too old. Or too ugly. Or both. It gave me a chance."

"Hey, at least you have a sense of humor about it."

"God helped me every day."

"*God?*" Jerome raised his eyebrows. "I don't see too much of God in the human trafficking trade."

"*I* saw Him. I mean, He was with me the whole time. All the kids upstairs . . ." She explained how she was assigned to feed the children, how she told them about Jesus and His love for them, then how she tucked them in at night. "I think it helped them. It helped me."

"I've never heard of a survivor doing such things. I mean, sometimes kidnapped people look after one another, but what you're talking about, it's just not done."

He grunted and smiled at her. "But I would agree with you. I think you helped them, too. Somehow. Look at this. See this boy's photo? We recovered him in Philadelphia last year, sold to an undercover agent. He said he came from Iowa. That's how I heard about him. He told an investigator that a nice lady who fed him each day told him Bible stories. The report stayed with me because it was so strange. I couldn't imagine that a kidnapper cared for the boy like that. I figured it must've been another survivor. That nice lady must've been you."

"Well, I don't feel like a lady. In my mind, I keep thinking I'm only fifteen or sixteen now."

"To that boy, and what he'd been through? You were an angel, no matter how old you feel." He closed his laptop. "We can get to my other questions another time. You're obviously handling all this pretty well, but you should probably see a counselor. Maybe they can help you deal with the trauma you've been through."

"I don't know what a counselor would do for me."

"Well, you can talk to them, get stuff off your mind."

"I do that with God when I pray. Why would I need a counselor if I already talk to God about everything?"

"Hmmm." Jerome squinted his eyes. "When you put it that way, I'm not sure I have an answer. How about we get you into a warm bed for the night? There are a couple of women's shelters we can check with. They take women your age."

"There was a man—PJ."

"The one you said beat you a lot?" He checked his notes. "Yeah, Pug Johnson. Imagine getting stuck with a name like Pug. No wonder he picked PJ instead. Believe me, his photo is all over the city. We'll hopefully have him in custody by Monday."

"He's got a limp." She blushed. "I gave it to him. I messed up his Achilles' tendon."

"Oh?" He made a note on his laptop. "That might help us. It's hard to disguise a prominent limp. That's good."

"Would it be okay if I, uh, stayed with you? I want to stay updated on the search for my brother—now that I'm free."

""Stay with me?" Jerome tilted his head. "That's probably not going to be appropriate. You should stay with the young ladies at one of the homes. As for your brother, I'll be talking to you often about the Dosier side of the GLOW network. Investigators are trying to unlock their phones. With any luck, they have records of guys and other rings. We might take down a whole network in the States—maybe in the whole world—with what we uncover with those."

"Can I have a phone? I mean, shouldn't I have a phone if we're going to be talking a lot? I have no money to buy one myself, though."

"Of course. I think we can swing that. Can you give me a day or two?"

A policewoman let her ride up front as she drove her to a downtown shelter and left her at the curb outside. Marcy walked in the front door and stopped. The front desk was empty. A woman with spiky hair was speaking on her phone in the nearby stairwell. Two other women could be heard arguing farther inside the three-story building. She smelled the sweet, acrid odor of weed. Her first instinct was to back out and find somewhere else to stay, but she knew no one and Jerome hadn't given her a phone yet.

Eight years. She held her few possessions closer and crept toward a doorway where she heard the sound of dishes. She'd survived this far. Maybe God would see her through this as well.

But danger nagged at the back of her mind—worse than even the fear of what people would think of her for being imprisoned for eight years. No, she couldn't shake the chill of PJ. He'd gotten away. Pug Johnson was out there somewhere. He would learn she was now free. And alone . . .

That night, she lay in a bed with four other women in the room. Two of them played on their phones, the glow from their little screens lighting the room just enough for Marcy to make out her surroundings. Crude posters hung on the walls. Two dressers stood by the door.

A man's laughter reached her ears, and she sat up in bed. The sound had come from somewhere downstairs. What was a man doing in a women's shelter at that time of night? Her roommates didn't react, so Marcy tried to calm her breathing.

Still fully clothed, she climbed out of bed, clutched her pillowcase, and approached the door to the hallway. If a man was in the women's shelter, then PJ could get in there, too.

"Where are you going now?" asked a woman whose face was lit up by her phone. "You just got here."

"I need a glass of water," Marcy said and crept into the hall.

The sounds in the building were strange—strange voices, strange noises. She couldn't make sense of it, and the unknown was terrifying. Maybe if she could find a little room and a stout chair to barricade the door, then she could finally sleep safely again. Her body was exhausted and still sore from PJ's last beating.

At the bottom of one flight of stairs, she found a common area with two sofas and a few chairs that faced a wall screen. The stairwell light dimly lit the room revealing that there was a man and woman giggling on one of the sofas. Marcy was about to pass the room by when she noticed a bookshelf—with two racks of books!

"Hey, get out of here!" The woman cursed at her, and her lover mumbled something. "Hey, I'm talking to you!"

But Marcy couldn't take her eyes off the bookshelf. It was like a library! One small black book in particular held her gaze. The lighting was bad, but she knew what the book was. Its binding was insignificant and it was wedged amongst a row of colorful novel covers.

"Hey, why aren't you in your room?" The woman stood from the sofa. "I'm talking to you, gal!"

Marcy reached the shelf and drew out the black book. Sure enough, the front read, *"Holy Bible."* Her hands trembled. This was it—the answer to her prayers and searching and years of hoping. She had so many questions!

She turned sharply toward the approaching woman and held up the Bible. The woman, her hair askew, appeared startled over Marcy's sudden about-face.

"Whose books are these?" Marcy asked.

"They're . . . everybody's. Or nobody's. What's wrong with you?"

"I found a Bible!" Marcy gasped, suddenly realizing she'd dropped her pillowcase somewhere. "Can I have it?"

"Will it get you out of this room?"

"Yeah."

"Then keep it."

"Thank you." Marcy held the Bible in one hand and picked up her pillowcase with the other. "Thank you. Sorry."

The woman muttered under her breath as Marcy left the common area.

Marcy crouched in the stairwell where a little light shined. She never imagined finding a Bible in an uncomfortable place like this. Who had left it behind? It was clearly used. The pages were brittle and a few corners were folded, but it was in better condition than most of the mildewy novels she'd found in the basement of Tory and Trey's house.

"Thank You!" Marcy whispered to God, sensing the Bible had been waiting for her all along. He was still answering her prayers, knowing what she most wanted.

As misplaced as she felt, the Bible had similarly been misplaced. She and it—they had a connection, a past, and hopefully a future.

"Two lost things found each other." She sighed. Her

tears ran with joy as she patted the cover of the precious book. "Nobody wants me, but God always rescues me."

Homeland Security Agent Jerome Wessel stood outside the human trafficking home in Davenport's east end and studied the brick house. It had always bothered him that criminals couldn't be identified on sight, and the house from which Marcy Nevins had escaped was no exception. The east end was home to an upper class of residents. This multi-story home seemed cared for with fresh paint, spotless windows, and a clean yard. Even the grass and bushes were artificial, which would've made for convenient upkeep for the kidnappers. The neighbors' houses next door showed no hint of criminal activity, either, but he wondered how many of them were harboring secrets just as wicked as this house, hiding human suffering in plain sight.

He mounted the steps to the porch, ducked under the police tape, and pushed open the broken door. The door was heavy, meant to contain rather than keep someone from breaking in. Nevertheless, whoever had kicked it in had used extreme force. And he'd worn size eleven boots to do so. The imprint was still on the front paneling. That person was still a mystery. Someone had found the trafficking house, broken down the front door, then anonymously called the police. Marcy had escaped, but she'd said nothing about who had left the door wide open for her. The police had found no one inside except the Dosiers on the foyer floor. And on the second story, the young kids had still been locked in their rooms.

From inside the foyer, Jerome took a photo of the door's broken frame and hanging padlock. This hardware had kept Marcy inside for many years. Jerome felt his temperature rise as he walked farther up a hallway, wanting such people to pay dearly for preying on the innocent. After serving as a Marine for twelve years, he'd discharged as a sergeant before joining Homeland

Security. He'd kicked down his own share of doors, but he really wanted to kick in someone's teeth. The kids had been recovered and Marcy was being cared for, but how many had suffered and died in this house?

Midway up the hallway to the kitchen, he found a door to a bedroom. The latch mechanism on the outside of the door indicated that someone had been held inside. From Marcy's description, this had been her room. Though she'd been treated as a type of maid off and on for years, he understood she'd been assaulted countless times. Even her face bore the scars of years of battery. To his fascination, she seemed to be the most placid survivor of human trafficking he'd ever spoken to.

Walking slowly through the room, he noted the bedding, the window with the crack in it, and the items in the bathroom. Detectives had already processed the room for their criminal case, but Jerome was there for a much different reason. He was Homeland Security. This was a hunt for him. Every habit, routine, and discipline of one trafficker might shed light to find the next one, which would lead to the rescue of more kids. The towels that the kidnappers gave the children had to come from somewhere. The food they fed the kids was purchased in bulk from someone. Had no one noticed or asked any questions?

Jerome partially closed the bedroom door at the sight of a mural on the wall behind it. The image was clearly drawn by a child. It was a boat on water, and a giant cross on the top of the boat. He backed up to the bed in the corner, eyeing the mural from where he imagined Marcy had slept for so many nights. This was her drawing. It had to be hers. The mural was awkwardly plain, yet he knew it held significance. Somehow.

Next, he stood in the kitchen for several minutes, studying everything from different angles. Marcy had cooked the meals here. The trays had come from the freezer there. She'd helped dispose of the dead boy through the padlocked back door over there.

In the basement, he used his flashlight to wander down aisles of shelves with clothes, books, and dusty household items. He picked through one bag of clothes that would fit three- or four-year-olds. It was all used, maybe from garage sales. The kidnappers had kept a stockpile of clothing on hand to clothe their victims without ever needing to go to the store. Appearances were carefully managed in the trafficking world. Tory and Trey had been experts, hiding their house and their activities in plain sight.

Hearing footsteps above, Jerome drew his sidearm. No one was supposed to be in the house. Detectives were done taking their photos as they now built their case for a trial or plea agreement. The location of the house had even been kept from media outlets, so far.

He climbed the stairs slowly to the main floor and aimed his handgun at the open door. No one appeared, but that didn't mean they were gone.

In the ground floor hallway, Jerome edged along the wall toward the foyer and stairs to the upstairs bedrooms. If someone was in the house, it was possible that—

A lamp crashed over his head. Lying on the floor, Jerome kept his eyes closed as his head spun. His gun had clattered somewhere nearby. His assailant had the upper hand, but Jerome wouldn't be shy about responding—as soon as he could sense where the perp was.

Behind him, he heard a footfall, then the scuff of metal on the floorboards as someone picked up his handgun. Jerome flipped over and swung his left leg hard at the person's calves. The leg sweep dropped the assailant hard, and Jerome was on him.

"Stay down! Stop struggling! You're under arrest!"

But this was a desperate person, and Jerome's commands weren't supported by control of his own sidearm. Jerome grasped the wrist of the hand that held the weapon, then straddled the man and slugged him once on the cheekbone. He was a dark-skinned black man, maybe Hispanic, not as muscled as Jerome, but definitely heavier.

The gun boomed. Jerome fought harder, trying a submission hold, failing, and finally being thrown against the wall. He lunged right back at the man before standing and grappling again for the weapon. With overwhelming strength, he twisted the gun from the man's hands, but such focus opened him up for a punch to the jaw that sent him rolling aside, his vision distorted. The man ran from the hall toward the back door. Jerome lifted his gun to fire, but he was too late.

Gasping for air, he tasted blood in his mouth. After holstering his weapon, he called for backup, and ordered that a perimeter be set up four blocks out.

"It's Pug Johnson," he stated. "He's been sighted again on the east end. Block every road—and don't let him cross the river!"

Jerome walked into the kitchen and washed his cuts and scrapes, trying to steady his nerves after the fight. His knees felt weak and his confidence was shaken by the man who'd gotten the jump on him. PJ had been so much larger. He couldn't remember the last time anyone had bested him in a tussle. How had Marcy fought off such an animal?

She would continue to be a key witness, he decided as he mounted the steps to the bedrooms above. Her mind didn't seem plagued by the scars of victimhood like most survivors, which made her objective view invaluable. She'd lived within a GLOW household for nearly a decade. He had to ask her more questions about Tory and Trey's ring. The way GLOW operated in one place was likely to be the same in thousands of other cities across America. Law enforcement could be notified to watch for such patterns.

Upstairs, on the third floor, he found what PJ had

probably returned for: thumb drives. About a hundred of them were scattered across the floor, spilt from a tote bag. It looked as if the bag had been hidden in the wall of the bedroom. PJ must've been in the process of recovering them when he'd heard Jerome in the house below. Jerome shook his head at his own carelessness. The trafficker had to have been upstairs the whole time!

He bagged up the thumb drives and returned to his car from which he called a squad officer to deploy someone to surveil the house from then on. PJ could come back.

While he waited for an officer to arrive, Jerome sat in his car out front and mulled over his battle wounds, past and recent. It wasn't his first time to have a physical altercation with a perp, but violence did seem to be escalating these days. More often now, cornering a human trafficker resulted in a gunfight. A couple decades earlier, traffickers were fewer and when approached by police, they usually accepted their fateful arrest.

"The whole world is going mad," Jerome mumbled and rested his head against his seat. But when he closed his eyes, he saw a boat and cross image in his mind. It was the one on Marcy's wall of captivity. He couldn't explain why some survivors found strength to emerge so stable when others emerged so debilitated. Although Jerome had taken all the psych classes and attended trafficking conferences, none of the "professional" explanations had made sense to him—why some victims recovered and some didn't. But Jerome had a sneaking suspicion it had to do with an outside . . . influence. Marcy had it and she knew it. The whole idea was unsettling to Jerome because he knew very little about God, but the idea was hard to deny.

The patrol car arrived, and Jerome walked over to the officer to give him face-to-face instructions.

"I've listened to the radio," he said to the young mustached boy, barely out of the academy, "so we know this PJ is still loose. Remember that face. He's a big guy, over six feet. Call for backup if you see him."

"No offense, sir, but it looks like you're the one who should've called for backup."

Jerome nodded, knowing his suit had blood on the breast from his scalp.

"Yeah, he got the jump on me. He doesn't fight fair, but we shouldn't expect him to. He's been preying on five-year-olds for years, along with the rest of his family. Let's not give him any more opportunities to do it again."

When he arrived back at the station, Jerome changed his shirt in the parking lot and left his bloody blazer in his car trunk. Inside the station, he weaved through officers and cuffed criminals alike without more than a glance. Federal money to fight trafficking ebbed and flowed on the whims of political agendas, so he'd adjusted to the discomforts of having an office amongst the locals. As a Fed, he'd shown his zeal to keep Davenport citizens safe, and that had earned their respect, though he knew their tolerance for Feds of any type didn't run too deep.

As he reached his office, he was surprised to see through the glass that Marcy was seated in a chair in front of his desk. He checked the corridor, but no one was available to explain how she'd gotten there or why. Since Jerome had no assistant, he had to depend on his own message service.

"Marcy, this is a pleasant surprise." He removed his sidearm and set it in his top right drawer, then sat behind the desk. "Everything working out? I've been meaning to come see you. I have more questions for you. I was just at . . .the house. Ran into PJ, but he got away before I could arrest him."

"That's why I'm here." Her face was grim.

He studied her closer. She wasn't a pretty girl, and it didn't help that she didn't seem to know what to do with her unruly black hair. That blackened tooth in the front was an eyesore, too. She wore her frumpy coat, and on the floor beside her lay the pillowcase he remembered she'd had last time—everything she owned.

"Was PJ at the shelter?" He reached for his phone. "Did you see him?"

"No, but I could've. I mean, he could just come right in there and kill me. Tory and Trey will send him after me, I know it. I can testify against them all."

"Well, yeah, but you're inside the shelter, so that—"

"Most of the girls there are prostitutes." Her face hardened. "You had to know that. Is that why I'm there? Is that what you think of me?"

"No, of course not!" He gasped. "They're just trying to get clean like you are."

"I'm not dirty, Agent Wessel!"

"That's not exactly what I meant. I mean, they're trying to get themselves together."

"I'm not using drugs. And no one there is trying to get clean. People walk in right off the street and deliver dope to them, and two different pimps for the others already talked to me about earning them some dough. As long as their clients don't care about my looks."

"That's terrible." Jerome felt his heart soften. "No one should speak to you that way."

"It's my experience that my looks have protected me more often than not. I'm not complaining to God about it."

"You should be safe from that kind of treatment in a shelter. It's my fault. I had you dropped there."

"Three days ago, you said you'd get me a phone, but I haven't heard from you. I can't do anything without a phone. It's like I'm back in Tory's house."

"I know. I've been busy following every lead about that place. Now I found a pile of new evidence—thumb drives. But it's not your fault, it's mine."

"While you're following leads, PJ could walk right in there and kill me or kidnap me again. I'm not going back."

Jerome couldn't argue with her. The whole system was broken. Billions of dollars were donated to supposedly fight human trafficking—the war on it and the recovery from it. But the money got lost somewhere between the sifting fingers of administrators, officials, and politicians. Human traffickers weren't the only ones taking advantage of the trafficking situation.

"I understand. I'll find somewhere else for you. In fact, something comes to mind right now."

"And I want to know what's being done to find my brother and parents."

"Wait. Your parents, too?" Jerome scratched his brow. "After all this, uh, you still want to find them? I mean, talk to them? That just isn't done."

"They're my parents. They were on drugs. I've read about it. They weren't thinking clearly."

"If you say so." Jerome checked his phone. "No results on searches for them yet. I'm guessing they're out of the country by now. GLOW relocates people pretty regularly. And your brother, after eight years, as young as he was—"

"He's sixteen now. That's not too young."

"Right. Well, it's been eight years. I've got to be straight with you, Marcy. Even with as much as we're doing these days to raise awareness and to fight trafficking, we still recover only about one percent of these victims. That means ninety-nine percent are . . . lost. Or they age-out of the trade. Or they, sadly, join the trade. A lot of victims are groomed to become part of the criminal network. For kids as young as your brother—"

"His name is Aidan."

"It could be all he knows now. He won't be the Aidan you remember."

"He's still Addy, and I want him found. He's still a kid and I'm still his sister. Is there someone else I should talk to besides you?"

Jerome pushed the offense aside.

"No, I'm it in Davenport. But I can put you in touch with support groups and awareness campaigns against trafficking. It can't hurt to get Aidan's picture out there as much as we're able. Maybe it'll give you hope—to search for him."

"Agent Wessel, my brother's a person, and people can be found!"

"We don't even know what he'd look like by now. I've put his old photo into the system and aged it eight years, but it's hardly perfect. Whoever he was sold to probably gave him a new name by now. Captors brainwash their victims like you wouldn't believe—by force or compulsion."

"He was old enough that he'll still remember his name. I read in the Bible where kids were kidnapped, sold, abused, and given new names. They didn't forget who they were or where they came from."

"That's in the Bible?" Jerome frowned. "Sounds . . . graphic."

"It's the truth. Different people deal with the truth in different ways. Some deny it and create their own, then live a lie. I chose to look it in the face and see that God still loves me."

"After all you've been through?"

"God didn't do those things to me. Sin and bad people did it. Remember, I got to mother a lot of kids that Trey brought through those locked rooms. You keep treating me like I'm damaged goods, Agent Wessel. It's not helping anybody."

"Yeah. You're right. You are . . . definitely unique." He swiped at his phone, then held it up for her to see. "Can you tell me about this mural you drew on that wall? What's it all about?"

"It's a story in the Bible. It's about God judging sinners, but He provides His Son Jesus as a rescue from the flood. I just read it in the Bible yesterday. My first Bible."

"You just read about it, but you drew it in that room? I don't understand."

"It was a story I heard when I was a kid, so it kept me sane when PJ was assaulting me all the time. It's about rescue."

"And you think God rescued you?"

"More times than you could ever know."

"No, I do know there's something different about you. Nobody comes out of what you've been through and still cares for the people who sold her—unless she's something special." He set the phone on his desk. "Can you remember anything about the moments before you escaped the house? We're still trying to piece together who called the police in the first place. Who broke down that door?"

"Okay, um . . . I was in my room. Trey and PJ were really worried about something that Trey saw outside. Tory and Trey were really afraid, then PJ ran out the back door. That's all I heard."

"The police were outside?"

"No, Trey and PJ called it something else. I don't remember what they called it. Then I heard the front door crash open. Arguing, then silence. And someone walked around in the house for a while. As soon as I thought it was clear, I ran out to find help."

"Whoever that was, they tied up Tory and Trey."

"Yeah, I saw them on the floor."

"So, that's what the police found when they arrived, along with the children upstairs."

"I don't remember anything else. I was barricaded inside my room. PJ had beat me a short time before that."

"Yeah, I remember the bruises you had. Okay. Thanks for repeating yourself. You've been through so much, I—"

"Why don't we just focus on finding Aidan?"

"Of course. I'll keep him at the top of my list. You have my word on that, Marcy. In the meantime, I might have the perfect place for you to go. You want help with your stuff?"

He headed to the door.

"No." She picked up her pillowcase. "It'd better not be another public shelter."

"It isn't. It's a foster home."

"I'm a little old for foster care, if I'm really twenty-one now." She followed him through the precinct floor. "Don't you think?"

"Carol Elroy is like you—a Christian. I think you can help her more than she can help you—but you'll be safe there. She's taken in some trafficked kids for us in years past, with mostly successful results."

"Why would she want my help?"

"It's just a guess that she will. Her husband recently died, but she still has three girls to care for. Almost teens now. PJ would never look for you there."

"And you'll look for Aidan?"

They reached his car and he faced her.

"You have my word, Marcy. I won't stop looking for your brother."

For the first couple months, Jerome checked on Marcy weekly, updating her about efforts to track Aidan and boys his age trafficked within the GLOW network the past few years. Jerome made additional rescues from these endeavors—in Chicago and Tucson.

But after two months, Jerome kept Marcy updated by phone calls alone. He simply couldn't face the young woman with such empty promises and unacceptable news any longer. Even his phone calls dropped off to texts every couple weeks. There was nothing to report. Forty million around the world were currently being trafficked. There was no measurable financial gain for anyone to turn in whoever had purchased Aidan, and Tory and Trey weren't talking. The DA wasn't offering them a sentence reduction for their cooperation, and the husband-and-wife team apparently didn't have a burdened conscience to volunteer such information.

Marcy qualified for a school grant and began to take

night classes at an adult business school, but mid-year, Marcy texted Jerome to tell him she'd dropped out to intern with a disaster relief ministry that was headquartered locally. Jerome felt that it helped the young lady to keep him updated, but often he didn't know how to respond to her inquiries about the search for her brother. Meanwhile, she helped her foster mother, Carol Elroy, with the three youths who lived in the home where Carol refurbished old quilts to supplement the dwindling government checks she received.

A year later, the country was ravaged by a virus that complicated international investigations even more, though global trafficking didn't stop. Jerome flew to Los Angeles to participate in the takedown of a GLOW massage parlor—only to find that they'd already cleared out. Over twenty women had disappeared. Due to further travel restrictions, agents were ordered not to pursue their only lead into Canada, and Jerome felt further hampered by pandemic bureaucracy to make headway on a monster that seemed unrestrained. GLOW was growing, and Federal efforts to combat the organization seemed limited to lip service and fundraisers. Meanwhile, victims suffered.

The night he returned from Los Angeles, he found a stranger parked in front of his studio apartment. But an instant later, he laughed at himself. No one ever visited him. Whoever was there was probably visiting one of the other three tenants in the complex.

As he walked past the car, the thin figure of Marcy emerged from the driver's door, but she didn't make a move toward him. He stopped on the sidewalk and set down his pack, wondering how he'd never actually pitied the girl. No, he almost envied her resolve. She had what few others did, including himself, even though he was driven to arrest criminals.

"Agent Wessel, I haven't heard from you in a while."

"Sorry." He nudged his bag with his foot in the dark.

She was so strong! "I sort of live my life trying to forget what I've seen and trying to shut down those who're to blame. As much as I try to help people, it's people who I forget about."

"I know you don't have an easy job. Maybe I've expected too much from you."

"Um, I'm . . . not sure how to take that." He picked up his bag. "I've had a long day, Marcy. Was there something else? It's good to see you got your driver's license."

He started to walk away.

"What's a Sladrick?"

Jerome turned back slowly.

"What . . . did you say?"

"What's a Sladrick?"

"Where did you hear that name?"

"So, it means something to you?"

"Yeah. It means something to me."

"What is it?"

"Sladrick isn't a *what*. He's a *who*." Jerome left his bag on the sidewalk and leaned over the car. "Where did you hear his name?"

"I finally remembered. That's who PJ, Trey, and Tory were so afraid of that day I escaped. Trey thought he saw Sladrick outside, but he wasn't completely sure. Why were they so afraid? Who is Sladrick?"

"Sladrick is a ghost. A legend in the war against trafficking. A phantom. He may be the only person in the whole world that GLOW really fears."

"They don't fear you?"

"Homeland Security?" Jerome cursed under his breath, then apologized for the crudeness. "GLOW knows our methods. They know every rule and law that restricts our access across borders and into homes. They use it all against us. Sladrick operates by something different. He knows no boundaries. Some say he works by contract, but no one's certain."

"Contract?"

"For pay. People hire him to find and retrieve people. GLOW fears him because rumor has it, he always gets his HTV."

"HTV?"

"Human trafficking victim."

"Oh. Would he go overseas, if they took Addy somewhere else?"

"I've heard Sladrick must've been born overseas. He could be a foreigner. He's comfortable out there where others, like myself, have no resources, contacts, or access. Everywhere Sladrick goes, he seems to have people, maybe his own network working against GLOW. It's far more advanced than what any country, even the whole United Nations, has been able to coordinate. But Marcy, if we knew how to find Sladrick, everyone in the government would be trying to use him, hire him, or ask for his help. There are just little pieces of intel we hear about him occasionally from HTVs. That's how I know a little about him. And from talking with other agents, I know he's gone by the codename RefugeGate. Some have thought there's more than one Sladrick, because he's all over the place. Maybe as many as a dozen people go by that name, but I don't know for sure. Nobody really knows."

"How would Trey have recognized him?"

"I don't know. GLOW is sophisticated. I've heard they send out alerts to their trafficking rings if there's wind of a raid. As sick as it sounds, GLOW owns some of the police and HT agency personnel."

"So, I need to find Sladrick, or RefugeGate, and he can find Addy and my parents."

"Marcy, I—" He shook his head. "I understand trying to find your brother, even though it's unlikely. I'm sorry. A guy like Sladrick isn't going to want to help you reunite with your parents. They're part of the problem. It's just not done."

"Sladrick is the reason I'm free, Trey and Tory are in prison, and PJ's on the run. I have to find him."

"Again, if just anyone could find Sladrick, we would have already—and GLOW definitely would have killed him. A man like him has no life because one side wants him dead and the other side wants to use him. You don't find Sladrick. No one ever has."

"Then how's he fulfilling contracts?" Marcy lifted her chin at the challenge. "God knows who he is, and I'll find him."

She climbed into her car, and Jerome stepped back, realizing she really was leaving that abruptly. Sure enough, she drove away, leaving him feeling like a pessimistic discouragement. What was she going to do, pray herself into finding Sladrick?

A moment later, as he let himself into his apartment, he realized that's just what she would do. That's what made people like Marcy Nevins special. She believed in things beyond herself. Yes, he definitely envied her. And if she actually found Sladrick, he'd envy her even more. Professionally, he'd never admit it, but Sladrick was a true-life hero.

Greg "The Rot" Rotz sat at a park bench in North Tampa, Florida, eating his lunch purchased from a taco truck. He chewed slowly, watching the skateboarders weave expertly around business people in suits in the eighty-five-degree weather with eighty percent humidity. The sidewalk was bustling with other people, too: transients panhandling, Hondurans seeking work, and working girls looking for johns.

Without looking, Greg tossed his taco wrapper at the garbage can. He heard evidence of another missed attempt.

"One of these days . . ." He retrieved his trash, gave it a critical glare, then dropped it in the can. Stretching his thin frame toward the hot, hazy sun, he prayed for stamina for the day and night to come at the TROAS apartments. Between Brody Sladrick's operations and

Binsa's aid requests, he had little time for himself. Sure, he'd signed on for this work, and he understood that the evils of the day demanded a faithful response, but when did he get any vacation time? How else was he supposed to improve his daily taco trash shot?

Yet, with no less enthusiasm than the day, week, or month before, he entered the high-rise apartment building behind him, leaving the Florida sunshine in exchange for the air conditioning of the twelfth floor. Once exiting the elevator, he strolled carefree in his faux leather sandals down the hallway of the eight apartments belonging to TROAS. The human Trafficking Recovery and Operative Assistance Service leased the whole floor, assuring the organization's necessary privacy.

The studio apartment belonging to Greg was the last one on the right, and it doubled as his office. He winked at the facial recognition camera above his head, then punched in a nine-digit code to unlock the reinforced door. Inside, he approached his desk, peeled off his shirt, and touched a switch on the wall that dimmed the double-plated glass windows beyond his screen. When he sat in his chair with custom lumbar support, he had to lean to his left to see out the window. Far below, he could see Interstate 4 where vehicles came and went between Tampa and Orlando.

"Everyone's on vacation but me." He tapped a key on his soft-touch keyboard. "How about you, Sister? Are you on vacation?"

"Good afternoon, Rottweiler," a woman's voice firmly greeted. "You have fourteen new messages and six overdue reminders."

"Sister, remind me later about the reminders. What's the first new message?"

The computer droned through texts and voicemails that had come in while he'd been out to lunch.

An Australian man was asking for help to recover his wife who'd been kidnapped and sold to a Middle Eastern man. Since the Saudi buyer was able to produce a "legitimate" proof of purchase, the Australian had no legal claim—so claimed the Saudi government. Greg summarized the situation and sent it off to Brody Sladrick. Dealing with the Saudis nearly always required a special operation since the Saudis never negotiated. Lately, Brody seemed to prefer the more dangerous and hopeless operations. Ever since his wife had died from the virus, Brody had been on the road almost nonstop.

In the next message, a Hungarian child had been trafficked to China and her parents had been killed. A world watch group suspected she'd become a child bride in the country short on women.

Several of the following requests were from various trafficking watch groups, pleading for help, praying that Sladrick could recover a loved one or lost one, since diplomacy or all traces had come to an end.

Suddenly, his computer speaker chimed.

"Sister, what is it?"

"We have a report alert on specified search parameters."

"Show me on screen left."

Greg studied the results. He was only twenty-three, but he'd developed his own botnets, which he called scorpions, to troll the internet for certain news, photos, enemies, faces, and other items. One scorpion was dedicated to scrubbing the internet of traces of TROAS, Brody Sladrick's face, or any trail that could lead back to Greg himself. Another scorpion functioned remotely from Iceland, compiling results on anyone who might be searching for them.

Someone in Davenport, Iowa, was using every available search engine to search for Sladrick. Greg pulled up additional searches made by the same person. Phrases like "human trafficking" and "recover people" were tried over and over again, sometimes on the same search engine, as if the user didn't understand how search engines worked.

People were always trying to find Brody Sladrick, but usually for nefarious reasons. Only a few private organizations had been trusted with TROAS' contact information, and Brody kept their actual physical location secret. Anyone else was a threat to the human trafficking retrieval expert that Brody had become over the last thirty years. Global Wares was always hunting for Brody, sometimes using actual kill squads or local gangs. Greg had seen them employ multiple traps in an attempt to capture their apex adversary.

But Greg doubted the Davenport user was a GLOW operative. This person was too sloppy. He tracked the account to a library, registered to a Marcy Nevins, age twenty-two. When he ran her through the system, he accessed her record from the previous year. It coincided with Brody's visit to Davenport when he'd broken up a small GLOW ring working the Midwest. Marcy had been an eight-year captive, yet Brody had apparently set her free. Greg hadn't seen her name on any of TROAS' reports, but that wasn't too rare since Brody didn't write operation reports. The people he rescued needed security, not a paper trail.

Marcy's search attempts didn't reveal why she was searching for Brody. Sometimes, survivors wanted to thank their rescuer. Brody never responded to such recognition.

Greg sat back in his chair and stared at the arrest photo of Marcy Nevins. All arrest charges had been dropped, but her photo remained. Then, he switched to her more recent driver's license photo. She was smiling in this one. It looked like she had a dead front tooth. Yet, she was nevertheless smiling.

This made Greg smile. He stood in his bare feet and approached the window to look down at the streets of Tampa, its parks, night clubs, and alleys. The world was so broken, but God kept reminding everyone that He was there. Marcy had been through so much, but she was grinning for her driver's license photo. Was it too much to hope for that her joy was from God? Did she know Jesus above and beyond the trauma? Greg knew that Christ offered the only real inner healing from such mistreatment, but was Marcy actually a believer?

"It wouldn't be the first time, Lord," Greg said, returning to his desk, "that You hid one of Your lights in the middle of the darkness."

Leaving Marcy's beautiful smiling face on one screen, Greg compiled her complete profile on another screen. His hopes that she was a believer grew when he saw she was interning with a disaster relief organization that smuggled computerized Bibles and study resources to believers in closed countries. All from Iowa!

He donned his headset and paced the apartment, praying for the right words to speak to Marcy. Brody didn't want him following up with past survivors, or overcomers, as he called them. Binsa, the woman across the hall, was supposed to do that difficult work. But Greg told himself that he wasn't certain why this young woman was searching for Sladrick. Maybe she wanted to thank them, or maybe she had an additional need.

"Or maybe I'm just lonely," Greg teased himself, "and can't resist talking to a pretty lady."

"Please repeat your last, Rottweiler," his computer requested of his audible voice.

"Uh, Sister, dial Marcy Nevins." He stopped pacing and watched the screens. Marcy's driver's photo stared back. She had dark eyes and unruly black hair, but there was maturity there, too. Wisdom and experience, not unlike himself. Sure, he'd never been held captive like Marcy, but they were both overcomers, both exposed to the horrors of humanity, and they'd emerged smiling. And she was just a year younger than he was. Anything was possible . . .

"Hello?" Her voice was innocent, feminine, and sweet. "Is someone there?"

Greg felt a cold sweat burst from every pore.

"Yes, I'm calling from overseas," he notified in his most manly voice. He used the server in Iceland as his primary proxy to safeguard TROAS' location in Tampa. "They call me the Rot."

"The *Rot?* That's so mean. Who calls you the Rot?"

"No. It's not mean." Greg frowned. "It's my handle. My online moniker."

"You made it up yourself? You call yourself rotten? Why would you do that?"

"No, the Rot. Not rotten. Like, the Rottweiler. I'm . . . the Rot. It's a name. People know it. I mean, some people. Maybe not normal people like you, but people in my field of—"

"I think I'm going to hang up now."

"No, wait!" Greg rolled his eyes at his attempted smooth talk. "Call me Greg."

"I'm confused. I think you have the wrong number."

"No, you're Marcy Nevins, right? It's really important I talk to you. Just as important is that you forget the first thirty seconds of this phone conversation. I'm an idiot. I don't normally speak to people like you."

"Uh, I don't know what you mean."

"You know." Greg's free hand tugged frustratedly at his dirty blond hair. "I live behind a computer. I don't interact with too many people face to face. If I tried to talk to someone like you in the park, I'd probably faint first."

"Someone like me? Why do you keep saying that? How do you know who I am?"

He heard the concern rise in her voice.

"No, please don't be mad. I saw you were searching for Sladrick. I work for him, er, with him."

"Sladrick? You know Sladrick? I was just searching for him!"

"I know. I'm sort of his . . . right hand man, you could say."

"I don't believe you. This is a trick."

"What trick?" Greg felt the blood drain from his hand. "This is no trick. I keep track of searches for my boss. We have a lot of enemies out there. I had to call and talk to you to see why you were searching for Sladrick."

"I'm not an enemy! Sladrick helped me escape some bad people last year. I think he can help me find my family. If anyone should be questioning anyone, it should be me questioning someone rotten enough to call himself Rottweiler."

"Hey, I thought we forgot about that." Greg chuckled nervously. She was feisty! He checked his screen. "Your family. Okay. Your brother Aidan, and your parents, Cole and Emma, right? You want to find them. I'm opening a file."

"I want Sladrick to find my brother Aidan first. Agent Wessel said Sladrick might be the only one who can find him, but he also said I'd never be able to find Sladrick. Nobody ever does."

"Well, you found him. I mean, I handle his operations. Well, he picks what ops he wants to do after I schedule them. I can talk to him for you."

"I need to talk to him myself."

"No, no, no." Greg ran a search on Agent Wessel—ex-Marine, now Homeland Security in Davenport. He was effective in the war against human trafficking, according to arrest and recovery field reports with his name on them. And his bank accounts and tax records matched his actual income, so he probably wasn't corrupt. "Sladrick doesn't really meet with people. He's private. That's what I'm for."

"But you said you're not very good at meeting people, Greg."

"I'm not. I'm actually much smoother when I'm typing emails back and forth. Talking to people on the phone isn't my forte. My mind races. I panic."

"And you tell people things like you're a Rottweiler, and that you'd faint if you saw me face to face."

"No, that was a compliment!" Greg gasped. "Please, listen to me. I never approach . . . attractive people. I mean, I'm the least attractive, so beautiful people just make me seize up. That's what I meant."

"You . . . think I'm attractive?"

"Please, don't be offended. I was just explaining why I said I'd faint if I approached you on the street or somewhere. On a computer, I'm a Rot. In person, I'm probably something between a weasel and a squirrel."

She laughed. Greg sighed. She was strong and quick and . . . amazing!

"So, where can I meet Sladrick?" she pressed.

"I actually can't remember the last time he met with a client. If he does, he doesn't tell me about it. He has secrets. It's important that he keeps them."

"I thought you two were close."

"Well, Sladrick isn't really close to anyone that I know of. It's the job."

"Right. Enemies and stuff."

"Yeah. All that stuff."

"It's been nine years since Aidan was taken. He's seventeen years old now. A stranger won't recognize him, so, I have to be with Sladrick when he goes looking for my brother."

"That's . . . so dangerous! Marcy, Sladrick goes to places where everyone's dangerous. They're killers—all those people who kidnap others."

"I'm not afraid."

"Yeah, well, maybe you should be. I know your story. Traffickers will try to take you again."

"They can try. I'll be with Sladrick. I know GLOW is afraid of him."

"Yeah, they are." Greg licked his lips. "Wait, you know about GLOW?"

"Personally. Eight years. You said you knew my story."

"Right. Okay. I need to think."

"Just tell me where you are. I can come to you, and whenever Sladrick is there, I'll talk to him myself. I barely started searching for him, and you already called me. Agent Wessel said this was impossible, so God must be helping me."

"God? So, you're a believer?"

"Of course. I wouldn't be alive or sane if I wasn't. Look, my whole life is on pause until I find my family. Nothing else matters. I'm not good for anything else. Um, I don't believe you're really overseas. Just tell me where you are, Greg, and I'll drive there. I have my own car now so I can sleep in it until Sladrick can see me. I'll never give up, I promise that!"

Greg squeezed his eyes shut. *Think!* Were there exceptions to their security protocols? Marcy was an overcomer, a believer, and she had a legitimate mission request. Trusting her at all was against Brody's unspoken rules, but . . .

"I'm sending you an address in Georgia. I'll meet you there."

"Thank you so much!"

"You, uh, probably need some money. Sorry for being so personal, but I'm looking at your financials. Can I wire you something extra for your drive? You can use your same debit card."

"That'd help a lot, Greg. I won't have to ask anyone else for help, then. Thank you so much."

He wired her several hundred from his personal account for her trip.

"Okay, I'll see you in Atlanta, Marcy."

"I'll see you, Greg. I mean, the Rot."

Greg turned off his headset and collapsed in his chair, exhausted. Marcy Nevins was the most amazing woman he'd ever spoken to!

CHAPTER THREE

Greg Rotz didn't get to be a field agent too often, but today was different. He was meeting Marcy Nevins and bringing her into TROAS. As he flipped a Frisbee in his hands on the park grass, his stomach was in knots. Maybe it was in knots because he hadn't told Brody Sladrick that he was pulling a rogue mission in Atlanta, Georgia. Or maybe he was queasy because he was about to meet the bold and attractive young lady from Davenport. Of course, maybe he was just self-conscious about his white chicken legs poking out like twigs from the new shorts he was sporting.

The park off Peachtree Street wasn't as crowded as he'd hoped for him to blend in. Pandemic rumors and city regulations were keeping people inside, but he was still counting on a few bike riders and joggers to offer him some cover. He was the only character with a bright red Frisbee, but he hoped from a distance he would appear like someone waiting for a companion.

He practiced tossing the Frisbee at a park tree where he'd left his backpack and phone at the base. The Frisbee wobbled and rolled from his clumsy throw, but in fetching the plastic toy, he knelt long enough to check his phone screen. Marcy hadn't used her debit card since leaving Birmingham. He'd tracked her by the card for three days, praying for her the whole way. By tracking her, he'd known just when to take the train from Tampa up to Atlanta to meet her at the determined address. Any second now, she'd pull up in her used blue Ford.

Hurling the Frisbee away from the tree, Greg walked slowly after it. He'd never been athletic. Anyone who looked too closely at his limbs would notice that, but he knew that being undercover was about playing the part in the right costume. He imagined Brody couldn't have taken better precautions. At least he wasn't bringing Marcy straight to the Tampa apartments.

A two-door blue car pulled off the street into the parking lot forty yards away. Only four other cars sat nearby. With the car still running, Marcy climbed out and looked around the park. She studied her phone, clearly concerned that she was at the right address—a park.

It was her. But Greg didn't run to her like he wanted to. He was an agent. What would Brody do? Surveil. Wait. Watch. TROAS had enemies, and Marcy had a few of her own as well. But she was a long way from Davenport and the trafficking ring that had held her for so many years. Surely, no one had followed her for—

Turning away, Greg tossed the Frisbee at an imaginary partner near his tree. A silver sports car had parked on the street. A male in the driver's seat peered toward Marcy and the park. Under his breath, Greg prayed for Marcy. She was in danger!

When Greg reached the tree, he dialed his phone without picking it up. Acting like he was tying his shoe, he listened on speaker to it ringing. Marcy picked up.

"I think I'm at the address," she said, "but it's a park, I think?"

"Yes, you made it. Can you sit inside your car for a few more minutes? I need to make sure you weren't followed."

"Followed?" He heard panic in her voice. She glanced around her. "All this way? Are you serious?"

"Just wait for me. I'll approach you when I know it's safe. Wait in your car."

Hanging up, Greg picked up his backpack, then walked casually toward the parking lot, using his phone to zoom in on the silver sports car. The man remained in the driver's seat, so Greg couldn't get a positive ID through the windshield glare.

With his backpack strap over one shoulder, he put his

phone to his ear and assured an imaginary friend he would see him that night for a cribbage game. He walked within ten feet of Marcy yet didn't look at her. The Frisbee was tucked under his left arm. Thankfully, she had listened to him and sat inside her car. From the side, he sensed her eyes following him for a few seconds, then she looked elsewhere.

Greg continued toward the silver sports car. No one else had arrived on the street after Marcy. Before he took her to Tampa, he had to make sure he wasn't just being paranoid, but he didn't see a way around identifying the driver without getting really close—revealing Greg's own face.

With that thought, Greg turned the bill of his hat frontwards and tugged it low over his eyes. Twenty more feet. He laughed obnoxiously on the phone.

"No, you bring the snacks this time!" he shouted to his cribbage adversary. "I brought the chips and sodas last week, remember? Loser brings the snacks. You know the rules."

Ten feet. Five. He stopped at the driver's door window, aimed his phone, and took a still photo—flash and all. Then Greg walked away. But he didn't need the phone now to ID the guy. He'd seen and recognized Pug Johnson very clearly through the window. He was someone from Marcy's past, and he knew her whole file.

Before Greg reached the sidewalk, he heard the sports car door open. PJ was a sizeable man, and Greg's knees felt like jelly when he imagined the man tackling him from behind.

"Hey, you! With the backpack!"

In that instant, Greg didn't see a way out of a confrontation. But he remembered what he'd learned from Brody about influencing a situation by remaining cool, calm, and confident in the Lord. All he needed to do was stand.

Greg stopped and turned. PJ stood in his open door,

his expression showing his bewilderment. A stranger had snapped his photo. Since PJ was a wanted man, Greg guessed the man's nerves were already overwhelmed.

"Who, me?" Greg looked left and right. "Did you call me?"

"Yeah, you!" PJ slammed his door and took a step toward Greg. "What're you doing?"

Greg dialed 911 with his thumb, barely glancing at the screen. He sent the photo of PJ to the emergency switchboard and left the line open.

"Oh, I was just making sure it was you." Greg stood up straighter, his gaze firm, remembering that God was with His people, even if they didn't always feel courageous. "It is you, isn't it?"

"What're you talking about?" PJ's eyes narrowed and darted about. "You don't know me. I've never seen you in my life."

"Maybe. But I know you, Pug." Greg held up his phone. "And now the authorities will know you're in Atlanta. Long ways from home, Mr. Johnson."

PJ's fury exploded on his face, and he started forward. His hands became fists and his shoulders rounded like he was a bull about to charge.

"Lord . . ." Greg muttered, barely containing his urge to dash away.

An instant later, caution seemed to return to PJ's mind. The brute froze, then he retreated to his car. After a visual sweep of Peachtree Street, PJ climbed into his car. His tires squealed as he raced out of the parking lot.

"Yes, this is Greg Rotz," Greg said to the 911 operator, then realized he was speaking to an answering service. It didn't matter. He knew they were understaffed, yet they recorded everything. "I've sent you a photo of Pug Johnson, a wanted fugitive from Iowa. Contact Homeland Security Agent Jerome Wessel for information. Johnson is in Atlanta, and he just turned west on Peachtree. He's driving a silver . . ."

By the time Greg reached Marcy's car, he'd left a detailed description of PJ's vehicle and license plate number. He tapped on Marcy's window, smiling at her. She rolled down her window an inch.

"Can I help you? I don't have any extra money."

"Money?" Greg's smile widened. "What?"

"Food?" Marcy reached across to the passenger seat where the clutter of fast food and gas station wrappers spilled onto the floor. "How about a breakfast sandwich?"

"Yeah, that'd be great."

"Here you go." She lowered the window another inch, just enough to squeeze out the sandwich. "Have a nice day."

"I will. Thanks." Greg tucked his phone into his pocket and unwrapped the sandwich. He didn't move from her window. "You know, I didn't eat all morning. I was too excited to get here to meet you on time."

Her mouth opened, then she nearly knocked him over as she pushed open the door. He backed away, grinning, his mouth full, loving the feeling of being the hero for a change—not just someone behind the computer screen.

She looked him up and down. He knew he wasn't much to admire, so he watched her eyes for disappointment. Instead, she threw her arms around his neck, knocking both sandwich and Frisbee from his hands.

"Oh, I'm so sorry!" She covered her mouth with her hand and stepped back as the Frisbee wobbled away.

"No, it's okay." Greg knelt to pick up his sandwich as she chased down the Frisbee. He couldn't remember ever being embraced by a girl his age. Nobody usually wanted to be around a socially awkward stick figure. But she was smaller than he was, and she didn't seem to mind his thin, pale frame. And she was so short, how could she even see over the dash to drive? "I can get another sandwich on the road. It's no big deal."

"I thought you'd be older." She handed him the

recovered toy. "You sounded older on the phone."

"I'm just twenty-three." He shrugged, taking in her wild hair, dark tooth, and bright eyes. "You look . . . great. Um . . ."

"So do you." Her eyes traveled up his face and settled on his cap. "Nice hat."

"It's part of my cover." He grinned and tossed the sandwich at a trash barrel, missed, then dropped it in.

"I usually just hang out in my apartment in my rags all day, but I put a lot of thought into this stuff today. Good thing, too. That Pug Johnson was totally fooled."

"*PJ?*" She seemed to shrink in size, her eyes widening. "You know him?"

"I just met him. That was him in that sports car. He followed you from Davenport."

"*What?* Where is he?"

"I took his picture and called 911. He was pretty mad, but he drove away like he was a chicken with an Everglades' alligator on his tail feathers."

"He's gone?" She sighed. "Wow. There were, like, two nights he could've gotten me. I slept in my car the last two nights!"

"God protected you." Greg shook his head. "I prayed for you the whole way, but you shouldn't take risks like that anymore."

"You . . . prayed for me?" She grinned. "The lady I live with, Carol, prays for me every day. I didn't think anyone else did."

"Well, you know . . ." Greg blushed and cleared his throat. "I took the train here, so I need to ride with you back to Tampa."

"Tampa? Sladrick isn't here?"

"No, he's still overseas. I didn't want to bring you straight to TROAS headquarters until I met you myself."

"TROAS headquarters? What's that?"

"I can tell you on the way." He pointed at the passenger seat. "Should we . . .?"

"Oh, no! All my garbage!"

"This? This is nothing. You should see my office trash. It's overflowing worse than this. Hey, it looks like we have the same taste in junk food!"

Brody Sladrick sat cross-legged at a street café along Sisowath Quay in Phnom Penh, Cambodia. He used a broad plastic spoon to eat his *ka tieu*, but his mind wasn't on the rice-noodle soup, even though it was delicious, seasoned with salt water. His mind was on getting away from the Pradal Serey gang on Sisowath Quay's riverside rail. They'd been following him since his arrival at Phnom Penh International Airport.

No less threat were the working-level police officers gathered at the nearest corner. Two of the five were still in uniform, but the other three were in plain clothes at that midnight hour. With corrupt cops and violent gangs after him, it would be a tangled night.

Taking a slow slurp of his soup, Brody gauged his exit point from the three-mile strip of road that hosted restaurants, bars, and hotels for tourists. He glared back at the seven gang members, all of them in their twenties. He knew they were Pradal Serey experts. Three even wore the weathered hand wraps of the Khmer kickboxing sport, usually unregulated in the underground shadows of Cambodia. They'd been hired to kill him, so they'd come for a fight. It was on their faces. The only reason they hadn't tried to get him yet was because they didn't know why he was back in the city.

That went for the policemen, too. They were dirty, probably paid by the same human traffickers who paid the local gangs to protect their industry. Until they knew exactly which establishment Brody was there to disrupt this time, they couldn't shore up their security and guard their interests.

It was an amusing situation to Brody, but he didn't laugh. He didn't even smile. In fact, he hadn't smiled or laughed for months, not since the funeral. His amusement was professional, like an expert lawyer arguing a case against an amateur. The enemy thought they had the upper hand, but he knew their skills and he knew his own abilities. But he wasn't about to broadcast his confidence. Even his eyes were hidden behind pricey Swiss sunglasses with round frames, keeping his foes unsure of where he was looking.

Shifting his feet, he waited eagerly for the right moment to run—which would be soon. A cyclo swerved in front of him, barely missed a moto, then continued on. Both bicycle and motorcycle rickshaw owners swore at one another, but the moment passed without much incident. No, Brody needed something more prominent to draw the eyes of his pursuers. If they really knew why he was there, they would've already arrested him—or tried to kill him.

Although he could wait all night, he preferred to make his move while it was still dark. The nearby police officers may have been corrupt, but Brody knew a couple police chiefs in neighboring provinces who were honest. One was even a Christian, and Brody preferred to work with that humble man whenever possible.

After another thirty minutes and a second bowl of *ka tieu*, Brody noticed the youths arguing. It seemed some wanted to abduct him right off the street, maybe hoping to beat the intel out of him about why he was in their neighborhood. The police seemed no less agitated by the waiting. Yet, no sufficient distraction had occurred on the street to use for his escape.

He signaled the matron of the restaurant, and she nodded in return. Brody took a deep breath. This was it. He'd have to cause his own commotion. It wouldn't be the first time.

"Hey, are you an American?" Two Westerners lurched over to him, one of them clearly drunk. Both men wore slacks and dress shirts. Their cheeks were tainted with smeared red paint—the cheap lipstick that the local prostitutes and child sex slaves wore. "Is this some city or what?"

"You boys had better sober up." Brody looked away, wishing he had the opportunity to teach them a real lesson. "Those policemen over there are looking this way. They probably suspect you came to Cambodia to have sex with minors."

"Yeah, well, what did you come here for?" demanded the one who was more drunk.

His friend seemed to take in the nearby policemen and Brody's warning more seriously.

"Hey, he's right. Come on. They're watching us. We'd better get back to the hotel."

Once they were gone, the matron approached his table.

"Yes, Mista Brody?" She bowed.

"You've been a wonderful hostess, once again." He counted out a number of U.S. twenty dollar bills, then rolled them up. "I'm feeling generous, Chantrea. Can you go to your rooftop up there and throw this money out onto the street?"

"Anything for you, Mista Brody. You give me back my Bopha. This money—it is offering for Pchem Ben? You get good karma?"

"No, it's not an offering to the ancestors. It's for the living. Here's twenty dollars for yourself. Please. I'll leave after you throw the money onto the street."

Bowing three times, she backed away, mumbling in the Khmer dialect used almost exclusively in the capitol city. A year earlier, Brody had rescued her teenage daughter Bopha from a child labor fish factory in Dangkao. He'd given the single mother a Bible written in Khmer, but she hadn't responded to the gospel as yet.

Removing his sunglasses, Brody busied himself cleaning them. But really, he didn't want the tinted things on his eyes while he was about to move through the dark alleys behind Sisowath Quay. He had to lose the police and the gang of youths, both of whom certainly knew the avenues better than he did.

The shimmer of paper money was caught in the streetlights over the café. The bills floated and fluttered from the night sky for a few seconds before a woman cried out. Tourists and locals alike scrambled to catch the drifting bills. For some of the residents of the city, a single dollar was a week's wages. Pandemonium ensued as rickshaw drivers and pedestrians joined them in the fray.

Brody dashed away while the ruckus separated him from his pursuers. His powerful six-foot frame propelled him to a full sprint in three seconds. He dashed down the nearest narrow alleyway, ducked under a laden clothesline, then hurdled an empty butcher's table. When he reached the next busy street, he slowed to a quick walk, weaving his way through the cinema and club crowd. Westerners mingled with locals. Against the backdrop of motorbikes, English, Khmer, and laughter blended together in a loud buzz.

Once across the modern street, he jogged up a narrow alley that was only the width of his shoulders. He climbed a ladder, then steadied himself on the tin roof of an animal pen. Two leaps later, he hooked his fingers over the edge of an apartment roof. Between two satellite dishes, he squeezed onto a balcony to look through a sliding glass door at a sleeping family. Their flat screen TV flashed violent images across their eyelids.

After climbing from one balcony to the next, Brody came upon an elderly woman sleeping on her balcony in a soft chair, a blanket over her lap. She startled awake, but he held up one hand to urge her to silence, and with his other hand he thrust his sunglasses into her wrinkled fingers. She held up the glasses and smiled a near-toothless grin.

Behind and below, he heard the hurried shouts of his pursuers who'd lost his trail. With the woman's blessing,

Brody gently touched her shoulder, thanked her in Khmer, then passed through the open door into her house. He avoided tall burning candles as well as smoldering candle stumps and incense sticks that choked his senses, to finally reach the front door.

Outside, he hustled along a raised walkway past other apartments, then descended a staircase to the next street. A *tuk-tuk* driver spotted his obvious Western tanned face and clothing and raced other rickshaw drivers to accommodate the American. Brody climbed into the seat and instructed the driver to head north without delay.

At the next intersection, he sank deeper behind the *tuk-tuk* canopy to hide his face from a number of police who were hastily setting up a checkpoint to catch him. Sighing, he relaxed in the seat after barely escaping their designs. It never ceased to amaze him when considering the amount of money and manpower corrupt precincts spent to suppress those who fought human trafficking—when the police could more easily fight human trafficking themselves. It seemed important to them to hide and protect the trade from outside influence. They were worried about saving face.

Ten minutes later, Brody paid the driver and climbed out. He was left to stand on a street with no streetlights. The houses here were either wood shanties or made of brick. Far away, electricity and tourism thrived, even at that late hour, but not here. Brody sniffed the air. Yes, something much different thrived out here in the suburbs.

Along the side street, there was no sidewalk and no parked vehicles. He walked up the street, his ears and eyes alert for an ambush as he drew closer to the smell of burning coal and cooking bricks. The sky above one building glowed from a furnace inside, and from a set of chimneys, sparks occasionally emerged through the gray smoke. Across from the brick kiln, Brody wedged his shoulders between two structures where he settled in to wait. Thanks to Greg Rotz's meticulous research and satellite photos, Brody recognized the buildings and streets around him, though he'd never been in that part of Phnom Penh before.

His heartbeat was slow and steady, hardly bothered by the chase from the waterfront. He quietly unwrapped a piece of gum and stuck it in his mouth as he watched a factory worker or resident walk down the middle of the street. A door slammed. A jet flew over the city, rattling the buildings and inciting a chorus of barking dogs for a few moments. The pandemic plagued the country, and movement restrictions were in place on paper, but there was too much money in tourism and slavery to shut down the city entirely. This was Cambodia.

An hour before dawn, a forty-year-old commuter bus lurched up the street. Only one of its headlights shined with a dull shimmer. The bus crept past Brody's position, then its squeaky brakes brought it to a halt in front of the nearest brick factory.

Brody crossed the street behind the bus as its brake lights glowed red. He reached an unlit staircase and ascended to a landing. On the right, a flimsy door barred his way. A rag stuck through a hole was meant to be used as a handle. But the door wouldn't budge at his pressure. As his intel had stated, it was padlocked on the inside. He heel-kicked it hard, splintering the particle board and causing more noise than he liked, but there was no way around it now.

He passed through the door and stood on a catwalk overlooking the brick kiln factory floor. Three ovens used for hardening, firing, and drying bricks glowed orange on the opposite wall, two stories below. Eighteen workers, strictly women and children in this factory, stood or crouched where they now paused their work, which was pouring and pounding bricks or hauling them out to a courtyard or roof to dry. Three guards postured with their long, thin batons. They were hardened, cruel men, their eyes as dark as their smoke-blackened faces.

The guards spoke quietly amongst themselves as Brody walked slowly toward the metal mesh stairs, which was the only way in or out of the factory. With heavy footfalls, he stomped down the metal steps to the dirt floor. One of the workers dropped a tool and backed away. A few others wiped their grimy hands on dusty trousers. The women's faces were nearly black, only their eyes were bright, differentiating them from the coal smoke that didn't completely drift up the chimneys.

"Who speaks English?" Brody asked the guards, standing in front of the three. "One of you speaks English."

"I speak English," declared the largest of the guards, his voice sharp, his knuckles tight around his baton handle. "This is private business, American. You broke the door!"

"It's time for that door to remain broken." Brody waved at the women and children. "These people are going free."

"No, American. These people owe the boss!" The guard glanced at his two companions, nodding at them to take up a similar stance with their batons. "You leave now or we make you leave."

Brody browsed the faces of the workers. He saw hopelessness in their eyes. They'd passed desperation long ago. The kiln owners had purchased whatever debts their families owed, and now everyone was forced to work. Ten thousand Cambodians were enslaved under such debt-based coercion.

"Ten thousand minus eighteen," Brody mumbled to himself.

"What you say, American? Leave! Now!"

"It's time you learned the difference between threatening a child and threatening a man with some holy wrath in his heart."

"Holy wrath?" The guard frowned. "What is wrath?"

"Get outta here." Brody signaled at the upstairs door. "Or you'll find out."

The two other guards stepped sideways, angling toward the stairs.

"No." Brody pointed. "Leave your batons and your phones. Then, you go."

The guards spoke among themselves. The larger one ordered something harshly, then leaped toward Brody, swinging his baton. Brody caught the baton inches from the end. It stung and bruised his palm, but he was too committed to care. He used the heel of his other hand to smash against the baton midway. Although he'd intended to force the weapon from the young man's hand, the baton broke in two.

Brody tossed his broken half over his shoulder and took a step, his hands held wide, blocking their escape.

"Phones! Now!"

The large guard's courage diminished with his broken baton. They drew their phones out of their pockets and set them on the floor. Brody waved them away, and they hurried up the stairs without looking back. They'd report him in a few minutes, but without their phones, he'd bought himself a little time.

"Go! Everyone!"

Though Brody's Khmer vocabulary was limited, the women and children didn't need much urging to grasp Brody's instructions. Mothers collected their children and glanced suspiciously at Brody as they mounted the stairs.

All but one child seemed to have a mother present. A girl of about eight stood alone, a single brick held in her arms like a child might cling to a teddy bear.

Brody pocketed the three phones. Lastly, he removed both of his shoes and twisted off the heels. After pressing the heel sections together, he ripped off a switch detonator and threw the device against the back of the middle kiln. This was the real reason the local toughs wanted to kill him. His use of crushing resources kept shutting down their businesses.

Turning his back to the kilns, Brody slipped his shoes back on, picked up the neglected child, and hustled up the stairs. He'd nearly reached the door when the plastique exploded. Half of the stairs collapsed below him, and from his knees at the door, Brody looked back at the three demolished ovens. There would be no more bricks from this factory for a very long time.

Outside on the street, the workers were loading onto the bus, and Brody set down the girl to join them. A plainclothes Cambodian man in his fifties approached Brody. They shook hands.

"Chief Narith," Brody greeted. "Nice night for a kiln fire."

"A better night to drive away from a kiln fire," said the police chief in accented English. He shook his head at the flames rising from the roof. "The guards were no problem? I saw them run in that direction."

"No problem. Here are their phones. You can check their records for contacts. How are things on your end?"

"I had the easy job." He laughed. "You protected my identity so I'm not harassed by my own people. They'll keep hunting for Sladrick." Narith gestured up at the bus windows. "Now, look what you have given them."

"You got all the men? The fathers?"

"All of them. The husbands and fathers and older sons work here during the day. The women and children work here at night. The separation keeps them from escaping. The older daughters are prostituted day and night until the debts are paid. But Sladrick, their debts are never paid, no matter how much they work, no matter how many bricks they dry. They die like this, and then their children's children continue the work."

"You'll get them out of the city?"

"Churches in the country will take them in. I'll drive them there myself today. They will learn the gospel love of

Jesus. In time, they will be thankful to God for their lives, instead of knowing only sadness from the ovens."

"Did you receive my other instructions? I need one family to be sent to America."

"Yes, one family of four. I have your instructions, and I will follow them." Narith chuckled. "You and I walk a strange path, my friend. Working for our earthly leaders but finding ways to please our Heavenly Father."

"It was good to see you again, old friend." Brody shook the man's hand, then walked away, up the middle of the street.

"Be safe, Sladrick," Narith called after him.

But Brody didn't look back. Sometimes the work was like this. Other people, other families, other couples—they all had happy endings. It wasn't so for him. The sound of joy of reunited family members heard from the bus rang in his ears for hours, even long after he climbed into a van destined for the border of Vietnam. Every operation seemed to shout his own loss louder. He couldn't run away far enough to escape his anguish. All he could do was what he knew best: to stand against the darkness in this broken world. Alone.

Marcy wandered across the carpeted apartment as Greg explained his daily routine of trolling for human traffickers on various levels of the dark web. The studio apartment was so wide open and bright! She'd never thought a home could have so many windows. The Florida sunshine seemed to offer something more than Iowa's gray days.

"So, it's easy to see why Sladrick picked Tampa as his headquarters." Greg said as he joined her at the window. "Tampa is the worst metropolis in the country, except for Portland, when it comes to the number of people regularly attending church services. It's no coincidence that Tampa's grade for morality is so low but this city's crime is so high."

"So, this is a good spot for a Christian ministry?" Marcy asked. "The view is nice, but around so much sin?"

"Sladrick says we're here to shine in the darkness, not shine in the light."

"But you guys are undercover."

"Not to the darkness, we're not." Greg grinned proudly. "Wherever Sladrick goes, the darkness flees. I try to do the same thing on the internet. You know, like a Rottweiler chasing away evil. We're just standing up for the Lord as soldiers where we're most gifted."

"Right. Greg the Rot." She watched his face, especially his eyes. She'd just met him hours earlier in Atlanta, but he hadn't ceased trying to impress her with the work TROAS was doing for God. He was especially proud of Sladrick, evidenced by Greg's lengthy reports of missions he'd shared with her during their drive south. "So, you have two beds over here?"

"Oh." Greg hustled to the far corner of the single room, spacious apartment and attempted to tidy up an unmade twin bed. "Sorry about this. I was so focused on leaving on time this morning, I forgot to make it."

"Who sleeps over here?" She stood over a perfectly-made twin bed on the opposite wall, the top Army surplus blanket stretched tight and tucked in. "For some reason, I don't think you made this bed."

"Oh, no. That's Sladrick's bed. I don't touch it."

"He lives with you?"

"No. Well, yes, when he's here, which isn't too often. He says he never had a home since he was a kid, except for a couple years when he was married to Gail. I told you what happened to her."

"So, now he has no home? This is it? It's so . . . sad, isn't it?"

"Well, maybe." Greg frowned. "He's like Abraham in the Bible, though. You know, he's a pilgrim and a stranger in this world because he's a citizen of heaven. Anyway, he says having no comforts in life keeps him committed to the next mission."

"You really think he'll help me?"

"Well, you can ask him. That's why I brought you here."

"But you say he's so busy."

"He is. I mean, there's an endless demand for his expertise and global contacts within the Body of Christ. How does he pick which mission he does next? I don't know. I just provide intel, and he chooses the next location."

A door closed next door.

"Oh, that's Binsa!" Greg darted to the front door. "Marcy, you've got to meet her." He threw open the door. "Binsa? Glad I caught you before you left. I want you to meet someone."

Marcy knew she needed to get over her fear of meeting new people, but for much of her life, she'd known only a few adults. For some reason, Greg seemed to like her company, and he was a follower of Jesus, so she decided to trust him when he wanted to show her off to others.

A dark-skinned woman in strange white and blue pants and blouse stepped past Greg. Her hands extended to Marcy, her big brown eyes seeming to smile as much as her lips. Uncertain whether to accept both hands or only one, Marcy opted to shake the woman's right hand. Yet the stranger came closer, completely embracing Marcy.

"I welcome you, Marcy." Binsa then held her by the shoulders and looked into her eyes. The woman was older, somewhere near fifty, judging by the lines around her eyes and mouth, but still beautiful. "I'm Binsa. It's a name for a woman who is fearless. But as I look at you, my sister, perhaps I should call you Binsa."

"Thank you, Binsa." Marcy felt her emotions rise. Such compassion and warmth! She glanced at Greg, not wanting to cry in front of him, but he probably wouldn't care. "I love your outfit. I've never seen anything like it. You're from Asia?"

"Nepal, yes. This is why my English is still . . . eh, so-so." Binsa stepped back and swished a purple scarf over her shoulder. "This is what the women in my country wear. It is called a *kurta suruwal*."

"I think your English is very good. You call other women your sister? I didn't know that was part of the culture in Nepal."

"No, it's part of the Christian culture, no matter what country." She leaned in. "I doubt very much that Greg would have you here unsupervised unless you were my sister in the faith. True?"

"Yes, Binsa." Marcy bowed her head at the motherly correction.

"But Binsa!" Greg stared wide-eyed, turning from Binsa to Marcy, and back again. "I was just giving her the tour. That's all!"

"It's been very special to meet you, Sister Marcy." Binsa touched her palm to Marcy's cheek, paused, then turned to Greg. She squeezed his upper arm. "Brother Greg, let all that you do be done in love."

"You're leaving?" Greg stuttered. "After telling us we shouldn't be alone?"

"Oh, you will not be alone." She passed through the door and looked back, her eyes full of humor. "The Lord is here, watching. And Brody will be here momentarily. He called me ten minutes ago from the airport."

Greg closed the door after her, his face downcast.

"She is amazing!" Marcy threw up her hands. "If I didn't already know God's love, I would see it just by meeting her!"

"Yeah, she's amazing." Greg turned his office chair and slumped into it.

"She helps you with TROAS?"

"She and Sladrick *are* TROAS. I just help them, Marcy. Binsa runs the trafficking recovery part. She probably travels as much as Sladrick—definitely more than me. She's the one who gets local churches to take in recovered people after Sladrick rescues them. Every believer Binsa finds and every person Sladrick recovers become assets for TROAS' future missions, especially those who are members of the Body of Christ. That's what makes TROAS so strong. We just use God's network of believers around the world. But I haven't met any of them. It's all Sladrick and Binsa."

"What are you moping about?" Marcy turned in a circle. "This place is . . . amazing. And you know all these amazing people. I mean, not personally, but you're a part of it. What's wrong?"

"Sladrick's here. I was hoping for a little more time to think about how to introduce you."

"Well, if he's anything like you and Binsa, everything will be just fine, right?"

"Sladrick like Binsa?" He frowned. "No, they're not too much alike. Binsa is all expressive and caring. Sladrick is the strong, silent type. And he's been pretty depressed lately."

"We're brothers and sisters, though." Marcy felt doubt creeping in. "That's got to count for something, right? I mean, Sladrick will care about my family, won't he?"

"Yes, he'll care. But I've never brought anyone here before. I'm thinking now I should've taken you to a hotel so I could explain everything to him first—about PJ and your parents."

His melancholy pierced her, and Marcy sat on the edge of his desk next to a blank wall where a TV screen might've belonged. There was no other furniture in the living room. She suddenly agreed with him, that she shouldn't be there. Binsa was right; she was impatient. Maybe she had pushed Greg too much for access to Sladrick. Her impatience could ruin everything. In minutes, she could be back to nobody wanting her, returning to Davenport empty-handed. PJ could get to her easier if she were alone again.

Someone used the secure keypad in the hallway. A few seconds later, the door clicked and swung open. Marcy stood slowly, barely breathing. If anyone could help her family, this would be her only chance.

Brody Sladrick stepped inside, carrying a gym bag. He was taller and older than Marcy had imagined. His shoulders were muscular and his forearms thick. After closing the door, he raised his head, revealing a weary, lined face and sad eyes, like Greg had described.

"Mr. Sladrick." Greg leaped to his feet. "Uh, welcome back."

Brody took in the room, his eyes pausing on Marcy before returning to Greg.

"Greg, how many times have I asked you to call me Brody?" Brody set his bag on the carpet. "This is a surprise. I can't remember ever having company here."

"Greg's still trying to figure out how to explain why I'm here." Marcy offered her hand. "I'm Marcy Nevins from Davenport. A year ago, you broke up a child trafficking ring on the east end. I was being held there. For eight years."

"Oh." He shook her hand gently, his face almost expressionless—except for the weariness. "Forgive me. I don't always stick around after I secure the scene and call in the authorities, especially here in the States."

"Yeah." She blushed. "That confused some people. I figured out it was you. When I searched the internet for you, Greg called me. I made him let me come here."

"You *made* him?" Finally, there was a hint of amusement on Brody's face as he watched Greg squirm, waiting to explain for himself. "I'm sure you followed some sort of safety protocols, Greg?"

"I met her in Atlanta first. She'd been followed from Iowa."

"He saved my life with a Frisbee." Marcy grinned,

confident she was helping Greg. "He's my hero."

"No kidding?" Brody turned and groaned softly as he stretched his back. "A Frisbee, huh?"

"It's a long story." Greg moved to stand in front of Brody. "Actually, it's not. I acted like I was playing with a Frisbee in the park. So, I was undercover when she pulled up. Then this guy PJ from her past pulled up. I called the cops and he sped away."

"Let me see if I understand this." Brody rubbed his face with one hand. "You found someone who followed her from Iowa?"

"Right." Greg's confidence seemed to build, but Marcy suddenly didn't like Brody's tone.

"You sent him running, then you drove straight down here to Tampa? To TROAS?"

"Yeah." Greg flapped his arms against his sides. "Totally secure, right?"

"What stopped this PJ guy from doubling back or changing cars to follow you two from Atlanta to here?"

"Um." Greg cocked his head. "What?"

"Tell me." Brody sighed, now including Marcy in his address. "This PJ guy . . . he's a dark-skinned guy about the size of a freight train? Almost bald. Eyes like an eagle. A little upturn of the upper lip. Maybe a scar on his left cheek?"

"I gave him that scar." Marcy shifted her feet. "How do you know that's what he looks like?"

"Just a guess." Brody rested his hands on his hips and looked down at the carpet. "I haven't slept in two days."

Marcy watched speechlessly as Brody kicked off his shoes and approached his bed in the far corner of the apartment. When he reached his bed, he fell rather than climbed into it. He didn't move again from where his limbs first settled on top of the blanket.

Shaking her head, she glared at Greg and shook her finger at Brody.

"What?" he whispered. "We'll tell him the rest later. He's tired."

"No!" she snapped back. "How did he know about PJ?"

"Um. Oh." Greg turned pale. "I think that was his way of telling us that he saw him. We . . . were followed from Atlanta. I'm so stupid! I didn't even think of PJ doing that!"

Greg sat down at his desk and swiped through screenshots of city streets and avenues.

"What're you looking for?" She moved up behind him. He was trembling, so she set her hand on his shoulder momentarily. He froze under her touch, then continued. "It's not your fault. We couldn't have thought of everything."

"Yeah, but this is security." Greg growled. "It's rule number one: guard yourself so you can guard others. It's even in the Bible. I'm trained for this."

"They have training for this stuff?"

"Brody used to train people all the time. That's where he met his wife, Gail. There was a place in Mexico. That's where I was trained, too. Oh, no. There he is."

Marcy didn't need to squint at the screen to see that it was PJ in a camera angle.

"Where is that?"

"Downstairs, outside the front door. I bet Brody walked right past him. That's where he saw PJ, probably realized the guy looked suspicious hanging around out there. PJ must not know for sure what Brody looks like."

"What should we do?" Marcy glanced toward the sleeping man across the room. "Should we wake him up? PJ is as bad as they come. He's murdered at least one kid that I know of, and he attacked Agent Wessel."

"I'm sending the police an alert and some of this footage." Greg's fingers flew between the keyboard and his touchscreen. "I don't know if this'll work. PJ's pretty good at dodging arrest."

"Why didn't Brody do something before he went to sleep?"

"I don't know." Greg glanced over his shoulder. "Maybe to teach us a lesson. Or maybe he has other plans for PJ. But we're safe up here. Even if PJ figures out what floor we're on, he'll never get into one of these rooms without the passcode and eye scan. I designed all this security. Not even a grenade could bust down one of these doors."

"As long as PJ is out there," she shuddered, "I sure don't feel safe."

For a few minutes, they watched PJ mill around outside. When he finally walked away from the apartment building, it was minutes before two police cars arrived. Marcy watched on the screen as Greg went downstairs and spoke with the officers for a moment. Though Greg didn't appear athletic or physically strong, he seemed to carry himself with confidence and she was glad when he returned upstairs.

"They'll leave a patrol car parked outside for the night," Greg reported, "then they'll drive by occasionally for the next forty-eight hours. They don't want this guy in Tampa any more than we do."

"Why would he still be following me around a year after I ran away?" Marcy hugged her midsection. "He's going to hurt me, I know it. I'm still a prisoner."

"No." He took her hand and faced her. "You're with us now. The GLOW network might span the globe and PJ might be a killer, but you're with TROAS now. Whatever happens, God is with us. Brody Sladrick isn't supernatural, but he has divine favor like you wouldn't believe."

"How can he sleep through this?"

Greg chuckled and joined her in admiring Brody.

"He was a missionary kid in West Africa. That's where he was raised. English isn't even his first language. It's

French, and I've heard him speaking other languages on the phone, too."

"Why'd he leave Africa?"

"From what little he's shared with me, as a teen, he helped his dad translate gospel tracts for the locals. That's when he first trusted Christ. After that, he started preaching the gospel, traveling alone to Ghana and Nigeria. He started bringing people to Christ, and it drew the attention of the Muslims. That's when people first started trying to hunt him down to kill him."

"Was he still young then?"

"He wasn't even twenty when they murdered his parents. He said they killed his family in Togo because they couldn't catch him. So, he left West Africa and started traveling around. The Middle East, Asia, and Eastern Europe. Everywhere he went, he visited Christian households and learned of their difficulties. That's when he first realized his calling."

"What was it? He didn't already know? He was a missionary."

"Well, all believers are missionaries, but he never really knew his personal calling until he began to help persecuted Christians, especially kidnapped or enslaved people. For him, he said it was simple after all he'd been through. I asked him how it was simple to face evil and retrieve kidnapped people."

"What'd he say?"

"He said the darkness hates the light and fights against it, but all the light has to do is shine. It's simple, he said, but not always easy. Once he told me that, I made it my life motto, too, I guess. Just stand. Usually, evil is used to trample everyone. But when it runs into someone who's willing to stand in God's strength, there's a dread that takes place—and it's not our dread of them, if you know what I mean."

"The righteous are as bold as lions!"

"Exactly. It's in the Bible. We just have to stand, not

even fight. God fights for us when we stand for Him. PJ is a predator, but he ran from me in Atlanta, and I'm not even intimidating. I just stood up to him."

"You might not be intimidating, but your confidence is a comfort." She shrugged. "I mean, it's contagious. If you're not afraid of PJ, then I'm not. He's already beat me so many times, and God brought me through it, right? And now I'm here."

"I'm sorry you went through all that." Greg smiled sadly. "Binsa always talks to the women who stay with us. She says their scars tell the story of Jesus. He carries scars of mistreatment forever. Our scars are a testimony of the spiritual battle between sin and Satan in conflict with God and His people."

"That's . . .beautiful, Greg."

"Yeah. We're not ashamed of our scars. Look at this." Greg pulled up his shirt to reveal his left side. "I was in Rangoon, Southeast Asia, with a friend of Brody's. We were using a North Korean offsite server to protect some believers. A bad guy stabbed me right here. There was so much blood, I thought I was going to die."

"How'd you survive?"

"I just wanted to finish the job, so I held my side with one hand. I taped it up later until someone could fix me up."

"I have a lot of those scars, too, but not from knives. I've been hit a lot—by PJ." Marcy touched Greg's ribs. "Most of my scars are on my face, though. That's why I'm so ugly."

"Ugly? You?" Greg frowned. "You're the most . . . beautiful person I've ever been around."

"Maybe you're not around too many people." Marcy smiled. "I'm not sorry for all these scars. Being ugly helps me see the important things in life a lot easier."

"So, maybe that's the real reason I can see the important things in life, too." Greg threw his hands in the air. "Here I thought I was gifted with special insight. Now I find out it's just because I'm ugly."

"I don't think you're ugly."

"Oh, well . . ." He looked away.

"So, women who Brody recovers stay with you guys sometimes?" she asked.

"Oh, all the time. In fact . . ." He eyed Brody for a moment. "Come with me."

He led her out to the hallway and down two doors.

"TROAS owns this whole floor, and all these reinforced doors have the same security, so you'll be safe in here. This is your apartment. For now."

"*My* apartment?"

"Here. Look. This is the code for this room. Memorize it and don't write it down anywhere. And don't share it with anyone."

Marcy watched him punch in the nine-digit code and repeated it several times in her head. Then, she followed him into a fully furnished apartment, not at all like the wide open one he and Brody shared. A separate bedroom door stood ajar off the living room. This apartment was clearly decorated by a warm and thoughtful woman. Colorful drapes hung on the walls with framed pictures of smiling people of all nationalities. She approached one picture and touched the glass that encased it.

"These are wonderful. Who are these people?"

"Binsa takes photos of the people she meets and helps through Brody. I've met some of them who've stayed here until they got on their feet."

"They're so joyful. And bright."

"I think the photos help her." Greg stood in front of a photo of an Asian boy, his grin as broad as his hands that cupped a bowl of rice. "Binsa is from Kathmandu. Her husband sold their daughter, then left Binsa behind. Brody heard about the case when he was over there and tried to retrieve the girl. But when he found her, she had died in another area of Nepal. That's how Binsa came to

Christ. Brody told her about Jesus, then she became a threat to the red-light districts in Kathmandu. Human trafficking is really bad over there. I guess it's bad everywhere now. But eventually, Brody brought her here where she could run the recovery program for TROAS and teach women how to start fresh, like she did."

"So, she lost her little girl, but now these are all her children." Marcy didn't bother to wipe away her tears as she moved from picture to picture. "It's the saddest thing and the happiest thing all at once. No wonder she has so much love."

Greg helped Marcy settle into her new room for the evening, then he returned to his own for the night.

Marcy hadn't spent the night alone in a room for over a year. Even living with Carol Elroy, she'd shared a bedroom with the eldest of the foster girls. Twice in the night, she opened the door to the hallway and peered down at Greg and Brody's apartment door. Their hall light was on, but she didn't venture to knock on their door. She was terribly lonely, but she didn't want to seem awkwardly needy to the people who she hoped would help her.

Inside the apartment, she stared at the wall behind the door. Two of Binsa's beautiful photographs hung there, but below them, there was empty space. In years past, when PJ had threatened her, she had clung to the promise of God being with her, represented by the boat-cross drawing on the wall. She missed that drawing, so it didn't surprise her that she had an inclination to draw the same sketch on the wall that night. Of course, she didn't, but she laughed at herself because she might have drawn it if she'd had markers or crayons.

Her thoughts of the house of bondage led her fingers to fondle the pink watch on her wrist. Tory had given it to her so she could perform her duties on time. The watch represented to her maybe what the pictures did for Binsa. But Binsa's daughter was gone, and Tory was still alive, somewhere up in Davenport, or maybe in the Iowa women's prison now.

Finally, her reminiscing gave way to her reading in the Psalms. In minutes, seated on a sofa near a lamp, she found renewed peace and confidence in God's good hands. Maybe these amazing TROAS people weren't in her life for long, but it sure seemed like God had directed her to them.

She fell asleep like that—her Bible open, her head resting on her arm, thinking of what God's will could possibly be for her and Greg. He thought she was beautiful, and she thought he was a hero. No one had ever said such nice things about her, not even her parents. In grade school, she'd never had anyone say they had a crush on her, or any such thing. The underprivileged girl with wild hair who dressed in poor clothes had been the object of much teasing and jeers, certainly not of silly teenage romance.

A knock on the door jerked her awake. Morning light streamed through the drapes over the windows. She wiped her wet cheek and smoothed down her hair, though she knew of nothing that could rule the unruly.

"Who is it?" she asked softly at the door.

"It's Brody and Greg," Brody stated just as softly. "Can we talk?"

"Okay." She opened the door a few inches to peer out. "But you have to wait for me. I just woke up."

"No problem."

Marcy heard them enter behind her as she hurried to the bathroom. In the mirror, she cringed at the dark rings under her eyes and the tangle of hair that poured from her skull. She'd never cared much for how she looked, knowing there was no real remedy for her features. But now she was concerned. Greg liked her. Somehow, she needed to make an effort.

After washing up, she used her fingers to wet and try to brush her hair out, but she only made it worse. Clumps of dark hair stuck out in one direction, and whole waves of hair flowed in another direction.

"Cut it all off," she mumbled. "Oh, Lord, help me. I'm such a mess."

Since she hadn't unpacked, she had no brush in the bathroom, and she'd never been interested in makeup, but maybe it was time to think about covering up those dark circles. Or the scars. And her eyebrows grew so haphazardly, they couldn't possibly be ladylike.

Finally, she pinched her cheeks like she remembered her mother doing to bring color to her pale skin, then she emerged to find only Brody there. He stood at the window, which faced North Tampa. The apartment door was wide open, which gave her a start, but PJ wouldn't be able to do anything to her as long as she was with Brody. Even Greg had conveyed to her that the retrieval expert would risk injury and even death to protect God's precious ones.

"Where's Greg?" Marcy patted her hair, hoping it would somehow accept some last-minute correction.

"He went to get his laptop." Brody turned, his hands in his pockets. "Sorry about last night. I don't sleep much when I'm on the road. When I'm here, Greg usually ignores me while I lay passed out for a day or two. Is your head all right? Did you hit it or something?"

"Oh." Marcy dropped her hand to her side, now more self-conscious than ever. "I just . . . need a haircut or something. It's never cooperated. Growing up, I didn't care much."

"But now you're a young woman." Brody approached her and eyed her critically. "Some people who're in captivity don't think much about their appearance. Others think too much about their appearance. You were just a kid when you were taken, so you didn't have the normal interactions to help you figure some of these things out."

"Yeah, but it's been a year." Marcy scoffed at herself but relaxed under his frankness. "I should know what to do with my own . . . bird's nest."

"You know what?" Brody backed to the door. "I think I have just the thing. Be right back."

Marcy smiled as he left, remembering what Greg had told her about all of the man's losses and challenges. Yet, he still had time to think of what was important to her.

He returned less than a minute later and held up a stumpy little navy-blue hat.

"This is called a beret. This one belonged to a female soldier in Israel. Now, take all your hair and draw it to the back. Good, now you can wear this straight or cocked to the side. People make their own fashion statements with these things. The point is, this'll hold back what may not be regulated any other way. Pull it down firmly. How's that feel?"

"Feels like a hat." Marcy touched her hair. "Everything's out of my eyes. That's new. What if the woman wants her beret back?"

"She won't. She was murdered by Hamas a few years ago. Died in my arms." He frowned at the memory. "I didn't realize till later that I'd tucked her beret into my belt, but she'd be glad you're using it. She was the type of person who would've given it to you herself if it made you happy. She was a sister in the faith."

"Well, thank you. Do I look okay?"

"Oh, yes. It works well on you. Keep it."

He plopped down on the sofa as Greg returned with his laptop. With his foot, the tech closed the door and continued into the room. When he reached the sofa, he glanced up. Marcy saw him take in her new appearance. He lifted his head like he was about to say something, then he turned his attention to his screen and sat next to Brody. She was pretty sure his reaction conveyed his approval, and that was enough for her. But it was Brody for whom she thanked God in her heart. Without causing a scene or embarrassing her further, he'd made a gesture—providing a simple hat—that she knew would change her life.

"Okay, PJ returned to the building outside early this

morning," Greg reported from viewing his screen. Marcy sat on the arm of a soft chair, facing the sofa. "He tried the front door, found it locked, and left. What do you think?"

"He'll keep coming back." Brody crossed his legs and tapped his chin with his finger. "The authorities want him behind bars, but like most cases these days, they can't commit the necessary manpower to catch this guy."

"So, do *we* catch him?" Greg asked. "You've caught others. I mean, can we catch someone like him?"

"I don't see what's so special about the man that we couldn't." Brody raised his eyebrows. "Is he special, Marcy?"

"He's big. And stronger than he seems. Especially strong. And cruel."

"We can deal with big and strong." Brody inhaled deeply as they waited on him. "But does he have nerve? Is he smart? Can he be persuaded?"

"I stood up to him in Atlanta," Greg said. "He could've squished me like a bug, but he got in his car and drove away."

"I don't think he's that smart," Marcy said. "Tory and Trey never trusted him with the business."

"That might just mean he's impulsive." Brody narrowed his eyes. "Greg told me about you trying to find your brother."

"And my parents. Before you say anything, I know they're the ones who sold us. I just have to find them."

"I won't try to stop you, but Greg says there's no real lead yet, and Trey and Tory haven't confessed anything to investigators."

"But you must know someone, Mr. Sladrick. The Homeland Security agent I know said you could find anyone anywhere."

"Call me Brody. And I can't find anyone anywhere. I work off leads and trails like everyone else. As far as knowing someone—I do. I know PJ." He suddenly leaned forward. "I think if we corner him, he might spill the beans on your brother. You want him found first, right?"

"So, you'll help me? Just like that?"

"Well, I haven't spent a lot of time around people for a few months." Brody sat back. "This might be God's way of kicking me back into being sociable. Greg told you about my wife?"

"He did. I'm so sorry. She must've been a wonderful person."

"She was. She was." Brody nodded and gazed out the window for a moment, then turned back toward them. "If she were here, she'd probably tell me that I'm too often a shadow in and out of people's lives. Yes, we could do this."

"Does that mean you forgive my security blunder?" Greg asked.

"You're forgiven," Brody said with a light in his eyes that Marcy hadn't noticed the night before. "Now, help us turn your blunder into intel. We can use PJ's presence. He's obsessed with Marcy. Maybe he'll remember what happened to her brother. All we need is a lead, then I can go get Aidan."

"But . . . how will you know it's Aidan unless I go with you?" Marcy pressed. "Nine years have passed. He's my brother so I have to be there when you find Addy. Since I know what happens to kids in those places, I can help him."

"Yeah, I understand." Brody stared at the carpet in thought a moment before looking up again. "I have a little experience helping these kids out of that kind of atmosphere. If PJ can point us in the right direction, Greg here will give me a location. When I go in, it'll be violent. Ugly. There won't be time for coddling. Sometimes, I have to smash and grab and run with a kid or two under my arms. Sometimes there's gunfire biting my backside."

"Addy's not a kid any longer. He's seventeen now."

"The point is, you can't be there when we go after your brother. You'd be a liability in the sense that I'd be worried about your safety. Chances are that your brother might still be in GLOW's hands. They'll want you back, too, or to silence you, if they figure out who you are."

"My brother's more important to me than my own life. But what about PJ?"

"We need to confront him. That's something, Marcy, that you may play a part in."

"Confront him?" Marcy's mouth went dry. "I've never seen him confronted by anyone."

"Yeah?" Brody folded his hands, totally calm about handling someone so large. "Well, I'd like to put him against the wall. When he realizes he has no way out, we help him understand the score."

"Um, I don't understand." Marcy shifted on the arm of the chair. "What's the score?"

"For PJ, he needs to understand that God is against him. Having you there, Marcy, might help his own conscience convince him of his need to change. I believe after I say what needs to be said, the Holy Spirit can do the rest—if PJ gives in to God's conviction of sin."

"Do I have to talk to him?" Marcy asked.

"Not if you don't want to."

"I don't know." Marcy looked from young man to aging operative. "After everything I've seen PJ do, I'm not sure he has a heart. And I don't know how you'd put someone like him against a wall."

"We'll trust God to work out the details." Brody stood and returned to the window. "It's strange how God keeps making room in heaven for us sinners. PJ might be one of those. Maybe it's our own hearts that need to be ready for that."

CHAPTER FOUR

Brody worked at containing his rage, even though someone connected to GLOW had come to his very doorstep. Pug Johnson was a threat to everyone TROAS had ever rescued, or would rescue, by whatever intentions had brought him to follow Marcy Nevins to Tampa. But any emotional reaction from Brody would cause more harm than good.

After midnight, Brody sat on the wet grass outside his apartment complex. He wore a faded, stained overcoat with a ski cap and a torn scarf. A plain cardboard box about the size of a microwave sat next to him. The box was torn, empty, and otherwise featureless, but the prop and the rest of his wintery costume needed to be convincing since PJ had just returned. The man was back, weaving his way past other transients on nearby sidewalks and yards.

Leaning on one elbow, Brody coughed raucously, as if he were an unhealthy alcoholic. It wasn't an easy detail to pretend since he was actually healthy, fit, and strong. PJ walked past him on the sidewalk without even looking at him. At the front of the building, PJ tried the door, then paced back and forth, occasionally leaning back and gazing up at the height of floors above. The man wanted Marcy badly and Brody wanted to know why. Actually, that was just one piece of intel he hoped to learn from him.

Shifting from his knees, Brody held the cardboard box in his left hand. In his right, he clicked a pen, causing the writing tip to be replaced by a water-soluble tranquilizer needle. Of all the non-lethal weapons the Commission of International Laborers had to offer, Brody preferred the easily-concealed tranq-pen.

Rising, he swayed to his feet. A youth on a bicycle

pedaled past on the street. Six cars lined the sidewalk fifty yards away. A siren drifted in the breeze from the direction of the bay. The warm humid air barely moved, and PJ didn't offer Brody more than a glance as the seeming homeless man started toward him.

PJ was so intent on trying to jimmy the building's locked door that he didn't respond to Brody until Brody had given the cardboard box an underhand toss towards PJ's head. As the man swatted at the box, Brody spun to his right, and with a reverse swing, he planted the tranq-pen firmly into PJ's thigh.

Continuing his motion, Brody finished his spin and came to a stop, his hands up and ready to defend himself. He clicked the pen twice, slipping a second water-soluble needle in place if it were needed.

But before the box settled on its side, PJ crumbled onto the pavement. Normally, only two heartbeats were necessary to carry the tranquilizer toxin throughout a person's system, but a sizeable man like PJ was unpredictable.

The front door opened and Greg's face appeared. Over his shoulder, Marcy, wearing her beret, peeked for a view of the fallen man.

"Are we in the clear?" Brody drew PJ's right arm over his shoulder, then lifted the man in a fireman's carry. "This guy needs to lay off the pork fajitas."

"Yes, everything's clear." Greg held the door wide for Brody to enter with his burden. "Hurry!"

Marcy ran ahead of Brody down the corridor and opened the door to a maintenance closet. Inside the closet, Brody gently set PJ on the floor next to a standby generator, facing an electric panel with tiny red lights glowing. From a bag of gear, Brody produced duct tape and tightly bound PJ's ankles and wrists, then securely covered the big man's mouth with two layers of tape.

Brody shed his coat, scarf, and hat, and handed the costume to Marcy, who stuffed everything into the recovered box. A few feet away from PJ, Brody sat on the floor and presented his wrists to Greg who loosely wrapped Brody's wrists and ankles in tape, then lightly pressed a single piece of tape over his mouth.

"Are you good?" Greg offered a thumbs-up, kneeling before Brody. "Your mic is on. You still have your tranq in your pocket? Okay."

Lastly, Greg emptied PJ's pockets—a phone, pocketknife, and a scrap of paper.

"How long until he wakes up?" Marcy asked.

"About another forty-five minutes." Greg set PJ's belongings in the box. "But someone his size, it could be sooner. Let's go. I want to start hacking his phone."

Before Greg and Marcy opened then shut the door behind them, Brody closed his eyes so his sight could adjust more swiftly to the dimness of the room. Only the red LEDs lit the room now, barely enough to make out shapes but no details. With a grunt, Brody fell sideways to his left shoulder where he rested, as if unconscious, and waited, his brow resting against cold cement. He wasn't afraid so his heart rate was slowing.

Instead, he found himself excited. It had been many months since he'd actually reveled in an operation. He couldn't be angry at the clumsiness of Greg or Marcy in Atlanta. They'd awakened within him exactly what he needed. His grief from losing Gail was no less, but working with people close to him in his own element the last couple of days had given him new life, new energy. It was undeniably the hand of God—dropping conflict directly into his lap to stimulate his spiritual senses and physical skills back to full measure, instead of the automated mode under which he'd been operating of late. Grief had numbed him. Oh, he so missed Gail! But having danger close by had lifted his head.

Forty then fifty minutes passed. PJ's feet jerked. Brody closed his eyes as PJ fully woke and fought his binds. For several minutes, Brody listened as PJ strained against the tape, testing it this way and that. Brody worried that the strong man might actually break free and ruin the plan, but in the end, PJ relaxed, his panting through his nose revealing his desperation.

Groaning through his tape, Brody rolled onto his back. A few feet away, PJ lay still. Brody had his attention now. With effort, Brody sat up and scooted over so he could lean against a wall panel. Finally, he lifted his bound hands and peeled away the tape from his mouth, but left it hanging from one cheek.

"Oh, that's better," he whispered and looked around, then froze. "Is someone there? Who's there?"

PJ tugged off the tape from his own mouth, clearly a more painful process if his gasps were any indication.

"Who are you?" PJ cursed and fought his binds, then was still again. "I think I was drugged!"

"This is ridiculous." Brody tugged against his loose tape, but not too hard. "It's getting so a fella can't even make a few sales on the streets of Tampa anymore."

"Who are you?" PJ asked again.

"Just a man whose life keeps getting interrupted by fools. Who're you?"

"That's my own business. Did you see who put us in here?"

"I got a look. I think there were three of them. One of 'em was a skinny kid. I seen him before. There was a girl his age—never seen her around, though."

"I know the girl but I don't think they did this." PJ swore. "It had to be someone else. You said there were three. My memory—I think it happened outside. They drugged me with something, but it's wearing off."

"We've gotta get free before they come back or call the cops." Brody loudly jerked his arms, wrestling against the tape. "How's yours? You got any play in the tape?"

"Nah, they wound it around my wrists too much."

"Maybe . . . I can get . . . one hand free . . ." Brody

fought and grumbled, then rested. "Just wait till I get my hands on that third guy."

"You saw him? What'd he look like?"

"I never saw him directly. Just glimpses. Like in reflections. He's sort of worn-out looking. Holds his hands low. He's older than I thought. Lines on his face. Shoulders like an ape. I don't know what else to say. Still moved like a cat."

"Sladrick." PJ cursed again. "That's his name. I bet it was him. This is what he does. Now I've got him. I know exactly where he is!"

"Actually, I think he's got us." Brody growled against his binds. "Are you working on that tape? Bite through it or something. Maybe it'll stretch."

"I followed the girl Marcy here. That little slut. She led me right to Sladrick. Good thing I made a call to some friends of mine."

"Friends?" Brody tensed. "They'll help us?"

"Well, they know where I am. One more call, and they'll come get me. And then Sladrick is mine. I'll finally kill that girl."

"I don't care about them. I just want to get free so I can start over with some other girls in another town. Tampa's too hot."

"You're movin' girls?" PJ asked. "How old?"

"Old enough to do what I tell 'em to do. Man, I don't need this drama. I try to stay outta the spotlight."

"Well, you're in it now, pal. Sladrick has pull with the police. He'll put us away unless we can think of something quick. You're smaller than me. Move over there. Use that cabinet to cut your wrist tape."

Brody followed his directions by scooting to the side and rubbing his wrists against a corner.

"Maybe I need to get outta this life altogether." Brody shook his head. "It ain't worth it. I was raised better. I've got to get right. Yeah, it's time."

"What's right is money in your pocket and a smile on

your face," PJ said. "Nobody else can tell you how to get that."

"God can. I know He's looking down on us right now. You feel His eyes?"

"I feel Sladrick breathing down my neck, but I'll have GLOW breathing down his neck in five minutes if you can get loose there."

"I think it's coming . . ." Brody sawed lightly, making little progress. "Getting arrested isn't the worst thing, I guess. Maybe it'll help straighten me out. It's been a while since I read the Bible. I'll get right with the Lord again in jail."

"Shut up with that!" PJ ordered. "Just get through that tape."

"I done some pretty bad things to people—young and old." Brody let out a whimper. "I'm gonna go to hell! I know it. Unless I trust in God for forgiveness."

"Oh, you blubbering idiot! Shut up and work. Ain't no God going to forgive us, not if you done what I done."

"Forgiveness is our only chance," Brody said. "I've heard we need to trust in Jesus—what He died for. Then He rose from the dead three days later. He must be able to forgive sins if He can conquer death like that."

"You need to put that tape back over your mouth and focus, now! I'm not going down because your conscience got to you!"

"Fine, then you talk while I work," Brody offered. "I'm getting close. What's this GLOW you're talking about? Your friends?"

"Associates. They want Sladrick as bad as I want Marcy. They can have him. I just want the girl. She's a witness against my sister. My sis can't fight her case while the state has a witness willing to testify. Can you point out Sladrick if you saw him again?"

"Yeah, I can point him out to you, but it seems you should stay far away from that Marcy girl. Forget your sister. Move on."

"No way. I should've killed Marcy when I had the chance. Nothing but trouble, that one."

"My arms are tired." Brody dropped his hands in his lap. "But I'm close. Real close. How'd you get tangled up with this Marcy person if she's so dangerous?"

"She's not dangerous!" PJ scoffed. "We got her and her brother years ago. Sold the boy. The girl was older than our people were moving back then. So, we kept her around."

"I'd be interested in that boy." Brody started again on his wrists. "Even if he's older now, he'll be broke in, right? I'll bet I'm free in less than a minute now!"

"The boy's gone."

"Yeah, sometimes the weak ones die too soon."

"Nah, I mean he's gone somewhere else. Bangkok doesn't exactly keep a filing system, you know."

"Bangkok? You really remember where one boy went all those years ago?"

"Special case. My sister took an interest. Would you hurry up?"

"Ah!" Brody peeled off his wrist tape. "Got it! Bangkok, huh? That gets us going in the right direction."

"What?"

Brody took the tape off his ankles, turned on the light in the room, then stood over PJ.

"Needing forgiveness, PJ—that was for you. The Lord already saved me by His blood. Now it's your time. Don't die without believing. Got it?"

"What? What is this?"

Opening the door to the utility room, Brody greeted two uniformed police officers standing at the ready with handcuffs.

"We got it all." Behind the officers, Greg tapped his earpiece, then gave Brody a thumbs-up.

Returning to PJ's side, Brody helped the man to his feet. He aided the officers in cutting the tape on his wrists, then they cuffed PJ behind his back. Only then did Brody cut PJ's ankles free.

"Your sin has made you foolish," Brody said as he walked out of the apartment building with PJ, the officers escorting him. Greg and Marcy stopped on the sidewalk. "Anything you want to say, Marcy?"

Marcy looked first at Greg, then at Brody. Finally, her gaze settled on PJ. She stepped a little closer.

"You've been a bad man, PJ. Mr. Sladrick is right. You need God's forgiveness. But maybe to start with, you need to know, I forgive you."

"What?" PJ's eyes glared at Brody. "You're Sladrick? *You're Sladrick? You?"*

PJ suddenly fought against his handlers, but they marched him away. Another set of officers waited to load him into a car.

"That's not easy, Marcy." Brody sighed as they watched them put PJ into the back seat. "But your forgiveness is more powerful than his wickedness. You wouldn't have really been able to live freely yourself unless you had forgiven him."

"I know." She smiled at Greg as he rested a hand on her shoulder. "But maybe he'll live free if he accepts God's forgiveness. That's what I'm hoping for."

"So, you're going to Bangkok?" Greg asked.

"We're going to Bangkok." Marcy nodded at Greg, then frowned. "Where's Bangkok exactly?"

"I'm going to Bangkok," Brody said. "Alone. You two heard PJ. GLOW knows more about us now. They'll be on the lookout. PJ might even reach out to them from jail."

"All the more reason for me to be far away from Tampa, right?"

"She does have a point." Greg hefted his case of gear to his other hand. "She's safest with you, Brody. I'll be fine."

"Bangkok is a mess right now, especially with this virus thing going on." Brody moved toward the apartment building. "There's no way I'm taking a young lady into the red-light district of that dark city."

Marcy couldn't believe Brody had caved in to allow her to come—with no small urging from Greg. In just a few days, Brody had her passport and papers in order for the overseas adventure!

She skipped to keep up with Brody's fast pace up a linoleum hallway in underground Albany, New York. Above her head stood the capitol building, and below, she witnessed tunnels and bunkers for hundreds of people if necessary.

Brody stopped suddenly at a door and Marcy bumped into him at the abrupt halt. He steadied her with one hand, then knocked loudly on a thick wooden door. Far, far back up the way they'd come, Marcy could see two security officers standing at the elevator. It seemed Brody had access to go where only few others went.

The door clicked open, revealing a carpeted office, furnished with a polished desk and wooden chairs with thick cushions. The balding, older aid who held the door wide bowed his head slightly as Brody entered. From behind the desk, a dark-haired man, his hair like a helmet, swiveled around in his chair.

"Brody! Come in, come in!" he said in a raspy voice. "Marvelous job you did on that Cambodia business. You sent back the perfect family to prove I'm an international crimefighter. I can always count on you to make me look good."

"Senator Madison, Marcy Nevins."

The man rose, shook Brody and Marcy's hands, then sat down heavily. The aide offered Brody and Marcy two chairs.

"It's getting harder for me to get in and out of Phnom Penh, Senator," Brody said, sitting down and crossing his legs. "The police and gangs are using better coordinating tactics."

"Is that because you keep breaking up their organizations, or because you keep rambling about your Jesus to everyone you meet?"

"Maybe some of both."

"Well, I don't blame them." The senator leaned back in his chair and picked at a fingernail. "I could do without your religious nonsense myself. But you get the job done. You keep making me look good, so I suppose I have to tolerate your angels and demons."

"I'm not doing it for you."

"You do it for the money."

"I do it for the souls that need help." Brody tilted his head. "If you want to pay me for it, that's your business."

"It's taxpayer business." The senator pointed a finger at Brody's face. "Don't you forget that. You work for the people. Okay, maybe we pay you with seized trafficking money, but still, we all get something out of it, right? I'm still a respectable senator, and you get your souls for Jesus."

Marcy watched Brody's face. It didn't reveal anything. During the flight to New York, Brody had told her they were meeting in secret with Senator Elliot Madison, who occasionally contracted Brody with odd jobs to make his ratings look good among voters who appreciated the fight against human trafficking. Brody had said he was a powerful senator, so Marcy couldn't imagine why Brody wasn't a little more in awe of the man's might.

"Your text said you had another job?"

"Yes, I do. I do. You'll love this one." Madison rooted around on his desk, nearly igniting several papers from a smoldering cigar. "Here it is. It's local."

He tossed a stapled packet toward Brody. Brody took the pages and read through them carefully, seeming not to care that others were waiting on him. It was then that Marcy noticed that Madison was eyeing her through his cigar smoke. With a wicked look, he smiled at her. Marcy didn't return his friendliness, since it seemed tainted with unhealthy interest.

"Who is this person with you, Brody?" the senator asked. "You've never brought anyone here before. I thought this arrangement was confidential for security reasons."

Marcy glanced at Brody, who didn't look up from his papers. The aide set a cup of tea in front of her, but she didn't reach for it. She felt herself quivering under Madison's attention and Brody's silence. This world of intimidating men and uncomfortable silences didn't set well with her. She preferred Greg's jabbering about his computer stuff over this any day.

"I'll take care of this when I get back." Brody returned the papers to the desk. "It can wait a few days. I've got something else that can't wait any longer."

"Does it have to do with her?" The senator blew smoke toward her. "Rather homely-looking, isn't she? Some hooker you just rescued off the street for your Jesus?"

Brody turned his head, and Marcy met his eyes. She didn't entirely understand his strength, but she knew he was a good man, so how could he work with such a creature as this senator? When Brody faced Madison again and spoke, his voice was no less strained than before, but his words were laced with something that gave Marcy a chill.

"Do you realize how quickly I could reach you across this desk, Elliot?" Brody didn't move a muscle, and the senator suddenly set down his cigar. "Don't you know by now that I serve God, and your gluttonous status here where you hide in your bunker from criticisms and the virus won't be able to restrain me once I put my hands on you?"

"You . . . wouldn't."

"I would . . . with pleasure."

"You're a Christian." Madison swallowed and cleared

his throat. "Everyone knows you're not like that, Brody."

"Maybe it's time you were reminded that manners aren't below you." Brody sat forward slowly, which caused Madison's eyes to widen. "And people aren't below you, either. Would a good old-fashioned thrashing around this office bring some courtesy back to your tongue, Senator?"

"I didn't mean anything by it," he stammered. "Come on, Brody. It's . . . me."

"Apologize."

"Right. Of course. I'm sorry."

"Not to me!"

Madison sat up straighter, then squared his shoulders and looked at Marcy.

"Forgive me, miss. I spoke impolitely a moment ago. Mr. Sladrick and I go back to the days before I was in office. Um, there's no excuse that I'm informal with him but abusive toward another guest. I'm sure if you weren't, uh, respectable and a pleasure to know, you wouldn't be with Brody. Please accept my apology."

"Okay, I accept it," Marcy said softly.

Brody rose to his feet, which made Madison flinch.

"I'll take care of your South Carolina problem when I get back. Give me a week."

"Sure. No problem." Madison stood and hesitantly offered his hand to Brody. "I'll make the regular arrangements with law enforcement and finances."

"Fine. I'll be in touch." Brody shook the man's hand.

Marcy thought she saw relief on the senator's face when Brody started toward the door. Once they were in the corridor, the aide locked the door behind them and Marcy felt her heart slow down.

"Don't be bothered by people like him." Brody gently took her arm and walked with her. "If he wasn't a coward, he wouldn't be hiding down here from society's struggles."

"Should I have done something differently?" she asked.

"Absolutely not. You were the perfect picture of grace.

It's my job to defend you. And you saw him change his tune, right?"

"Yeah. Real quick. Why do you work with him if he's like that?"

"He provides government access to things that need to be done, even though his motives for doing them are far different from ours."

"What're his motives?"

"Himself. Last year, when I was in Davenport, I was there because he sent me to break up that GLOW ring with Trey and Tory. He uses me to gain the favor of governors and other senators around the country, even around the world."

"And you let him use you?"

"Are you kidding?" Brody smiled a warm smile. "I get to rescue people all over the world. Then I talk to those people about Jesus Christ and His free gift. Who's using who? That's how I see it. We can tolerate Senator Madison for the sake of Christ. It doesn't mean we agree with his ways. You wouldn't be free right now if he hadn't sent me to Davenport last year."

"Can we go to Bangkok now?"

"Yeah, we can go now. But there are uglier things than Madison waiting for us there."

Marcy rocked to the motion of the BTS Skytrain as it clicked along into the heart of Bangkok, Thailand. Although the train seats were filled around her and Brody with interesting people, her eyes kept drifting back to Brody, watching his posture and face. She wondered if he were praying as she was. Nothing he did seemed accidental. Every movement was intentional. Even where he placed one hand on his upper thigh was probably positioned there to yank her out of harm's way or to draw out a tranq-pen. At the airport, he'd given her a tranq-pen of her own, and that non-lethal weapon had awakened her to the very real dangers they were about to face.

At the airport, Marcy had been impressed with Brody's perfect familiarity with several customs agents. He'd even spoken their language and passed an envelope to one official. "Tactical access fee," he'd called it. Marcy guessed they could've passed through the airport's checkpoints without notice, but Brody left nothing to chance, and no one bothered them.

"The city doesn't look too bad," she observed through the window at her shoulder. "I mean, it looks clean. Nice buildings and clean cars."

"From a distance, these kinds of places always appear innocent." His voice was low, his head turned toward her, but his eyes were watching the train passengers. "When we get down to ground level, even in this daylight, you'll see every sort of wickedness imaginable. Russian gangs control about five thousand prostitutes in this country, most of them in the city sector where we're going."

"Russians?"

"You won't find that in the travel guide we bought you. They'll kill us to keep us from taking their assets. And they're not the only ones. Every brothel, casino, and entertainment facility trafficks in people. The 14K Triad dominates this country's sex trade even more than the Russians. About thirty thousand prostitutes under the age of eighteen are right here, and that's only about forty percent of the prostitutes where we're going."

"How are we going to find Aidan with so much of that happening? Greg said you probably have a plan."

The train slowed at a Siam station, and the two Westerners weaved through the crowd to board another sky train. This train cruised east for a few blocks, then swerved south. Outside the window, the city was canvassed with Buddhist shrines, foreign embassies, and sparkling hotels. Shopping centers announced their wares with bright signs and taunting images. Several parks zipped past the window, green and lush with vegetation and colorfully-clothed people. Everyone seemed modestly dressed on the train, just like Brody had told her to dress. He'd explained the dress code of Thai society: covered shoulders and covered knees, with a high neckline. The facade of morality, Brody had explained, disappeared when visitors discovered the city's many vices.

"The plan isn't that complicated," Brody continued now from their new seats.

Opposite their aisle sat several Americans or Europeans, men in slacks and collared shirts. They spoke English, so Marcy caught several words, all vulgar regarding their plans for the night.

"Human traffickers sell their people to specific vendors at the local level. If Aidan was truly sold to someone in Bangkok as PJ said, there are only a few establishments who take young white boys for prostitution. It was eight years ago, so he may have been exchanged a few times, even exported."

"Or killed," Marcy stated.

But Brody didn't react to her directness.

"We'll find a lead here. That's my hope."

"Because you know people."

"I know the GLOW network. People change all the time."

Marcy wiped her sweating hands on her cotton trousers, but every part of her was sweating, even her scalp under the beret. Thailand was hot and humid. No one wore jeans—they were just too hot. Brody was the only one on the train who wore light boots, but she wore tennis shoes with no socks—also Brody's recommendation.

"Here's Sala Daeng," Brody said as the train slowed.

She remembered the name from the map he'd shown her on his phone at the hotel. It was the nearest station to the Silom sector that Brody wanted to check first. Since they carried no belongings, they exited the train without hindrance and descended the stairs to street level where a few vehicles crept through the throng of merchants, pedestrians, and tourists. Children in shorts and sandalled feet weaved through the adults, offering trinkets with Buddhist symbolism.

Brody took Marcy's arm and pulled her faster than she could've moved alone. She didn't want to be a burden to him in his search for Aidan, but he'd made it clear at the airport that her life was in danger. He'd booked a large suite for the two of them. Though she had her own bedroom, he said she wouldn't be safe in her own suite.

"No one wants someone like me," Marcy had told him. "I'm too ugly."

"No, you're not." He'd checked the hotel doors and locks. "Maybe in the States, the Davenport smuggling ring didn't want to bother with you. But here, a young white woman is priceless. There are probably already runners being sent to watch us."

"Watch me?"

"You're traveling with an older man. It's not normal. They might think I've brought you here to sell you, or they might hope to catch you alone to kidnap you."

"Is it GLOW?"

"Maybe. GLOW is plugged into the airport's passenger system. I paid to bypass security, not for secrecy. They probably already know to watch for me. But you—they just see you as a money-maker."

"That's sick. I'll fight them like I did PJ."

"Then they'll drug you, and you'll still service ten to fifteen clients a day, which is normal for sex slaves here."

That conversation had taken place the night before in the safety of the high-priced hotel suite, but Marcy still remembered Brody's every frank word. Whether she liked it or not, she was a burden on this mission, though since GLOW knew their whereabouts in Tampa, she'd felt no safer there, either.

On Silom Road, Brody drew Marcy to the side of the street until they could stand with their backs against a shuttered shop.

"Some of these places have closed since I was here a few weeks ago."

"Is that good or bad?" Marcy couldn't see over the flow of people.

"It's the virus. People are afraid. If travel restrictions tighten further, it'll choke off the sex industry. Tens of thousands will go hungry. Only about two percent of the prostitutes here are eligible for government aid. Their pimps and owners will force them into another trade to earn a quota, or they'll turn to another kind of crime."

"What about Aidan? He's a teenager now. What'll happen to him if all these customers have to leave the country?"

"You need to brace yourself, Marcy. Anything is possible. Come on. I see a place I know. Keep your pen in your hand for now."

As Brody led her by the left arm into the street, she dug her tranq-pen out of her pocket. If anyone grabbed her, she knew what she was supposed to do. She clicked the pen twice to prepare the tip to tranquilize. But the pen was a small security. It was God's providence in which she needed to rely.

Brody pushed through a metal door. Two fighting figures poised in a martial arts stance were stenciled on the front. The door swung closed behind them. The sweet smells and bright colors on the street were replaced by foul odors and drab fixtures of an alley. They passed two young men who were crouched over a drain and a hypodermic needle. Neither looked up at the strangers.

Sounds of shouting and rhythmic drumming came from ahead of them. The noise echoed down the narrow walls. Brody led Marcy into a courtyard of about forty shirtless, sparring men. The nearest pairs stopped fighting and backed away from the newcomers. Marcy had read on the plane about Thailand's *Muay Thai* fascination. It was hard to read the fighters' faces. Some appeared to want to attack them, and others bowed their heads and clasped their palms together in the *wai* gesture of reverential greeting.

"Brody?" Marcy whispered as Brody led the way into the midst of the fighters.

"It's okay."

"I think they want to fight you." She noticed one man with a bamboo staff twirling it threateningly. "No, I'm *sure* they do."

Everyone in the courtyard had now stopped sparring. They gave Brody ample space as he passed through. At the opposite side of the courtyard, another corridor waited, but instead, Brody stopped and faced the still fighters.

"They might want to fight," Brody said, "but they won't."

"Why not?"

"They already tried that."

Brody offered the *wai* to them collectively. Most returned the gesture, then stood still as Brody continued into the corridor. But Marcy paused and watched the fighters, wondering with awe what must've happened during one of Brody's previous visits for such hardened youths to steer clear of the aging American. She couldn't hold back her smile. God had gone before them to find Aidan.

She gave them the *wai*, and many returned it to her, then she jogged to catch up to Brody. Behind her, the sounds of sparring continued from the courtyard.

They arrived at another smaller courtyard, this one empty except for two bonsai trees and a serenity pond. Brody approached one establishment door and knocked on it. Marcy tried to gauge where they were by looking up at several stories of cheap siding and fogged windows. The camera orbs at several intervals on the four walls were hard to miss.

The door opened, and the face of an older Thai man withdrew a few inches in obvious surprise. He peered around Brody's broad shoulders, noticed Marcy, then his eyes searched beyond her. She guessed he was disappointed at the security failure by the *Muay Thai* fighters.

"*Sawasdee-khrap*. I'm here to see Khun Somchai," Brody said. "Tell him Sladrick is here."

"I know who you are." The man hesitated a moment in thought, glanced over his shoulder, then widened the door. "*Mai pen rai*. Welcome to Khun Somchai's home."

Brody removed his shoes, and Marcy followed suit, leaving them beside the door with a collection of others. They stepped into a dimly lit interior smelling of incense.

The doorman led them down a short hallway lined with shelves of dolls and candles. Marcy stopped to examine one doll with human-like hair. Brody returned to her side.

"It's called a *luk thep*. A child angel. Thais believe it's inhabited by the spirit of a child."

"Creepy. Look at its eyes."

"To them, it's good luck for business. Come on. And put away your pen. Don't let them see it here, even if we need to use them."

Marcy slipped her tranq-pen into a front pocket and followed him into a wide room of wood and a low dining table. More incense burned against the wall where fruit, money, and bowls of food sat on a desk. Three men in red shirts reclined at the table, attended to by a white woman dressed in traditional Thai clothing, a long colorful skirt with a matching blouse, and a shawl of silk. The center man of the three was obese, his jowls hard not to stare at, but Marcy knew to divert her eyes.

Everyone exchanged the *wai*, then the doorman whispered in the fat man's ear, though it was clear from the look on Somchai's face that he both recognized Brody and was startled to see him.

"Khun Sladrick!" Somchai smiled broadly. "Sit, sit. This is a pleasant delight. The spirits have blessed us. Eat. Your friend as well."

His English was perfect, though with a British accent.

"You are very kind, Khun Somchai." Brody seated himself and gestured that Marcy should sit next to him. "You honor me by this welcome for my unexpected visit."

Marcy did her best to direct her eyes away from the jowls of the fat man by watching the white woman moving about the room. She appeared to be about thirty, her skin ruddy, maybe too old to work as a prostitute, if Somchai was indeed a trafficker. The woman, upon orders in Thai from Somchai, retrieved food from the altar of incense against the wall and set the bowls before Brody first, then Marcy.

When Marcy raised her hand to take up a fork, Brody reached across her and gently pushed her hand to her lap. Her mind screamed. Had she broken one of the many Thai rules or superstitions? She couldn't remember from what she'd read.

"I've told you before, my friend," Brody said almost cheerily to the man, even though Marcy sensed this wasn't friendly company. "I'll not eat the food offered to your spirits. My companion and I here have a different Spirit within us—the Spirit of the living God, Creator of all things. Perhaps you forgot?"

"No, I did not forget." Somchai jiggled as he chuckled. "Something makes me keep testing you."

Their host waved at the female servant to return the food to the altar.

"Thank you," Marcy whispered to the woman, who kept her head bowed and her eyes low. But for just an instant, those eyes strayed to Marcy's, and Marcy saw in them both kindness and shame. "Brody?"

"Yes?" Brody leaned close for her to speak in private.

"You know I once served under lock and key. I recognize it."

"I understand," Brody said, and sat up straighter, looking across the table at Somchai. "My companion was noticing your helpful hostess. Might I ask her name?"

Somchai barely restrained his frustration yet smiled through it.

"Khun Sladrick, we are both men who prefer the smoothest road possible. It's the Thai way, is it not? *Mai pen rai.*" He shook his large head. "Tell me what brings you to my simple home and how I may help you on your way."

"Nine years ago, a boy from Iowa was brought to Bangkok. Marcy?"

Marcy set her phone on the table and slid it toward Somchai. The man picked it up, studied the photo, then showed the screen to his dining friends who flanked him.

"Nine years is a long time for such an innocent looking child." Somchai returned the phone to the table. "He probably isn't so innocent any longer."

His two friends smiled, and Marcy clenched her teeth before her jaw trembled with fury. Brody didn't move or speak for several seconds, but learning what little she had about him, she knew he was holding back something tremendous that had ruined smuggling rings around the world.

"Khun Somchai," Brody finally said, his voice unbelievably ripe with patience and courtesy, "you pay dishonest police to look the other way. I know honest police who would love to look closer. Do you wish to test me further?"

Brody gave the phone back to Marcy.

"You shame me in my own house?" Somchai's smile disappeared. "Those are not the words of a grateful guest."

"Oh, but you shame yourself. Tell me what I want to know, and the three of us will leave."

"What three?" Somchai frowned. "Who else have you brought?"

Marcy followed Brody's gaze to the white female servant.

"Go, collect your things, young lady," Brody said to the white woman. "We're leaving in a few minutes."

"No!" Somchai barked.

The woman froze in her activity, her body tense and her eyes downcast as her fate was being decided.

"No?" Brody leaned forward. His shoulders seemed to swell as he placed his knuckles on the low table. "Did you just tell me no?"

"Khun Sladrick, please." Somchai held up his open palms. "Your last visits, and now this? I choose the smooth path with you. Show mercy, I beg you. This one is mine—from a debtor. It's an important transaction between friends that she remain here."

Marcy no longer cared if her gaze was deemed disrespectful. She openly watched the white woman, Brody, and Somchai's faces.

"Where are you from, young lady?" Brody asked the servant.

"I am come from Ukraine," she said with a humble head bob. "Now I go?"

"Go with her, Marcy," Brody said. "Help her collect her things. No one will stop you."

"Khun Sladrick, please!" Somchai's voice rose. "I have asked you to respect my wishes! She is legally mine."

"The longer I am here," Brody said, "the more I will take. Tell me about the boy. His age and origin are unique. Now you've seen his photo. You know everyone in Patpong."

Though Marcy wanted to stay and listen, she moved out of earshot through the house with the Ukrainian woman. In a master bedroom she walked into a closet with an open lock on the door. The woman knelt to collect clothing and hygiene articles scattered over a deflated blow-up mattress on the floor. Realizing the woman had been kept in the closet, Marcy held back her tears by kneeling and helping her bag up her belongings.

With everything collected, they stood together and Marcy embraced the woman, then held her cheeks in her hands, even though Marcy was a little shorter.

"God has sent us today. Don't be afraid."

"God?"

"Yes, the one true God. You know the cross?" Marcy made a cross sign with her fingers. "Jesus. You're safe with us now. Brody Sladrick works for God."

They returned to the main room where Somchai spoke softly, even apologetically, to Brody.

". . . I'm not saying it's him, but it could be. Others have been getting outsourced to the countryside for agriculture. It's this virus. I couldn't tell you where everyone goes."

"But you know who owns them," Brody said. "If this boy in Lumphini isn't who I'm looking for, I'll be back to collect more from you."

"Please, Khun Sladrick! This is everything I know. Bangkok is more than just Patpong. Speak to others, I beg you!"

"But you and I have such a fine relationship." Brody rose and gave a *wai* to the fat man. "Until we meet again, Khun Somchai. May you turn from your evil deeds and seek the kindness of the God of the Bible. Don't wait to seek His forgiveness when it's too late, my friend."

"Please . . ." He shook his head. "Go your way."

Instead of leaving the back way through which they'd come, Brody instructed the doorman to fetch their shoes, and they left out the front door, past another doorman, and into the street. Marcy felt supercharged to be the Ukrainian woman's escort and the one to whom she clung for assurance. But a few yards up the street, Marcy had to stop Brody.

"Did he tell you where Aidan is?"

"It's a long shot." Brody drew out his phone, swiped the screen, then pocketed it. "It might not be him. Many have scattered or run away. The pandemic is disrupting a lot, even though things might seem the same."

"What about her?" Marcy kept her arm around the older woman. "Do we take her with us or what?"

Brody nodded at someone ahead. Marcy had to look twice at two suited Thai men who were walking on either side of Binsa, the TROAS Nepalese woman! Binsa seemed to ignore everyone but the Ukrainian woman, whom she approached with open hands.

"I'm Binsa, a friend. We have a safe place for you. Can you come with me now?"

Stepping back, Marcy gave Binsa room to come alongside the Ukrainian woman. Binsa's two bodyguards fanned out and stood before and behind Binsa. Their eyes were never idle, their heads swiveling, constantly checking passersby for weapons, danger, or aggression.

The Ukrainian woman started away with Binsa.

"Stay close," Brody said to Binsa as she moved past him.

"We'll be ready," Binsa assured him without looking back.

Marcy moved up closer to Brody as the bodyguards walked calmly away on either side of Binsa and her new friend. In seconds, they were out of sight in the press of shoppers and shopkeepers.

"Don't be too shocked," Brody said as they walked north. "The bad guys aren't the only ones who utilize their network to plan ahead. God gave us each other to work together for His sake. The body of Christ is like that."

"I thought we were alone in Bangkok."

"I rarely go after a ring without a support team available to take in either criminals or captives who need our help."

"Except a year ago in Davenport. You were alone then."

Brody was silent for a moment, and Marcy regretted her accusation.

"There are occasions when my courage borders on over-confidence." Brody led them under the skyline, where the shade offered a little respite from the humidity. "Davenport was one of those occasions. It wasn't as cut and dry as I'd hoped. I handed off the kids in your house of captivity to the authorities, but I overlooked you."

"But God didn't."

"True." He smiled and glanced down at her. "He seems to do that pretty regularly."

"What did Somchai say to you about my brother?"

"Someone who might be Aidan was turned out when the first wave of the virus hit Bangkok. He became a beggar in Lumphini Park. It's within walking distance, but it's a big park. Last time I was here, there were thousands living in the park, most of them kids."

"We have to stay until we find him."

Marcy noticed that he didn't respond. She knew what it meant. They might find the boy, and it might not be Aidan at all. But if he was alive, he was out there somewhere. He'd been through nine years of horror. She begged God that this was the end of Aidan's suffering. Finding her parents would be a whole other challenge.

Lying in the dirt of Lumphini Park, Aidan Nevins picked at a scab on his arm. The gnats were especially numerous that night. Instead of lying on top of his *sabai* on the ground, he'd chosen to use the shawl as a cover for his upper body to protect himself from the bugs. During his first night sleeping in the park, he'd taken the *sabai* from another child—a dead child.

The scab came off and he felt the wetness of blood in the darkness. Aidan couldn't remember how he'd hurt himself. He was always tripping and falling, then crawling until he could find something to help him climb back to his feet. Although he didn't remember how he'd injured his arm, he remembered why he couldn't move the left side of his body. Arthit had beaten him, and that last time, his wife Preeda hadn't stopped him.

Aidan struggled to remember his life before Thailand, before embarrassment and cameras, before small rooms and an evil man. He had a vague recollection of a girl, his sister, always reading or studying on her side of the bedroom. She'd been older, but he wasn't sure how old. And though he'd forgotten her name, he remembered that she'd fixed him meals and washed his clothes. A sister? No, maybe she'd been his mother.

He had the fuzzy recollection of the plane ride from America, though he wasn't sure how long ago that had been. The small room in Thailand where he'd been kept was vivid in his memory since he'd only recently left it. The bed mattress had covered the whole floor, wall to wall. The two cameras had been mounted to the wall, and he'd learned the hard way not to touch them. His toilet had been a bucket with a lid, and his only pastime had been the three video games on the console on the foot of his bed.

For an indeterminate number of years, he'd played those video games. He knew every pixel of every frame of them. But they'd lost their appeal. Now, lying in the dirt of the park, the humidity causing his *sabai* to stick to him, he didn't miss that room or the games, and he certainly didn't miss the visits from Arthit and Preeda.

They'd come most often when he was asleep and they would wake him. He never knew if it was day or night. His only gauge of time had been the two meals he was fed probably daily. Arthit was a dirty, smelly man and Preeda was the boss because she knew what viewers wanted. Aidan had known that the cameras were watching everything, but after a while, he'd stopped caring.

The only time the cameras were off, he'd learned, was when Preeda told Arthit to beat him. She didn't want the beatings to be recorded.

There were only two rules in the little room. First, he was never to touch the two cameras. Second, he was to participate in the activities Preeda staged for him and Arthit. Breaking either rule resulted in a beating. Arthit used a strap most of the time, but sometimes he used his fists.

Aidan sat up in the dirt and used his one good arm to shake out his *sabai*. It was so hot here on the edge of the clearing! If there were grass, it would be cooler, but the grassy areas of the park were occupied by adults and older kids, meaner kids. He was different, weird, and smelly. They never beat him, but they would shove him around until he fell down or left their area.

Preeda and Arthit had been wealthy, he'd determined, and in their privileged place in society, they'd spoken English. Aidan had never needed to learn to speak Thai until now, but since his mind didn't work too well, and one side of his mouth and face didn't cooperate, learning and speaking Thai hadn't come naturally for him. Life was hard now, harder than it had been living in the little room, but he would rather die than return—even if they wanted him back.

Arthit had literally thrown him into the street for three reasons. He knew those reasons because they'd explained them to him. First, because of the abuse from Arthit several times a week, Aidan's bowels no longer worked right. He was in constant abdominal pain, and his regular accidents had required Preeda to wash far more laundry than she could tolerate. She'd cursed him for his filth, saying he was far messier and more disgusting than the others. This had been how Aidan had learned only recently that Preeda had other kids in their home. That explained why he thought he heard crying sometimes through the walls.

Second, when Aidan had refused to participate in one of Preeda's painful activities for him and Arthit, Preeda had become particularly enraged since she said they were "live" at that moment. Preeda had turned off the cameras and ordered Arthit to beat him. In the absence of his strap, Arthit had used his fists, blow after blow on the boy's skull and back. The result had been paralysis on one side of his body, but Preeda hadn't discovered this until two days later, after she saw he was struggling to sit up, chew food, and drink water.

About that time, the Meridia Virus fears had swept through the neighborhood. The costs to house and feed a crippled youth who could no longer care for himself wasn't worth their time. Arthit himself had carried Aidan into the street and dropped him in the gutter. It had been raining that day. The gutter water had pooled around him until he'd crawled away.

Aidan decided that night in the park that he needed to relocate on account of the bugs. Perhaps in the darkness, the others who lived there wouldn't notice if he found a little patch of their cool grass to lay on. Of course, the boys would bother him less if his body were clean, but he'd given up trying to wash himself. He soiled his clothes so often, unable to control himself that he just stood limply in the outdoor bathing areas to ladle water over himself. Getting dressed and undressed was too difficult. Cleanliness was a hopeless pursuit for him now.

After crawling through scratchy bushes to use a tree to aid him to his feet, he shuffled toward the lights at the edge of the park. Yes, there was a street there. He wanted to sleep, but maybe his night would be better spent begging, if there were any generous people in the area that evening. Without charity, he would've died during the first week of living in the park. But receiving charity was a challenge of patience and location. The best locations were taken by younger kids protected and guided by older kids. They occupied train platforms or crossroad corners. Aidan was left to sit on street curbs where people usually streamed past without noticing.

And since the pandemic had started, fewer sympathetic tourists gave him money, trinkets, or food. Some tourists asked him outright if he would have sex with them. But if they didn't realize that he was crippled and soiled, he would tell them that he hadn't bathed in days. That always made them go away. Anyone who made such offers to him, in his mind, were just like Preeda and Arthit. They were dirtier than he was. He didn't want to be mistreated like that anymore, cameras or not.

On the west side of the park, the night life was still busy, regardless of curfews across the rest of the city. Aidan found a swept area of the curb along the street and clumsily sat down. Most streets didn't have curbs, so he counted himself privileged. Sure, he wasn't at an intersection, but foot traffic on this street was moderate.

"Food, please?" he asked in English and Thai, holding out his only functioning hand. "Food, please."

He never asked for money from passersby anymore. His only hope at survival was if they gave him something to eat, though most people were hustling past on their way to one of the shopping centers, sex shops, or parlors. Some had food they were eating as they walked, and sometimes they didn't mind giving him part of their meal. Aidan never cared that the food was already half-eaten.

"Food, please."

Then Aidan spotted a Western man and a Thai woman coming from the right, and he set his gaze on them. The woman carried a cup with the Royal Bangkok Sports Club logo. She used a plastic spoon to take slow bites of something as she and her lover visited and laughed. She was a beautifully painted prostitute, but Aidan didn't care. If he could catch her eye . . .

It was some kind of soup. Aidan trembled with eagerness as he held out his hand, leaning out over the street toward the couple.

"Food, please?" he called louder as they neared.

She noticed him as she laughed at something her lover whispered in her ear.

"Food, please!" Aidan pressed, willing to merely lick the inside of the cup if its contents were gone. He hadn't eaten the previous day.

Her walk slowed, even though her companion hadn't looked up from his affections aimed at her. She glanced at her cup, then at Aidan. He nearly gasped as she cut away from her friend and held out the cup to him. This was it. He'd survive another day and night. With a cup like this, he could even carry drinking water from the fountain!

"Thank you! Thank you!" He bobbed his head, unable to offer the proper *wai* since he couldn't raise his other arm. Instead, he clutched the cup to his chest, intent on disappearing into the park where he could eat it in his awkward way since his mouth was partially paralyzed as well.

She smiled at him an instant before her lover tugged her away. Aidan didn't look after her to see if she looked back. He smelled the soup. The cup was nearly half-full! He didn't want to spill a drop or miss a single noodle, vegetable, or sliver of meat.

After rocking back and forth on the curb to gain momentum, he rose to his feet and steadied himself. He turned toward the park and stepped carefully onto the sidewalk. Though he was very focused on not spilling his cup as he shuffled forward, he noticed the band of youths approaching. By the look of their faded clothing and uncut hair, they were also park dwellers. Yes, at least one of the boys among them was familiar. He'd forced Aidan away from the train station a week or so earlier. Now, they were coming straight after him!

Aidan panicked. They wanted his soup! He hustled faster, moving over the uneven ground toward the park's interior. Afraid that he would have his soup stolen altogether, he determined to get at least one mouthful. Without stopping, he put the cup to his mouth and tipped it back.

But before anything reached his lips, his lead foot caught on a root or some protuberance on the ground. He pitched forward. His elbow hit bare ground, and the cup crumpled against his face. Everything spilled out around him.

An instant later, rough hands rolled him over. The

boys spoke Thai, but it was clear they wanted what he had. One carried a flashlight. Their cruel hands searched his shirt, then pushed his face into the dirt. As they parted with nothing, they intentionally trampled the bits of soup and the cup into the dirt.

Sitting up, Aidan licked his arm where some of the soup juice had spilled. It tasted heavenly, even mixed with his own sweat. Only then did he look hatefully after the boys. By treating him this way, he wondered if they understood they were killing him slowly. How could he survive without begging and eating? Maybe if he relocated to another area. There had to be other parks in the city. But there might be other gangs as well.

If it had been light, Aidan might have still tried to pick bits of noodles off the ground, but he couldn't in the dark. Instead of trying to rise to his feet, he remained where he sat in the soup puddle. What was the point of continuing? It was hopeless to even try. No one cared. He could die and no one would mourn him.

Lying on his side, Aidan's will to live was now gone. In a final sense of defeat, he realized he'd forgotten his *sabai* at the last place he'd tried to sleep in the park. He'd never find it in the dark, and by morning, someone would find it before he could.

He closed his eyes, welcoming nothingness. Living was too miserable. Death seemed much more inviting, and certainly inevitable.

When he opened his eyes again, it was still dark, but there was a light drawing nearer from the middle of the park grounds. It must've been the boys, circling about. They were coming back. Aidan wondered if they would just kill him this time, so he didn't need to crawl into the bushes to die more slowly.

The flashlight beam reached his face and his eyes flinched at the brightness. Instead of ridicule or abuse, someone was kneeling over him.

"He may have been beaten up," a man's voice said, as

he held the flashlight. "We came through here an hour ago, and he wasn't here."

"Does he look white?" a woman asked. "I think this is a white boy. Aidan, is that you?"

Aidan shrunk into the ground, wanting to disappear. He couldn't remember Preeda or Arthit ever using his name.

"No, just . . . leave me," he mumbled.

"I don't think he knows English," the man said.

"Wait," she said. "I think something's wrong with him. Look."

A gentle hand lifted and dropped his paralyzed arm. Aidan used his functional arm to draw his limp arm against his torso.

"It might've been a stroke. Here, hold the light." The man grasped Aidan's right wrist and forced his hand onto the flat screen of his phone. "His fingers are dirty, but his prints should still work."

The second the man let go of his hand, Aidan withdrew it and used his good leg to push off the ground, scooting himself a few inches toward the nearby vegetation. Even in the dark, he knew it was there. If he could just hide, maybe people would let him die in peace.

"It's him, Marcy," the man said. "It's Aidan."

"*It's him?* Brody, you're sure?" The woman crawled after him through the soup remains. "Aidan, it's okay. It's me. It's Marcy, your sister."

Aidan raised his arm in front of his face. For years, the only person who'd been this close to him was Arthit, and abuse had always followed. He didn't want anyone to be close to him again.

"Take your time," the man named Brody said. "He's been alone out here a long time. Give him a little space, Marcy. Let him come to you."

"But he needs me!"

She was crying. Aidan recognized the sound because he'd cried many times. Why was she crying?

"Just hold your hand out to him," Brody said. "That's it. We don't know what he's been through. It might take days for him to get used to you, even weeks."

"No, I'm his sister." Her hand remained outstretched toward him. "Hey, Addy. How you doing, little brother? You want to take my hand? See? It's me, Marcy. We're going home now."

Aidan almost reached for the hand. The woman's voice was so sweet. But suddenly the flashlight left him, and he heard the voices of the homeless boys. He couldn't understand what they said, but the man called Brody spoke back to them in Thai and stood his ground. The boys backed away, and Brody shifted the light back on him and Marcy. He'd made the cruel boys go away, and this woman didn't seem to wish him any harm. At least they hadn't asked him for sex.

He slowly laid his hand in hers.

"That's it, Addy," she said through her sniffles. "You're safe now, little buddy."

Aidan didn't pull away as she leaned closer. She embraced him lightly, and after a few seconds, she didn't even gag from his stench or shudder from his soiled clothing. When she released him, she looked up at Brody.

"We have to get him back to the room. I need to clean him up."

"I've alerted Binsa." The man knelt and patted Aidan's leg. "Hey, big guy. A minute ago, you spoke. Can you talk a little? Do you remember English?"

"Yeah." Aidan nodded. He tried to enunciate past his mouth not working right. "English is all I know."

"Okay, that's good. Can you tell us where you've been for the last few years? Do you know where you've been living?"

"Brody, you can investigate later," Marcy said.

"No, sometimes there isn't a later. Besides, we're leaving tomorrow. Aidan, do you remember where you were? How about a building? Did you make any friends? Do you know any names?"

"Preeda," Aidan said.

"Pretty?" Marcy asked. "I think he said pretty. He can't pronounce words very well."

"Preeda," Aidan repeated. "And Arthit."

"Preeda is a common Thai name for a woman," Brody said. "Arthit is a man's name. Aidan, were these your friends, Preeda and Arthit?"

"No. No! Not . . . my . . . friends!" He hid himself in the embrace of the woman. This was safe. No more Preeda. No more Arthit. No more cameras.

"That's enough, Brody," Marcy said. "We found him. It's over now."

"It's not over." Brody rose to his feet. "Get him back to the train. You have your tranq-pen if you need it. Aidan's been missing for nine years. Someone knows where he's been."

"Preeda and Arthit," Aidan repeated. "Preeda and Arthit . . . they're . . . bad."

"I hear you, pal," Brody said. "I hear you loud and clear."

Another woman and two quiet men arrived, spoke briefly, then escorted him and Marcy away. Aidan looked back. The strong man had left the flashlight with Marcy and had walked alone into the darkness.

CHAPTER FIVE

Brody Sladrick woke to his coworker Binsa's touch. "My brother, it is morning."

He sat up in the back of a rented minivan and acknowledged Binsa's two Christian bodyguards in the front seat, watching him. The floor of the van smelled like fuel, but Brody had slept in worse places.

"Good morning," he greeted.

They nodded and faced the front. He guessed his behavior was strange to others, but he'd lived and slept like this so often since his late teens that he was completely acclimated. It hadn't bothered him at all that as he'd slept on the floor of the van, the two Thais had visited quietly in the front seat, and Binsa had texted or spoken with people on her tablet and satellite-uplink next to him.

A glance out the window showed that it was daylight in Bangkok. After finding Aidan in the park and sending Marcy with Binsa back to the hotel, Brody had gotten only about three hours of sleep, but this wasn't his first sleep-deprived mission.

As if reading his heart, Binsa leaned close to him.

"I've been praying for clarity in God's direction for you." She closed her eyes, as if praying even then, and after a few seconds, she opened them. "I know the challenge of grace before you."

"Thank you, Binsa." He took a moment to straighten his clothes and finger-comb his close-cropped hair. Binsa handed him a thermos of strong tea and a protein bar. "The Ukrainian woman? Sorry, I forgot to ask you about her when I got back to the van."

"The Ukrainian embassy isn't open in Bangkok,"

Binsa said, "so we went across the street from the U.S. embassy to the Czechs. They owed us a favor for the Prague incident last year."

"They remembered we brought a couple of their kids home?"

"With some help, yes, they remembered." Binsa smiled. "They took her in and will return her to her family. I've contacted believers in Kiev who'll connect with her when she returns."

"Okay, good. Well done, Binsa, as usual." He gulped several swallows of cold tea. "Anything from Marcy?"

"We got them safely to the hotel. The boy's traumatized, nearly catatonic."

"Nine years." Brody's heart felt heavy. "The Lord will need to help him in a special way."

"Marcy cleaned him up. Deja General Hospital said we can pick up a bundle of adult diapers for him on the way to the airport."

"That's fine." Brody nodded, not needing her to explain. Young boys who'd been raped sometimes lost control, but surgery usually corrected the problem. "I'm not too sure where home is for them now. The way GLOW is these days, word'll get around about the brother and sister who're now free."

"They'll be safe with us at the apartment. True?" She nodded once, as if it were settled, and turned his attention to her tablet screen. "Greg found government tax records of a Preeda and Arthit Somdet living here. And the dark web identified years of videos for sale from Arthit Somdet. He didn't even disguise his name. Some of the videos have Aidan in them, so we know we have the right couple. Do you know this area?"

"Evergreen Laurel? I know it. It's not far from where we were in the park last night."

Binsa watched his face without speaking for so long that Brody sensed what she wanted.

"Are you sure about this?" he asked. "There could be

other kids there, like there usually are in these places. They need your attention more than these people who are holding them. It could be dangerous."

"I know, but to care for those broken souls, Brody—" She bowed her head and one hand went to her mouth and her voice broke. "I want to help the abusers this time."

"Well, you know what to expect." Brody gestured to the two men in the front. "Can they help with the kids, if we find any more?"

"They both have wives who are sisters in Christ. I already called them. They're available and they can meet us there. Thank you, Brody. I won't get in your way. I feel . . . I have love to show them, even if it's as you've said before—tough love."

"Love is what they need." Brody sighed. "But love isn't what some of these traffickers want. The darkness is so thick here, Binsa."

"I know. But God—He can cut through it. True?"

"He's the only one who can." Brody took her hand in his and closed his eyes. "Lord, we need You and not ourselves in this moment. Let Your grace break through where man's wrath or my own anger have no effect. We trust You to move, because Your Son defeated death for us. Amen."

"Amen."

Brody climbed out of the back of the van and took in his surroundings. While he'd slept, the van had relocated. They were parked across from the boxing stadium near the Suan Lum Night Bazaar. Binsa gave instructions to her escorts to fetch their wives and to meet her and Brody several blocks to the west. She closed the door and stood beside him on the street as the van pulled away.

"They're good men," Brody said. "Dependable."

"The finest for God in Thailand," Binsa agreed, "along with their wives. Precious ones. True? Remember?"

"That's true. I remember them. Amazing cooks, too."

They joined the drifting foot traffic, bicyclists, and

vehicles heading west on Suthon Tai Street, then turned north for quieter walking. Brody felt his tranq-pen in his right trousers pocket, and he guessed Binsa had one of her own. As a woman who had come from a culture where women and children were sold regularly, she knew well the dangers they could face. But this wasn't Binsa's first rescue, though it would be her first confrontation. Normally, she came in to assist trafficked survivors only after Brody had torn an establishment to pieces and dealt with the traffickers.

"Do you think they sense their lives are about to change?" Binsa asked as they reached the massive shopping district. "I would expect they sense something."

"Sin often blinds sinners, but if they do sense what's about to happen, they're in a state of fear right now. Satan has no claim on us, and we're about to interrupt what he's been doing in their lives."

Behind one building, they climbed a set of metal stairs so steep they could've been considered a fire escape ladder—to reach the second floor. Through the apartment building door, the interior was less like a slum building and more like a four-star hotel. The doors in the hallway were numbered and labeled with family names. At the far end, they arrived at the Somdet residence.

"Appears harmless," Brody said softly, inspecting the door for security, then moved aside. "It even looks innocent."

"They always do, don't they?" Binsa stood close to him where he'd moved to a window at the end of the hall. They watched the sellers outside quietly order their stalls for another day of market. "Sin often escapes our attention because it's wrapped in the unexpected. True?"

"True."

A few minutes later, Binsa tugged on his arm.

"They're here."

Brody acknowledged the two bodyguards and their Thai wives approaching up the hallway. Since in Thai culture shaking hands wasn't accepted, Brody offered the *wai* first, and bowed slightly, as a sign of respect, even though he was older and in charge. They all returned the *wai*, and the men greeted with *Sawatdee-khrap*, and the women with *Sawatdee-kah*.

The women were wide-eyed and nervous, though Brody had called before upon the Bangkok fellowship to help him respond to trafficked survivors, whom they called overcomers or "the found," so as not to engender weakness or a victim mentality.

"Wait out here," Brody said to the men. "Binsa and I will call you when it's time, if there are children."

The four understood, and Brody went to the Somdet door. He quietly tested the bronze door knob and found it locked. He inspected the frame closer, and then gently applied his weight to the flange on each side of the door. There was flex in the fabricated wood. It was cheap but made to appear strong.

Where the deadbolt might've been, Brody placed his shoulder, then coached the two men to push at intervals on his opposite shoulder. The effect was like a soft battering ram, but in the civilian apartment, the gentler approach was best.

After a dozen heaves, the wood cracked. The next two surges split and tore the wood off the doorway. There'd been very little sound. Brody swung the door free from the splintered wood and swept a few fragments of particle board aside with his foot. He and Binsa stepped inside and closed the door behind him, leaving the two Thai couples in the hallway.

Their entry had been so nonaggressive that Brody came upon a seated man in shirt and pants at his kitchen table but still barefooted. Neither Brody nor Binsa removed their footwear, which was considered either rude or even sacrilegious, depending on the household's superstitions. But Brody wasn't there to honor their Thai customs.

The man appeared to be about forty and was fit and clean-shaven. His attire looked clean and pressed, and his complexion was darker than most Thais Brody had seen. He may have been from Indian descent. Such was his surprise at his home invaders—and certainly of a white man—that he didn't object or rise from his chair when Brody sat across the table from him. The burning incense at a Buddhist altar reached his nose. The kitchen was clean, the furniture new, and the living room nearby was stocked with a Chinese TV screen and sound system.

Binsa paused in the kitchen only briefly, then continued into the living room alone, beyond Brody's sight. He suddenly heard a woman shriek. Arthit Somdet started to rise, but Brody slammed the palm of his left hand onto the tabletop. His mouth agape, Arthit lowered himself slowly back to his seat.

A moment later, Binsa drove the woman of the house into the kitchen. The Nepalese woman had Preeda's left arm twisted behind her back, controlling her whole body to seat her beside her husband. Preeda cursed Binsa in Thai, but Binsa wasn't thin-skinned, and she didn't respond. Instead, she left to scout the residence.

In her absence, Brody alternated his gaze from husband to wife, trying to communicate through his eyes the seriousness of the situation. He didn't glare since he didn't hate these people, even though their crimes were heinous and many. Even they could be forgiven, so Brody left their eternal plight in God's hands.

Several doors slammed in the rear of the apartment. When children's voices reached the kitchen, Preeda and Arthit shared a look, then settled their eyes on the tabletop, as if meeting Brody's gaze was too difficult. It was shame, Brody guessed, which was a good sign. The exposure of their sin was shameful to them, but that didn't mean they were ready to repent before the Lord.

In his peripheral vision, Brody noticed Binsa escort three children past the kitchen and to the front door. She spoke quietly to her Thai counterparts, then she closed the door. When Binsa returned, she cupped her hand over her mouth to whisper into Brody's ear.

"Two boys and one girl. They're going to the hospital. Mattresses and web-cams like we've seen in other countries. I touched nothing."

Brody nodded, then Binsa stood idly on his right, blocking the way from the kitchen. She folded her hands and waited.

"We are friends of Aidan Nevins," Brody stated so softly in English, Preeda and Arthit leaned forward to hear him. "Aidan Nevins sent us."

Preeda whispered to her husband, then looked back toward Brody, but diverted her eyes in the custom of Thai culture between a woman and a strange man.

"We don't know anyone by that name," she stated.

Brody watched their faces. They probably really didn't know or remember Aidan's name, even though they'd held him long enough that Aidan had learned their names. The grooming and manipulation of trafficked people often included a rejection of their past identity. Many were given new names by their captors.

"It's right for you to be fearful right now." Brody sighed. While he allowed his words to sink in, he checked the counters nearby for possible weapons the couple might lunge for. There was nothing in sight that seemed threatening. "You have been caught. Your lives will now never be the same."

Arthit licked his lips and looked to his wife, maybe for a reaction. Brody read the couple and understood that she was the dominant party. She wasn't a collateral witness to Arthit's sex enterprise; she was probably directing it, since he was taking his cues from her.

"Thailand is under a lot of international pressure right now to punish sex traffickers," Brody continued. "They'll want to make an example of someone to show the world that they treat traffickers without mercy."

"Those were our children," Preeda said firmly. "What right do you have to remove—"

Brody slammed his palm down on the table again.

"Silence. The cameras in their rooms speak for themselves, as do the injuries to the children. They'll be returned to their families or adopted by loving parents. But you two—you have no defense. You need hope and forgiveness. Without it, you'll most certainly die horrible deaths in shame and guilt."

As suspected, the husband gasped in his weakness. His face contorted in a sob that was interrupted by a stern glare from his wife. With obvious effort, he recovered and returned to his downcast posture.

Standing, Brody walked along the counter until he stood directly behind the pair. It had the effect that he wanted. They both stiffened.

"Perhaps you know a few corrupt officials," Brody said, as he often brought to the attention of traffickers. "Perhaps you think you'll pay your way out of it this time. But, no. I most certainly know more powerful officials in this country than you, and my officials can't be bought."

"There must be something—" Preeda began.

"Quiet, Preeda," Brody said. "You'll both be punished. There's no way around that. All of the evidence in this apartment will condemn you both. The only question is: will you live the rest of your lives in guilt or in grace?"

Brody rested his hands on Arthit's shoulders. The man's body trembled under his touch. In Thai culture, it wasn't polite to touch another person, especially someone who wasn't a family member.

"You deserve to have done to you," Brody said, "what you've done to those children. Perhaps in prison, that will be done to you after all."

"We fed those—!" Preeda stated.

"No words!" Binsa snapped. The woman leaned across the table. "There are no words to excuse what you've done."

Returning to his seat, Brody folded his hands on the table. Binsa planted her feet again.

"What hope do you have now?" Brody shook his head. "I'm looking at two condemned souls, destined to suffer agonies for eternity. No peace. No love. No joy. This has been your choice—wickedness and evil and crimes unspeakable. The consequences will still be difficult, but there's only one way for you to escape the wrath to come."

"Money?" Preeda asked. "We can pay you. We are wealthy."

"No, you have no money. By now, my organization has found all your accounts and set it aside for the children who will need help in their recoveries, including Aidan. All of your internet clients are also being tracked down. We know their names and IP addresses. Because of you, they'll be arrested, fined, maybe jailed. They'll blame you. But your punishment will be more severe than everyone else's. Unless . . ."

Brody wondered if he had sufficiently established their need for rescue. Arthit was clearly shaken, but Preeda was so hard and cold, she was still looking for a way out that cost her little or nothing. Their loss of wealth might have softened her resolve. By now, Greg had reallocated the couple's bank balance for TROAS recovery efforts.

"There's a story of a shepherd who had a flock of sheep," Brody shared. "One day, two thieves came into the valley and stole a lamb. The thieves took the lamb into the nearest town where they put a chain on the lamb's neck in the town square. They shaved the lamb and began to beat it. They charged money for the townspeople to watch them beat the lamb. The lamb begged for mercy, but the thieves only laughed. The lamb bled and cried, but the thieves only charged more money.

"One day, the shepherd came to town and found his little lamb being beaten. With unmatched authority, the shepherd dismissed the townspeople and took the chain off his lamb's neck. He placed the chain on the necks of the two thieves, and he handed down the judgment."

In silence, Brody sensed he had even Preeda's attention now. When she could wait no longer, she spoke.

"What was the judgement?" she asked.

"After everything the thieves did to the lamb," Brody said, "how would you judge the thieves if you were the shepherd?"

"Say nothing, Arthit!" Preeda ordered in Thai. "He's speaking about us."

"Yes, it's true," Brody admitted. "The story is about you. But it's not just about you. It's about me, too. It's about all people. We all mistreat others. We all victimize and steal and destroy. We must all admit what we truly deserve as thieves before we can take the next step to heal. What do you deserve, Arthit? How should the shepherd respond to the thief who has harmed his sheep?"

"This isn't healing!" Preeda said. "What game is this?"

Brody acknowledged Arthit's discomfort, even though the man didn't answer, then he addressed the man's wife.

"It's not a game, Preeda. My people tell me that you're not in the videos with the children, but yours is the voice behind the films—hundreds of them. You're directing your husband. You're responsible. You're caught. You're the thief. Even if you're too proud and stubborn to speak it, you know what you deserve."

"I'm a businesswoman." Preeda scowled and looked away.

"But just because we deserve death, doesn't mean that mercy isn't available. Arthit, there's mercy available to you. Preeda, there's mercy available to you—even you. But it must be received."

"What . . . will happen to us?" Arthit asked, then he began sobbing, his head bowed.

Preeda scolded her husband in Thai. Brody nodded his head at Preeda as he spoke to Binsa.

"Take her into the other room. Maybe you can talk some sense into her, but I want to talk to Arthit alone now."

Binsa forced the Thai woman to her feet. Brody drew a black zip tie from his back pocket and tied her wrists behind her back. Once Brody was alone with Arthit, he moved around the table and knelt next to Arthit's chair. The man openly wept, though Brody could only trust God that the man's sorrow was headed in the direction of true repentance and not just shame.

Brody set his hand on Arthit's forearm. The man didn't pull away.

"I'm here, Arthit, to bring you hope. For your crimes against children, you'll suffer the consequences in the hands of your government. Patiently accept that punishment, but you need to know that when you die and pass into the afterlife, there will be a time of judgement. You'll one day soon stand before the Creator of all things. He is the only God, and His justice and compassion are shown to all people. He is the reason I'm here to speak to you about mercy, even though you deserve death for your crimes. Do you understand?"

Arthit's nose ran unchecked, but he nodded solemnly with his eyes closed.

"God sent His Son to earth as a Man to save all people from the death that all people deserve. The Son of God's name was Jesus. He died for us, Arthit. God died for you, my friend, because He loves you. And because Jesus is God, He didn't remain dead. He came back to life, and He wants to welcome all those who believe in Him into His arms of mercy and forgiveness. It's important that you receive this gift of forgiveness, Arthit. You receive it by trusting God that He died for you. That's all. Take hold of God's mercy by faith, and it becomes yours.

"When you believe, when you know that you have received God's mercy, you must trust Him to help you live a new life. The old gods and spirits of your ancestors must be set aside. Those old superstitions won't help you. You must become a new person, Arthit. Trust in the Creator to forgive you."

Brody stood Arthit upright and embraced him. After a few seconds, Brody turned Arthit around and zip tied his wrists, then sat him down again. Arthit sat quietly, but Brody could hear Preeda's mockery and evil tongue from the next room as she derided Binsa.

Using his phone, Brody called an official on the police force who he'd relied on in years past. As far as Brody and Greg had been able to discern, the policeman wasn't corrupt, though he wasn't a believer. He had a wife but no children of his own, yet he'd taken a special interest in arresting the sex ring leaders in and outside the GLOW network in Bangkok. That morning, he promised to send Brody two squad cars and an investigative team to process the house for evidence.

Binsa led Preeda out of the apartment, and Brody followed them with Arthit, though Arthit didn't resist. Preeda chastised her husband all the way to the street where officers took them into custody in separate cars.

"Her heart is bad," Binsa said, looking in at the woman in the back seat. "Her husband may be helped. True?"

"True. We'll have the local church reach into the jail system to find him in a few days. A Bible may do him some good. He seemed receptive, but we'll find out in glory."

"Marcy wouldn't approve of what we do—offering such wicked people the forgiveness of God."

"She's forgiven PJ, so she's understanding that forgiveness is God's to give." Brody sighed. "Nobody has to approve of God's forgiveness, even when He offers it to those we know have been cruel."

"I need to get to the hospital to look after the three children."

"I'll ride with you there, then go to the hotel." He

raised his hand for a taxi. "I'll see you back in Tampa, huh?"

"Marcy and Aidan will live with us now?" she asked. "At the apartment?"

"If that's what you want, Sister." He chuckled and held the taxi door open for her.

"It's what I want." Smiling, she climbed into the back seat.

Before he joined her, Brody looked up at the steep staircase where the investigative team climbed to the second story. Sadly, Preeda and Arthit's trafficking residence was only one among hundreds across Thailand. But that day, there was one less, and that mattered a great deal to three young children they'd rescued.

Marcy closed the door to the cabin in the back of the private jet. There was no turbulence as they flew east, but the vibration of the plane made Marcy feel like she needed to hold out her arms as she walked up the narrow aisle to where Brody sat in a swivel chair.

"Aidan's sleeping," she reported as she plopped into her own chair across the cabin from Brody. "All these years of praying to find him, I never imagined the condition he'd be in. I just knew we needed to be a family again."

"He's blessed to have you," Brody said over his tablet, then set it on his lap. "His mental state will improve over time, but it'll take patience on your part. You're learning that he needs you to be a nurse more than a sister right now."

"Well, I bathed a lot of the kids back in Tory and Trey's house. I can handle it."

"I believe you." Brody smiled and picked up his tablet again. "You might even say that God prepared you for this time of helping your brother."

"Yeah."

Sitting back, Marcy pondered such a plan from God.

That Brody would even suggest such an idea told her how well he knew God. Her years of hardship and abuse had indeed prepared her to help others recover from their own hardships and abuse. Now, if she trusted God about her past and her future, her mind could be free from caring about herself so she could care for Aidan.

"I didn't want to ask you in front of Aidan . . ." Marcy said. "Sorry to keep interrupting you."

"It's fine." Brody set down his tablet again. "I'm reviewing another operation that needs my attention."

"The senator?"

"He gives us certain access, but we'll keep him our secret."

"Then we can go look for my parents?"

"Greg is already on that. I think you should stay back with Aidan. He's in no condition to be traveling, and right now, he needs you at his side, not strangers."

"But I have to be the one to help my parents." Marcy felt a mixture of sadness, anxiety, and anger at the situation. "It has to be me. They won't listen to a stranger. No offense. I need to tell them that I still love them."

"You can't care for Aidan and go wherever we may need to go to get your folks. By God's grace, Marcy, I'll bring them back to Tampa. It'll give me time to talk things over with them. I may be a stranger to them, but I'm not a stranger to what they've done. Binsa will be at the apartment to help you and Aidan get situated. Don't worry, it's gonna work out. That's what you wanted to ask me?"

"No." Marcy tried to set aside her disappointment, but of course he was right. Aidan was her priority now. "You didn't tell me what you did to those people who did stuff to Addy."

"What do you mean, what I did to them?"

"Well, you're like a . . . secret agent, right? I know you did something to them."

"I suppose I did. Binsa and I found them—a husband

and wife team of traffickers. Using the internet, they were abusing children on camera. Some countries like North Korea do the same thing to thousands of children, so we weren't surprised to see it in Thailand. We found three kids locked up in different rooms. They were sick and injured like Aidan, but Binsa had friends in the Bangkok church to look after them."

"What did you do to the husband and wife."

"What did you want me to do to them?"

Marcy watched his face. She hadn't known him long, but she recognized he was testing her.

"I had a chance to kill PJ once when I was at Tory and Trey's house. He'd beat and raped me more times than I know. But I didn't kill him."

"Why not?" he asked.

"Something in me—I don't think God wanted me to."

"I think you're right. Feelings of revenge and murder don't come from God. Followers of Jesus Christ are more inclined to forgive and show pity rather than try to destroy since His spirit lives in us."

"It was still hard not to hate him."

"Yeah, I understand. I do. In my arsenal, I have a variety of abilities that can cripple, maim, or kill an enemy. As a child running with African shepherd boys, I learned how to throw spears and make knives. Just because we can hurt someone doesn't mean we should. I agree with you. But I think God wants something that reflects Christ when we confront these evil hearts."

"So, you didn't hurt them—the people who hurt Aidan?"

"No, we didn't hurt them. Binsa and I sat them down in their kitchen and told them the gospel as clearly as we could."

"And they just listened?"

"Hearing and listening are two different things. Preeda, the wife, didn't want to hear anything about the gospel. But her husband, Arthit, wept through most of the end of our time with them."

"He cried?"

"His sin was exposed. But the Thai culture is so saturated by Buddhist mysticism and strange superstitions, it's challenging to introduce them to a God they've probably never heard about before."

"But you tried, at least."

"Yeah. Other Thais who're believers will reach into the jail wherever he ends up. There's a strong possibility that the forgiveness and mercy I described to him—and showed him—touched his heart."

"And you didn't kill him?"

"No, I didn't kill him. I try to follow the Holy Spirit's guidance over my new nature when dealing with these kinds of people—or all people. I'm often firm like a stern father with this type. But there's no glorifying God in the death of unbelievers, even if they deserve it. God is looking for repentance and a true broken heart for His Son's sake. A criminal like Arthit who comes to Christ is more useful to God than an unbeliever who never committed such a crime. Americans are generally a self-righteous lot, so this approach with Christ's gospel of forgiveness isn't too popular back home."

"But it works for that senator."

"Senator Madison wants results, so he tolerates the means I use." Brody chuckled. "Even Joseph in the Bible served God as a priority yet benefited from being submitted to the pharaoh of Egypt. This jet is a sample of one of the benefits, but it's not about luxury. Using a private plane, I can get in and out of countries a lot easier, especially with recovered friends. With virus quarantines and restrictions rising all over the world, VIP privileges play an important role in this work."

"I have another question. About Aidan."

"Okay, I'm listening."

"What do I do for him? He's seventeen now. Does Tampa have a program I should take him to or something?"

"You could take him to a program. There are many. Most will have him on five different psych medications in a week, and either indoctrinate him about how he's damaged goods now, or that he's deserving of endless pity because of what he's been through."

"So, no program? I don't want him on a bunch of drugs. Does he need them?"

"Binsa knows which doctors to take him to for the stroke he's had, but as for his emotional and mental health—the Lord has provided already what Aidan needs to grow up. He might be seventeen, but he's been locked away for nine years. He didn't mature like you did in your situation. So, we'll help him, treat him like a normal boy. To reach normality, we operate normally."

"Like it all never happened?"

"No, we never ignore things like this. Instead, we face it with him, and we don't treat him like he's a victim—or he'll live his life like a victim. We need to treat him like the man he should become. Our means is dictated by the end goal, not by the past events."

"I don't know anything about making him into a man."

"You and Binsa take care of him with what you can do—without babying him. And Greg and I will take care of the rest. We might know something about being a man."

"But Aidan wears diapers now."

"Oh, that's nothing." Brody shook his head. "There might be a surgery that'll help him with that, but if there's not, he'll learn it's not what you wear or what happens to you that makes you a man. He'll learn all that from us, especially as we introduce him to the Lord. God will teach him his identity and calling and future."

"It's all so strange." She turned in her chair and

peered out the starboard window. "The little boy who only cared about video games is gone."

"We'll walk beside him as he continues to grow up."

Marcy envisioned her little brother all grown up. He wasn't yet, but maybe God would help him like He had helped her. It seemed all the more likely that Aidan would become what Brody envisioned if he, Greg, and Binsa helped her.

"But we still have to get my parents," Marcy pressed.

"One step at a time, little sister." He raised his tablet. "One step at a time."

Homeland Security Agent Jerome Wessel sat in his parked rental car in North Tampa. Less than a block away stood the apartment building where he understood Pug Johnson had been arrested. At least, that's what the police report said. Marcy Nevins' blue car was parked at the curb behind him, so he guessed he had the right place.

His window was down, and the fireflies were out. What a contrast to Iowa! Everything was green and humid, unlike Davenport with its rationed water program and dry, dusty air. But even his preference for Florida's climate couldn't erase the discomfort of living in the rental car the last two days. He felt foolish for even coming down here to Tampa. What was the point? PJ had been arrested. Marcy had apparently found safety and reliability in Sladrick's mysterious network, and Jerome should've been in Davenport tackling his next trafficking case.

After two days and nights of sitting on the apartment, he hadn't seen any sign of Marcy. At that midnight hour, the only thing moving besides a couple transients, was a heavyset skateboarder on the street. He was a big kid, with his sideways baseball cap and baggy clothes, who'd zoomed up and down the perpendicular avenue for the past hour. The highschooler seemed too overweight to practice any skating tricks, so he seemed to be practicing his turns at the end of each straightaway.

Jerome rolled his eyes at his impatience and checked his mirror, which captured the front of the apartment building. No one had come or gone from the building since the skateboarder had exited an hour earlier. Maybe it was time to return to Iowa. Using his sick days to take a week off had been a waste of time. Instead of a much-needed restful vacation, he was bleary-eyed from a sleepless and fruitless surveillance exercise.

He dug his hand into a bag of cashews and glanced up in time to see the skateboarder zip past his driver's window. The crazy kid didn't even have elbow pads or a helmet. Jerome had never trusted his own coordination on such unruly wheels. There were no brakes. At least while skiing, there was snow to fall on, not the unforgiving asphalt.

Suddenly, his passenger door opened, the ceiling light blinked on, and the skateboarder swooped into the passenger seat with more grace than he'd been skating all hour. The youth reached for Jerome, whose right hand was filled with cashews. He dropped the nuts and grasped for his sidearm in the shoulder holster. As soon as the passenger door closed, the ceiling light turned off. Cashews clattered and settled in the cracks of the center console. Jerome's fingers brushed the grip of his gun, but a firm hand gripped his elbow, prohibiting his arm from proceeding.

"Relax, Agent," the youth stated calmly—his voice more mature than expected. "I'm not your enemy."

Remaining still, Jerome tried to make out the features of the man beside him and the danger he presented. Apparently, his voice wasn't the only mature thing about him. The stranger took off his cap and ruffled his hair, revealing in the streetlights the chiseled face of a man in his fifties.

"If you're not my enemy, then . . .?"

"Brody Sladrick." He let go of Jerome's elbow and

pointed up the street. "Our enemy is up there, the white sedan with three men in it."

"What?" Jerome frowned and slowly lowered his hand to his lap. "I didn't see anyone pull in."

"Well, they're there. Probably been here longer than you. Or they pulled in when you were catching a few winks."

"Yeah, I guess so." Jerome's heart rate slowed, and he rubbed his face with his hands. "Sladrick, huh? So, you're real."

"Last time I checked."

"I knew there was something weird about that kid on the skateboard."

"An associate said there were two teams surveilling the apartment." Brody took off his baggy outer shirt, revealing a firm upper body and muscled shoulders. "Figured I'd better counter-surveil before heading upstairs. You checked out. They didn't."

"Is it GLOW? I've heard they don't like you any more than they like me." Jerome squinted at the white car forty yards away, in front of two other vehicles at the curb. "I don't see any movement."

"They're there. And yes, GLOW was my first guess, too. PJ probably called them from jail. Their car has stolen plates, and the photos I took while cruising past them identified at least one of them as a Russian ex-con."

"And you figured all that out on a skateboard?" Jerome scoffed. "Maybe I need to rethink my undercover skills."

"We're only as sharp as our resources are available." Brody gestured at the apartment. "My guy Greg is upstairs. Between my phone and his directional cameras, we patched together the suspects' faces."

Jerome sat quietly next to the man he'd thought of as a ghost for years. Except for their abrupt meeting a moment earlier, Jerome felt at ease with the veteran. Though Jerome was a decade younger, they spoke the same trade language, had the same goals, and cared for the same people.

"I'm assuming Marcy is safe in there, too?"

"She's safe, but not in there. She's at the hospital with her brother. We just returned from Thailand."

"You already got her brother?" Jerome whistled. "Of course, you did. How'd you find him?"

"Caught a break in Bangkok after PJ admitted to something. That and the overwhelming grace of a mighty God."

"God?" Jerome snorted. "What God?"

"The God who's always been, Agent Wessel. Just because society has become materialistic and humanistic doesn't mean He's been any less present and available for His creation. Don't tell me you've been living your life in ignorance of your Creator."

"I—" Jerome eyed the man carefully. "No one's put it quite that way before. But the world's too crazy for me to check in with religion. Too much for me to do."

"Yeah, I hear you about being busy." Brody ran his fingers through his hair. "I'm pretty sure I slept a few days ago, but I'm too sleep-deprived to remember. And I need to be in South Carolina for another take-down."

"What's in South Carolina?"

"A Saudi national is pushing in on domestic trafficking in the U.S. Who would've thought the Arabians would be one of the leaders of trafficking in America?"

"They're organized and well-financed." Jerome found a few cashews on his seat and popped them into his mouth. "Everyone blames the Russians, Asians, or the cartels south of the border, but I've known the Saudis were involved in some way here in the States. They import a lot of kidnapped women into their own country, so why not others if there's money in it? How did you track them down?"

"We use a system matrix," Brody explained. "Every trafficking organization uses a business model and other industries. When we notice organizations using social media, hotels, transportation, and a heightened number of work visas, we look a little closer. The larger the trafficking network, the more resources across society they require."

"Never thought of it that way. So, they think that intertwining themselves within society's framework creates subterfuge, but that's exactly what you're using to identify them?"

"It's not that complicated to confront evil, Agent Wessel. It just takes guts—the guts to handle what's ugly."

"Ugly I know too well."

"You ready to look into its face again?" Brody drew his phone and held it up. The screen showed a remote-control device. "We've got three boys up there who need their lives interrupted."

"If they're professionals working for GLOW, they won't talk."

"We can't avoid confronting evil simply because it may not reveal what we're looking for."

"Touché. What's your plan?"

"Greg put together a little gift package upstairs. Watch, and get ready to move."

Brody shared his phone view with Jerome as a drone with a camera launched from the nearby apartment. The screen showed the lawn in front of the apartment, then the line of cars at the curb.

"There we are," Brody said. "And there's the white roof of their car. I have an arsenal of two."

"Two what?"

"Water balloons." Brody switched to a targeting screen while the drone hovered. "Filled with red paint—an undiluted, quick-dry mixture."

"Is the paint toxic?" Jerome asked excitedly. "You're going to poison them?"

"Toxic? No. Why would we want to poison them?"

"Well, what good is it otherwise?"

"If I splash it just right on the front and back of their car, it'll run down their windows."

"So, it's like a message?" Jerome smiled. "Blood? They'll think it's blood. It'll cause them to panic."

"No, nothing like that. The color doesn't matter. Red's just what Greg picked up at the hardware store."

"Oh, then what's the point of splashing them with paint?"

"If their windows are covered with something, they can't see out of them to drive away or shoot us. What do you think I am, some crafty genius with James Bond tricks? Water balloons and paint are as sophisticated as we get around here."

"My mistake." Jerome swept his arm from right to left to give way to the simple approach. "Paint-bombs away."

Brody pressed "release" on the screen. Then, he adjusted the drone to the rear of the car and dropped the second load. He punched a homing function for the drone, then put away his phone.

"I didn't hear anything." Jerome leaned forward and put his ear to the open driver's window. "You sure it worked?"

"You're asking a guy dressed like a highschooler who rides a skateboard?" Brody climbed out of the car. "Let's go see."

Jerome drew his sidearm and joined Brody on the sidewalk. Brody wasted no time approaching the rear of the target car. The front and back windows were indeed splattered with dark red paint. The paint had adhered so rapidly that only a fraction had run down to drip on the asphalt. The rest had dried in a sheet of crimson, and the side windows were well-baptized as well.

Brody crouched at the rear bumper where Jerome joined him.

"Anatoly Rudenkov!" Brody called, then spoke in Russian.

"What'd you tell them?" Jerome whispered.

"We only know one of their names, but I told them all to open their doors and set their guns on the pavement outside, that they're under arrest."

"I have only one pair of handcuffs."

"One's enough."

"You said there's three of them."

"It's okay." Brody cupped his mouth. "Anatoly! *Davai, davai!*" Then to Jerome, "That means, let's go. We don't want them overthinking this process."

With that, Brody slapped the trunk of the car, which produced a string of Russian words from within the car.

"Uh, you don't want me to translate that," Brody said. "Get your handcuffs ready."

"We should call the local police."

"When we're done with them, we will."

The doors opened and three men exited the car with their arms raised. Jerome leapt upright and covered two of them on the driver's side as Brody patted down the third man on the other side of the car.

"Come over here on the grass and sit down," Brody ordered. "Move it! I know you know English, boys."

"Sladrick!" One of the thugs cursed in Russian, but he kept his hands on his head. "Of course, it is you."

Brody searched them for weapons as they sat side by side on the grass while Jerome covered him.

"Cuffs," Brody called.

"This ought to be good." Jerome tossed him the cuffs.

Shoving the men around, Brody arranged them so they sat in an awkward triangle back-to-back. He tucked the cuffs through the back of the belt of the middle man, then cuffed one wrist of each man on the sides of him.

"I think you just invented a new cuffing protocol," joked Jerome as the three gangsters scowled at their plight. "Looks like they left their guns on the floor of the car."

"Yeah, they're clean." Brody crouched in front of them. "GLOW must be getting short on intelligent soldiers if they sent you three to kill me. We just ambushed you with a couple water balloons filled with paint."

Jerome holstered his gun, realizing Brody didn't even appear to be armed. The Russian men were in their thirties. In the streetlights, their prison tattoos showed clearly on their arms and necks. They wore jeans and t-shirts, except for one who wore a tank top. All had military haircuts.

"You can't arrest us for sitting in a car," Anatoly said, his accent strong. He had narrow shoulders with deep-set eyes. "We've done nothing wrong."

"Maybe not tonight," Brody said, "but Anatoly, you've got a warrant for battery up in New York. And you other two—my Interpol friends will be glad to put you two away after we track down what bad business you've been up to."

"Sladrick, you're a dead man," Anatoly threatened.

"Well, we're all dying." Brody moved from a crouch to sit cross-legged before the men. "And since we're all dying, it's reasonable that we consider the afterlife we'll face when we get there. God probably isn't too pleased with you three right now. Is it reasonable to assume that you mock death with each other, but when you're alone, you do your best not to think of it? Death is final, boys. After death comes the judgment. There's good reason to fear death if you haven't trusted in Jesus Christ to save you from an eternity of hell. Jesus is your only hope, my friends."

The Russians put their heads down. Jerome wondered if they were as perplexed as he was by Brody's strange interrogation tactics.

Brody sighed loudly, as if he pitied them, then stood and searched their car again. He emerged with three phones. One at a time, he plugged the phones into a keychain thumb drive.

"Get all that, Codefighter?" Brody asked no one—until Jerome realized the operative must've been linked up with an earpiece to another operator in the apartment.

"Roger that, Rot. See you in a bit."

"What'd you find?" Jerome nodded at the phones. "Anything useful?"

"Oh, they're all locked up, but Greg has pass-keys for these things. It'll take time, but he'll get them open. That'll help in the prosecution." Brody tossed the phones into the car. "Greg called the authorities. They're on their way."

"That's it? You're not going to question them?"

"It's like you said in the car: as professionals, they won't talk. I've said to them what they most need to hear, even if they don't want to say anything to me. Their phones will give us more than they will."

"We should make them talk."

"That's outside my level of interest, especially since if they talk, their own people will kill them. That's their code."

"So, we give them a pass?"

"They're being arrested. Nobody's getting a pass. It's their right to keep their mouths shut. Besides, we already know why they're here. PJ probably told them to kill me and Marcy or take Marcy back after killing me. Their playbook is like Satan's—not too complicated, even if they're skilled at what they do."

"*Satan?* And you're preaching to them about trusting in Jesus?" Jerome rubbed his brow. "I didn't expect this from you, not from what I know of your reputation."

"Oh, yeah? What's my reputation?"

"Just—" Jerome frowned. "To be honest, I don't even know. I just expected something different."

"So, you thought I'd be taller?"

"You . . . have a strange sense of humor doing this kind of work."

"Blame Marcy. She's got me interacting with people again for the first time since my wife died. You could say I've been shut off for a while. Maybe my sense of humor is still trying to find its groove."

"Maybe my biggest expectation was for you to work

adjacent to law enforcement not just invent new ways to use one handcuff to cuff three men.”

“Well, stick around, Agent Wessel,” Brody said. “You might just find that I appeal to a much higher standard than you realize. That’s why I talk to men like these three about Jesus Christ. They need a heart change not just a dose of right acting.”

Anatoly and his comrades lowered their heads even more. Two squad cars arrived, then a detective took their statements and processed the Russians’ car. It was three in the morning before Brody picked up his skateboard and stood idly next to Jerome’s car.

“So, why’d you come down to Tampa, Agent Wessel?” Brody asked.

“I suppose we could blame Marcy for that, too.”

“She’s a special girl.” Brody rested the skateboard over his shoulder. “Now she wants us to go get her parents next.”

“Us?”

“Oh, I assumed you were joining me. On Marcy’s behalf. My mistake.”

“No.” Jerome sighed. “I’m with you. I’ve wanted to pick your brain about things for years. It’s probably the real reason I’m here. I don’t seem to be making much of a lasting difference in Davenport. But you do.”

“Wessel, I know your history. You catch a few traffickers every month.”

“You catch them every week.”

“It’s not a competition.”

“Tell that to GLOW.”

“GLOW isn’t my real enemy. Those three Russians— they’ll be back on the street in no time. That’s not due to GLOW’s ingenuity or even their network necessarily. It’s because not many in authority really care about the innocents enough to incarcerate these kinds of criminals for too long. But you’ve got to care about the crooks as well—which means addressing the actual moral depravity involved not just jail them.”

“I care about the innocents, sure.” Jerome shook his head at the sky. “But how can you ask anyone to care for the crooks? Do you really care?”

“Yeah. They’re in a terrible state of bondage, so I definitely pity them. All people are in a terrible state of bondage, but GLOW soldiers are especially trained to exploit people. What they don’t realize is that everything they do to others just sinks themselves into deeper shame and guilt. They’re rapists, thieves, and murderers. If I don’t care for them, who in the world will? I think they need our compassion more than anyone, but certainly not our approval for what they do.”

“That . . . may be the craziest crime-fighting philosophy I’ve ever heard of.”

“Well, I’m not a crime fighter, Wessel,” Brody said. “I recover what was lost, and that goes for people who’ve lost their way, not just those who’ve been kidnapped.”

“Your heart may be right, but the world doesn’t work that way.”

“I’m not talking about how the world works, but how God and His judgment works.”

“You’re not going to love these people to the point that they give up their lifestyles?”

“Oh, not alone, I won’t. God goes before us in these situations. When I speak to Anatoly and men like him about eternal judgement and the Savior of all people, I’m casting a net for hearts that’re already provoked about their sins.”

“Don’t ask me to care for men like that. I’ve seen too much to do anything but put them away. I don’t care about them or what happens to them after I put them away. They can rot in hell for all I care. I’ll be professional, but they deserve my hatred. Nothing else.”

“They deserve a lot worse than your hatred, Wessel, but showing them grace speaks to their souls—if they choose to listen. And speaking of grace," Brody continued, "you could probably use a shower and a shave, huh?"

"What's that have to do with grace?"

"Because by the smell of you, you deserve a fire hose, but I'm offering you a civilized shower nozzle instead."

Jerome laughed like he hadn't laughed in years. Coming to Tampa hadn't been a mistake, even if he couldn't fathom Sladrick's philosophy regarding human trafficking.

Marcy sat upright, fully clothed in the dark, trying to remember where she was. Sometimes, she woke with a sense that she was in the locked bedroom where Tory and Trey had kept her. She never cried out during these moments, since she knew her wits would return in a few seconds. Sure enough, her terror passed.

"Thank You, Jesus."

She stood from the cot the clinic nurses had brought in for her. Aidan was still asleep. The battery of tests the day before had wearied the little guy out—something called a sigmoidoscopy and other things she couldn't pronounce. Of course, Aidan wasn't little anymore. He was a young man, but in Marcy's mind, he was still a child.

Binsa had introduced Marcy to the medical staff two days earlier. The small specialty clinic in Tampa dealt exclusively with trauma patients who needed reconstructive surgery, no matter the anatomy. Though she was twenty-two now, Marcy felt especially grown up being trusted with all of Aidan's needs. With nothing more than a kind word and embrace, Binsa had left her in the clinic's care with Aidan.

Sitting back down on the cot, Marcy felt both loneliness and wonder at her new life. Aidan's physical abuse for so many years had left him impaired in other ways—so much so that Marcy didn't feel like he would understand what she was doing for him. The minor surgery the day before was meant to correct his incontinence issue, and Brody had said the boy would continue to mature as any other boy—but Marcy had her doubts. So many years of abuse and neglect!

But suddenly, like the hand of God on her doubts, she perceived the Holy Spirit reminding her of all that she'd been through herself. She didn't want others to think of her as damaged goods, so if she treated Aidan as she wanted to be treated, maybe she could join Brody in his optimism—his faith in how God healed the mind beyond what the body had been through.

"I'm trusting You, Lord," she mouthed in the dim lighting of the room. With spiritual comfort and fresh resolve, she lay back down to rest. God had never forgotten her. He was still with her now. And He was with Aidan.

In the morning, Marcy was startled awake by a nurse who came into the private room to check Aidan's vitals and take his blood. Aidan remained asleep, and Marcy lay there until the nurse left. When her phone vibrated, she expected an update from Greg or Brody. But she was surprised to receive a message from her old Davenport acquaintance, Agent Jerome Wessel. The agent was in Tampa working with Brody! His text conveyed his happiness that Aidan had been found, and that after a short operation in the Carolinas, he and Brody were going on the search for her parents, aided of course by Greg's invaluable intel.

Marcy covered her mouth as she cried. And she'd thought she was alone? No, she was surrounded by a wonderful team of believers. And if Jerome was at Brody's side, it was just a matter of time before even he was taken to the cross of Christ for forgiveness of sins.

"What's the matter?" Aidan asked, his speech slurred. He hadn't stirred, but his eyes were wide open.

"Nothing's the matter." Marcy laughed and wiped away her tears. "I'm just happy we're back together. Did you miss me?"

"You're my sister."

"Yeah, I am. You remember me?"

"I forgot your name. But you told me on the plane."

"It's okay. I forget things sometimes, too. My name is Marcy."

"Oh, yeah. Marcy. I knew it was something like that."

"Are you hungry? The doctor said you can begin to eat real lightly today."

"What . . . should I eat?"

Marcy held back a sob. He didn't know what to eat. He couldn't even talk normally. This was going to be a long journey.

"The doctor said yogurt would be good for you. Do you remember yogurt?"

"No. Is it good?"

"Yes, it's delicious. They have so many flavors these days. Peach, kiwi, strawberry, blueberry. And toast with a little peanut butter spread on top. The doctor said that would be good for you."

"I know toast." He rolled his head away from her. "I was gone a long time."

"Nine years. But I thought about you all the time. I prayed for you ten times a day, once I learned to pray to God. He brought us back together."

"What about Preeda and Arthit?" He wouldn't meet her eyes. "And Mom and Dad?"

With trembling chin, Marcy realized that he'd spoken of his abusers in the same way as his parents.

"The man who helped us is named Brody. Brody said Preeda and Arthit are in jail. They didn't treat you very well, but you survived. Brody says you're an overcomer. You're now a man."

"I . . . don't really want to be alive."

Marcy took his hand, and only when he tried to pull it away did she remember this was the arm that still worked normally. The other side of his body was partially paralyzed, the neurological remnant of a head injury, the doctor had said.

"You might feel that way right now, but now we're together. I'm your older sister, and it's my job to look after you. No one's going to split us up again. I won't let that happen. Look at me, Addy. We're going to start over now."

"But, I'm all . . . messed up."

"The doctor says that with some hard work, you'll be able to live a normal life. You had a surgery so you won't have as many accidents. It doesn't matter, anyway. I'm here to help you, and our friend Brody said he'll take you on some adventures someday soon, like going sailing. He's a real-life hero, and he doesn't care if you have some little physical problems. Addy, he's one of the best people you'll ever meet, and he's super strong, too."

"He's your friend?"

"Yeah. Your friend, too. He's the one who found you in Thailand. Oh, and Binsa. She's amazing times ten! And beautiful. She loves everyone. You'll see."

"The brown lady."

"Yeah. She brought us here. You remember. And there's Greg, this really nice guy about my age. He wants to meet you, too. Oh, and Agent Wessel. Nobody has more muscles than he does. His first name is Jerome. He's here in Tampa to help look for Mom and Dad."

"Mom and Dad?" Aidan's face twitched.

"We have to find them, Addy. Things got so messed up when we were kids. Mom and Dad were on drugs. They weren't very good parents. I mean, they were the worst parents. But it was a long time ago. I think they feel bad about how they treated us. If they knew we forgive them and we're back together, maybe we can be a family again."

"I don't want to be a family again."

"It won't be like it was before, not ever again. Mom and Dad are old people by now. Like forty-five years old or something. We need to help them, because they're probably really messed up still."

"You got really smart, Marcy." He sighed. "I remember you liked school."

"Yeah, I've read a lot of books. And I got my GED last year. I had to study for the math test, but I passed it. You should take some classes, too."

"I'm not going to school!" Terror swept his face. "Not the way I am."

"Well, I can teach you what to learn. There are classes on the internet you can take. There are video games that can make learning fun."

"No, I don't like those games anymore. Preeda and Arthit made me play them all the time, the same three."

"Okay, so, no video games. We'll figure it out along the way."

"Without Mom and Dad." He pulled on her arm. "Just me and you."

She hid her frown and held him tightly.

CHAPTER SIX

Agent Jerome Wessel sat in the driver's seat of his rental car, parked in the West Ashley district of Charleston, South Carolina. Brody Sladrick sat in the passenger seat, leaning forward slightly as they watched the front and alley access doors of an import business. The two men shared a bag of cashews between their seats. Jerome was happy that his usual snack was appreciated by his new companion.

"That's twelve immigrants in the last hour," Brody said, speaking for the first time in twenty minutes. "They have no idea what's going to happen to them in there."

Jerome eyed a tablet screen mounted on the car dash. It displayed a surveillance view of the business's main office, including audio. Brody had infiltrated the building and installed the camera himself two days earlier while Jerome had kept an eye on a security guard who was checking on a back lot. From the camera inside and watching the outside, they knew exactly who and what to expect inside.

"I think we're ready." Jerome picked up his phone. "Make the call?"

"Do it. But we won't wait for these boys to toss the evidence the instant the police show up."

Calling his Homeland Security liaison in Charleston, Jerome gave the green light for a raid to commence on the business. The SWAT team was still twenty minutes out, though warrants had already been secured.

"Plenty of time for us." Brody climbed out of the car and stretched. "We're here for the visas, but I have a spiritual agenda as well. Follow my lead and stick to the plan."

"All right."

Jerome had learned that Brody's faith drove his every move, especially when in the field. Even in the hotel room the night before, he'd asked Jerome to leave the television off so they could prepare their hearts for the following day—without the distractions of the world in their ears. Beside his bed, Brody had knelt, his back to Jerome. He'd known the man was praying, but he hadn't been prepared for how long Brody would remain there. When Jerome had washed up and gone to bed, Brody was still on his knees.

Instead of weariness, Brody exhibited an air of calm ease and confidence in his every action. It was an impossible force for Jerome to argue against, even if he didn't like it, since Brody seemed to have such clarity about the details of the operation. Was it possible that Brody actually received counsel from God as he claimed? It seemed like cheating, Jerome laughed to himself, but he couldn't explain it otherwise.

The two men reached the intersection and crossed the street. Charleston Harbor was just a few blocks away where the Port of Charleston was frequented by ships too big to transit the Panama Canal. And not far away, Union Pier Terminal hosted the cruise ship departures to and from the Caribbean. The import business was thriving in Charleston, regardless of pandemic fears. Unfortunately, the massive hub aided in human trafficking.

Reaching the front door first, Jerome opened it for Brody. They entered the business waiting room. A pretty assistant sat behind a counter and offered a Southern welcome to the strangers. But Brody didn't return the salutation. He planted one hand on the counter and vaulted over it. In the same instant, Jerome drew his sidearm and held it on two men sitting in the waiting room who looked up from playing on their phones. Someone with an unknowing eye might've thought they were customers waiting on an appointment, but Jerome knew better.

"Keep your hands in sight," Jerome ordered the two men, approaching them briskly. "This is for your own protection."

He used his free hand to jab a tranq-pen into the first man's thigh, clicked the pen for a second water-soluble needle, then jabbed the next man, who was too stunned to move. In just two heartbeats, the men slumped unconsciously in their seats. Jerome looked toward Brody to see how he was doing. Brody had tranqed the assistant—sufficiently surprising her before she could press the warning button under the counter.

As rehearsed, Jerome holstered his sidearm and collected firearms and cell phones from those unconscious, stowing them in a small pouch strapped to his front. Brody moved to the door that led to the rear of the building, now that the false-front had been neutralized.

"This pen works faster than I thought!" Jerome smiled, realizing his heart was pounding like he was in a firefight back in Afghanistan. "I'm ready."

Nodding once, Brody displayed pure confidence on his face. He didn't even seem to be breathing hard. Jerome had been piecing together the man's past from bits he'd shared, so he knew this small Charleston business raid was small potatoes for the expert. But Jerome was Homeland Security, an investigator who normally called in Federal or local law enforcement to handle risky raids like this, so it was a thrill to be leading the charge himself!

When Brody opened the door, Jerome followed him into a hallway lined with several open office doors on the left and right. The far end of the hallway opened to a larger warehouse space, which he and Brody had only scarcely investigated two nights earlier. They suspected the crates hid illegal or smuggled items within them, but that was for the Port Authority to track down later. He and Brody were there for people.

Brody barged into the first office on the right, then swiftly slipped into a chair that faced the wide desk. Jerome disciplined his eyes from looking at the ceiling to locate the camera they'd hidden there. A thick-necked, balding man in a blazer sat behind the desk. Maybe he'd been a weightlifter in the past, but he'd let himself go as he'd climbed the ladder of his organization. This was Scott Grint, front man for the import establishment.

Jerome took up a position at the doorway where he could see inside the office yet keep an eye on the hallway. Four other employees were somewhere in the building, and at least twenty immigrant workers.

Sitting to Brody's left in the office was Jerome's main interest—a Saudi Arabian national with dual American/Saudi citizenship. Zayed Aziz was the sponsor of hundreds of Middle Eastern employees on the eastern seaboard. The man was dark-skinned, and his eyes revealed a cool demeanor. His federal file showed he had a permit to carry a concealed firearm, so this man was highly dangerous. Jerome couldn't wait to see how Brody would confront him. The Saudi wore Western clothing now, but Jerome's investigations the day before had revealed that the human trafficker had diplomatic ties to the royal family in Riyadh. From photos on the internet, Jerome discovered that a younger Zayed had worn the traditional robes alongside known leaders on the peninsula.

"You don't know me," Brody said to Scott Grint, ignoring the Saudi for the moment. Brody held his right hand across his front in such a way that he could reach Zayed if the man made a move for his concealed weapon. "I'm a concerned private citizen. A very concerned private citizen—the name's Sladrick."

Checking Grint and Zayed's faces, Jerome saw no recognition, as expected. The Saudi trafficking ring was separate from the GLOW network. Nevertheless, Grint's eyes revealed his caution as they darted to Zayed, then back to Brody.

"How can we help you, Mr. Sladrick?" Grint folded his hands on top of his desk. "Concerned citizens are important to us. We're a family business that looks after the community here."

"I'm glad to hear you say that." Brody turned his head and stared at Zayed long enough to draw a frown from the Saudi businessman. "Does Saudi Arabia share the same concerns for families in our community?"

Zayed shifted in his seat, but his right hand rested on his knee. Jerome wanted to draw his own sidearm and hold it at his side, just to keep everyone in order, but Brody had made it clear he wanted no one hurt during their inquiries. The police were coming, and they could make arrests when they arrived.

"Who exactly are you, Mr. Sladrick?" Grint asked. "And how have you come to know our Middle Eastern friends?"

"I know you keep a purse with you at all times, Mr. Grint." Brody's voice was so soft, the men had to focus to hear. "Right now, it's in the second drawer on your right side. Open the drawer, pull out the purse, and set it on the desk. And don't open the first drawer where you keep a semi-automatic nine-millimeter."

Grint's eyes widened. Jerome wondered what the crook thought of Brody's intel-gathering ability.

"You don't want that purse." Grint's jaw muscles rippled and his thick neck seemed to bulge thicker. "It comes with more trouble than you can imagine."

"Who sent you?" Zayed spoke for the first time, his voice scratchy, as if his throat were constricted. "You're robbing us? Do you know what's in the purse?"

"Of course, I know." Brody pointed a finger at Zayed's arm. "The same way I know if you reach for that gun under your arm, I'll put you against the wall before you can—"

"They're *our* visas," Grint interrupted. "Go get your own workers. This is our operation, our livelihood. We brought them over. We put them to work. Their visas are useless to you unless you have a system of your own. Who sent you?"

"They're not your visas, and they're not your workers." With Brody's left hand, he tapped the tranq-pen on his knee, but Jerome knew the two traffickers couldn't guess what the pen actually contained. "You brought them from overseas by misrepresenting their jobs and residences. Take the purse out and set it on the desk. Now."

Jerome flinched at movement up the hallway. A man walked two immigrant women with coats and backpacks from the warehouse to one of the offices. Their eyes reached Jerome, but even the man, clearly a Grint employee, didn't react. So as not to escalate the situation, Jerome tried to appear casual as if standing in the boss's doorway. He and Brody were certainly outnumbered in the building. Grint and the men in the waiting room had been armed, so the others up the hallway probably were, too.

"You're law enforcement?" Grint asked.

"I told you, " Brody said, "I'm a private citizen."

"Then, I'm not giving you the purse." Grint sat back, crossed his arms, and smirked at Zayed, as if he were showing off for his business partner. "And you can't do anything about it without us hunting you down, Mr. Sladrick. You've shown us your face and given us your name. That's going to be your undoing."

"Oh, you're mistaken," Brody said patiently. "I offered my name to forego this nonsense, since my name is well-known in some circles. At least, you should be aware enough to know that someone like me who gives you his name isn't concerned about what you might do with it."

"We've never heard of you," Grint said. "I think you're

lying. Maybe you're a concerned citizen. Maybe you're our competition. I think you're a dead man—you and your whole family."

"That threat may work against some, but my life isn't in your hands. I'm a follower of Jesus Christ and a servant of the needy. That includes you. If you'd like a more thorough biography of me, I'll happily supply it, including my longing heart to see both of you turn from your dark ways and stop hurting God's precious people."

"Your longing heart?" Grint guffawed. "God's precious people? Are you some kind of local do-gooder or what?"

"Enough stalling." Brody sighed resolutely, then addressed Zayed in Arabic. What he said was brief, only two sentences, and Jerome wished more than ever at that moment that he knew Arabic.

Zayed shifted in his seat, obviously unsettled to hear his native language spoken by someone who Grint treated as a common citizen. The Saudi responded nervously in Arabic, with just a couple words, and Brody responded in what seemed like a one-word affirmation.

Jerome didn't miss the shocked look on Grint's face. Suddenly, Zayed drew out his sidearm with the fingertips of his left hand and set it on the floor. Without looking at Grint, Zayed stood and left the office. He passed Jerome and exited quietly through the front. Brody turned partially in his chair to look up at Jerome.

"He would've been trouble," Brody said. "He agreed to meet with us later."

Before he protested, Jerome clamped his mouth shut. It seemed naive of Brody to believe the Saudi wouldn't run for his life. Even though Jerome was a government agent, he didn't feel like he could contradict Brody. This was the Christian's show, and Jerome felt chained to his agenda.

"So, what offer do you have for me?" Grint asked, looking from Brody to Jerome.

"You have no bargaining power," Brody said, "because you have nothing to offer us but lives that aren't your own. Hand over the purse. No more discussion."

"What? You let Zayed walk, but you're holding me?"

"Zayed wasn't the one keeping the purse from us." Brody stood upright. "An associate of mine will send you a Bible while you're in prison, Mr. Grint. I advise you to read it and trust in your Savior from eternal judgment."

"But you said—!"

Grint shrieked as Brody swung his arm over the top of the desk. The tranq-pen stabbed into the trafficker's deltoid muscle. Grint's face displayed shock—perhaps that he'd been attacked, or because a man Brody's age had moved so quickly.

As Grint was still sighing into unconsciousness, Brody took the purse from the second drawer and unzipped it. Jerome remained at the door to cover the hallway, but he could partially see into the purse.

"There must be forty or fifty work visas there!" Jerome gasped. "It takes the whole Department of Homeland Security a year to make a bust this big!"

"I don't care about the bust." Brody zipped up the purse and slid the strap over his head and across his chest. "Let's clear this building, then we need to meet Zayed."

Brody hopped onto the desk and unscrewed the fire alarm. He plucked out their camera the size of a pair of dice and pocketed the device.

"But you just let Zayed go."

"It's temporary. If you want, you can still arrest him."

"You can't really believe he'll meet us." Jerome checked the frustration in his voice. "You should've tranqed him while he sat next to you."

"I could've tried, but Zayed is a fighter. If he would've struggled, the others in the building would've been alerted and innocent lives would've been put at risk. You're concerned about the bust, Jerome. But I'm concerned about the lives of the trafficked as well as the traffickers."

Jerome didn't approve of Brody's methods, but Brody

wasn't asking for his permission or opinion. This was just like he'd dealt with the Russians in Tampa! Instead, Jerome followed Brody as the operative moved quietly down the hall. In each office, one of Grint's men was processing migrants and confiscating their visas to control their livelihood and defraud them of their income. Brody greeted the office workers like he belonged in the building, then rapidly tranquilized each of Grint's men. He moved so quickly that Jerome wasn't given the opportunity to participate, and none of Grint's men were given the opportunity to resist.

With the enemy neutralized, Brody gathered the two dozen migrant workers—all recent immigrants to the States—into the back of the warehouse space and instructed them to sit down. They consisted mostly of Middle Eastern men and women, as well as one or two from Lebanon, Mexico, India, the Philippines, and Colombia. Jerome stood off to the side as Brody spoke in various languages to communicate instructions and returned their visas. When he was finished, the purse was still full of visas belonging to workers already employed in the field.

"Go out front," Brody said to Jerome, "and tell SWAT the building is secure, but Grint and his boys will need to be arrested."

"And Zayed?" Jerome pressed. "He just gets away?"

"God is watching, so no one gets away. Besides, I told you that you can still arrest Zayed. You'll see."

Brody turned away to speak with a woman from India. Whatever language it was, Brody didn't seem to know it well, but well enough to communicate something about Jesus to her since Jerome heard His name mentioned before he left the warehouse.

Though Jerome followed Brody's orders, once he reached the fresh air outside the front door, he grumbled under his breath. How could Brody make all these critical raids and not think long-term by focusing on getting all the perpetrators he could off the streets and behind bars? How could someone so effective at what he did have such different priorities than his own? Brody's tactics made no legal sense to Jerome, and allowing Zayed to slip away without a fight was a violation of Jerome's ethics.

The authorities arrived in stellar fashion—twelve vehicles and two ambulances. Two federal agents received Jerome's intel, then a team entered the establishment to make arrests. Barely had Jerome completed an explanation to a superior than Binsa arrived in a Suburban with one other woman. Jerome had met Binsa at Brody's Tampa apartments, so he stood aside as the Nepalese woman offered her credentials as a victim's advocate. She had of course been waiting around the street corner, Jerome guessed, for Brody's call. The man had orchestrated everything for his own motives. Sure, those being trafficked were getting much-needed care, but the criminals needed to be—

"Everything in order?" Brody stepped up next to him.

Together, they watched Binsa and her friend guide recovered immigrants over to her vehicle. Medical personnel joined Binsa as she prioritized federal resources like she was a trauma team nurse.

"Yeah, you scripted this out beautifully." Jerome pouted. "Everyone gets mercy in your book, but no one gets justice. Is that it?"

"Showing mercy never precludes justice, Jerome," Brody said. "The wrongs committed are always paid for— by someone."

"By someone? What does that even mean? Zayed is a wanted man and now he's in the wind. You let him go. How's he paying for his crimes?"

"Sin always comes to light, Jerome. A perceived escape may actually be a route to confrontation."

"Now you're speaking in riddles. Is that what you do instead of admitting you're wrong?"

"You said I have everything scripted out." Brody

gestured in the direction of Jerome's car. "Are you ready to meet with Zayed to find out if that's true?"

"Zayed isn't going to meet us just to be arrested."

Brody stared blankly at Jerome for a moment, then walked past him to the car. Jerome surveyed the scene and saw no further reason to remain there. He'd file a full report with his office soon enough, but he didn't know how to explain to anyone how a civilian like Brody was calling the shots in such a situation. It could get him disciplinary action as an agent!

He climbed behind the steering wheel and started the engine.

"Where are we supposed to meet him?"

"Under the Ravenel Bridge in Mount Pleasant."

They weren't far away, but it took thirty minutes to drive through downtown Charleston to reach the cable-stayed bridge over the Cooper River. On the east side, Jerome pulled the car onto a side street and eventually reached the growing shadows and sandy bank under the eight-lane bridge.

"I don't believe it." Jerome stopped the car thirty yards from the water to face Zayed Aziz, who was standing in front of a black Mercedes—no doubt the product of extorted foreign laborers. "He actually came. The guy must be crazy. I'm going to arrest him."

"Let's hear him out first." Brody climbed out.

"In English this time?" Jerome requested.

Jerome first noticed Zayed's hardened gaze as they drew close. Then Brody went up and actually shook the man's hand! But Jerome didn't get that close. He hooked his right thumb on the pocket of his trousers, ready to draw his sidearm if needed. Zayed's own hands were in his pockets, rather than shifting toward his own weapon—which he no longer had, he hoped, since Brody had disarmed him earlier.

"Thanks for meeting us out here," Brody said to the

Saudi national. "Things went badly for Grint after you left."

"Yes, I watched from a distance." Zayed's English was perfect, a Middle Eastern accent barely discernable. He looked out over the water. "I lost a lot of wealth today. But maybe . . . I gained some perspective. You're different, Sladrick."

"Oh, I'm just another man like you who needs the help of God Almighty to navigate the traps of sin and the flesh."

"Your God . . . is different than my god," Zayed stated.

"I think," Brody said carefully, "your god allowed you to do the things you did, even to your own countrymen. You certainly see the problem with that, and I think you may be ready to accept the mercy and love of the God of the Bible."

"The Christian God?" Zayed sighed. "My family, those who still speak to me, would disown me. I know about *Isa*, or Jesus in your language. But following Him would cost me everything."

"*Not* following Him will cost you your soul for eternity. Perhaps you should consider again the value of what is lost against the greater value of what is gained. I'll help you. You'll gain me as your friend to begin with, and a clear conscience by accepting God's forgiveness of sins because of Jesus Christ's sacrifice on the cross. That's more than Allah's anger could ever give you."

"You know . . ." Zayed paused and looked away. "This is the third time this week someone has spoken to me about Jesus. Before that, I don't remember hearing His name spoken meaningfully for twenty or thirty years."

"Like I said, I think you're ready." Brody crossed his arms. "I think God's been preparing your heart, hasn't He? He's tugging on your soul right now. I hope you're listening."

"How could you ever be my friend? Our entire lives have been lived in opposition to one another."

"I read you in that office, and you had enough curiosity to accept my invitation here. Let me help you, Zayed. Let God help you. A new life is before you."

"Brody, this is ridiculous," Jerome said, taking a step closer. "You don't have the authority to offer him amnesty for his crimes."

"He's partially right." Brody nodded. "Any pardon you receive can't be given to you by man, Zayed. You need to get on your knees before the holy and loving God who wants you to trust Him with your life."

"That's *not* what I meant!" Jerome rolled his eyes. "Zayed, you're under arrest."

"I have done a lot of wrongs," Zayed admitted to Brody, ignoring Jerome. "There are sins that can't be removed. Lives . . ."

"You can either cling to the sin that leads to death, or cling to the promise of the Savior who defeated death by His resurrection. Sure, you've heard the story, but I assure you that it's factual history. He's alive today. I know it because He's alive inside me. That's why I believe my offer to you today will reveal a whole new life to you, even if you must face the authorities for what you've done."

"What about him?" Zayed nodded at Jerome.

"He's important to me." Brody turned and acknowledged Jerome. "But it might help him if he understood why I let you leave the office to meet you out here."

Jerome felt his face burn with anger. He was a skilled federal agent, and they spoke about him as if he were a child? He would put a stop to this nonsense once and—

Zayed withdrew his left hand from his jacket pocket and tossed a pear-shaped object in a high arc to Jerome. He caught the shrapnel grenade in one hand and stared at it for a few seconds before realizing what it actually was. The pin hadn't been pulled, but the deadly item was no doubt live if Zayed was carrying it around for his own protection.

Looking up, he saw Brody and Zayed waiting for his response. But Jerome had no response. Only now was he putting together more of the story—which he'd overlooked in his own haste for justice. *Zayed had had a grenade in the office!* Brody must've glimpsed it or suspected it, choosing to spare all their lives by letting Zayed go free. Such was Brody's care in the moment that Zayed hadn't run away. He'd remained to speak to the man who had offered courteous mercy instead of blind wrath.

"It seems we three are coming to some understanding here," Brody said for them all. "Zayed, I'm not going to ask you to do something you don't want to do. But I'm telling you of Jesus' invitation to you to become a new creature by the gift of the Holy Spirit. You'll have much good to offer people, but only if you become a vessel for God's love and peace."

"And my crimes?"

"Jesus paid for your sins, but your crimes on earth among men will require you to face the judgment of men. I'll request that you face those consequences by helping us stand for the light and against the darkness in this life from now on. The authorities I know have the power to use you as an asset instead of throwing you away in a prison cell. But you must repent from your unbelief."

Zayed took a deep breath.

"Well, I already gave you my gun. And he has my grenade, which I would've used earlier rather than be taken alive."

"I believe you."

"I'm skeptical."

"I'm not." Brody chuckled. "I've served my God for a long time, and I know what He can do with a submitted man."

"Maybe . . . I'm interested," Zayed said. "What happens next?"

"Dinner. I'm hungry! You, Jerome?"

"I could eat." Jerome shrugged and tucked the

grenade into his pocket. "I'm just as curious as Zayed as to what you have planned next—and who you think you know who'll give him a license to work with you."

Jerome waited for Brody to respond. This was the first time he'd heard actual evidence of someone in authority, presumably within the government, who could pardon a human trafficker. Someone was backing Brody, and Jerome needed to know who. His superiors needed to know, too. How could this be legal?

"This is about discerning God's will," Brody finally said. "We'll get there only through faith and humility, but I think we're on the right path. There's a Cajun restaurant I saw up by the highway. Let's make an evening of discussing the details."

As Brody and Zayed each went to their separate cars, Jerome shook his head. He didn't understand what could change Zayed so thoroughly, simply from Brody's offer of forgiveness for his crimes, but it was a perceptible change. Brody still wore the purse of captured visas across his chest, but he hadn't processed them. Apparently, Zayed's soul was more important.

It was difficult for Jerome now to think of his life without having met Brody Sladrick—or the love that Brody was offering to all people. He couldn't go back to Davenport—not yet. Nor could he write his report yet. Jerome felt like he was only now waking to something weighty—more than the weight of the grenade in his pocket. His life had been spared. Was there really something to Brody's words?

Aidan Nevins rode in the elevator next to the man Marcy said was named Brody. It was fuzzy in his memory, but Aidan vaguely recalled Brody being with his sister in Thailand, then on the trip home, they'd flown in the same jet.

"I've never thrown a baseball before," Aidan said. "In

school, I played dodgeball, but I was never very good at it."

"Every young man should know how to catch and throw a baseball." Brody twisted and folded a baseball mitt. "I grew up in Africa. My dad taught me to play catch. Then I'd play with the boys on the goat farms around the area. You'll have this mitt broke in in no time."

"But my—" Aidan glanced down at this left side. "I only have one arm."

"I'll teach you how to do it," Brody said. "I've seen one-armed men play baseball before. You just have to develop a technique. It's like anything in life."

Aidan doubted it was possible for a one-armed person to play catch, but this man seemed determined to include him in something. Marcy had told him it was important to try new things, especially now that he had an adult-sized body. Truly, Aidan was still adjusting to his height. He'd grown to be six feet tall while in Thailand. Binsa had just measured him upstairs, right before giving him a haircut in her kitchen, with Marcy watching. His shaggy blond hair was gone. And even though he was as tall as Brody, Aidan had a hard time thinking of himself as anything but a frightened boy in Preeda and Arthit's shadow.

Outside the apartment building, Brody led him onto the mowed lawn beside the sidewalk.

"Throwing and catching—" Brody said, "the two parts to tossing a baseball back and forth. The more accurately we throw, the more often we'll catch the ball and chase it less. Right now, you have a tough time picking things up off the floor, but you'll get better at that. The doctor said the meds you're on might improve your paralysis, too, right?"

"Yeah." Aidan looked toward the apartment building.

"You forget something?"

"No," he quickly answered, then turned toward Brody. "I'm ready. Show me how."

He didn't admit his worry that he'd need the bathroom—and that they were so far from the toilet. Marcy helped him clean up when he had an accident, but he wanted to be normal. The doctor said it would take a few weeks of trial and error until he learned to control himself, since the surgery.

"When you throw with your right hand," Brody explained, "you step into the throw with your left foot. You can't take a big step, but you can swing your left leg forward, right? Try it. Good. Now back, and step forward. That'll give your whole body some momentum to throw the ball. Now, here's the ball. Throw it to me a couple times. Let's see where you're at."

Aidan hefted the baseball in his hand. He never realized his hands had grown so large. Maybe he could even palm a basketball now!

He limply tossed the ball, getting the feel. Then Brody walked it back to him. After several throws, Brody walked the ball back and picked up Aidan's mitt.

"You're a natural, Aidan. You're already ready for the glove."

"I don't know . . ."

"It's okay. Your form when throwing will continue to improve, but now you need to develop a system to throw, then catch. Look here. Fit your glove on like this. Nice and snug?"

"Yep." Aidan opened and closed the glove.

"Now take it off by sticking it in the armpit of your other arm. Fit it in there. Now work your hand out. There."

The mitt dropped from Aidan's armpit, and Brody picked it up.

"I get it." Aidan tried again and again, getting faster and smoother each time. "What about the ball?"

"That's the trick, see?" Brody dropped the ball into Aidan's mitt. "Let's say you just caught the ball. Now, slide the mitt off, but you've got to get the ball into your hand to throw it back. Try it."

For ten minutes, Brody stood in front of him,

coaching him as he practiced positioning the mitt under his arm, then recovering the ball.

"There's only one thing left to do," Brody finally said, taking the ball with him and backing away from Aidan. "You ready? You look ready. Tell me when."

Aidan stood determinedly on the lawn and held up his glove. The ball was about to fly toward him. A hard object would race at his face, but he was armed now to stop it. He couldn't back down, even though he was afraid. He was becoming a man. Men didn't back down. Men were brave, Marcy said. Men like Brody and Greg.

"Okay." Aidan trembled. "Throw it."

Flinching away from the ball, Aidan didn't catch it, but he did stop it with his glove. Brody remained where he stood this time and didn't help Aidan recover the ball. Aidan understood Brody was teaching him now by not doing it for him. This was about independence, and Aidan felt excitement that he was doing something without help. *He was really doing it!*

Ten throws later, Aidan caught the ball for the first time. He nearly wept as he held it up for Brody to see it in his glove. Then, carefully, he fit the glove under his arm, plucked out the ball, and tossed it back.

"Good! Now you've got it," Brody praised. "Watch my form when I throw. That's how we learn—watching how others do things well. You can learn a lot about life and other people just by playing catch."

"You can?"

"Sure. We tell each other about ourselves. When you care to throw the ball directly to me, aiming with intention, you show that you're courteous, that you don't want me to chase after the ball unnecessarily. And when you try to catch one of my throws that's not too accurate, you tell me that you're not afraid of a good challenge. You don't give up. Even if you don't catch every ball, you make an effort. People who make an effort in life are a pleasure to be around. They're not a burden."

"What if my throws aren't accurate—like that one?"

"Well, you can make up for it with your next throw. Some people can't throw well at all, but it's important that they listen to instruction and try to improve. When someone throws a bad throw, you forgive them. You don't complain. You don't even need to mention it. You just fetch the ball and keep playing. Here, let's try some high ones. These are called fly balls. You ready?"

"I'm ready." Aidan licked his lips and held his mitt high and open. "Let it fly!"

Aidan was so focused on catching, chasing, and throwing the ball that he didn't notice the people who'd lined the sidewalk to watch until they cheered when he caught a particularly difficult throw. But he caught it! And he raised his glove again in triumph from the grass where he'd tumbled.

Grinning, he righted himself and climbed to his feet. Brody joined him as the people nearby dispersed.

"We'll have to continue another day when there's more light." Brody rubbed one eye. "My old eyes are struggling to follow the ball in this darkness."

"I didn't notice." Aidan didn't even want to take off his glove. "This was way better than video games."

"Oh, absolutely. But dinner's waiting. Greg may be skinny, but he'll eat everything in sight if we don't show up for whatever Binsa and your sister are fixing."

"Greg is nice, huh?"

They walked side by side to the front of the apartment.

"Yeah, I think so. God didn't give him any baseball skills, but he's coordinated in other ways. Greg's a computer genius. He's saved many lives by finding people through network systems."

"He likes Marcy, right?"

"You're perceptive." Brody held the elevator door for him. "I think Marcy likes him, too. Do you think so?"

"Yep, I've seen her face when he's around."

"There's nothing wrong with that. They're both keeping their priorities straight."

"What's that mean? What priorities?"

"God designed us to enjoy serving Him with others. That's our priority. But most people set the wrong priority by serving themselves by using others for their own fulfillment."

"Marcy talks a lot about God to me in our apartment. It's weird."

"Well, she's learned a lot about God from reading many books and the Bible. Since she cares for you, she wants you to learn about Him, too. We should all try to share the good things in life with others—especially the truth."

"You want to play baseball tomorrow?"

"That depends on what Greg says at the meeting tonight."

"What meeting?"

"Greg said he's got news on his search for your parents. You should be there to hear. The new guy in the other apartment, Jerome, will be there, too."

They reached the twelfth floor and started up the hallway.

"Marcy wants to find them, but I don't."

"Some people we may not want to see again, but they still need to be found—because they're lost. Your parents may not deserve your love, Aidan, but they sure need to be loved. I guess that goes for all of us in life. We all have a past. We all want to satisfy only ourselves—until we entrust our lives to God. Sure, we don't deserve God's love, but He loves us because it's His nature to love, and He knows we need to be loved."

"Well, I don't hate Mom and Dad."

"That's good."

"I just think selling your kids is wrong. It makes me mad now that Marcy told me more of what happened."

"Yeah, I understand." Brody stopped in front of their

doors. "But Marcy only explained all that to you so you could understand your parents were in a selfish state of being. It could be that they're still in that same state. That's why Marcy wants to find them—to help them, not to criticize them."

"So, it's like playing catch."

"How so?" Brody tilted his head.

"If someone throws you a bad throw, you said you forgive them. You don't complain or criticize. You just pick up the ball."

"And you keep playing." Brody laughed and set his hand on Aidan's shoulder. "You're figuring out life faster than I did, my friend."

Binsa's apartment door opened, and Marcy stood there with a scowl. Sweet scents of food wafted into the hall.

"Where've you two been?" Marcy pointed her finger. "The food's been ready for twenty minutes. Get washed up. Everyone's waiting."

She left the door open and spun around.

"Women don't always understand men and baseball," Brody confessed quietly as they entered Binsa's apartment. "But you already know what we've got to do."

"Forgive 'em and don't complain?"

"Exactly. And wash your hands. Women can spot unwashed hands from across the room!"

When Marcy entered Greg and Brody's studio apartment after their dinner, she was pleased to see Greg notice her, even though after smiling at her, he immediately returned his attention to Jerome who sat at the tech's computer terminal.

"Hey, Marcy." Aidan approached her, his baseball glove under his limp arm. He held up his functioning hand. "Check out that blister. It's from my glove."

"That's . . . nice, Aidan."

"I'm getting another one over here on my thumb.

Brody said it'll turn into a callus if I keep practicing. I want my whole hand to be a callus so it's as tough as a glove."

"Okay, now that's just gross."

Aidan wandered off to the window, where he fit his mitt on and off again, and flexed his glove.

"Sit next to me, Marcy?" Binsa patted the carpeted floor where she'd set up her laptop on a recently-purchased coffee table. It was the only furniture in the living room area.

"Um . . ." Marcy glanced toward Greg, still engaged in conversation with Jerome. Where would Greg be sitting? She wanted to sit next to him. "Okay."

Plopping down, she wondered if she should've come prepared to take notes like Binsa. After all, the people of TROAS had all just eaten dinner together, and Brody, Binsa, and Greg were involving her in the operation's intelligence reports. She belonged to something amazing now within the fellowship of faith. It was so exciting—and she got to see Greg every day!

Marcy caught her breath when she noticed Brody speaking to a man she didn't recognize in the far corner where Greg and Brody's beds sat. That man hadn't been at dinner. Was he part of TROAS, too? He was olive-skinned, with a rigid jawline and frowning, dark eyes. Brody spoke so softly that Marcy couldn't hear a word, but in Brody's hand was a Bible, so they were certainly speaking about God. Although Marcy was uncomfortable about a stranger in their midst, if he were a believer, then she figured it was okay. Jerome wasn't a believer—evidenced by his questions about prayer over dinner—but Brody and Binsa seemed to be involving the agent to bring him on board to some degree.

Brody and the stranger stood and moved toward the living room area, a signal that Greg caught and directed Jerome to join the others in a wide circle on the floor. Aidan made a point to sit next to Brody, who casually supported the teen's light frame as he collapsed to sit with them. Jerome sat next to Marcy, much to Marcy's disappointment, but she could still look across the circle directly at Greg.

Only the olive-skinned stranger didn't sit with the other six. He remained standing, the Bible Brody had used now in his folded hands where he leaned against the wall by the door. Brody and Binsa didn't seem too concerned about the new face, and Marcy didn't want to be rude, so she tried not to stare—though her curiosity was certainly aroused.

"We're here to share intel on the next operation," Brody began, his hands on his knees where he sat cross-legged. "Normally, this process is completed more privately between myself, Binsa, and Greg. But this involves Marcy and Aidan's parents, so we're breaking protocol this time to share the planning tonight more openly for their sakes. Let's pray."

Reverently, Brody bowed his head. Marcy lingered an instant to see Jerome's eyes narrow critically and Aidan mimic his new hero—Brody. Their leader prayed softly, asking for God's guidance and comfort, even if they heard difficult news or experienced challenges ahead. When he concluded, Brody gestured at Greg. Greg was leading the briefing! Marcy beamed with pride as she directed her complete attention toward the young man who'd said she was attractive. She'd never forget that. And he'd said that even before she'd begun to wear the beret to keep her springy hair in check.

"For days, I've been scouring the net for leads on Emma and Cole Nevins." Greg used no visual aids or notes. "I've gotten glimpses of them from over the years, sometimes in the States, and sometimes overseas. Sometimes it's just from an apartment they rented, a car they drove, or a bank account they opened. From all these things, I've been able to deduce that they aren't together anymore, but the details of their relationship are sketchy since they've both lived off the grid more often than not."

"What's that mean?" Aidan asked.

"Mom and Dad are probably divorced," Marcy translated, "and they've probably been using fake IDs and living quietly in areas with criminals."

"That's a pretty good assessment." Jerome raised his eyebrows. "Greg already briefed you, huh?"

"No, I—" Marcy gulped, realizing all eyes were on her. "I've read a lot and thought for years about how they might be living. That's all."

"Well, Marcy's right," Greg said. "At least one hospitalization for an overdose can be traced back to Emma Nevins in Philadelphia four years ago, but I also have a plane ticket under a stolen visa—with her face—that indicates she flew to Paris not long after she was in Philly."

"Mom's in Paris?" Aidan asked.

"Could be." Greg shrugged. "I have some feelers out for her face and name with other agencies, but nothing else has come back that's recent. Emma Nevins is still in the wind at this point, but Cole Nevins is another story. I found your and Marcy's dad."

Greg grinned triumphantly. Marcy sat in awe that he seemed to care and enjoy the search to reunite loved ones as much as she wanted them found.

"Overseas?" Jerome asked. "If he was Stateside, I think he would've been easier to find with the search apps you've written."

"He's in Ukraine. It's a medium-sized city called Chernivtsi in the west where the war hasn't been as destructive or disruptive."

"You're sure he's there now?" Brody asked.

"Two months ago, a hospital did some blood work on him. Last week, they did another panel. I don't know what the tests show, but Cole Nevins gave them his home address. We know exactly where he's living."

"Do you have his blood results?" Binsa looked up from her tablet.

"Yeah, but there's no physician's diagnosis in the database, so we can't know what the blood test shows. Besides, it's in Ukrainian."

"Let me see it, please?" Binsa requested.

Greg hopped up, plucked a printout from his desk, and handed it across the circle to Binsa. Marcy leaned in to see the page with columns, numbers, and abbreviations, some of them written in Russian lettering.

"Can you read it?" Marcy asked.

"I was hoping to be able to." Binsa shook her head. "I'm sorry. I'm not an expert. The numbers look normal to me."

She offered it to Brody.

"May I see it?" The stranger from against the wall suddenly stepped forward. His voice was scratchy, his movement fluid.

Brody received the paper from Binsa, and without looking at it, handed it to the stranger. The man held the results against the Bible. Everyone watched him, especially Binsa. He was a handsome man, in a rugged sort of way, and about Binsa's age. Marcy thought she saw more than curiosity in her eyes.

"It's a routine blood test," he said. "This must be his first test from two months ago, yes?"

"Yeah," Greg answered. "How'd you know?"

"There's not much to notice, except one number. Show me the second test results from last week."

Again, Greg jumped up and returned with the other. The stranger knelt on the carpet and laid the two pages side by side.

"They found antibodies against mitochondria," he said. "That's in the first test. This second test contains results from a biopsy to confirm the first test."

"Is it cancer?" Jerome asked. "You said antibodies."

The stranger spoke softly to Brody. Marcy listened closely but heard them exchanging words in another language. After a moment, the newcomer left the two pages in Brody's hands, then returned to stand against the wall, his eyes downcast.

"It's cirrhosis of the liver," Brody announced. "Cole Nevins must be a heavy drinker. Or he was. The second test, the biopsy, shows that it's progressive."

"What's that mean—progressive?" Aidan asked.

"Your father is dying from liver failure, Aidan," Binsa stated.

Marcy bit her lip. *Her dad was dying.* No wonder the stranger didn't want to share that news himself.

"There are transplants available," Jerome offered. "He could get a transplant."

"Even if a living match were found," the stranger said from behind Brody, "a transplant patient rarely lives more than a few months."

"But he's alive right now," Marcy said, pleading with her eyes at Brody, "and we know exactly where he is."

"Yes, we do." Brody nodded resolutely. "Greg, do we know anything else? How about this address he left at the hospital?"

"Yeah, I searched it and mapped it out for you. There's a functioning trolley bus to this area of the city, but the neighborhood is rundown. Ukraine's been hit by virus quarantines, and the whole Russia thing . . ."

"So, you're going, right?" Marcy pressed. "He could be dying. We need to get to him before he dies."

"We will." Brody handed the medical pages back to Greg. "But it's like Greg says. Ukraine isn't the Eastern European country it once was. Conflicts with Russia, refugees everywhere, elevated crime, and the recent protests—it won't be a smooth ride, even though we do have fellow believers in the country."

"I can see if Homeland Security has any contacts in this city—Chernivtsi," Jerome offered.

"No, but thank you," Brody stated, looking sternly at Jerome. "TROAS keeps our affairs private until we want to bring the authorities in. Let's surveil the neighborhood and draw up a plan to intercept Cole Nevins with as little outside attention or interference as possible."

"Bring Dad back here," Marcy said. "We can take care of him here if he's dying."

"Well, I'll need to talk to him first," Brody said. "It's a sensitive situation. Just because we've found him doesn't mean he'll want to come back or even want to see his family again. We'll need to brace ourselves for that possibility, right, Marcy?"

"All the more reason," Jerome blurted, "to have official backup! It could develop into a police matter. He's a wanted man. It's best to have the police on alert."

"Hold it, Jerome." Brody raised a hand to halt the agent. "No need to move faster than the intel we have. Remember Charleston. We move slowly until it's time to move with haste. Cole could be in the middle of a GLOW hornet's nest, or he may be all alone. There's no way to know yet. As far as backup is concerned—we have all we need."

"Who—*God?*" Jerome scoffed.

Even Marcy was offended, and she stared at Brody, who she guessed would fire back and put the over-eager agent in his place. Instead, Brody smiled patiently, like he'd done with Senator Madison.

"Yes, God. But the State Department has placed Zayed with us for a probationary period of time, since he turned himself in to us. He's repented from his old life and he's under my authority. Zayed'll be our backup."

"Five days ago, he nearly killed us in Charleston!" Jerome fumed. "And I remember the grenade very well. Do you remember Charleston? I can't believe this. A Saudi human trafficker is our backup going into an Eastern European hornet's nest where GLOW has the upper hand?"

Marcy eyed the man Brody had called Zayed. He was Saudi? The stranger didn't move a muscle or lift his gaze from the floor, but Marcy doubted it was because he was afraid. Jerome was muscled and had Homeland Security on his side, but Zayed appeared fit, too. And if Brody stood up for him, and Brody was on God's side, then Jerome didn't have a chance of winning in his criticism against the new guy.

"Yes, Agent Wessel, last week, Zayed was involved in trafficking domestic workers along the East Coast. Today, he's our ally, willing to share his skills and resources with us for good instead of evil. He understands that he may die in the process of helping others besides us. Depending on a person's faith, some limit God to work in them over many years, and others open wide to allow the Holy Spirit to transform and refine them much more swiftly—in a matter of days or weeks. If you read your Bible a little more—"

"I don't even have a Bible," Jerome said, "and I don't want one."

"Well, if you did, you wouldn't be so shocked that someone who once harmed people is now able to help people. This is what God alone can do—change a man from the inside out."

"It's baseball," Aidan whispered to Brody, but loud enough that Marcy heard him.

Brody nodded to Aidan and set a hand on the young man's shoulder to acknowledge his comment, but he didn't change the subject.

A lot must've happened in Charleston, but Marcy hadn't heard any details. Clearly, the way Brody did things conflicted with Jerome's professional opinion.

"I just—" Jerome licked his lips as he looked around the circle. "We should be going after the GLOW network, crumbling it from the top down. It's just I'm not used to taking such risks in the field, especially with those I work with."

"We're followers of Jesus Christ here," Brody stressed. "Making ourselves vulnerable for others' spiritual and physical benefit is our whole purpose. We couldn't possibly honor our Lord any other way except through sacrificial love. That's who we are. It's the whole reason Marcy has us going after her parents, even after what they've done. From what we know, they're probably part of GLOW, yes, so we're not ignoring that network, but they're very low on our list of priorities."

"It's just not done," Jerome said. "No offense, Marcy, but this isn't the way the world works. We can't rush into a dangerous and unstable country like Ukraine and expect your God to protect us all."

"God doesn't promise our protection while we serve Him," Marcy stated softly. "He offers us the privilege to serve Him. Binsa said that Brody knows he could die on any mission, and it sounds like Zayed is aware of the same thing. It doesn't mean God won't be with them, but it also doesn't mean they shouldn't keep going out there."

"If you go to Ukraine with us," Brody said to Jerome, "it'll be with the priority of reuniting this family. There'll be other opportunities for us to fight against GLOW. I'm sure you'll get some arrests and bring criminals to justice again soon."

"You mean you won't be trying to prosecute Cole Nevins?" Jerome asked. "I'm legally bound—"

"Stop speaking." Brody's face was expressionless, but this command was too abrupt to be ignored. "You've been invited into our midst, Jerome, to expose you to an effective, biblical approach to confronting the *cause* of human trafficking, not just the *symptoms* of it. Until you receive God's wisdom, truth, and love as revealed in the Bible, you have no say in how God's people behave in life or respond to those needs. TROAS combats sin, but we aren't an extension of human government. The body of Christ is an extension of Jesus Himself. His Spirit lives in us, and we are motivated to love and forgive, not to arrest and condemn. Sure, we're willing to cooperate with authorities in any nation that intends to act morally, and sometimes that leads to arrests. But where we are able to show mercy, we show mercy. Now, it's getting late. There's a trip to plan and pray about. We can discuss this more in the morning."

Brody rose to his feet first. Marcy watched the veteran cross the circle and offer his hand to help Jerome to his feet. Jerome was more than capable to climb to his feet alone, but this was Brody's way, and Marcy glowed with pride at the man who led them. Jerome's eyes lingered on the hand for just an instant, then he accepted it. That easily, Brody made the tension vanish between the two men. And it was a good thing since Marcy heard Brody tell Zayed that he was bunking that night in the apartment next door with Agent Jerome Wessel.

Cole Nevins knew he was dying, but that wasn't the worst part. He was alone in Chernivtsi, Ukraine. Emma had left him a couple years earlier when they'd been living in Odessa, partying at night and seducing tourists during the day. Ukraine's sex tourism trade had been thriving before the pandemic fears struck, but Cole didn't care what was happening out there in society now, and no one out there seemed to care about him anymore, either.

He pushed the pile of marriage applications away from him. His kitchen table was covered with printouts of letters from lonely men seeking Ukrainian wives. This was what GLOW had reduced him to—a secretary processing vulnerable targets for a marriage scam. Gone were the colorful festivals and his own drunken laughter. *Laughter?* Even with the couple of women that GLOW had sent to accompany him in his new assignment, he'd found them not only sickly but joyless. Death weighed on him. There was nothing to laugh about anymore. Not even the prospect of scamming Westerners out of their life savings could lighten the dusk that had settled over his soul.

Wandering into the bathroom where the brightest light bulb shined, Cole examined in the mirror the yellow nodules of skin around his eyes. He was jaundiced and his whole body itched constantly. The doctor had told him these were common symptoms of liver disease—cirrhosis. His arms and legs felt heavy, he had no appetite, and every morning he found more hair on his pillow. From an English brochure he'd discovered that his lower back pain was probably a sign of his kidneys failing as well.

Cursing his wife's name, he turned off the bathroom light. She'd actually abandoned him—even though he hadn't hit her in years. Maybe she was in worse shape than he was since her drug use had been so much heavier. But his drinking had been worse. Her craving for mind-numbing junk had kept him broke for much of their marriage, but at least she'd been at his side. Now, GLOW had set him down in a remote cultural city, and Emma could've been living with a prince for all he knew. Though she'd never been particularly pretty, when sober, she could be compassionate and creative—a warm spirit to be around.

Skirting a picnic table in the living room, Cole reached the bay window that faced the street. Who'd furnished the house with a picnic table, anyway? It seemed to be a joke. He would never use the thing since he preferred the small, round dining table in the kitchen to work on the marriage applications. They hadn't even given him a computer, only the printouts from the GLOW scam site.

The bay window was dusty on the inside and scratched on the outside, but he could still see the littered one-lane street that led into the city to the right—or deeper into the poor suburb to the left. Beyond the other duplexes and apartment buildings nearby, he could see the beech trees around the bank of the Prut River, and higher up, the lighter green of fir trees in the summer. It almost looked like a park in Davenport. That was a time in his youth when he'd been carefree and innocent—riding bikes as kids and chasing squirrels at the edge of the neighbor's yard. Another life. Another country. A happier time.

Movement on the street caught his eye, and a car door slammed. No, it was that van he'd noticed the day before. It was parked halfway in the ditch about fifty yards down the lane. Two white men had come and gone from the front seats, men who ate their meals and drank coffee in their vehicle. Cole recognized policemen who were on surveillance, but these two men seemed far too obvious to make any effective impact. Though he hadn't been living on this street for long, Cole wasn't aware of any nefarious neighbors. Besides, GLOW paid off all the local magistrates to steer clear of any of their safe houses. It could be drug-related surveillance, maybe a manufacturer of meth, spice, or something exotic that GLOW had no hand in, so it didn't concern him.

Turning from the window, Cole bumped his shin on the picnic table bench. Of all the furniture to put in an apartment!

Limping, he returned to the kitchen table where he rubbed his shin. The marriage requests were piling up. They arrived in the mail once a week from a GLOW office somewhere in England, so he should've been processing them faster, but he kept reading and rereading the letters of lonely men. Men like himself, seeking companionship, a human touch, someone to love, and someone to love them in return. The closest he'd come to being near someone who cared for him was a Ukrainian doctor who'd told him he was dying, yet he kept mispronouncing his first name.

His processing job was simple. All he had to do was respond to the letters with a stock photo of a woman promised to the prospective husband and write a handwritten letter inviting the man to come to Ukraine. When the man arrived, he was to have ten thousand U.S. dollars or Euros in cash to pay for the supposed debt of his bride. By saving his future wife from debt servitude, the man would find a thankful and obedient wife.

But there was no debt. And there were no women involved. The photos were prostitutes, young women smiling during happier times. When a man showed up at a Ukrainian address to "rescue" his fiancée, he instead found a shotgun in his face, then came the beating and robbery. That all happened in Kiev, normally, far from where Cole processed and sent out the responses. He knew GLOW was paying him only a small fraction of what he was earning for them, but who was he? And what would he spend money on now? He was just a dying man, abandoned by even his own wife.

Cole picked up his pen to draft the next letter, then imagined if the van down the lane were actually there for him. He'd been on the internet and seen federal warrants for his arrest in the States. It was about time. Someone may have finally discovered what he'd done with his kids all those years ago. Maybe Aidan or Marcy had been found in a landfill, which was pretty standard for GLOW victims. An investigation could've revealed that one or both kids had been sold to his old connection in Davenport. The money from that sale hadn't lasted two months, but at least they'd gotten out of Davenport on GLOW's dime. They'd partied in New York City, then caught a flight to Paris where GLOW needed them to manage a brothel for underage girls.

The enterprise had failed miserably, though. He and Emma had spent all the profits on dope. When GLOW had come for their cut, Cole had claimed they'd been robbed. They'd beaten him so badly he'd ended up in the hospital. Self-discharging a day later, he'd returned to the brothel to find that his wife had been hurt badly as well. GLOW had reassigned them elsewhere—Greece for a couple years, taking in migrants from Syria and Africa, smuggling the men into Europe to work and the young women into the sex shops. Some had been used to harvest their organs. Though he'd been high most of the time, Cole had been shocked how gullible people were to his promises of citizenship and fair wages for whole families. Later, GLOW split up every man, woman, and child. Many of the immigrants wished they'd never left their country of origin, but that wasn't Cole's problem.

Unless that van outside was Interpol and they were on to him. But who was he compared to a real GLOW mover like the man known as the Executive? Or maybe the Executive was a woman. He'd heard only rumors. But he and Emma had been GLOW underlings, with managers and henchmen of the Executive levels above them. Now, he was even lower in the GLOW hierarchy since he was dying.

Well, at least he was sober. Coughing, he wrote a lonely Nebraskan man who promised to take care of a Ukrainian woman in need—answering an online ad placed six months earlier. Cole almost felt sorry for the poor fool who was thirty-nine years old, working construction for nineteen years, even attending a church for a decade. Naïve and willing, he would come to Kiev and lose his life savings—and maybe a couple of teeth. He couldn't go to the police. Well, he could, but they wouldn't care. If the police charged anyone of anything, they'd cite the man for attempting to traffic a Ukrainian woman—though there would be no woman—and he would return to Nebraska broke, bruised, and alone.

Cole lifted his head. Someone was on the doorstep. While on drugs and booze, he'd either been lethargic or paranoid. Now sober, he had to discern between fantasy and reality. His senses had to be retrained even though his body had detoxed.

Sure enough, the front door opened. Cole was tall, always priding himself in being three inches over six feet when he wasn't stooping. Some men were intimidated by his height, even though he'd been unhealthy and slender most of his adult life. But the man who entered with groceries in his arms barely glanced at Cole, caring little for his size. The visitor wiped his feet on the indoor mat. He was a broad-shouldered man in his fifties, a hard face but with gentle, blue eyes. Maybe sad eyes.

"Hey, Cole," the visitor said, then moved farther into the house. "A little warm out there today."

"Yeah." Cole frowned and scratched his arm through his flannel shirt. "You left the door open."

"It's all right. Jerome's right behind me."

"Oh." Cole turned in time to see a muscled black man enter carrying two sleeping bags instead of groceries.

The first man reached the kitchen, so Cole stepped into the room to see him setting his groceries on top of the marriage requests and letters on the table.

"Getting lots done?" the stranger asked.

"Yeah. You know." Cole ran his fingers through his hair, knowing he looked ill.

The black man was in the empty back bedroom, probably unrolling their sleeping bags on the floor. These had to be GLOW people. They spoke English and acted like they owned the place. Definitely GLOW since they knew his name.

"How long you guys staying?" He picked up a head of lettuce. "What's with all the vegetables?"

"Figured with your health, protein and sodium is out." The man stowed what he could in the fridge, notoriously small all over Ukraine. The rest he placed under the counter in the food box. "I'm not a bad cook. Jerome says he makes a mean stir-fry."

"Protein and sodium?" Cole asked.

"Didn't the doctor tell you to cut back on anything metabolized by your liver? I'm a steak and eggs kind of guy, but for you, we'll eat something from the garden. Who knows? Maybe it'll catch on and we'll all live longer."

The man chuckled while Cole studied him closer. He didn't seem to be armed. That was strange for a GLOW thug. And this guy's attitude was much more friendly than other GLOW foot soldiers who usually treated Cole like a mark more than a peer. But he wasn't complaining. Cole could use a little company, even if they were GLOW soldiers in town on some assignment.

"Are you hungry now? I'm Brody by the way."

Cole shook the blue-eyed man's hand.

"Uh. Pleasure, Brody. Yeah, I could eat."

"And that's Jerome." Brody gestured to his partner who left through the front door. "He's just getting a few more things."

"You should know there's been a surveillance team down the lane." Cole went to the bay window. But instead of finding the van parked down the street, it was parked in front of his house! "Oh, it was you guys!"

"Yeah. Strange how that works. For years, you feel invincible, then in an instant—bam! Your whole world comes crashing down. It could happen to any of us. Are you doing a lot of reflecting lately? I know I would be."

Brody wasn't much shorter than he was, but since he was standing so close, Cole looked down into those blue eyes. There was concern in his voice. Genuine concern. And he sensed he really wanted an answer.

"Oh, I guess I have been." Cole looked away, back out the window. "It's strange what comes to mind after a doctor tells you that you have only twelve months to live."

"They say anyone who has no regrets at the end of his life lived perfectly, or he's too arrogant to admit his wrongs."

"You have a funny way of saying things." Cole didn't want to answer the stranger, but he also didn't want him to leave. "Do you guys know anything about my wife? Have you heard anything?"

"No." Brody cocked his head. "We've actually been trying to track her down. If anyone knew about her, I thought you would."

"How would I? You guys took her in Odessa two years ago."

"It wasn't me or my people," Brody said. "You seem

confused about who sent me. Hey, Jerome, let me help you with that."

To Cole's surprise, his guests hung a small flat screen TV in the living room on the wall at one end of the picnic table.

"Finally, some entertainment," Cole said. "I was starting to think I'd need to learn Ukrainian and get a book to read or something. You guys got satellite or what?"

As Brody set things up, Cole examined the tech.

"Nah, just some videos we downloaded. Should be interesting."

"That's everything." Jerome wiped his sweating forehead. "Now what?"

Cole wanted to know the same thing. Brody was clearly the boss, so they looked to him.

"Well, why don't I start cooking in the kitchen. That's where Cole's been working on that paperwork, so he can tell us what he's been doing. Later, we can eat while watching a video."

Sitting at the kitchen table, even in his melancholy, Cole was only too happy to share what he'd accomplished. He had a whole box of letters to mass-mail all over the world, inviting potential grooms to Ukraine for their brides-to-be. First, he showed them the ad on the internet that attracted the lonely marks, mostly in Europe and the Americas. Then, he showed them how he responded to marriage requests via postage mail, so he couldn't be traced as easily through the digital world. After that, he read aloud his latest letter to the Nebraskan, revealing his creativity at crafting such a hook to the mark.

"I didn't know you had such a gift with words," Brody said. "There must be thirty letters here. How many will make the trip with ten thousand to buy a wife?"

"On average, only about a quarter of them these days."

"That's seventy-five thousand dollars." Jerome paged

through the envelopes. "What about the women in these pictures?"

"Prostitutes. Some of them are even dead." Cole thumbed through a stack of photos like a deck of cards. "It doesn't matter. They posed for whatever we wanted, and now they're the bait that lands the fish."

"How long have you been doing this?" Brody asked.

"Just started about two months ago. Ever since you guys, er, the higher-ups heard I'm sick, this is all I've done. Hosting Westerners in Odessa was getting hard for me. I was missing appointments. Just didn't have the energy, especially at night."

"Hosting Westerners?" Jerome asked.

"I speak English, and some say I have a trusting face. You probably know about Odessa. It was party central before the war. I'd average two grabs a month, if I planned carefully."

"Grabs?"

"Mostly kids or teenage girls. There'd be an investigation afterward. You know, by the kidnapping division. But all those guys were getting a cut. We just went after foreigners, so the locals looked the other way. You guys must be in town for something big if you're not familiar with all the little stuff we've been doing at the local level here. Setting up something new? You obviously came prepared for a stay."

"A job like this takes patience." Brody nodded. "Thanks for being a good host, Cole."

Cole winced through a smile, realizing Brody had dodged his efforts to find out what GLOW had sent them to do in Chernivtsi. But it didn't really matter if he knew or didn't know what they were up to, Cole decided. He'd be dead soon, so a little company was welcome.

CHAPTER SEVEN

Zayed Aziz stood in the moon shadow of a beech tree and watched the house where Brody Sladrick had entered hours earlier. Homeland Security Agent Jerome Wessel was in there with Brody as they visited with Cole Nevins. Nothing contrary seemed afoot since their arrival in Ukraine. The peace and quiet of the cool European summer night pleased Zayed perfectly. He was still adjusting to this new life—which had been a whirlwind since first meeting Brody in South Carolina.

For two nights, Zayed had slept in the van with Brody and Jerome as the three had surveilled Cole's apartment building in shifts. They'd suspected GLOW owned the apartment building, maybe to house their aging workers, yet to keep them still involved in some money-making schemes. Cole's neighbors hadn't seemed concerned that the three men had been lurking about the street, even sitting in the van all hours of the day and night. Brody had even spoken with some of the neighbors in Russian, buying fresh milk from them. Everyone he met, Brody seemed to touch in a unique way. Zayed knew it was God, and he wanted to be a part of that.

"Isteslemna," Zayed said aloud in Arabic into the night. It was a prayer of surrender to his new God and Father of the Nazarene, Jesus, who was also God. And Brody had explained that the third Person of the Godhead now lived inside him. *"Isteslemna.* I surrender."

As a general practitioner in Saudi Arabia years earlier, Zayed had immediately recognized Cole Nevin's liver condition from his blood results they'd researched in their Tampa headquarters. Owning his own medical practice in Riyadh seemed like a lifetime ago, especially with all the twists and turns he'd taken in the West—and now coming to the feet of Jesus—or *Isa*, in his own tongue. He probably would've still been in Arabia if he hadn't been so close to the royal family when he'd misdiagnosed a beloved relative of the prince. The woman had died, and Zayed had expected to be executed. Instead, the royal family had stripped him of his credentials and exiled him from the country.

And how far he'd fallen since then! Eventually, he'd ended up in South Carolina, sponsoring foreigners to immigrate to America, then exploiting them like slaves. He'd even begun carrying a handgun and a grenade for protection, weapons he knew well since his youth in the military, where he'd first met the Saudi prince and become friends.

Zayed had confessed his shameful past of death and abuse to Brody, but the man hadn't pushed him away. Brody had simply expressed the enduring love and forgiveness of God with greater fervor. Now, even if he weren't already exiled, he'd never be welcomed back into Saudi Arabia. He was a *Nasara* now—a Nazarene, as his people often called Christians.

After a slow-moving car passed on the lane, Zayed crossed to the front yard of Cole's apartment building. Since it was dark outside and light inside, Zayed could see inside easily. Brody sat with Cole at a picnic table, and they watched one of the videos Brody had downloaded for the man. Jerome sat in the kitchen, sorting through papers and envelopes. The agent suddenly left the kitchen and joined Brody and Cole in the living room.

So he could see the screen better, Zayed moved to the side of the house. The picture showed the Grand Canyon, then various images like galaxies, a butterfly, and the human eye. It was a strange approach, but Zayed understood what Brody was doing. He was exposing Cole to God, the Creator of heaven and earth. The video was a documentary about the wonders of nature and humanity's purpose—all designed by God.

The other videos Brody had brought included an archaeology report on historical locations in the land of Israel. Another was about the life of Jesus—a real historical Person whose first coming had changed the world, and whose second coming would begin with His reign over the world. Zayed looked forward to seeing the videos himself, but Brody had explained what they were about and how he hoped they would touch Cole's life. Ultimately, they wanted to win him over and return him to his daughter and son in Tampa.

In that moment, Zayed prayed to his new God about Cole's spiritual need. Brody had shown him texts in the Holy Bible that revealed how Christian prayer mattered a great deal to his relationship with God. To Zayed's surprise, Brody had shared how he'd often prayed for those he'd not yet met, and that Zayed was a product of that kind of expectant faith! Zayed had never known that God could answer such prayer so personally, so dramatically. In a single day, Brody had recruited Zayed and introduced him to the gospel. He'd even stopped carrying his lethal weapons for protection. Now, he carried only one of Brody's tranq-pens—to preserve the lives of others rather than violently take the lives of his enemies.

He also carried a small Bible, also a gift from Brody. The pen was a weapon, but Brody said the Bible was even more powerful. Zayed was learning how and why a little more every time he read from its pages.

If God could answer Brody's prayers for him, then Zayed believed God could answer even his prayers for Cole, who was a similarly lost man. After all, the Bible explained that all people were born into the guilt of Adam, positioned against God until each person chose to accept the salvation offered. Leaving all to faith because of God's good grace made Zayed's soul ache to learn more about his Savior. Unlike the religion of his Saudi fathers, his eternal destiny no longer relied on an angry god. Nor did it depend on his own perfection to keep the five pillars of Islam.

"*Isteslemna*," Zayed whispered, and he walked away from the apartment window.

When he reached the van, he sat in the driver's seat and watched the street. He liked living in the background like this—a good man like Brody counting on him to ward off evil so he could plant the seeds of truth. This was where he belonged, where he felt needed, even loved. Even the girl Marcy had embraced him before he'd left Tampa. And the beautiful Nepalese woman, Binsa, had promised to pray for him while he was gone. If they had known all the wicked things he'd done the last few years since leaving Arabia, he guessed they wouldn't have shown him concern upon his departure. Or maybe that was the forgiveness Brody had told him about. As Jesus had forgiven them, so His followers were inclined to forgive others.

It was too beautiful not to surrender to such a truth. *What a God!*

"*Isteslemna!*"

Brody stood in the doorway of the back bedroom in the Chernivtsi house in Ukraine. It was nearly three in the morning, the moonlight peering in several uncurtained windows, but he couldn't sleep. It wasn't a matter of inability to sleep as much as it was necessary that he not sleep. Sometimes sleep needed to be forfeited because spiritual needs were more important.

From where he stood, he could see into Cole Nevin's room where the man tossed and turned in his own bed. As Brody prayed for God's intervention on the dying man's soul, he could almost imagine the dreams God might be using to shake the criminal's desperate soul. With things as they were, Cole was dying in his shame and guilt as a sinner.

Behind Brody, Jerome sat up in his sleeping bag and cursed.

"This is ridiculous, Brody!" Jerome hissed in a whisper. "We don't have to sleep like this. There are hotels in town. This guy's done things to people that only a sadist would do. He's literally kidnapped people to sell them. Hundreds. He bragged about it because he still thinks we're with GLOW, which seems ridiculous that he could still think that after watching those videos with you."

"Faith is a choice of the will," Brody said softly. "Just because the truth is staring you straight in the face, that doesn't mean you accept it in a way that changes your life."

"How can you spend this much effort and money on someone like him?"

"You can go sleep in the van with Zayed if you want." Brody didn't move from the doorway. "God values this man's soul as much as yours or mine."

"I highly doubt that." Jerome slapped the sleeping bag. "The floor is uneven in here. I can't sleep like this."

Brody didn't respond. He felt as if he were losing the agent. Jerome didn't have the Spirit of Christ in him, so his internal guiding system of spiritual and eternal matters was completely skewed. The man had even complained about the length of the three videos Brody had brought for them to watch, all while Cole had watched in silence, asking no questions and making no comments. The last video, which had described the historical life of Christ, had also explained a direct gospel invitation to lost sinners—and still Cole hadn't criticized the documentary.

"Just tell him why we're here already!" Jerome stated. "Do it now. Wake him up and tell him. Then we can leave this mad man's house and get back to civilization. I swear, Brody, I've gone to a lot of lengths to help trafficked victims, but this is too much. It just isn't done. He's the victimizer!"

Jerome rolled over, continuing to grumble as he sought a comfortable position. Brody quietly drew the bedroom door closed, leaving his companion inside while Brody stood alone in the chilly hallway. When he turned his attention back to Cole, he noticed Marcy's father was sitting upright in his bed.

"I heard voices," Cole said.

Smiling in the dark, Brody wondered if maybe the Lord had touched the man's heart in his sleep and he'd heard Him speak.

"Sorry. We didn't mean to wake you."

But Cole didn't lay back down. His breathing sounded coarse, like an invalid who was struggling to inhale past the pains of his body. Brody moved from the hallway to Cole's bedroom door, opening the door a little wider.

"You're not like other GLOW friends I've known," Cole said. "You're different. There's something almost familiar about you, but I can't place it."

"You and I are the same, Cole, except I really embrace the truths in the videos we watched tonight."

"I don't . . . think about that stuff. I don't get it. If God is real, He's gonna do what He's gonna do. I can't worry about it."

"Cole, I've seen you when the lights are on. You haven't seriously cared for yourself in a long time, if ever. If you were worried about dying, you'd prepare for it."

"I prepare in my own way."

"How are you preparing to meet your Maker?"

The man didn't speak for a few moments.

"It's my business. I'm the one who's dying."

"We're all dying, my friend. That means we all look out for one another. Death chases all of us, so we stop to help those it's about to overcome."

"So? I can't escape it."

"Death comes with a serious sting for those of us who've never recognized our need to be made new. Our whole lives, we live in sin and wickedness—unless we come to the cross of Christ for God's forgiveness."

"I'm not going to come crawling to God just because I'm about to die."

"I can't think of a better time to come to Him in humility, Cole." Brody walked into the room and stood at the window where he could see the van in the driveway. "Sometimes it's our own pride that gets in the way of us giving up and letting go of the person we've been for so long."

"You've given up?"

"Yes, I gave up when I was a teen. I recognized that God is my Savior, and He's my Savior because I needed saving. Without Him, Cole, we're not just doing evil things; our whole identity is on the wrong side from God. We need to be forgiven, yeah, but we also need to be made new."

"And you think you're new? You're still in the life, just like me."

Brody turned from the windowpane.

"I'm not with GLOW, Cole."

Cole swallowed audibly.

"You're *not?*"

"No, I'm not."

"Okay, now that makes sense."

"What does?" Brody asked.

"I was trying to figure out how someone in GLOW would be watching those Jesus videos unless they were seriously questioning their life choices."

"The truth about Jesus is meant to make us all question our life choices. There's a choice all of us dying people need to make, and we need to make that choice before we face that final judgment day."

"It's not that easy."

"Pride tells us it's too hard."

"No, it's hard because I can't make disappear the things I've done."

"Nothing anyone has ever done can be made to disappear on their own. That's what those videos revealed tonight. We need Someone so mighty, so strong, because there's some heavy lifting, impossible lifting to do if we're to be transformed from sinners to saints. We need a miracle, Cole, and that means we need the One who performs miracles."

"Saint?" Cole chuckled. *"Me, a saint.* There's a thought. You think you're a saint?"

"I know I am, but not because I made myself one. I'm a saint because God has pulled me aside for Himself. When I gave up who I was, He gave me the purity of Jesus. He died for me so I could choose to live forever for Him. Jesus died for you, too, Cole. It's time to believe that. That's faith—that He can do that heavy lifting about your past and make you new."

Cole sat very still for a moment, and Brody prayed through those few seconds. He could sense all the baggage that had weighed on Cole's soul for so many years.

"There are a lot of things I've done," Cole said, "that I can believe God might forgive me for. But there's one or two things that . . . Let's just say I wouldn't win any father-of-the-year awards."

"Oh, I understand." Brody sighed. "I get it. You need to witness God's love and forgiveness for yourself. You need to see it in action, feel the radiance of His glory upon your own dead spirit."

"I . . . wouldn't have used those words, but yeah. I want to know what I'm getting myself into."

"Then we leave in the morning." Brody stalked to the bedroom door.

"What?"

"Sometimes we need to take a few steps up to that ultimate choice." Brody turned in the doorway. "Watching those videos was a first step. Tomorrow is your second step. We're leaving this place and everything it represents."

"Wait." Cole swung a leg off the bed. "If you're not with GLOW, who are you?"

"I'd like to tell you, Cole, but you'll get more out of the answer if you come with me to find out. You need to witness how amazing and wonderful our miraculous God is. Then, you need to trust Him as your Savior like I did. We'll leave at dawn."

Brody closed the door. In the hallway, he found Jerome standing against the wall, his sleeping bag draped over his shoulders.

"I'm leaving. Zayed can drive me into town."

"We're all leaving in the norming," Brody said. "Just wait a few more hours."

"No. I'm not returning with you. I'm done doing anything your way."

"Oh. You're serious."

"Why are you playing games with this guy?" Jerome whispered, but his words sounded punctuated as if he were yelling.

"If I tell him who sent us, then his shame will get in the way of his conviction for being a sinner before a holy God."

"He should feel ashamed!"

"This isn't about what he feels about his daughter and son as much as it is about him and his Redeemer."

In the dimness of the hallway, Brody couldn't see Jerome's eyes, but he could feel the man's confusion, maybe even his hatred. Something had switched inside the agent.

"Get some rest," Brody said, moving past Jerome toward their bedroom. "We pull out at first light."

"No!" Jerome gripped Brody's upper arm. "I'm not going back with you. Didn't you hear me?"

"I was hoping we could move through this together, see it to the end."

"All this is wrong. This man should be in prison for his crimes. There are warrants. How can you overlook that?"

"The same way Marcy does," Brody swiped the

muscled agent's hand off his arm. "I'm thinking of his soul, and you're still concerned about his crimes."

"I'll report him. And you."

"That's something you can explain to Marcy yourself. I'm very sorry we're parting ways like this, Jerome, but I know you must do what you feel you must. I can't say I didn't see this coming since you have such a controversy with God's merciful love toward the undeserving."

"They're undeserving. Exactly! It's the deserving who get God's mercy, *not* the undeserving!"

"Then you have a real task before you, Agent Wessel," Brody said, "if you really think you've got to reach a point that you deserve God's favor to qualify for His forgiveness and heaven."

Brody sat at the picnic table while Jerome left everything behind and Zayed drove him into the city. An hour later, Zayed returned, parked outside, and walked into the living room.

"We have made an enemy." Zayed sat across from Brody. Only the kitchen light remained on.

Taking a few minutes, Brody quietly shared the conversation he'd had with Jerome before he'd demanded to leave.

"But I'm glad you're here now," Brody said. "You're someone who can relate to the gravity of the situation."

"Cole is ready," Zayed stated softly, "as I was."

"And Jerome has pushed away."

"It's his choice."

"Yeah." Brody shook his head. "While you were gone, I was reviewing all my time with the man. Maybe the whole time, I was fostering an enemy instead of a friend. The signs were there. He resisted from the first moment. Or maybe he had different expectations for me."

"If he is an enemy, he is a powerful one," Zayed considered. "Will God protect us?"

"Physically? That's not something God promises. Persecution will come. But spiritually? The Lord has our souls. We're secure that way, even if we go through the fires of persecution in the flesh."

"So, we need to have strong faith." Zayed folded his hands. "I am with you like Silas was with Paul in prison."

"I know you are, Zayed." Brody bowed his head, overcome with emotion. "It's good to have someone beside me who understands. I struggle with dread still about allowing Jerome into our inner circle. Now, it may cost us all."

"Then we'll make sure it's a worthwhile cost."

"What do you mean?" Brody felt like the student for a change.

"We have a few hours until dawn. Shall we pray?"

"Yeah. Nonstop, my brother, nonstop.

Binsa wiped her eyes and looked away from the picture frames that cluttered her desk in her apartment. The pain was still there, even after all those years. Seneeya, her daughter, was truly gone, but she'd never owned a camera in Nepal, so she had no photo. Maybe the agony in her heart would be less if she could only remember Seneeya's face. The six-year-old had been a smiling child, a gap in her front teeth as her child-sized mouth adjusted for her adult teeth. But Binsa couldn't remember her eyes. Or the shape of her face.

She'd never told anyone, but that was the real reason she surrounded herself with the photographs of recovered men, women, and children. Her daughter's face was there somewhere among them, still smiling in her awkward way.

Taking a deep breath, Binsa refocused on the next mission Brody had given her. He seemed to understand her need to aid in the rescue and recovery of trafficked people. She understood she wasn't responsible for losing her own child when her husband had sold her, but she felt purpose in the work she now did within TROAS. Now, she fought against the very trade that had caused her so much pain and had taken her Seneeya away.

The next mission was in France. Binsa would need to leave before Brody did, since she wanted to meet with two small churches in Marseille and equip them with the knowledge to better minister to the trafficked and traffickers of their great city. Binsa's French was inadequate, but she'd spoken to women at both churches who spoke fluent English. They would be waiting for her, and then they would all wait for Brody to rescue the lost.

Her phone vibrated. The text was from Brody. He and Zayed were back. And Cole Nevins was with them! Binsa closed her eyes that instant.

"Open hearts and minds, my Lord," she whispered. "Heal the wounds of this poor but beloved family . . ."

A second text followed. Cole wasn't yet aware of why Brody had brought him back from Ukraine. Binsa licked her lips, her heart beating faster. Marcy didn't know her father had been on his way yet. Brody had sent them only one update from Chernivtsi to explain that he was sharing the gospel with Cole where they'd found him living alone.

Binsa organized her desk and tidied up her apartment, since Brody said he was bringing Cole there first. It was strange, but Brody hadn't mentioned the watchful Agent Jerome Wessel. Perhaps the man needed to return to his work in Davenport. It was rare, even dangerous, for Brody to reveal and expose TROAS to so many outsiders lately, but Binsa knew it might've been his way of growing from his own loss. After grieving for his wife, he was beginning to open up again, to connect with people, and to care for them personally instead of merely as a private shadow operative.

When there was a knock, Binsa rose, smoothed down her *kurta suruwal*, and opened the door. She recognized Cole Nevins from the file Brody had opened when Marcy had first asked TROAS to find him. He was much taller than she, but his frame was stooped a little—she guessed because of the pain of his illness.

"Welcome to my home, Mr. Nevins." She took both of his hands in her own and looked up into his weary face. "I have been waiting for you."

She guided Cole inside, leaving the door open to the hallway where Brody and Zayed remained. Binsa could always count on Brody to understand the security she expected him to provide for her—but he also understood the way God often used her to confront souls in private.

Still holding his hand, she guided Cole to the dining table and gestured at a chair. She seated herself at the head of the table where she clasped her hands together and studied the downcast man before her. He was only a couple years younger than her own forty-seven years, but to her, he seemed like just a boy in a man's body. Looking at him in those few seconds, she peered beyond the misery he'd caused his children, beyond the abuse he'd afflicted upon strangers, and beyond the crimes he was certain to be arrested for if drastic intervention by Brody didn't take place.

"You may call me Binsa. I'm from Nepal. May I call you Cole?"

"Yeah." His eyes only met hers rarely, as if he were a child already caught and under the gaze of a knowing parent. "That's fine."

"Tell me a little about yourself, Cole. I want to know your heart in this quiet moment."

He fidgeted and glanced over his shoulder at the doorway. Even though the door remained open, Brody and Zayed were out of sight. Binsa desperately wanted a report from both men, especially on how Zayed had performed on his first mission, but Cole's soul was her priority.

"I . . . don't know what I'm doing here."

"It's okay. You're among people who care about you. Tampa's sunshine is better than Western Ukraine's weather, isn't it?"

"Yeah. You know about me already?"

"So, tell me about your work in Ukraine."

"The marriage scam?"

"Yes, tell me about the marriage scam. Do you like that kind of work?"

"It was paying the bills, but I feel like I got thrown away once GLOW found out I'm sick. I have cirrhosis of the liver."

"I see. And GLOW—you like working for them?"

"Yeah, I guess." He shrugged. "Why? You guys got something better?"

"What would be better in your opinion?"

"Oh, I don't know." Cole scratched at sores on his arm. "I miss the life, ya know?"

"And what life was that?"

"You know. Partying. The, well, the women."

"Aren't you married to Emma?"

"Yeah." His face sagged. "But I haven't seen her in two years. You know a lot about me already."

"Did Brody talk to you about Jesus?"

"Jesus?" Cole frowned. "Yeah, but what's He got to do with this?"

"I think Jesus has everything to do with why Brody brought you here. He didn't explain that to you?"

"Well, I mean, he said I need to be forgiven and get a life, basically."

"To receive new life?"

"Yeah. That."

"How honest are you with yourself when you're all alone?" Binsa turned her head a little to eye him from another angle. "Do you believe you have contributed good things to those around you?"

"I've . . . done what I wanted in life, mostly."

"That wasn't my question."

"I guess I haven't done much good for anyone."

"Now, you're sick. You must be thinking about facing God after your death."

"Well, I wasn't. But Brody talked about it so much, it's

all I'm thinking about now. He's a lot more serious than you are, you know."

"And you're comfortable with God judging you? Our choices and behavior in life reveal the truth about our souls."

"I know I haven't done much good. What do you want me to say? That I'm no good? I told Brody I wouldn't win any awards as a father. I'm not proud of what I've done."

"But you said you missed the life. Maybe God allowed you to get sick to open your eyes to what you've done with your life. Have you thought of that?"

"Yeah."

"If God hadn't gotten your attention, maybe you'd still be lost in that life of partying and chasing women. True?"

"Yeah."

"Tell me about your kids."

Cole lifted his head.

"Why? They're . . . not in the picture anymore."

"Are they dead?"

"I—" He swallowed. "I don't know for sure."

"When did you last see your children? I was a mother. As a parent, I think all the time about the last time I saw my daughter, Seneeya."

"It was a long time ago. Besides, my kids were better off without us. We were in a bad way back then."

"Do you think maybe God will treat you the way you treated your kids?"

"What? No, I hope not. Why would you ask me something like that?"

"So, you have regrets?"

"Yeah."

"So, it isn't all about Cole Nevins living for himself. You actually care about how you've mistreated others."

"Of course. I'm not an animal."

"But you've treated others like animals. That's what GLOW does, doesn't it? For almost ten years, you've stolen and sold people for them. Now, you scam people over marriages somehow. Maybe it's time to stop treating people like animals. True?"

"Yeah."

"Our conscience can be hardened, but it never really goes away, Cole. One way to keep a clear conscience is to behave as God intended. Do you understand that?"

"Yeah."

"But our behavior doesn't erase the evils we've already done or the wicked heart that we have."

"That's what Brody said."

"I'm sure he did. We read from the same book—the Bible. Have you ever read from the Bible?"

"No, not that I remember."

"Are you ready to be made new? To be forgiven by God? He loves you dearly, Cole Nevins. It's time to be embraced by your Savior before you die in your sins."

"I don't know . . ."

Cole raised a single hand to his brow. His shoulders jerked as he sobbed softly. While he wept, Binsa spoke plainly what he needed to do to be born again. Faith alone would see him saved from the penalty of eternal hell, but salvation was a gift from God that Cole himself had to receive. When asked if he recognized he was a filthy criminal before God the Judge. He nodded without speaking. When asked if he believed Jesus had died for Him so he didn't need to be punished for his terrible sins, he nodded again.

"Why don't you pray aloud right now, Cole," she urged. "Tell God your heart. It's humbling, I know. I'm right here, but you need to allow God to clear the air and bring peace to your tired soul. Pray, my son."

He remained silent for so long, Binsa wondered if he would pray at all. Maybe he wasn't ready.

"God," he finally said, "I'm really messed up. I have no idea what I'm doing, but I don't want to die and go to hell. I'll try to be a better person now, but You'll have to fix all my . . . past stuff. I've done . . . all the bad things. If there's forgiveness for me, I really, really need it. *Really.*"

"Ask Him to come into your life and tell Him that you believe He'll make you new."

Cole blubbered through a few more incoherent statements, until he could no longer speak at all. Binsa moved to stand behind him and placed a hand on his shoulder, but his real comfort needed to come from God now. She was thankful Brody hadn't rushed to reunite Cole with Marcy. This way, his soul's most desperate need could be addressed without the emotions involved from such a reunion. But with his godly sorrow in place, he was ready.

"Brody?" Binsa called.

"I'm here." He walked into the room, Zayed a step behind him.

"Sit with him," Binsa instructed. "I'll get her."

She crossed the hall and knocked on Greg's door. He answered in shorts, a t-shirt, and bare feet.

"Hi, Binsa." He turned and walked back to his computer terminal where Marcy sat. "You should see how many people responded to our new trafficking site. Reports are pouring in from all over."

"We need to vet most of them still," Marcy said, "but TROAS is ready to open new files on two we've already vetted."

"Good work, you two. Marcy? May I introduce you to someone? Greg, you come as well."

Binsa was trusting God with what had occurred thus far, but she couldn't stop the nervous trembling in her belly as she led Marcy back to her apartment.

Brody tapped Cole on his shoulder.

"Someone's here to see you."

Cole turned at the same instant Marcy must've recognized him, because she stopped just inside the door.

"Oh, no," Cole muttered, rising slowly to his feet as he wiped his eyes with the back of one hand. "Marcy."

Marcy stared at her father for just a second more, then she opened her arms and rushed to him.

"Dad!"

Binsa wished she had her camera to capture the shock on the broken man's face. That shock froze him in unresponsive stillness until his arms seemed to lose their paralysis. He embraced the girl who was hugging him, and then his knees seemed too weak to support his weight and he dropped to the floor. Together, they huddled on the carpet, Cole gasping from sobs, clinging to his daughter, while Marcy consoled her father.

Wiping away tears of her own, Binsa's smile remained as she took an arm of Marcy and Cole and guided them to the sofa in the living room.

"Take your time." She touched their heads. "You've both been through so much." Binsa looked up and nodded at Brody.

"Is he next door?" Brody asked.

"Yes, in Marcy's apartment."

Brody left the room, and a moment later, she heard his muffled voice in the hallway. Marcy had a heart softened by the compassion of Christ, so she'd been trusted to respond in the midst of the surprise. But Aidan was still adjusting to the wonders of forgiveness, so it was wise that Brody coached the boy a little before meeting his father.

Aidan hesitantly entered the room, Brody's arm over his shoulder. Looking up from his daughter, Cole checked his emotions. Aidan shuffled closer, glancing at Brody for support.

Cole stood from the sofa and faced his son. Binsa wondered who looked frailer—the aging, dying father, or the boy recovering from years of abuse—still gripping his baseball glove in his good hand.

"I always wondered if this day would ever come." Cole set his jaw and shuddered. "Sometimes, I wanted it to happen. Other times, I didn't. I can see you've grown into a fine young man, son."

Aidan looked away. Binsa hoped he was reviewing in his mind the spiritual lessons Brody had taught him through playing catch.

"Marcy said she wanted to find you." Aidan tucked his mitt under his limp arm, then hung his thumb in his waistband. "I'm still trying to remember what happened when we were kids."

"Your father was a . . . coward." Cole's lip quivered. "That's what happened. I was a coward about being a father. I should've been a man who took care of his family, who protected his kids."

"Where's Mom?" Aidan asked.

"I don't know. Brody?"

"We'll find her," Brody vowed.

"I'm sorry, son." Cole shook his head. "I can't— I'm just so sorry."

Binsa sensed the two had been estranged for so long that they'd need to work things out, so she approached Aidan and took his hand in hers.

"Why don't we visit over some sherbet, okay? Marcy, would you get the bowls, please?"

Aidan seemed skeptical about everyone's friendliness, and he watched his father with guarded eyes, but the atmosphere was otherwise light, even jovial. Marcy was carefree, like her eight years of trials had been nothing out of the ordinary. Cole had an air of relief about him, and his very posture showed that something had changed.

After Marcy served everyone, Binsa noticed only Zayed standing aloof, a bowl and spoon in his hands and a paper package under his arm.

"You don't want to sit, Zayed?" she offered.

He shook his head. Binsa approached him as those at the table admitted they had brain freeze from eating the cold dessert too quickly.

"It's good to see you have safely returned, my brother." Binsa searched Zayed's stoic face. "As I promised, I prayed for you on your first journey with Brody. God has made him a strong man for the sake of others. It says much about you that he wanted you with him."

Zayed seemed uncomfortable with her comments.

"The Ukrainians are a peculiar people," Zayed said. "They have many strange superstitions and rituals. We spoke to some at the airport while departing. Their hand-embroidered shirts are unlike anything I've seen anywhere in the world. They're called *vyshyvanka*."

He handed her the package.

"A present for me?"

She unwrapped it with eagerness that surprised even herself, revealing a white blouse with red, blue, and yellow embroidery up and down the sleeves. Flowers, flags, and designs perched unevenly across the shoulders, and the sleeves ended in ruffles and elastic.

"Oh, I love it, Zayed! I've seen these costumes often in Ukraine while there, but I never slowed down to buy one. I'm flattered you thought of me while you were away. My gift for you is much less . . . decorative."

"Me?" His dark brow rose in surprise. "I'm not worthy of a gift."

"Wait here." She walked quickly to her bedroom and picked up a pear-shaped metal object. Hefting it in her hand, she returned to Zayed and gently set in his hand.

His face was an instant mask of dread as he recognized the object: a fragmentation grenade. He dropped his bowl and spoon to delicately hold the grenade in both hands. For an instant, he eyed it as if examining an egg for a fractured shell.

"It's okay," he announced to the room. "The pin is still in place."

"Oh, I'm so sorry!" Binsa exclaimed. "I thought you would appreciate this thing." She knelt to pick up the bowl and wipe up the ice cream from the carpet.

Zayed looked from her to Brody, who was standing rigidly nearby. He cradled the grenade as if it were a baby chick.

"Binsa, that's a grenade." Brody walked closer to examine the device while it was still in Zayed's hands. "That could've killed everyone in the room."

"No, I made sure it was disarmed." She felt sorry for their concern. "You said Zayed used to carry a grenade. I bought this one from our military friends in Pensacola and disarmed it myself. Now, Zayed can carry it as a harmless weapon—though of course, his enemies won't know it's disarmed."

"You disarmed a grenade?" Brody gently took the device from Zayed's hands and inspected it himself. "Where did you learn to disarm a grenade?"

She felt her neck warm from the attention in the room.

"I'm very sorry to have frightened all of you." She gestured to Zayed. "It was meant as a surprise for Zayed. A gift."

"Oh, I'm . . . very surprised," the Saudi assured.

"My grandfather was in the Nepalese militia," Binsa said. "He used to change grenade fuses on the kitchen table. It's not difficult. Zayed can use it during his travels with you."

"Huh." Brody's eyes narrowed, as if he were seeing her in a completely different light. He felt the weight of the grenade in his hand a few more seconds, then tossed it back to Zayed. "Binsa disarms explosives. Who would've thought?"

Those at the table breathed easier and returned to their sherbet. Binsa washed her hands of the spilt dessert, and Zayed joined her at the sink.

"I like it." Zayed tapped a fingernail on the grenade casing. "Very clever. Perhaps I should've gotten you something different—a dagger with a serrated edge, perhaps? Or an RPG tube?"

"No, of course not." She smiled and clutched the embroidered blouse closer. "I didn't know you were getting me anything. This is perfect. Thank you. Brody never buys me any mementos when he travels."

"Hey, I heard that," Brody called from the table. "I bring you lots and lots of things. I bring you people, including Zayed there. Don't they count for anything?"

"Were we supposed to get each other gifts?" Marcy asked. "No one told me."

"I didn't get anyone anything," Greg said. "What'd I miss?"

"Listen," Binsa said firmly. "No one was supposed to get anyone anything, okay?"

"Then why did you and Zayed exchange gifts?" Brody asked, a knowing gleam in his eye.

Saying nothing more, Binsa stalked from the room to lay the embroidered blouse in her room. But Brody's question remained in her ears. *Why indeed?* Zayed had thought of her, and she'd thought of him. It was completely unexpected. It had been years since she'd thought about anyone . . . this way.

Later that night, Binsa busied herself in her kitchen as Marcy and Greg sat with Cole in her living room. Aidan stood near the window in the corner, his eyes revealing his skepticism toward his father. Marcy was doing most of the talking, counseling Cole in how she hoped he would proceed in life, and what it meant to her to find her father after so many years, no matter what he'd done.

Binsa could hear every word in the quiet apartment, so she didn't approach them. Rather, as in past situations of this nature, she'd found it best to get out of the way once she'd brought people to the table. God could be trusted to reconcile where Satan had initially caused ruin. Marcy was proving herself a sound minister of God's truth, since the Holy Spirit had quickened her spirit years earlier in her captivity. She'd even read the Bible in its entirety in the past year. The severity of life's events for the young lady had refined her zeal as well as her love for God.

Greg mostly listened, though he offered small comments to affirm Marcy's explanations regarding God's eternal purpose for all of their lives.

It was late now. Brody and Zayed had left after finishing dessert. Binsa had almost forgotten about her awkward gift exchange with Zayed until she heard a light knock on the door. She opened it to find Brody. He surveyed the living room to find Greg and Cole still there with Marcy and Aidan.

"Can I steal you away for a few minutes?" he asked softly so as not to disrupt Marcy's monologue.

"Of course." Binsa wiped her hands on a sink towel and closed the door as Brody led her back to his apartment.

"You might consider some living room furniture soon," Binsa advised, "if you're set on holding meetings so often in here. True?"

"Oh." Brody glanced about the room as if he hadn't noticed before. "Greg found Emma Nevins. You'll want to hear this."

He seated himself next to Zayed, who sat cross-legged on the floor. Zayed set aside his tablet to offer Binsa his hand in support as she lowered herself. Only when she was halfway seated did Binsa notice that Brody had held out his arm to her as well, but she'd accepted the newcomer's help instead. Another awkward moment involving Zayed, Binsa reflected, but Brody didn't make an issue of it. He was wholly focused on the next mission.

"Emma is in Nepal," Brody began, sharing his tablet screen with her.

"Nepal?" Binsa couldn't hide her surprise. "No wonder we're talking. I'm going home? What about France?"

"Zayed and I can handle France. You already connected with the church there, so we can coordinate the rest. I'd like you to do recon on Marcy's mother before we go there next."

"Of course. I'll have Greg make arrangements tonight. The rest of Emma's information seems to be here. Anything else?"

"Unfortunately, yes." Brody and Zayed shared a look of concern. "Jerome had a falling out with us in Ukraine."

"I guessed something had happened since he didn't return with you."

"He couldn't fathom our pursuit of Cole's repentant heart. Jerome could see no value in it. It seems our Homeland Security friend is too focused on law enforcement to appreciate what we do for Christ."

"What's happening in my apartment is a miracle. True?"

"True," Zayed agreed. "It is a miracle, like God saving me."

"Which Jerome also opposed," Brody said, "even though legally, Zayed, you're serving an undisclosed sentence in the custody of TROAS. It's been approved at the highest level of the U.S. Department of Justice, where we'll also need to go to speak to them about Cole. Cole will need to turn himself in and face his crimes under the law. If he cooperates with them and he's truly repentant, he won't serve much time. His health will be good reason for the state to leave him with us. We'll trust God with his future."

"I deserve a death sentence," Zayed said, "but here I am with . . . Well, I'd rather be nowhere else on earth."

"And I think Cole will feel the same way," Brody said.

"What's your policy," Zayed asked, "on people like Jerome who become adversaries? This can't be the first for TROAS."

"We must remain Christ-like toward him," Binsa said.

"Yet remain guarded," Brody added. "In an effort to win Jerome, I let him into our circle. He resisted, but I kept trying. We're more vulnerable now because I tried to help his needy soul and failed. Now he says he'll report us, whatever that means."

"But we must do the same thing again for another person." Binsa smiled at Brody. "Even if it's a risk, we would do it again. True?"

"Yes, I would. Since we're safe in Christ, we can allow ourselves to be vulnerable while trying to help others. God fights our battles, and we take precautions by not being careless with our security."

"Keeping our doors locked doesn't mean we don't trust God," Binsa said. "It means we stand in faith, and we won't test God over what He promises. God gives us the pleasures of responsibility like this."

"If Jerome comes after us, now knowing we're not law enforcement like he expected, there may be repercussions, legal or otherwise."

"But you have contacts," Zayed said. "We'll be fine, right? With your Justice Department friends or someone?"

"God doesn't promise we'll be fine physically, but he does promise we'll remain secure spiritually," Brody reminded. "That's where our rest is—in Him. It shouldn't surprise us when assurances on earth break down under outside pressures. What I'm saying is, even our friends in the government who use our organization for their own reasons, might not stand with us or for us if someone powerful enough targets us."

"True. We are aware and prepared," Binsa said. "You and Greg have done well to keep us secure."

"We mustn't become distracted." Brody folded his hands. "Let's pray right now. Cole has a long road ahead of him. From what Greg uncovered about Emma, she's no less entrenched in the GLOW network. What began with selling her kids for drug money has brought her to becoming a madam in a brothel in your own hometown, Binsa."

"Maybe even with the people who killed my own daughter."

"I should go with Binsa to Nepal instead of to France with you, Brody," Zayed said. "She would be safer in that country with a man by her side."

"Legally, Zayed, you're supposed to remain at my side. Binsa knows what's waiting for her in Nepal. Besides, the French authorities asked that I bring someone I trust to accompany me. It's a serious op. Binsa, I don't want you to move on Emma in Kathmandu until we join you. This won't be like sneaking up on Cole in Ukraine. No one from GLOW was even watching him. But Emma is tied in with GLOW security, Greg believes. There may be violence, but Zayed and I will handle that part when we arrive."

"I'll stay with our friends in Kathmandu," Binsa said in submission, "and I won't contact anyone in my old neighborhood until you both arrive."

"The world is panicked about the spreading virus," Brody said. "They should be frantic about their spiritual depravity, but instead, they're frantic about trying to control what can't be controlled. Let's pray we don't get distracted by the fears around us, whether those fears are orchestrated or legitimate. Hell has a gaping throat. Sin and Satan are our primary enemies. If we can see people delivered by Christ from these enemies, then any other concerns begin to pale in comparison."

Binsa closed her eyes and waited for one of the men to begin praying. In her heart, she was already thanking the Father for allowing her to accompany such men of faith—Brody, a veteran, and Zayed, a spiritual newcomer. Like Zayed, she wanted to be nowhere else but serving the Lord within TROAS.

The same morning that Binsa left for the airport to catch a commercial flight to Nepal, Brody and Zayed departed in a chartered jet for France. Senator Elliot Madison had a crime-fighting appearance to uphold, and

Brody didn't mind being used on a contract basis as long as his faith wasn't compromised or his ministry restricted.

Sixteen hours later, he and Zayed stood on the terrace of the Notre-Dame de La Garde Basilica overlooking the Old Port of Marseille, France. From the height of the nineteenth century cathedral, they could see the fringes of central Marseille all the way out to the blue-green sea of the Mediterranean.

Brody appreciated Zayed's quiet demeanor as they took in the city of their next mission, surveying it in the daylight. During their flight from Tampa to Paris, they'd spoken mostly of Bible truths and a believer's proper behavior. Since Zayed wasn't a nervous man, he hadn't asked Brody much about the mission ahead. All Brody himself knew was that the French wanted to lay a trap to catch a GLOW leader in their country, and Brody was supposed to be the bait.

"I've been down there." Zayed pointed at the Old Port, packed with small sailboats and tourists that looked like toys and ants below the limestone hillsides. "The two forts on either side—I took a ferry from one side to the other and back again."

"Work or pleasure?" Brody asked.

"During my medical school days, I was a young sightseer. I wanted to see where my people once invaded."

"Your people?"

"Muslims. Some Arabians among the Africans. Still my people, but no longer my beliefs."

"Yeah." Brody checked the rock terrace beside and behind him. Tourists with cameras and a few drifting lovers wandered past. "I've recovered survivors from all over this area. It's what we once called the French Connection. Heroin was smuggled here from Indochina through Turkey. It was product all destined for the United States."

"I've heard of the French Connection."

"Now, they smuggle people along the same route. The

GLOW network controls it through the Nigerians, Bulgarians, Romanians, Chinese, and locals. Lover boys work the clubs along the street there, offering romance to young women."

"Predators."

"Kidnappers with smiles and nice haircuts."

"Where do they take them from here?"

"There are migrant camps all over France that make great holding places for traffickers. Migrants rarely speak up, even though they know what's going on, because they don't want to get involved and potentially get thrown out of the country. Kidnapped women are put to work among the ninety thousand prostitutes already in the country. Younger girls are moved through the railway system all over Europe and beyond."

"GLOW is far more organized than what we had in the Carolinas." Zayed became tense. "Two people are approaching us. They're not tourists."

Brody didn't look.

"People are probably saying the same thing about us, that we don't look like tourists."

"Mr. Sladrick?" called a man's firm voice with a rich accent.

Turning, Brody was about to greet their French contacts, but instead, Zayed stepped forward and offered a hand to a tall Frenchman, his gray stubble making him look older than his fit forties frame appeared.

"*C'est moi.* It is I. We've been expecting you," Zayed said, shaking the Frenchman's hand. "Jean Perec?"

"*Oui.* I am Captain Jean Perec. This is my associate, Specialist Colette Quinon. She has worked trafficking cases for many years."

"I am pleased to meet you, Monsieur Sladrick," the captain greeted in French. The woman's face was narrow but pretty, her blond hair pulled back in a messy ponytail. When she shook Zayed's hand, her sidearm was revealed in a shoulder holster. "I have had my doubts you even existed."

"I'm sure the legend is greater than the man." Zayed bowed his head slightly. "This is my associate . . ."

Brody offered his hand to the captain, who was also armed, his concealed sidearm in the holster under his light jacket.

"You may call me Eutychus. I'll be Mr. Sladrick's second for this operation, as you requested."

"Very well. *Commencons*. Let's commence." The captain directed their attention out to sea. "We have on satellite a boat due in port after midnight tonight. See the Frioul Islands there? The two larger ones side by side are Ratonneau and Pomegues. They are connected by that narrow land bridge, which is not lit at night. That is where the boats land. The immigrants then walk into the island's interior. In the morning, they will take a ferry to the shore here. *Voila*—they are in Europe, undetected." He turned and addressed his associate. "Specialist?"

Colette rested her hands on her hips. She was slender like a distance runner, a determined gaze on her face as she eyed the beach.

"Once on shore while undocumented, they become prey. If the traffickers have not already taken everything from them, their new handlers now do. You know GLOW better than we do, Mr. Sladrick. Their network reaches far beyond our nation's borders, but we want to make a difference right here."

Nodding, Brody looked to Zayed for a response. Zayed hadn't told him that he was switching identities with him, but since the man had initiated the ruse, it was necessary to live up to it.

True to form, Zayed lifted his chin thoughtfully.

"Then this is where we will lay the trap? On the islands or on the shore?"

"When we heard you were responding to our invitation," Colette said, "we were hoping you would allow yourself to be taken. Your captors could perhaps lead us to someone more valuable."

"What about the immigrants?" Brody asked.

"We're not concerned about them tonight," Jean said.

"Some friends of ours would like to take them in," Zayed said. "They're locals who'll keep them safe and help them follow the immigration laws once they're here."

"That's fine." Jean pointed at Zayed. "But we want to use you while you're here. Once GLOW realizes who you are, they'll take you somewhere to meet someone in authority, hopefully in Marseille, but we're willing to follow you wherever they take you."

"We believe a leader is here in Marseille," Colette said. "It may not be the one known as the Executive, but perhaps one of his generals."

"I didn't come here to be a bystander," Zayed said with more bravado than Brody thought he himself had. "How will I be taken and tracked?"

"Our undercover team is on standby," Colette explained. "Like us, they're all Parisians and probably unrecognizable. But we are French. The façade will be more believable to GLOW people if your associate, Eutychus, takes lead on the capture. You can do it at the shore where the ferry arrives. GLOW smugglers will be there to welcome their unsuspecting immigrants."

"Also, we have a dedicated drone to track you via thermal imaging." Captain Jean Perec shifted only his eyes skyward. "We will not rely on tracking devices on your persons, which may be taken from you."

"You must know enough about GLOW, Mr. Sladrick," Colette said, "for your associate to impersonate one of their agents for a few hours."

Zayed frowned and glanced at Brody. Brody wondered if the Arabian was now questioning his switching places with him earlier.

"Yes, we can do it," Brody stated. "GLOW has hunters who work internationally, performing counterintelligence. I know their reputations and a few of their names, so I can impersonate one of the GLOW hunters for a few hours, and push my way in."

They looked to Zayed for his approval, and he nodded. They spoke of additional details that would contribute to the conclusion of the operation once they were satisfied that a high-ranking GLOW leader was identified.

"All right then, we dare not be seen with you any further," Colette said. "Watch where the ferry docks this evening, and you will know where to be at dawn. You will not see us until after we recover you, but we will be watching your every move, Mr. Sladrick. Please know you will not be alone."

"I'm honored to work with you all for such an important operation," Zayed bowed his head again. "God is certainly with us tonight."

Colette smiled.

"We've heard from survivors whom you've rescued that you are a preacher of Jesus the Christ. I'm an atheist, but I've learned that you have become a refuge for many lost people. Law enforcement have also referred to you by the codename, RefugeGate, therefore, we're calling this Operation RefugeGate for that reason."

"As long as it's understood Jesus is our refuge, not me. I'm simply a man who points others to the Gate of Refuge. *He* is the one in whom all people should trust."

"Regardless." Colette dismissed his words with a wave of her hand. "This is Operation RefugeGate for us because you are here, Mr. Sladrick. It is an honor for us. You are the one with superior experience, so we will not instruct you further."

Leaving the basilica hilltop, Zayed leaned closer to Brody.

"That's it? No more planning?"

"Of course not. You're the great Sladrick, Mr. RefugeGate. You don't need to be told what to do, do you?"

"I should've warned you." Zayed sighed. "I thought it best to protect your identity in public. Now, I'll need you to protect my life in private. I am *not* Sladrick."

"Well, I appreciate the gesture." Brody chuckled. "But you made your bed. Now you have to sleep in it."

"You're laughing?"

"Yeah, I'm laughing. I wouldn't want to be you!"

"But, I'm you."

"Tonight, you're going to be the most hunted agent finally captured and turned over for torture by GLOW operatives. Thanks, by the way. I didn't feel like having a bloody nose tomorrow morning."

"A bloody nose?"

"You don't think I can turn in Sladrick to GLOW without evidence of a struggle, do you?" Brody put his hand on Zayed's shoulder. "Let's go have a look at that shoreline, then prepare for Operation RefugeGate. One of our advantages is that GLOW doesn't know we're coming. We'll watch the ferry land tonight, then go back to the hotel to sleep for a few hours and call Greg. Binsa should be in Nepal by now, and that's where our focus will be after tomorrow. But first things first."

"It's not too late for you to be Sladrick," Zayed said. "You know better how you should act in front of them."

"No, your instinct was right. We're both acting tonight. I'll be a GLOW enforcer, and you'll be Sladrick, the hated disrupter of human trafficking. And along the way, we might actually point some souls to the real Refuge Gate."

As dawn broke on a clear Mediterranean day in Southern France, Zayed stood in an alley of Marseille and presented his face to Brody. Deep in the Arabian's heart, he swelled with pride at the opportunity to sacrifice himself in this way.

"Do it," Zayed said. "It's necessary."

"Yeah, I know." Brody made a fist and looked at it,

then he looked at Zayed's face. "This could hurt."

"A little of my pain will save others from much more."

"I was talking about my hand." Brody frowned. "I don't want to hurt it."

As Zayed cracked a smile, Brody punched him at a sharp angle across the bridge of his nose. Blood poured from his nostrils as he doubled over, dripping crimson onto the alley floor. He spit and raised his head, allowing the blood to trickle down his chin and onto his shirt front.

"How's your hand?" Zayed asked, his eyes watering.

"Better than your nose. Sorry." Brody gently gathered Zayed's hands behind his back and zip tied his wrists with a black tether. "The cut in the plastic is on the inside. When it's time, clasp your hands together and force your wrists apart. It should break at the point of the cut."

"I understand." Zayed sighed loudly and faced Brody. "Okay, I'm ready."

"Are you regretting that you volunteered to be Sladrick?"

"The bigger picture is more important. Your face will remain a mystery to most, and we're removing part of the GLOW network today. The French get to make a few arrests, and we help some immigrants connect with the French church. I've said before: I'd rather be nowhere else."

"Me also, Brother." Brody turned him roughly to face the street. "This is where it gets tricky."

"You've seen my soul saved and secured in the arms of our Shepherd," Zayed professed. "If something goes wrong, if they shoot me dead on sight, I go to a place of glory without shame."

Zayed noticed that Brody didn't respond, which made him wonder if the veteran operative was getting emotional as he had through the night. When they'd prayed in the hotel room, Brody's heart had been touched by the magnitude of suffering happening in the city very near to where they knelt. In that peaceful moment, Zayed himself was moved to tears as well, but also to boldness—knowing that God was with them in their stand of love against the horror and selfishness of human trafficking.

"So, you have one tranq-pen in your pants pocket," Brody reminded, leading Zayed to the waterfront. "Hopefully they overlook it. I have your fake grenade, another pen, a knife, and a gun as props for my role. But killing people isn't an option. Not for us. Remember that, even if it costs us our own lives."

"I understand."

Even as his eyes watered and his nose bled, Zayed walked with his head held high. Few French civilians were out so early. The merchants who passed them on the pavement looked at him with criticism. Brody kept a hand on his left arm, as if he were an officer escorting a crook down to the waterfront.

The ferry from the Frioul Archipelago was nearly to shore. There were no customs officers or officials in sight, even as potentially dozens of illegal immigrants were about to arrive.

Then Zayed spotted them—three SUVs parked on the shoulder of the street near Canabiere, the historic street ending at the old quarter of Marseille. The street was mostly filled with pedestrians, but the four dark-clad men who stood outside their vehicles didn't seem the type to follow local customs.

Brody stopped Zayed next to a boat house. Hundreds of sailboats lined the Old Port, their masts undisturbed by the natural harbor's still morning air.

"Timing is everything," Brody said under his breath. "We need to wait for the moment of optimal pressure, when they're forced to act rashly and accept what I tell them in the moment."

Zayed looked from the ferry to the four men near the SUVs who were also watching the ferry. The ferry was yards away from the dock. It appeared crowded with passengers—obviously more than should've been arriving from the communities of the small islands. As he watched, Zayed noticed most of the passengers were carrying backpacks and clutching heavy coats, like they'd been traveling from far away and had slept outside for days.

"Now," Brody said, and pushed Zayed forward.

The men at the SUVs were so focused on the ferry that they didn't notice Zayed until he was a few yards away. Zayed felt fear deep inside his pounding chest. His hands were bound and he was a captive. These men wanted him dead. Sure, he could break his binds, but then what? The four men were armed, and GLOW had intentionally sent men who appeared intimidating to bully the illegals to do their will.

"Look who I found snooping around!" Brody shouted in French, then shoved Zayed into the largest of the four toughs, a bald man with a neck tattoo. "Put him in the cab. We'll take him with us."

The four men jostled against Zayed and seemed unsure about their response. Two put their hands on their sidearms. The bald one grabbed Zayed by the collar. Zayed was two hundred pounds, but the bald barbarian jerked him around like a child.

"Who are you?" asked a clean-cut Frenchman, signaling his men to remain calm. "And who is this?"

"I work for the Executive," Brody said. "And . . . that's Sladrick."

"Sladrick!" The clean-cut man visually measured Zayed's features. "Greek? Or Italian?"

"Does it matter?" Brody held out a hand toward the ferry. "Get him loaded up. Here they come. We'll discuss it up at the house."

"Get him inside," the man said in agreement.

The bald one opened a rear door and hurried Zayed into a back seat, but left the door open for the approaching men, women, and children. The plastic cut into Zayed's wrists behind his back. He guessed with just a little more pressure, he could break the tether along the cut Brody had provided, but it was too early to spring their trap. The French special forces were watching from above and nearby. They were relying on him to bear up until it was time. Brody was obviously playing his part in a convincing way.

"Welcome to France!" the four men greeted the new arrivals.

Zayed watched as even Brody offered a hand to the immigrants, directing them into the three vehicles. An entire family of five joined Zayed on the seat. Between the three SUVs, it appeared that nearly forty were crammed into every conceivable inch.

Finally, it was time for Brody and the four GLOW traffickers to load up. One took to each of the driver's seats, which left Brody and the bald one to pile inside. Brody climbed into the middle seat, forcing a mother and her child to stand awkwardly until he closed the door. The woman had nowhere to sit except on Brody's knee, and the child on her lap. The refugees didn't speak, but Zayed saw their furtive glances. They were nervous. Stern men with guns had just taken them into their vehicles. Surely, they'd heard in their countries of origin how immigrants were mistreated.

Suddenly, the door next to Zayed opened. The bald Frenchman manhandled Zayed, thrusting him off the seat onto his side on the floor of the back seat. Zayed gasped for breath, momentarily panicked by the dim crowded space on the floor amongst the feet of the people—who had nowhere to rest their feet except on top of him. An instant later, the bald one pressed his size onto the seat where Zayed had been, and the brute placed his heavy boots on Zayed's legs.

Closing his eyes, Zayed prayed for calm. A little discomfort was acceptable. The lives of others were more important. His sacrifice was saving Brody from such treatment. Together, they were standing with God against

Satan's darkness in the world. This was a battle not of flesh and blood . . .

"Where are we going, Momma?" a child asked in Arabic, the language of Zayed's own childhood.

"Shhh, Avrim, not far," the mother responded.

Zayed could tell by their dialect that they were probably from Syria or Lebanon. During his own trafficking schemes, he'd taken advantage of such people searching for safety and a new start. Now, he wondered if any of the people that day in the vehicle with him were Christian brothers and sisters fleeing persecution. Some were Africans, and others from farther east, Persians and Afghans.

The SUV swerved along city streets, then climbed the hills that contained old Marseille against the sea. Zayed opened his eyes, ignoring the feet resting on him, and tried to track their whereabouts out of the city. The road was paved for a stretch, probably in a suburb of the city, then they slowed. The sun was lost as the vehicle drove into an enclosure and parked. Doors opened. The bald one ordered everyone to get out and line up against the wall.

One of the men grabbed Zayed, dragged him out of the SUV, and dropped him heavily onto the cement floor of a small warehouse. He didn't stop depending in his heart on the comfort of God. He wasn't alone. His Savior had suffered far worse for him, so he could suffer a little for others. This was his new calling.

CHAPTER EIGHT

Brody climbed out of the SUV in the warehouse in Marseille, France. As if he were a GLOW enforcer, he joined the other four GLOW aggressors to line up the illegal immigrants, their backs against the outer wall. Gone was any pretense of friendliness they'd displayed on the shore. It disgusted Brody to impersonate the darkness for even a moment, since he'd worked as a light in the darkness since his teen years.

When a Syrian man stepped away from the wall to gather a little girl to him, Brody shoved him back with overwhelming force. The girl finished collecting a dropped backpack, then ran back to her father. But Brody had a facade to project. He drew his sidearm, a Beretta nine-millimeter, and pointed it straight-armed at the man's forehead.

"No, no!" The clean-cut boss of the Frenchmen hurried to Brody's side. He gently touched Brody's arm and pushed the weapon down. "They're no good to us if they're dead. Whatever he did, let it go for now."

"I . . . did nothing," the Syrian said in broken English. "My daughter . . ."

After glaring at the Syrian, Brody holstered his weapon and turned to the Frenchman.

"Been on the hunt too long," Brody grumbled. "I see the enemy everywhere."

"Relax, man. These people aren't our enemies. They're our money machines." The Frenchman gestured to the larger bald man who stood over Zayed. "Florent, collect their papers. Search them. I'll take these two to see Duke. You there, bring Sladrick."

Wrestling Zayed to his feet, Brody didn't like leaving

the immigrants alone with the other three, but the operation needed to be fulfilled.

They left the garage space of the warehouse and walked through a set of swinging doors. A middle-aged, thin man in a wheelchair sat at a card table with a laptop and camera before him. A tapestry of a tropical island hung against the wall nearby. It was obviously the backdrop for photographs.

"Duke," the clean-cut one said in French, "we made it with everyone. No problems. Florent is collecting their papers. But these two were at the shore. This one says he works for us. And he says this one is Sladrick."

"Sladrick?" Duke studied Zayed critically. Though his lower body may have been crippled, his face displayed he was a vigilant, cautious man. "Henri, why did you bring him here?"

Brody kept a hand on Zayed, whose head was slightly bowed, but his eyes were busy. Zayed's posture was that of a broken man. Though he'd been roughed up some, Brody was certain he would be ready to act when it was time. Henri seemed at a loss of an answer for Duke.

"I tracked Sladrick here," Brody said. "He appeared intent on intercepting this morning's transports. I'm not being paid to hold him. Kill him or catch him. That was the contract."

"And who gave you the contract?"

"Who else?" Brody scowled. "Don't test me. I have no patience for this. All my contracts come from the Executive."

"How long ago?" Duke sat up straighter. "How long ago did the Executive give you the contract?"

"Look, I'm not here to be questioned," Brody stated. "I've already been paid. You have him now. I have another job waiting."

"What do we call you?"

Brody had contemplated an identity through the night. A couple years earlier, he'd heard that one of

GLOW's hired assassins had been arrested, then killed while in prison. It was possible that GLOW hadn't confirmed his death. But it was a gamble . . .

"Hawk."

"Hawk? You're Hawk?" Duke palmed his phone. "This is a rare moment. Hawk and Sladrick, two men no one's seen in a long while, both now making an appearance in my city."

As Duke made his call, Brody waited. He checked the rest of the room, empty except for a row of high windows set in the metal wall. Whoever Duke was calling had to be a superior, maybe even the GLOW Executive himself. He didn't want to risk his photo being taken—or to be driven somewhere else that separated him from Zayed or from the refugees in the back. The French secret police would just have to work with whoever they could arrest here.

"The sky is blue," Brody said to Zayed the moment it sounded like Duke had connected on the phone.

Lunging forward, Brody kicked the flimsy table into Duke's chest. The man in the wheelchair fell over backwards, his limp legs airborne for an instant before they fell on top of the paraplegic's upper body. Just as swiftly, Brody batted the table aside and drew his tranq-pen. With the crippled man lying on his back, Brody easily slammed the tranq into his ribs.

He turned to confront the clean-cut man, but Zayed had broken through his wrist binds and drawn his own tranq-pen. Henri was no match for Zayed, who may not have been a veteran operative, but his heart was determined. As Henri backed away, Zayed settled for pricking the Frenchman's arm. The man slumped unconsciously a breath later, his sidearm half-drawn.

Facing the swinging doors, Brody expected company, but the three with the refugees in the larger room must not have heard their scuffling. At least Duke and Henri hadn't cried out.

"Eutychus?" Zayed pointed to the phone where it had

fallen a couple inches from Duke's fingers.

Licking his lips, Brody picked up the phone. It was still connected.

"This is Hawk," Brody said, disguising his voice behind a British accent. "You there?"

There was silence on the line. Brody thought perhaps it had been disconnected after all.

"You used to text me," the voice of a woman said. "Nothing for almost two years, and now you call me . . . from *this* number?"

"I have Sladrick." Brody held up his hand for Zayed to remain perfectly silent. *A woman!* Her English was American—a Westerner. "The Marseille office has fallen. I'm standing there now."

"This phone is secure. Is Sladrick alive?"

"Until you say otherwise, but I believe authorities are near."

"If it's fallen, get out of there. Go somewhere. I want Sladrick questioned."

"That's not part of the contract. I'm no interrogator. It's getting too hot. I suggest we wash our hands of him entirely. They'll find his body floating in the Med."

"No. Can you get to Paris?"

"I have no plans."

"Bring him. I'm texting you an address."

"I'm on my way. You'd better make it worth my while."

"Oh, I will."

"Wait." Brody checked the phone screen, thinking on his toes. "I'll use this line exclusively to stay in touch from here on. Not that you'll need me again. You'll have Sladrick."

"There are others. I'll have more contracts for you. I don't like people interrupting my business."

Brody barely breathed as a chill went through his body.

"The Executive is thorough," he tested.

"I'll have a team waiting in Paris for Sladrick."

He ended the call first, more intent on holding to his identity than speaking any further, which could draw her suspicions.

"That was the Executive?" Zayed asked softly.

"Yeah, I think so. It was a woman. She sounded older. And American."

"What? An American woman runs GLOW?"

"She wants me to take Sladrick to Paris."

"So, we go to Paris?"

"Not us." Brody memorized the address she'd sent, then pocketed the phone. "The French police can follow up further leads. The Executive probably won't even be there. She said she's sending a team. But now we know the Executive is a woman. I'll never forget her voice. Maybe the French even recorded her voice. If they did, Greg can run it through voice recognition. Her words were controlled, polished, and cautious. Definitely educated. I'd bet she has a position in the public eye, living a double life. This certainly changes everyone's hunt for the GLOW leadership."

"Now what?" Zayed asked, fondling his tranq-pen.

"Binsa is waiting for us in Nepal."

"I mean, about them." His eyes signaled the swinging doors.

"The French are watching, so they're probably on their way. Might be best if we neutralize those three before there's any gunfire."

"Two of us, three of them?" Zayed nodded.

"Whichever two are farthest away, they're mine. You take the closest one."

"Okay, I'll follow your lead."

"How's the nose?" Brody moved to the swinging doors.

"Worth it." Zayed smiled, then flinched from the pain it caused.

Brody led the way through the doors. The illegals

were now seated against the wall. Bald Florent had a plastic bag full of visas, passports, and phones he'd collected. Their plan was that all travel documents and IDs would be held hostage to keep the new workers in compliance. Duke was probably set up to photograph and assign each person, even the kids, to different jobs—domestic labor for older adults and the sex trade for the rest. Others might've been held to harvest their heart, liver, lungs, and kidneys, depending on blood type.

Moving quickly past the first tough guy, Brody approached Florent. Thankfully, no one had his firearm out.

"Duke is ready," Brody announced. "Let's get them processed. Who's first?"

Florent compared an ID photo with the people in front of him. He suddenly looked past Brody and confusion sparked his face over the presence of who he thought was Sladrick. At that instant, Brody reached him and jabbed him with the tranq. Committed now, Brody charged the farthest man, who was already scratching for his sidearm under his jacket. But Brody was faster and tranqed the man in the shoulder, then held his arm so he couldn't raise his sidearm as consciousness slipped away. Brody looked back. Zayed's man was down as well.

The immigrants huddled more closely together, fear in their eyes. Brody crouched in front of the Syrian who even now held his daughter protectively in his lap.

"You're safe now," Brody said in Arabic. "I'm a friend. My name is Sladrick and I serve Jesus Christ, the King of kings, my Savior and Lord. Please forgive me for frightening you earlier. It was an act. Actually, I'm here to help you all find safety and start new lives. The French authorities will be here soon. Since you've arrived illegally, you'll need to be processed through French customs, okay? But my friends serve Jesus, and they will help you through the process."

Brody held out his hand. Hesitantly, the man placed a weathered hand in Brody's.

"That's good. Now, we're brothers. Come now. Help me take photos of everyone so we can follow them through wherever they're sent after today. We also need to return everyone's papers to them, so help me identify everyone."

Zayed dragged the three unconscious ones into the front room, and Brody spread the identification papers on the hood of an SUV. He took a quick photo of each paper, then a photo of the matching person. Gradually, with the help of the eager Syrian, the newcomers relaxed and began to visit with one another and with Zayed, whose Arabic was far better than Brody's. When the French authorities arrived, the warehouse was secured without drawn weapons.

"Thank you, Mr. Sladrick." Captain Jean Perec shook Zayed's hand. It's been a pleasure to see your results."

"Our people recorded the phone call," Specialist Colette Quinon reported to Zayed, but included Brody. "She used a proxy server to place the call, but we now know much more than we did, and we'll be sharing it with Interpol. Hopefully, we'll find out more when we interrogate these five men. Thanks to you, we'll arrest more in Paris in a few hours."

Brody stepped aside as several officers in black facemasks escorted the five in cuffs out of the warehouse. Duke was cuffed in front, his hands in his lap, as a policeman pushed his wheelchair outside. All five appeared duly humiliated rather than defiant.

"We have to be somewhere else," Zayed said. "Paris is your operation."

"And what if the Executive calls you again?" Colette asked Brody. "You have the phone now, the phone she'll use to call you. To her, you are the Hawk. When the Paris operation falls apart when she thinks she's getting Sladrick, she'll suspect you."

"I can't control that, Specialist," Brody said. "But

know this, we want the same things for these people. What happens with her or to her may be out of your jurisdiction, but not mine. I'm willing to share transcripts of calls, but I think we'll hang onto the phone for now."

"What jurisdiction do you two have?" Jean asked.

"When I'm in France again," Zayed shook their hands, "I'll give you a call."

Remaining a mystery, Brody and Zayed made their exit to the street. Brody drew out his own phone as they walked toward the city. Zayed hailed a cab.

"Zayed!" Brody called and held up his phone for him to see a text message from Greg.

"*Binsa never reached Nepal?*" Zayed's face turned gray. "Where is she?"

As they climbed into a cab, Brody dialed Greg.

"Greg, it's me. We're done in Marseille. Just got your text about Binsa. Tell me what you know."

"It's a long flight to Nepal with multiple connections," Greg said. "I thought she was just taking her time to check in with me once she got there. There was no reason to suspect anything was wrong."

"We left Tampa at the same time, Greg," Brody said. "That was a day and a half ago."

"I know. Backtracking from Kathmandu, I found she never made any of her connecting flights. Brody, she didn't even board the plane in *Tampa!*"

"She's still in the U.S.," Brody said. "We're coming home, Greg. Find some answers before we get there."

Brody turned off his phone and looked into Zayed's concerned eyes.

"They took her?" Zayed asked. "While we were ambushing them, they ambushed her?"

"Don't jump to conclusions."

"But she's missing."

"Someone may have taken her, but we don't know it was GLOW. Greg will check hospitals, jails, everything he can between the apartment and the airport. There are cameras."

"Who else could it be but GLOW?"

Brody gazed out the taxi window.

"We should've sent her in the jet, and you and I could've chartered another flight or taken a commercial flight."

"You couldn't have known, Brody."

"Well, we know now. The world is getting more dangerous for us. Whoever it is, they're interfering with our work for the Lord. That's not going to go well for them— since God doesn't take lightly the suffering of His people."

"I'll do anything to get her back," Zayed said. "Brody, I'm afraid . . . that I would kill right now for her."

Removing the dummy grenade from his pocket, Brody returned it to Zayed.

"We're all being tested right now," Brody said. He could tell Zayed was clenching his jaw, but then he relaxed and looked away. There was nothing more to say, so they didn't speak again until they'd arrived at their hotel to pack. Then they drove in silence to the airport, though they were each deeply in prayer.

Sister Binsa had been kidnapped. Brody felt responsible. He had to get her back, but in God's way. Occasionally, God used a whirlwind to accomplish His goals, Brody remembered, and he certainly didn't mind being the force behind that wind right now.

Agent Jerome Wessel studied the calm St. Petersburg neighborhood through the living room front window. The house at the edge of a Florida suburb had been on the Homeland Security inventory of assets, used for years by other departments as well, sometimes as a safe house, sometimes as a surveillance outpost. It had a basement, and that's what mattered to Jerome this time.

Nothing significant moved on the street outside, but

he was still edgy. He kept telling himself that he had nothing to fear, since he was upholding national security interests. But far deeper than his ethical fortitude, he was afraid Brody Sladrick could expose him, or Greg Rotz might discover him. However, TROAS' attempts to interfere wouldn't matter once Jerome got what he wanted. He would bring TROAS down to its knees!

He popped a couple cashews into his mouth. *Fear Sladrick?* Scoffing, he cursed himself for ever idolizing the man. It sickened him to think about being in the self-righteous man's presence again. Christians like him seemed okay at first. Yes, they were very moral, but underneath that layer of kindness, they were a liability to national security. Jerome had personally witnessed how Brody had confronted dangerous criminals, and instead of bringing them to justice, the man had embraced them! Zayed Aziz was of course a prime example. But Cole Nevins was the filth of the human race—and Brody had welcomed him into the United States for Marcy's sake.

Sure, Jerome thought, he understood why Marcy wanted to reunite with her father, but it should've been after he was in prison. Brody had operated as a private retrieval expert long enough to know that governments couldn't possibly allow such criminal elements to infect its communities, just because Brody said they'd had a "spiritual awakening." Spiritual awakenings weren't part of Jerome's training because they were pure fantasy, weren't they?

It didn't matter, he decided. Religion needed to remain separate from the Justice Department. Brody needed to go down, his power revoked, his expertise exposed as the threat that it was. Someone was protecting Brody, however, even motivating him and contracting his skills. Whoever that someone was, needed to be exposed as well. Then, TROAS and Sladrick would be isolated and vulnerable. The whole TROAS network would tumble and fall. Even Greg would go to prison if Jerome had his say.

Turning from the window, Jerome acknowledged that he wasn't alone. A local Homeland Security agent stood quietly at the open basement door. His name was Wes Spader, a wiry blond man in his thirties with a definite sadistic side. Maybe all interrogation specialists were a little bit demented. Jerome had already held Spader back from going too far the last couple days.

"She's ready, sir," Spader said, his blue eyes sparkling like he was enjoying himself more than he should. "Sleep deprivation is the bedrock for chemical interrogation—when there's enough time like now to use it."

Jerome slipped his bag of cashews into his blazer pocket and gestured to Spader to lead the way back into the basement. As they descended to the brightly lit basement, Jerome wondered if that descent was a symbol of his own moral decline. He'd crossed a line that he couldn't uncross—he'd betrayed an intimate friend. Never would he be able to call something righteous that he knew was wicked.

No! He shook himself. Now he was thinking like Brody had spoken. *Righteous* and *wicked* were terms for churches and traitors. This was the U.S. government, and sometimes ugly acts needed to transpire for the good of the nation.

They arrived in the basement where Binsa was bound to a chair, her wrists strapped to the chair's armrests. Spader had lain out plastic tarps underneath her. Soiled and isolated, Binsa had surprisingly endured so far, refusing to answer their questions. Jerome had even taken shifts with Spader to keep her awake, shooting her up with adrenaline, slapping her, placing headphones on her ears that made such horrific noises that no one should've been able to sleep.

On the table nearby, Spader had lain out a number of devices he hoped to use soon to extract information from the forty-seven-year-old woman. Three vials and syringes had already been used, and others remained. And there were tools. When Jerome had requested an interrogation specialist, the department had apparently sent their most depraved, but maybe some dangers needed to be fought with the slightly deranged applying their skills.

Nodding off, Binsa's eyes were half-open. Drugged, she was on the edge of consciousness. Jerome pulled on a pair of rubber gloves, then lifted the woman's chin to look into her face. Her lip was swollen from Spader hitting her, but Jerome couldn't reprimand the younger agent. Other lines might still be crossed. It was Binsa's fault. She withheld what he needed to know to proceed against TROAS. This was an investigation. That justified everything.

"Binsa?" Jerome called to her in her delirium. He remembered her sweetness when first meeting her, her aura of compassion. "Who does Brody know in the U.S. government? Is someone helping Brody Sladrick? Focus, Binsa. We'll let you use the bathroom and clean up as soon as you answer me. Don't you want to sleep? Does Brody rely on someone in the government? This will end if you tell me. You're doing this to yourself. Just talk to me."

Her lips moved.

"She's saying something," Spader said from where he stood next to a camera tripod. He'd hung a sensitive microphone from the ceiling to capture any confession or response. "What's she saying?"

Jerome placed his ear closer to Binsa's mouth.

"Shame . . ." she whispered. "You . . . shame."

He stood upright like he'd been slapped.

"What'd she say?" Spader asked.

"Nothing important."

"Sladrick . . ." Binsa said louder, "coming . . ."

"How can she threaten us?" Jerome fumed at Spader. "She's supposed to be out of her mind by now, rambling information incoherently. You said she wouldn't even know reality from fantasy!"

"I could give her more." He glanced at his table of

syringes. "But I already gave her more than normal. Her system seems resistant. She's so . . . passive. It's strange, like something's interfering."

"That's how these people function." Jerome turned away. "They embrace adversity and call it a gift, and they think justice is resolved on some cross instead of taking responsibility for their own crimes."

"She's received a toxic dose already," Spader said. "We've kept her awake for forty-eight hours. Even I'm exhausted. And giving her more serum could, uh, fry her permanently."

"Oh, now you want to show restraint?" Jerome shouted. "I've been holding you back, remember?"

"The more permanent the damage we do," Spader said, "the harder it'll be to deny our involvement. A toxicologist will be able to see what we've done. I'm committed to getting answers, sir, but deniability is one tunnel that will get smaller the further we go. If you want me to give her more, we may need to dispose of her, you know, entirely, or we'll be leaving too much evidence. People won't understand. Even our own people. Seriously, I don't care, but it's your show."

"Sladrick's too careful." Jerome considered the tools on the table. "He has a sixth sense. It's legendary. We may never get another chance at someone from his inner circle. It's now or never. This is it. Make her talk today. Whatever it takes. Stopping Sladrick is in the interest of national security."

"It's your call." Spader picked up another syringe. "I can make her talk."

Jerome stepped aside to let the sadistic little man administer his next horror. Binsa didn't seem like such a strong person. If he didn't know any better, he'd guess something stronger than herself was resisting every attempt to disclose the secret connections that permitted them to operate TROAS without seeming oversight on American soil.

As Spader spoke soothingly to Binsa, Jerome tuned his ears for noise upstairs. He didn't like not knowing where Brody was and what he was doing. After taking Binsa, Jerome had covered his tracks, but still, this was Sladrick he was trying to fool. And Greg wrote his custom scorpion programs that could cruise the internet like no spyware Jerome had ever seen. Even in her delirium, Binsa kept insisting Brody was coming, which was ridiculous.

Cursing, Jerome climbed the stairs to check the street again. He wondered if having a dozen more security agents and an electric fence outside would make him feel any safer. There was just no telling what unconventional methods Sladrick might use to track down Binsa.

Brody sat on the edge of his bed in the apartment he shared with Greg. They'd arrived back in Tampa overnight, but he hadn't slept except a little on the jet. He'd had enough time for the Lord to settle his emotions from expressing anger to expressing mercy. Whoever had taken Binsa would need all the grace he could muster, not his rage.

On the living room floor, Marcy and Zayed sat close together, facing one another with closed eyes, their quiet voices barely heard as they prayed. Brody had been with them only moments ago. It was an amazing sight, the two of them—an ex-human trafficker and a rescued young woman united in heart for a missing sister in the faith. That was indeed miraculous.

Meanwhile, at his computer desk, Greg rubbed his eyes, then leaned closer to one of his screens. For twenty hours straight, Greg had been on the hunt. They'd deduced together that for all traces of Binsa's disappearance to be removed from city cameras, someone in authority was involved rather than the GLOW network. The recent acquaintance made of Jerome Wessel seemed to be the likely culprit. This was further confirmed by

Jerome's own disappearance after returning to the States from Ukraine over a week earlier.

Suddenly, Greg pushed away from his desk and froze. Brody stood abruptly. Greg pivoted in his chair and stared straight at Brody, Greg's look communicating the desperate heart he had for Binsa's recovery. She'd been like a second mother to him since joining TROAS.

Brody stalked swiftly to Greg, drawing the attention of Marcy and Zayed, who hopped up to join them.

"There's one thing no crook or country's government can ever really erase," Greg explained, dark circles shadowing his eyes. His voice was throaty instead of triumphant. "Everyone leaves a money trail. I just had to narrow it down and exclude about a thousand resources Homeland Security could've used in this type of situation."

"You think that's it?" Brody pointed to an address on the bottom of the screen. "She's in St. Petersburg? That's just twenty minutes from here."

Zayed turned toward the door, with Brody on his heels.

"Wait, Brody!" Greg called, stopping his boss momentarily. "It was Jerome. He requisitioned the residence as well as additional personnel. I can't tell how many personnel, but Jerome's not alone."

"I don't think that matters right now." Brody offered a sad smile. "It's Binsa. They could have an army, but I've got Zayed with me. Jerome has sown the wind. He'll reap the whirlwind!"

After holding the door open for Brody, Zayed closed it as they entered the hallway. They had no gear beyond what they'd used in France, and they hadn't showered or changed their clothes. Even Zayed's eyes were blackened from the punch Brody had given him. The cut on the bridge of his nose was scabbed, but dried blood still stained his neck.

"He's provoking you for a rash response," Zayed

warned in the elevator. "The man will justify shooting us if we go without an invitation."

"When he took Binsa, he sent me all the invitation I needed."

"You have an idea?" Zayed drew his new grenade from his pocket. "All I have is this useless grenade."

"Jerome has underestimated the number of people Binsa has recovered over the years—and he's overestimated his own authority to face the people who care about those recovered people. We have assets we normally never use."

They reached Brody's car and started south. The afternoon sun was setting over the bay.

"Revenge is a difficult temptation," Zayed admitted.

"Don't focus on Jerome. Focus on Binsa."

"I want Jerome to suffer, the same as you do."

"Vengeance is God's responsibility," Brody said. "God will make sure those that sow will reap. We focus on living as Christ, even now. That doesn't mean today is about being passive servants. It's about being assertive disciples."

"It'll affect Jerome's life?"

"Undoubtedly, but only because he's placed himself in the path. We recover Binsa from whatever sinister plot Jerome has designed against us. The consequences of our care for Binsa are on his own head."

Brody dialed his phone. He usually called the senator only when he needed legal influence, as in transferring Zayed's custody for the sake of his own human trafficking efforts. But this was an instance where the government needed to rein in one of its own, and Brody guessed the senator would enjoy flexing his authority for his favorite contractor.

"Who're you calling?" Zayed asked.

"Someone who cares about our work more than Jerome misunderstands what we do."

Zayed replaced his grenade as Brody raced south.

Binsa floated in the fog of the medication she'd been given. Somewhere on the fringe of consciousness, she acknowledged Jerome was snapping his fingers in front of her face, but she struggled to keep her eyelids open or her ears alert long enough to identify what he wanted. She knew he wanted something from her, but instead of giving it to him, she could only pity the terrible choices he was making.

In her more lucid moments, she'd recognized he was torturing her. She felt the pain, but strangely, something inside her didn't allow her to care. It was God, she knew, who was debilitating her from revealing any truth, therefore frustrating Jerome's plans.

She blinked as she tried to focus on the IV inserted into someone's arm next to her. No, it was her arm. Oh, yeah, the chemicals. Jerome held up a tool in front of her face. He wanted something. Names. About Brody. TROAS. The government.

"Who is protecting Brody Sladrick?" he questioned, then took hold of her hand.

It didn't seem like her own finger since the feeling was so far away, like down a long hallway. God was helping her, protecting her, guarding her from doing harm to . . . someone. Brody! Yes, someone named Brody needed her to remain silent. About what? The person in front of her was speaking too slowly. She tried to read his lips, but her eyes closed.

He slapped her. Jerome. Her senses cleared. The drugs were wearing off. The pain rose in her face and up the length of her arm from her fingers. Two fingernails had been removed. She was never one for fingernail polish, anyway.

"This isn't working," Jerome said to a young blond, mousy man. "You gave her too much. Look at her. She can't even understand what I'm saying."

But Binsa could understand. Maybe her mouth wasn't

working right, or her eyes were wandering, but she was back from the fog. Jerome was torturing her for information. She gasped in thankfulness to God that they were still torturing her. If they had stopped, it would've meant she'd revealed some secret in her delirium. Though she couldn't recall what secrets she possessed, she didn't even want to bring them to mind, since what came to mind might trickle from her lips. Think of something else. Yes, her daughter's birthday. Carefully, she mumbled aloud the numbers.

"Seven, nineteen, twenty, twelve."

Jerome gripped her whole head with his hands.

"Did you hear that, Spader?" Jerome asked his companion. "Numbers. A code! Finally, she's giving us something. Write it down."

"We're recording, sir. You can just play back the video later."

Binsa recalled the first place she'd met Brody, a man who'd become closer to her than family.

"*Hanuman Dhoka,*" she remembered. "*Hanuman Dhoka.*"

"What's that?" Spader asked. "Her native language?"

"It could mean something in Nepalese. I think she speaks a few languages. She travels all over the place like Sladrick does. Binsa, can you hear me? Who helps Brody? Who in the U.S. government gives Brody legal privileges? Do you understand?"

"I understand," she slurred, then changed to Dutch. "*Wat is van my is van jou.* (What is mine is yours.) *Hoe kan ik je helpen?* (How can I help you?)"

"Is that German?" Jerome asked.

"No, I know a little German," Spader said. "That's something else."

"*Ik he been medisch onderzoek nodig.* (I need to see a doctor.)"

"It's European," Jerome said. "Is it Portuguese?"

"I'm an interrogator, sir, not a linguist. Who knows what this lady is saying?"

"*Watashi ni nanika goyo desu ka?* (How may I help you?)" she asked in Japanese.

"Binsa, English!" Jerome shouted. "What are you saying?"

"*Nichevo* (Nothing at all)," she said in Russian.

"Was that a different language?" Jerome frowned, his eyes pleading into her face. "What are you saying?"

"*Was du erlebst, kann keine machtder welt dir rauben.* (What you have experienced, no power on earth can take it from you.)"

"That was German," Spader said.

"What did she say?"

"It wasn't real clear, but I think she's messing with you."

"No way. You gave her way too much junk."

"*Bog vam blagoslovi* (God bless you)," Binsa pronounced, repeating the only Serbian phrase she could remember.

Binsa closed her eyes, believing her vision was betraying her. It must've been a vision from God. A third person had descended the stairs behind Jerome. She recognized him. He had come for her.

"Jerome," she said softly, then tried her best to open her eyes again to make sure her eyes weren't misleading her. She didn't want to miss this moment. "Jerome?"

"Yes, Binsa? I'm here. Tell me what I want to know. Tell me how Brody has such influence in the government."

"Oh, Jerome." In an attempt to reach up and touch his face, she found her arms still strapped down. Her tears flowed. "Jerome, you are so loved. Don't forget that. That may not be what you want to know, but it's what you need to know. And . . ."

"And? And?" Jerome and Spader leaned closer. "And what?"

"Brody, don't hurt them."

Jerome frowned.

"Binsa, Brody isn't here. It's me, Jerome. Remember?"

"Oh, Jerome, you are so lost." She sighed. "You should know that God is here . . . And so is Brody. He's right behind you."

Zayed froze on the basement steps. The scene before him was one of his nightmares. Binsa was strapped to a chair, her face swollen, her shirt front bloodied. Jerome and a smaller, wiry man hovered over her, demanding that she answer their questions. Dressed in a white collared shirt, Jerome's sleeves were rolled up, and his right hand held a pair of needle-nosed pliers.

And though Zayed was shaken by what they found in the basement, Brody didn't seem to be as much. Zayed had trafficked domestic workers for a few years, but Brody had been recovering survivors for decades. He'd seen both the trafficked and their traffickers in the most extreme conditions.

As smoothly as a prowler, Brody moved up behind Jerome, and where a camera tripod stood, Brody unclipped the digital camera and tossed the whole device to Zayed. By instinct, Zayed caught it, his attention remaining on the Nepalese woman below who'd captured his affections the last couple of weeks. He cradled the camera in one hand but didn't trust himself to continue silently down the stairs. In his flesh, he wanted revenge. But in his spirit, he sought God's aid and comfort so he could remain where he crouched.

The instant Binsa told Jerome that Brody was behind him, Jerome turned, and Zayed saw the agent's face. *Caught. Exposed. Terror.* His gaze darted to the tripod, and his mouth opened in uncertain shock. Then he noticed Zayed, and Jerome shut his mouth. He appeared determined to speak, to explain himself, but no words came to the man.

"You." Brody pointed to the blond man nearest a tray of syringes and stainless-steel tools. "Lie down on your belly on the floor and don't move."

The young man dropped to the floor like he'd been shot and laced his fingers behind his head. Zayed watched Jerome's gaze drift to the nearby table where his shoulder holster and sidearm lay.

"How unfortunate for you," Brody said, acknowledging the man's pistol too far away to be of any threat. "You have taken a path far away from the caring heart I'd hoped you'd develop."

"I know you won't hurt me." Jerome shifted the pliers in his hand, pointing them at Brody. "You don't believe in hurting people."

"Now how could I hurt a man who's harmed himself as much as you have?" Brody signaled with his thumb. "Step aside. Move."

Jerome backed away. His face revealed an internal struggle, maybe the humiliation of being caught mixed with professional self-righteousness to complete his objective at any cost. Zayed had seen atrocities in Saudi Arabia, but this moment pierced his very soul. Torturing such a gentle woman like Binsa?

Unstrapping Binsa's wrists, Brody then unbuckled the strap around her ribs. She fell into his arms.

"Brody, you're an angel or a dream," she gasped.

Leaping down the last few steps, Zayed took Binsa in his free arm as she rose to her unsteady feet. Her lips revealed her dehydration.

"She needs a hospital," Zayed said to Brody.

"No." Binsa looked over her shoulder at Jerome. "We don't need a medical record of what he has done to me. He knows. Just get me home."

Zayed gave her the camera to hold, then he picked her up in both arms.

"This was justified," Jerome finally stated. "This was

a federal investigation. You are a threat to national security under section—"

"Stop talking," Brody ordered, but without volume. "If this were a legitimate investigation, you would've filed a custody report with any DHS office. But you didn't, so this isn't official. This was personal to you—hurting a woman close to me because you couldn't get to me."

"I didn't file a custody report because Greg would've found me too quickly!" Jerome wiped his nose on his arm. "It's that kind of authority that's too dangerous for you to have."

"So, I'm dangerous, huh?" Brody scuffed his shoe at two bloody fingernails on the plastic sheet on the floor. "I already mobilized the authorities, but I'll call them off. We have what we came for. And I'm keeping the camera. Do we understand one another?"

Jerome licked his lips nervously. Zayed turned and climbed the stairs with Binsa. Brody followed him. When Zayed looked back, the young man still lay on the floor, and Jerome stood holding the pliers, his gaze on the empty torture chair.

"Oh, I'm a mess," Binsa said when they emerged to the ground floor.

"It's nothing." Zayed paused for Brody to open the front door to the residential house. "I'm a doctor, remember? We'll have you washed up and comfortable in bed in no time."

Outside, Brody took the camera from her then opened the back door of the car. Zayed laid her on the back seat, then climbed in to cradle her. Brody drove away while speaking on the phone to his federal-level contacts— the senator's people. But Zayed knew better than to ask questions.

"I thought he was going to kill me," Binsa mumbled.

"He tried, I think." Zayed touched her bruised cheek. "I got a look at those vials on the table."

"What were they?" Brody asked from the front. "You recognized them?"

"Sure. A small amount of any of them—she shouldn't be conscious right now, let alone coherent."

"So, I'm dreaming?" Binsa asked.

Zayed just held her.

Brody called ahead for Marcy to be ready to receive their patient.

"Between Marcy and you," Brody said to Zayed, "we can take care of her better than an over-crowded hospital."

"She needs fluids to flush her system."

"We have medical supplies at the apartment. You can start an IV and hang a bag."

Nodding, Zayed took a deep breath. They'd recovered Binsa. And God had restrained him from hurting Jerome.

"What does this mean for TROAS?" Zayed asked.

Though Brody's eyes in the rearview mirror betrayed his concern, he didn't reply. But Zayed understood. Jerome wouldn't stop. He would keep coming, make a case against Brody or TROAS and try another angle to ruin them. Using the law, Jerome would continue to attack them. The man was driven by professional policies and disgust of Brody's principles. GLOW was no longer TROAS' only powerful enemy.

In Tampa, Zayed carried Binsa into the elevator and to their floor. Marcy was ready and took the woman into her own bathroom. Zayed followed Brody into his apartment where Greg had already laid out a store of medical supplies.

"Is she going to live?" Aidan asked, his baseball glove on his left hand.

"Yes, she will." Brody stood aside as Zayed picked through both first aid and meager surgical supplies—more than enough to treat her dehydration and mangled fingers and facial abrasions. "The Lord guarded her more than we may ever know."

Once Marcy called on Zayed, he carried Binsa in a towel to her own bed. With only Marcy present, and Binsa in and out of consciousness, Zayed examined the woman for further injury. Then, he helped Marcy dress her, start an IV, and bandage her fingers. Once finished, he stood beside Marcy, looking down upon the sleeping woman.

"Angels shouldn't be treated this way," Marcy said, tears in her eyes.

"The world is cruel."

"It was really Jerome?" Marcy wiped her eyes. "What'd Brody do?"

"Brody did what Brody does best. He left Jerome to his own destruction, and he brought Binsa home."

"No one knows more about survival than Binsa," Marcy said. "God still wants her on earth, not in heaven yet."

"Yes. Not yet."

Marcy remained with Binsa, and Zayed found Brody in his apartment, speaking quietly on his phone while Greg and Aidan looked on. Brody pocketed his phone, then picked up the camera recovered from the government house. He drew out the memory card and handed it to Greg.

"Nobody watches this video but you when you're all alone. Understand?"

"Yes, sir." Greg accepted the card along with the burden that was sometimes demanded that he carry when needing to watch certain surveillance.

"I want a transcript of only the audio from the video," Brody continued. "Then upload the video to TROAS' secure database, and make sure it's encrypted. Though I don't believe in blackmail, this leverage may protect the people we love and the work we do. Jerome would be arrested for kidnapping and worse if this gets out. That's what he may deserve, but I still have hope for his soul. We must keep praying for him. Once Binsa wakes up, she'll agree. A little roughing up hasn't changed her heart, I'm sure."

"And the memory card?" Greg asked.

"Burn it."

"Are you going to wait until she's better," Greg asked, "before you go to Nepal, or . . .?"

"Fair question." Brody thrust his hands into his pockets. "We have a window of opportunity to get to Marcy's mom before she relocates again. I say we go now. Binsa could've offered invaluable insight to where we're going, but we know our job. Zayed?"

Lifting his head, Zayed respected Brody even more that he was giving him a voice in the matter.

"Can we wait another day?" he asked. "I'd like to monitor any residual effects from the drugs she's been given."

"Good idea. Then tomorrow, Greg, line up the jet and housing in Kathmandu. Let the church know we're coming and we'll need them on standby."

"I'll arrange it."

Greg went to his computer, and Zayed returned to Binsa's apartment to sit beside her. Marcy stayed with him, which he didn't mind, even though they didn't talk. The young woman had a peace about her that Zayed recognized must come from her faith in God. He knew her story. She had personally experienced more trauma than he had, but the Lord had brought her through it for purposes like this.

"Binsa will be stronger from this," Marcy said suddenly, smiling. "She will be, you'll see."

"I believe you." Zayed nodded, trusting her Christian insight and praying she was right. He didn't want to lose Binsa, not while his heart was still warming to the angel.

❧

Brody walked slowly through the Nepalese bazaar known as Thamel, a tourist center in Kathmandu. The locals around him were wearing jeans, sneakers, and similar Western clothing. It was early evening, and though there should've been more tourists about, the pandemic fears had stunted the tourist trade in the high country that relied on tourism as its central trade.

The single-lane street under Brody's all-purpose boots was hard-packed dirt. Maybe there was pavement underneath, but he couldn't see it. Everyone he'd met in Kathmandu had been friendly since his arrival two days earlier, but the city was in economic straits. Forty percent unemployment plagued the country, and though the people tried to accommodate Chinese investors and Western interests, the Asian country seemed trapped in its Hindu and Buddhist traditions.

He paused next to a sign that read, "Massage Parlor." From his vantage point, the buildings on both sides of the narrow street were three stories tall. But they were barely visible behind the hundreds of signs written in various languages, including several in English. There were so many signs, in fact, that Brody could see only about half a city block ahead before the street faded in a collage of signs, prayer flags, afternoon shade, and dust. Dozens of local men crisscrossed the lane, most of them merchants. Women weren't outdoors much here, unlike the rest of the city of Kathmandu with a population of one million. And he saw no children.

Locals, with brown eyes of suspicion, hid their glances toward Brody, but he read their faces. They thought they knew why he was there on that street. Curry houses, pizzerias, bars, bakeries, and ice cream parlors offered their enticements, but it was for sex that many foreigners came to that part of Thamel. The odor of cow dung lingered in the air, overpowering the incense burning. But even that assault to the senses didn't stifle the base lusts of visitors from being appeased.

The sex industry in Kathmandu was "training ground" for its seven thousand girls and women they exported just to India alone each year. An additional thirty thousand women were groomed in those very shops for export to the Middle East, elsewhere in Asia, and to Sub-Saharan Africa. South Korea and China accepted their share of exploited women for marriage, all with promises of good family life, citizenship, or job opportunities. Since prostitution was legal and trafficking wasn't exactly illegal in Nepal, Brody had found its women mistreated all over the world. Under debt bondage, men were inclined to sell their children, even their own wives. That was Binsa's story, so Brody felt personally touched by the filth of the Nepalese trafficking industry.

If Brody thought too much about the horrors being committed behind those signs and flimsy boards, he would've been overwhelmed with grief. Binsa had come from these streets, hampered by a caste system that diminished the value of life in general and recruited men, women, and children with offers of freedom.

Looking back down the street from where he'd come, Brody could see Zayed's tall, dark frame standing taller above the shorter Asian crowd. The Saudi was visiting with a shop owner, maybe in English, or maybe in a local dialect. Brody was still learning that Zayed had vast knowledge and experience, having been raised in Saudi's privileged class beside the royal family. The two men had stayed together in a hotel overlooking the city's "holy" Bagmati River, which was swollen with garbage and mud, but here, Zayed had agreed to return to his role as backup, like he'd been in Ukraine.

Brody ducked under a line that was burdened with a dozen prayer flags in red, blue, white, green, and yellow. It seemed everywhere he went in Kathmandu, he was ducking one form of paganism or another. South of Thamel was one of the Durbar Squares, and it hosted no less than fifty temples! The rest of the city was the same, claiming a harmonious existence while catering to Buddhists and Hindus simultaneously. But that harmony was supported by a passivity, Brody suspected, rooted in shame, depression, and desperation. Sadly, one of the most paganistic countries in the world was also one of the most abusive and impoverished, but few saw the connection between beliefs and conditions.

He passed through a curtained doorway into a dimly lit massage parlor. The pollution and mud of the ancient city was left behind for silk pillows and Eastern music biting the air from a scratchy speaker in the wall. A white woman in a Japanese *kimono* shuffled forward, her hair up in a blond pile of curls over eyes with too much mascara. Brody saw Marcy in her mother's face. Emma was shorter and wider than her daughter, and she looked more classy than Brody had expected to find in an ex-drug addict, as Marcy had described her.

"Welcome to Himalayan Paradise." She held a sheaf of menus in her hands. "English?"

"Yes, English."

She offered him a menu, and he accepted.

"Please, sit."

Wading through Indian pillows, he reached a low couch with a wide back, more like a bed, covered in some sort of soft hide.

"Is this your first time to Kathmandu?" she asked, then served him tea that smelled like chamomile.

"No, I've been here many times." Brody studied the menu. It offered not food but massage techniques, all of which included sensual descriptions. "It's not as busy as I remember from a few months ago."

"We've mostly recovered from the earthquake," she said, standing at a polite distance, her hands folded, "but now with this virus business . . ."

"Of course. But you have massage girls here?"

"Oh, yes, they're ready to serve. You're our first customer today, so we can accommodate you fully—for a price, you understand."

"I understand." He looked up from the menu. A shadow passed in front of the parlor curtain. Zayed was hovering. "There's a price I'm willing to pay, but not for any . . . massage. How much to buy you out?"

"Excuse me?" Emma took a step back, one hand straying to her throat. *"Buy me out?"*

"Yes. You, the girls, this whole place. How many girls do you have working here?"

"Nine, but that's not the point. They're not for sale."

"Everything and everyone's for sale, isn't it? What's your life worth?"

"My life?" Emma frowned. "Who are you?"

"I'm someone who's offering to buy you out."

"Well, I don't own this place. I just . . . run it for them."

"Them?"

"The owners. Associates."

"Locals or foreigners?"

"Some of both. I mean . . ." She glanced over her shoulder. "Maybe with how slow things are here, we could give up half the girls, but not the whole place. Do you want me to get one of the owners?"

"Yes, please, but I'd like you to be a part of the conversation."

Her face showed confusion.

"Okay. One moment, please."

She left the room. Brody stood and crossed to the beaded hallway to hear indistinguishable voices, at least one male, maybe two. Multiple doorways lined the hallway. The wallpaper and ornaments portrayed local customs, but otherwise, it was just like any other brothel Brody had infiltrated.

He returned to the couch a few seconds before a man entered wearing a traditional *daura*, a light blouse, and a *suruwal*, the baggy trousers of Nepal.

"I am Toofan," a bright-eyed, short Nepalese man greeted. "Our wonderful Emma tells me you have a business offer to make?"

Brody eyed the man, thinking how he could easily handle the fifty-year-old without much effort—when a younger, barrel-shaped man emerged from the back. This one was a giant, his hair carelessly kept like Brody imagined the Sherpa caste might have. The giant was obviously the parlor's security, a much greater obstacle than Brody had expected, but not one he hadn't prepared for.

"Yes, I have an interest in this part of Thamel," Brody said. "I'd like to buy this establishment as an investment and convert it into something more . . . helpful. Of course, I'll pay for everyone who works here—except you two men—I'll have to let you two go."

"But we are not selling." Toofan smiled uneasily. "You are very generous to offer to purchase this luxurious business, but we are a thriving company. We already have investors and many local clients."

"You're not thriving." Brody surveyed the room. "You have no customers. No income. You're losing money every day. Tell me: you have nine girls in the back. How much for all of them together?"

"We would never let them go." Toofan's smiled faded. "I am a businessman. No one leaves without a replacement."

"Replacement? Please explain."

"The girls here have been purchased. When their debt is paid, they may leave only when they find a replacement. If I sold you my nine, you would pay me for the nine, but I would require nine more. You see? I am a businessman."

For a moment, Brody was stumped, so he prayed for wisdom in what to say next. He knew what was necessary, but he wanted to ease into it.

"How much for Emma here?" Brody asked.

"I'm not for sale!" Emma stated. "I manage this place. That's all."

"Twenty thousand Euros," Toofan blurted, "and she is yours."

"Toofan!" Emma looked from the owner to Brody.

"No, I'm here to manage and help with recruiting. That's all! We have an agreement."

"This is business, and you are a woman." Toofan shrugged. "Agreements change."

Emma appeared trapped. The giant behind Toofan grinned, perhaps familiar with forcing the females under their roof to do whatever they wanted.

"Agreed," Brody said, and rose to his feet, though he wasn't sure he could respond too swiftly on the pillow-strewn floor. "But I'll want the other nine to stay on."

"No, they are not for sale without replacement."

"They're staying here," Brody said, "but I don't want to replace them. I'm buying them to remain here for a different job than they're doing now."

"There . . . seems to be some confusion here." Toofan chuckled uncomfortably. "Sir, you're obviously a man of wealth."

"Oh, I am."

"This is a business. You may pay for Emma and leave with her. She is not too old yet. That is the agreement. Leave with her—without the others."

"Hmm. No. That won't do." Brody wagged his finger. "You're right. Agreements do change. I am inclined to think we may not reach an agreement at all for any price. It may be best if you go ahead and leave, Mr. Toofan. Emma will be my new manager, if she agrees, and I'll simply have no use for the two of you. Thank you for your service."

Toofan looked to his security man, maybe to explain what was happening, but neither had an answer.

"We are not leaving." Toofan's voice rose. "You are leaving now, without Emma at all!"

"No, you're the one who is confused." Brody stepped carefully away from the pillows. He took Emma by the arm and guided her to his side, then moved up close to look down at Toofan. In his peripheral vision, Brody could see down the hallway where a broad-shouldered Arabian man approached in perfect silence. "I've had dealings with GLOW recently. Now, today, I'm here to take over Himalayan Paradise. Besides, I'm sure Emma and the other girls will like what it'll become. Maybe the Himalayan Clothing Shop, or something where they don't need to sell their bodies any longer. Would you like that, Emma?"

"You work for GLOW?" Emma asked. "Are we restructuring again? If we are, I want to go back to Europe."

"We'll get to that." Brody watched Toofan's face as it transformed through various emotions. "First, Toofan and his water buffalo need to leave. Toofan, if I see you around here again, well, you can imagine the amount of fury I might express."

"GLOW did not send you," Toofan responded. "No one called me."

"And why would they? Look." Brody scoffed at the room. "You waste your money on decorations instead of advertising. You have no customers and you've made no money today. You're not a very good businessman, Toofan."

"I will not leave." Toofan jabbed his finger into Brody's chest. "You leave, American!"

"Are you telling me that you want my bodyguard to throw you out onto the street? Or will you leave quietly?"

Emma cried out in surprise the instant they noticed they weren't alone. Zayed emerged from the hallway, his grenade in his left hand. Toofan and his man backed away, but Zayed approached the barrel-chested giant directly.

"Did you say you were leaving, Toofan?" Brody grabbed the man's shoulder and turned him to face him again. "You should know, I have friends in the government. If this shop or any of the girls here are harmed, I will know you've created the problem. Look at me, Toofan. Do I seem like a serious man to you?"

Toofan eyed the grenade held delicately by Zayed.

"Yes, you are a serious man."

"If we meet again, I will be very, very unhappy."

Toofan pulled his brute with him as they left, both showing angry expressions as they passed through the door.

Brody used his phone to call a local number as Zayed went to the door, took down the curtain, then tore down the Himalayan Paradise sign.

"This is Brody," he said on the phone. "Come on in. Everyone is waiting for you."

He hung up and nodded at Emma.

"You're really ready to go back to Europe? To be with your husband again or what?"

"Do you know Cole?" Her face lifted. "Is he mad at me?"

"I haven't asked him about that, but he returned to America. Last week, his daughter found him. She's taking care of him before he dies, which seems inevitable. He has liver disease."

"*What?*" Emma steadied herself by reaching out to hold onto his arm. "Marcy? Marcy is with Cole? *My* Marcy?"

Brody watched her painted face. Her eyes still revealed some maternal care. She hadn't been lost altogether, though she'd run far from her past.

"Your daughter's name is Marcy?" Brody nodded. "Good to know. Maybe we could get her to come here and work for you, huh?"

"What? No! No, she should stay in America. Cole . . . probably needs her."

"Yeah, maybe you're right. But what about you? Don't you need her, too?"

She looked away, but not before Brody glimpsed tears.

"They're here," Zayed announced from the front door.

"Who's here?" Emma asked.

"Friends. Friends of mine. And friends of yours."

CHAPTER NINE

Emma Nevins felt like she'd entered another reality. She watched the one who called himself Brody take charge of her brothel like he was a coach taking charge of a sports team.

"Make sure the back door is secure," he ordered his dark-skinned friend who'd come through the back. "Are all nine girls in their own rooms? Emma? The girls are in their own spaces, right?"

"Yes. Um . . ." She touched her hair, wondering what kind of boss this Brody would be. Some bosses were cruel and others were gentler, but all had made it clear that she was there to be used. Even when she'd been with Cole, she'd been required to have sex with some of the others in GLOW leadership. Twice, she'd been raped, even while she was supposedly trusted to manage GLOW's commodities. "Yeah, they're all here. They live here with me."

"Okay, help me get all these pillows off the floor. We'll have company in a few minutes."

Emma stooped with him to pile the love-pillows in the far corner next to the couch. She studied Brody's face and hands while he helped her. His hands seemed gnarled and a little meaty, definitely calloused. His voice had been firm with Toofan, yet now he wasn't exerting his power, only some authority, but she wasn't sure who'd given him the authority to take over the brothel.

"Am I yours now?" she asked quietly before his friend returned. "Usually, I come with . . . the furniture. I mean, you seem nice. I'm just trying to figure out what to expect. You . . . know my family, but . . . uh, I don't know what to expect."

"Yeah, you said that." He held his hand out, palm up. "Give me your hand."

She set her hand in his. His were definitely a laborer's hands, but when he closed his fingers over hers, and placed his other hand on top, she felt weak from her head to her knees.

"You're Cole's wife, are you not?"

"Yeah. I mean, we never got divorced. But I've . . . GLOW has passed me around with the different jobs. It's always been that way."

"Well, that's over with now, okay?" He patted her hand. "You and the girls—I'd like you all to take this time to look at life in a new way. The past has been pretty bad, right?"

"That's . . . an understatement."

"You've made some really bad choices, and others have made bad choices that impacted you, too, right?"

"Um . . . yeah. Big time."

"Well, that ends today. Unless you want to run off to be passed around like the furniture again."

"No. But what do I do now?"

"This is Zayed, my close friend."

The Middle Eastern man stepped up. But instead of offering his hand, he bowed from the waist.

"It's a pleasure, Ms. Nevins. I am your servant. Marcy and Aidan have become recent friends of mine. They anticipate seeing you again soon."

"Aidan?" Emma's hand went to her throat. It was hard to breathe. Her eyes misted. "And Marcy, too? They're really okay?"

"They've been through a lot—for years," Brody said. "We found Aidan in Bangkok, and Marcy escaped that place in Davenport where you left them. Yeah, they still have some healing to do, but they'll be fine in God's loving arms. Aidan throws a mean baseball, I tell you."

"He is inseparable from his baseball glove," Zayed said with a smile.

"Baseball?" Emma gasped, then turned away. "No, it's not true. I mean, it's not right. I . . . can't . . . You don't understand. They can't want to see me. What I did . . . Who I am . . ." She flinched when Brody set a hand on her shoulder from behind.

"They remember, especially Marcy. And they have scars. They've been hurt. But they've survived. Not many do. They're overcomers. Marcy found strength by trusting in God and His Son who was sent to comfort the brokenhearted. Emma, they don't hate you. This was all Marcy's idea—to find you."

"It was?" She turned to face him.

"Yes, she sent us." Brody chuckled. "She's a stubborn one, that young lady."

"She looks good? I mean, she grew out of her . . . goofiness? Marcy's a woman now? She must be almost twenty-three now."

"Marcy's a fine young lady," Brody assured.

"What about GLOW?" she asked.

"GLOW may always be around," Brody said. "Do you know the name Sladrick?"

"Of course. I've been around enough to know about him."

"So, what do you know of him?"

"He . . . takes back what GLOW has made its own."

"Yeah, I suppose that's what I do." Brody smiled. "I'm Sladrick, Emma. Brody Sladrick."

"You're Sladrick? You?"

"Yes. Now do you think I know how to deal with GLOW?"

"Huh." She looked around the room. "I'd say you have some idea what you're up against. I've never seen Toofan kneel to anyone before. You're really Sladrick?"

"I'm just a man God chooses to use. And that's what gives us our edge. We have what GLOW could never have."

"What's that?"

"God's mighty support."

"You keep talking about Him. I don't really . . . know anything about him."

"The GLOW network tries to replace what God has provided: family, love, intimacy, security, purpose. GLOW counterfeits what God intends to be true and real and pure. Those who live in God's reality will always stand more firmly than those who make up fairytales in sex rooms to cope with life's challenges. May I ask you about your health?"

"My health?" Emma clutched her midsection. "What about it?"

"I've seen old photos of you. You were skin and bone then, unhealthy-looking. But you seem to have put on some healthy weight—the right amount, I mean, if I'm any judge at all of these things. Are you still using or are you clean?"

"No, I haven't . . ." Emma touched the inside of one elbow where track scars still remained. "When I left Cole two years ago, I cleaned up. Well, in some ways. I should've stayed with him. You said he's dying?"

"He's not well, but he's in Marcy's good hands until you're there to help. If that's what you want."

"Is Cole with the . . . God stuff now, too?"

"Well, he's coming around." Brody grinned. "Your kids can be very persuasive when they know what's best."

"I wasn't even a mother to them." Emma gazed at the far corner of the room, remembering a different time. "I think it's too late to be their mother now."

"Nope." Brody frowned. "Kick that foul kind of thinking out of your head. As long as anyone is alive, it's not too late to repent and reconcile."

The front door opened, and three Nepalese men and three Nepalese women walked in, their arms full of bags of clothes and food.

"Brody!" one of the men shouted and shook Brody's hand heartily. "How are you, my American brother? And how is Binsa? Did she find herself a husband yet? When will we see her again? Has she forgotten this is her home?”

“Slow down!” Brody laughed. “One question at a time. How about this place? Can the church here keep this place running the right way?”

“No problem.” The Nepalese man rested his hands on his hips and admired the room. “Now that you’ve run off the traffickers, we will make it a productive business for the girls. A clothing store, you said? Yes, something to bring the light of Jesus to a dark street. True?”

“True.”

“You must be Emma,” one of the Tibetan wives said, with the two others gathering closely. They were modestly dressed, but they didn’t seem to shy away from her, in her figure-clinging *kimono*. “Can you introduce us to the girls in the back? Do you think they will leave their old lifestyle? Are their debts large or small? Would they like to become clothing retailers? We have many ideas for this place. Do you know how to operate a sewing machine?”

Speechless, Emma looked to Brody for help.

“It’s overwhelming, I know.” He waved his hand. “Just go with them. Everything will be fine. This isn’t the first brothel in Kathmandu they’ve repurposed.”

Emma was swept into the back hallway by the Nepalese women who conversed excitedly in English and Nepalese interchangeably. When she looked back at the front room, Brody and Zayed were looking after her. It must’ve been God, she realized right then in awe, who’d brought them here. They had opened impossible doors, doors she’d thought could never be opened again. Hope had returned to her life of slavery, bondage she’d welcomed in moments of drug-induced sensuality.

Her family, her children—they wanted her back!

Though Emma didn’t know the women around her yet, she fell upon them, weeping uncontrollably. And they comforted her. She couldn’t remember the embrace of anyone who wanted only to help her, but they held her in those moments, moving her into a new reality, as Brody had talked about.

When she finally recovered, she began to learn their names, then called out the working girls from their rooms.

"These women will help you get a fresh start," Emma introduced.

"Yes, we will help you learn a trade," one woman explained, "and our husbands will help protect you. You will be safe here now. Some of the people in our church are city administrators. We know policemen and at least one mayor we can trust. And we will teach you all about Jesus, who rescues us all from the shame and guilt of sin!"

The nine girls, normally reserved and shunned, began to speak all at once—to Emma and to the three newcomers. It didn't seem possible that a place that had dealt the girls such fear and pain could now offer them care and promise.

Emma checked her emotions. It was one thing to give these girls a fresh direction and healthy employment, but America and her family were a long way away. She didn't want to place too much hope in what Brody had told her about her family wanting to see her again. How could they have anything but hatred for her? She'd abandoned Cole in Ukraine and sold her children years ago. No, it wasn't possible to be their mother!

But, if there was a chance to be with them again . . .

Aidan threw the baseball in a low arc to his father, aiming for his chest like Brody had taught him. His father threw it back with precision Aidan hadn't expected. They were playing on the lawn in front of Brody's apartment building, the Florida sunshine comfortable that mid-morning.

"Who taught you to play catch?" Aidan asked.

"I played baseball in junior high," Cole said. "My coach taught me, then I played with my friends a lot."

"Why didn't you ever play catch with me?"

He didn't mean to accuse his father, but Brody had assured him that with the right heart, he and his dad might need to talk about some of the messy things as they got to know one another, then forgive and move on forever. Although Aidan was pretty sure he'd already forgiven his dad, he was still curious about many things from his youth.

"Probably because I was more interested in getting high with your mom. Mostly, I was just stupid, Addy. I should've done a lot of things differently."

"Oh."

Aidan tossed the ball back. He could've backed up to throw the ball from a greater distance, but this was the right distance to play catch and still talk without having to yell.

"Brody said he'd take us sailing when he gets back with Mom. Have you ever been sailing?"

"Nope." Cole dropped the ball. Weakly, he picked it up, reminding Aidan how sick he was. "Not too many oceans to sail in Iowa."

"There are *no* oceans in Iowa," Aidan said. "That's geography."

"Yep, that's true. You're gonna be ripe for college at the rate your sister is schooling you."

"But I don't want to go to college. You and Brody didn't go. Marcy says I can serve God any way I want, as long as my heart is pure."

"Yeah? So, what are you going to do?"

"I want to do what Brody and Zayed do."

"What does Brody do?" Cole stopped throwing and walked closer. "Do you know what he does, Aidan?"

"Well, not really. I guess he helps people like us, right?"

Cole sat down on the grass next to Aidan. The man seemed winded.

"I've never known men like Brody and Zayed, but if

you want to be like them, that would make me a proud father."

"So, what do they do exactly?"

"They go into dangerous places and help people, like you said. From what I understand, Brody and Greg teamed up first. Then came Binsa. I'm still trying to figure out what Jesus is all about, but He seems to be their inspiration."

"God forgave us all so we can all be better people. Marcy knows a lot more. She's teaching me to memorize verses in the Bible."

"Bible verses, huh?"

"And Binsa tests me on what I learn. There's Samson, Paul, David—he killed a giant—and a guy named Moses who couldn't speak right, so God gave him his brother to help him."

"Yeah, it sounds like you're learning it all."

"That's not all—Math, world history, English. Yuck, man, I hate grammar."

"The Nevins men have never been too sharp on grammar."

"I think I need to study other languages, though. Binsa said she'll start teaching me after she gets better. She said she's learned a little bit of a lot of languages traveling with Brody, but Brody knows more than her. Brody didn't even learn English until he was my age, she said."

"They're good people. You're definitely on the right track, Addy. You know, if I could live my life again, I'd try to do it like you are right now."

"Yeah?" Aidan looked at his dad, his chest swelling with joy. "Baseball and learning Bible stories?"

"Yep. It's better than all those video games I bought you when you were a kid."

"Now I hate video games." Aidan felt himself scowl. "Those people who had me in Thailand—that's all they gave me—three stupid games to play. For years. It was torture, let me tell you. But not as bad as that other stuff."

Cole didn't say anything for a moment, then Aidan realized his dad was softly crying.

"Sorry, Dad. I didn't mean to bring it up again." Aidan patted his dad's arm. "Marcy says that blaming others doesn't help anyone, so I don't blame you. Brody said I'm a man now, so I need to take responsibility and trust God to use the bad things to make good things in life. He said it's like taking a bunch of mud and building a house out of it. God takes the useless and makes something useful. That's why I can use what happened and help others. And that's what Binsa said she does, too. God helps people like her. We don't have to stay in the mud like pigs."

The front door of the apartment building opened, and Binsa walked out with Marcy. The two sat on the bench that faced the sun.

"Binsa's face is healing," Aidan said. "She's not mad about what Jerome did to her. Would you be mad?"

"It would be hard not to be mad." Cole sighed. "Their faith in God makes them strong, I guess. You stay on that path, son. You'll keep getting stronger."

"Marcy said Brody and Zayed must've set Jerome straight, but they didn't hurt him. How do you figure they did that?"

"They didn't share any details with me, but they're men of honor. I'm sure they did it right."

"Yeah, I'm sure, too. I'll ask Brody sometime when we're alone. Hey! There's Brody!"

Struggling to his feet, Aidan watched as Brody pulled up in his car. But there was a blond woman in the passenger seat, and Zayed sat in the back. He felt a queasiness in his stomach.

"Dad? I think that's Mom. But I'm not sure I remember what she looks like."

"Help me up." Cole used Aidan's growing strength to reach his feet. "Yep, that's your mom."

Aidan looked back at Marcy and Binsa, who hadn't noticed Brody's arrival yet.

Brody climbed out of the car, followed by Zayed and Emma. Zayed and Brody fetched luggage as his mom stood nervously on the sidewalk. Aidan watched as she admired the park-like grass, despite the homeless people camping nearby, then she turned her face up toward the sunshine.

"You think she remembers me?" Aidan asked.

"Remembers you?" Cole grunted. "Yeah, she's your mother. She's probably thought of you every day of your life, you and your sister."

"Should I wait for Marcy?" Aidan licked his lips. "Mom hasn't seen us yet. I'm going to go to her. You okay?"

"Yep. You go ahead. I'm right behind you."

Aidan started forward. His mother was so short! He guessed that was because he was so tall now. Suddenly, he stopped and looked back to where his father stood. The baseball and their mits remained on the grass. It was the first time he'd been without his glove since Brody had given it to him. But he was a man now. He didn't need his glove right now, not with his mother here.

As he approached her, he held his head erect and his shoulders back, the way Brody had told him that dependable men presented themselves to others. His mother saw him, her eyes lingered, then moved past him. For an instant, Aidan realized she hadn't recognized him because he'd indeed grown up. But then her gaze returned to him, and her hand went to her throat as if she were struggling to breathe.

"Mom!" He grinned and held his good arm wide long before he reached her.

"Oh, Addy!" She stumbled forward across the grass.

The instant she started to fall, he caught her and held her upright. Her head reached only to his shoulder. His own mother seemed so weak, so fragile, so important to protect. He turned and waved his arm.

"Marcy! Come on! It's Mom!"

One month later, Marcy sat uncomfortably at the low table in the Iowa State Women's Facility south of Des Moines. She and Binsa had rented a car to reach the prison. But she wanted to do this alone, so only Marcy had gone inside the correctional facility.

The visiting room was only sparsely filled, mostly with children visiting their mothers or boyfriends visiting their girlfriends. A correctional officer in the screening wing had said the virus was scaring people away, so it was a slow visiting weekend.

Marcy touched her wrist from where she'd had to remove her watch to enter. It had been the pink watch that Tory Dosier had given her to schedule her chores in the house of bondage. For a year, she'd worn it out of convenience, but she'd realized she'd actually worn it for a different reason. The watch, much like her scars, reminded her from where she'd come, from where God had brought her.

And at that instant, Tory passed through an electronic door. The small woman was clothed in blue pants and smock. Tori searched the visiting room. The processing officer outside had said this was the first visit the poor woman had received since being given her lengthy prison sentence.

Rising from her seat, Marcy waved at Tory. From that distance, she saw Tory's recognition of her, then her lips moved, obviously with a curse. The woman glanced at the pair of officers who sat at the elevated desk nearby, perhaps wondering how monitored the visit would be, or if Marcy would be protected if she were to attack her.

But Marcy wasn't afraid, even if Tory did attack her. Instead, when Tory reached the table, Marcy stepped close, smiled, and gave the woman an allowed brief embrace, then backed away.

"So, you're surprised to see me." Marcy gestured at the chairs. "Sit. I bought some snacks from the vending machines. You want the chicken sandwich or the steak quesadilla?"

Tory sat uneasily, her frown impossible to miss.

"What are you doing here?" Tory grunted and checked the other tables of visitors. "We're not family. People are going to think you're my daughter. I don't want anything from you."

"Oh, I know." Marcy smiled, then took a deep breath. "But we have history together. I feel like I grew up around you. We've seen each other at our worst. When I heard you'd been sentenced, and I hadn't been called to testify, I thought I'd come see you anyway."

"For what?" Tory scowled. "No one else is going to visit me. I had to sign a plea agreement. Even my stupid brother tried to testify against me for a lighter sentence."

"He may have testified against you," Marcy said, "but it didn't help him. PJ received a much, much longer sentence than you did, so he'll never get out."

"Neither will I." Tory looked away.

"Do you remember all those books from the basement I used to read?" Marcy waited.

"Yeah. So what?"

"There was one subject that I read about more than the others. It helped me in my place of, well, captivity. Now you're being disciplined in your place of captivity. I think what I learned will help you and give you hope, too, Tory."

"Hope? In here?"

"Yes, even in here. You think this place is worse than me being locked in a room where PJ abused me for so long? I still found hope, and so can you. It's a true story about a boat and a man named Noah."

"Noah?" Tory frowned. "The Bible story?"

"So, you've heard of it?"

"Um, yeah." Tory narrowed her eyes. "Our parents

were Bible freaks. I remember all those stories. Why would you want to tell me about Noah and the ark?"

"Your crime and your sentence, Tory, are nothing compared to what's coming. There's a flood of judgment coming. God wants you to get ready for that. Heaven is real, but hell is, too."

"You've lost your mind, Marcy. PJ hit you too many times."

"Well, I can't argue with you there." Marcy smiled. "I mean, look at my face, right? But look, I might be the only real friend you've got. And we have some food here for us on the table. Why not visit awhile?"

Tory wrestled for a response.

"Okay. Whatever." She picked up the chicken sandwich. "At least this is better than the noise back in the unit."

"Do you have your own room?"

"No, I wish! I live in this eight-person dorm. My bunky is this woman from Arizona. Tattoos all over. Head to toe."

"Tattoos?" Marcy laughed. "You're not going to get any, are you?"

"Yeah, like I need a disease from one of those needles!" Tory scoffed, chewing on her sandwich. "She's not that bad, though, my bunky, since she shares her TV. We watch soaps together."

Marcy nodded, listening to Tory as the needy soul she was, rather than the woman who deserved punishment. She waited for God to steer the conversation back to the gospel, Noah, and judgment. But for now, she listened. Tory had never visited with Marcy in her youth. Now, they were both women, both sitting in a prison visiting room, each with a tangled past from the same horrid place.

But God wanted even Tory to become His child. Marcy wasn't returning with Binsa to her new home in Florida until she'd fully shared the real reason she'd come to visit. It was only because of Jesus Christ that Marcy still cared for Tory Dosier, the human trafficker.

Greg stood at the helm of a forty-foot sailboat beyond the mouth of Tampa Bay. It was midday, the air was still, so the sails were hanging. He had his shirt off, his slender frame showing his bones through his skin, but Greg didn't care what he looked like. He was happy to be out with his friends, even if there was no breeze at the moment. Contentedly, he listened to the casual chit-chat of his friends.

Zayed sat with Cole near the bow, and Brody and Aidan lounged middeck in front of the mast, wearing only swim trunks. It was a perfect day, the first time the five had been out on their own without Binsa, Marcy, or Emma—though Greg really didn't mind Marcy's company at all. In fact, he was mustering the courage to talk to Brody about asking Marcy to marry him. It wasn't likely he'd find a more wonderful woman, he guessed, so he should just pop the question and get an apartment of their own on the floor TROAS owned.

But that opened up a can of worms: apartments. Since Emma had arrived, Zayed had been bunking with him, Aidan, and Brody. Marcy and Binsa were each living in their own apartments, while Emma and Cole were staying in Zayed's apartment. But Cole didn't have long to live. That day, Zayed had carried the man onto the sailboat, his legs too weak to support his weight. Binsa was making hospice arrangements openly, like nobody expected anything else. But the family was together. They had a past uglier than Greg had ever heard of any family having, but with Marcy on one side, and Binsa and Brody on the other, they'd pulled together. Emma was even talking about God, though never without tears in her eyes.

"I want to rescue people like you do," Aidan suddenly said to Brody that lazy afternoon.

"Yeah?" Brody didn't open his eyes, nor did he lift his

head from the deck. "You've got to be content with what God has brought you through."

"I am."

"You've got to have such focused faith in God's goodness that you're not limited at all by anyone to do His will."

"I've got faith. I'm learning all about Jesus from Marcy."

"And you'll have to suffer. It's part of being a follower of Him."

"Well, I've been through a lot," Aidan said. "I'm ready. I mean, my body doesn't work too well, but Binsa says that's okay. I've got God now, so I'll be fine."

Brody leaned up on one elbow.

"There's some training you'll need to start with. But you'll never stop learning. That's what God does. He trains us on the job—getting us ready for Christ's appearing, and we help others get ready for heaven, too."

"Yeah, I could do that." Aidan yawned. "Greg says I'm pretty strong. And I'll get stronger. I'm almost eighteen. He wasn't much older when he went to Asia for his first mission."

"I remember," Brody said. "I had the privilege of training Greg down in Mexico. Quite a few of the others who were in his class are now in international prisons, or they've been killed during their own missions."

"If God wants me to, I'd die for others, too," Aidan said.

"That's a good attitude to have." Brody glanced at Greg and winked. "I suppose there's only one thing to do then, and that's your initiation into the TROAS Training Camp, eh, Greg?"

"Yeah, the T-T-C," Greg said, playing along. "It's initiation time, Aidan."

"What's initiation?"

Zayed sat up from the bow.

"Don't listen to them, Aidan," the Saudi believer said. "They're up to something."

"It's the TROAS plunge," Brody said. "You can't really start your training without it."

"The TROAS plunge?" Aidan rolled over. "What's that?"

"Well, do you see that sea gull up there?" Brody pointed.

"Where? I don't—"

As soon as Aidan turned to look, Brody rose to a low crouch, scooped up Aidan's lanky frame, and leaped overboard, throwing Aidan as they plunged together.

Aidan surfaced, sputtering and laughing.

"I can't . . . *swim!*" Aidan managed to scream between shrieks of laughter.

Brody scrambled back on board and offered his hand to Aidan. He hauled the youth back on deck.

"Congratulations, Master Aidan!" Greg saluted from the helm. "You've been initiated into the TROAS Training Camp!"

"Okay." He faced Brody, still coughing. "What's first?"

"Well, I don't see how we can get started without giving Zayed an initiation of his own."

"Now, stay away from me." Zayed jumped to his feet." "You two, stay back!"

"It's the TROAS plunge!" Aidan cheered, driving Zayed farther up the bow.

Greg smiled and watched the sails fill then ebb in the wind. It was a perfect day, but only because they'd gotten away from it all. Soon, Brody would go out again, maybe to hunt GLOW's Executive. Zayed would go with him, and then Binsa would help the survivors recover. And Marcy would be there to help, somehow. And it seemed that Aidan would be as well. Only time would tell what God had in store for Cole and Emma.

TROAS had changed a lot in the last two months because of the people who'd joined their cause for Christ. As long as TROAS was there, they would help repentant people learn of God's love and forgiveness, no matter what earthly crimes they'd committed, or the suffering they'd endured. Yes, TROAS could do that, since it was made up of believers who'd suffered sin's consequences but had overcome through Christ. And every step of the way, they'd never been lost from God's hand of love and care.

Until Christ came for His church, there would always be another mission for TROAS. The lost were out there. They just needed to be found.

Thanks for reading!
I pray you have been blessed by *Hidden Humanity*.
Please leave your comments wherever you bought this
book. That will help me know if I hit the mark
with my writing. Thank you!—*David Telbat*

WHAT'S NEXT?

Book Two, *SHADOW SLAVE*, is next
in the *NEVER LOST SERIES*. Enjoy the teaser below.

Shadow Slave
Book Two

Ram Garrity is arrested and charged as an adult for selling stolen goods when he is only seventeen years old. Due to California's soft-on-crime policies, he spends only two weeks behind bars. But that is long enough for him to connect with other criminals who can better satisfy his lust for money and power.

When Ram is released from jail, instead of returning home to his praying father, he travels to the southern border in a stolen vehicle. There, he connects with junior bosses in the Mexican cartel who smuggle drugs and people into the U.S. The professional criminals find Ram to be both daring and cruel in their border enterprise. But it is in his ingenious methods to smuggle humans that promote him to a junior boss within a year.

The following year, Ram grows in influence and violently takes over his peers' responsibilities. His fame and viciousness spread, while law enforcement hunt him day and night. Civilians live or die at Ram's word, and that draws the attention of recovery specialist Brody Sladrick.

Brutally, Ram has risen to power at a young age. His

generals fear him and obey his every word. He keeps them wealthy and satisfied with money and women, and they keep him in power and influence. But Brody Sladrick—alias RefugeGate—interrupts Ram's life and forces the troubled youth to examine from where he came—the childhood he ran from, the father he left behind, the faith he abandoned . . .

Join Brody Sladrick and the TROAS network of believers as they confront human trafficking at the U.S. southern border in Book Two of the *Never Lost Series: Shadow Slave.*

God never loses those who are His!

END NOTES FOR HIDDEN HUMANITY

Reaching the Trafficked
who are Never Lost to God

VISION BEYOND BORDERS

"I believe God wants to bring this subject into the light and get people praying and involved in helping."
—**Patrick Klein**, founder of Vision Beyond Borders

Please refer to the Author's Note at the front of this book for more info & links. The following are just parts and pieces of the greater picture. Let's all be praying.

A FEW FACTS

➤ Many tribal girls from Laos, Burma and Vietnam are taken as child brides to China.
➤ Unsuspecting parents think they are sending their kids to the city to work and are instead sending them to the wolves. China has been used to destroy many lives.
➤ Many victims are women and girls who are especially vulnerable due to lack of education and limited work opportunities. Desperate for a way to feed themselves, they are coerced and then trafficked for sex.

Nepali Women Currently
Trafficked Around the World:

- 54 women are trafficked out of Nepal every day.
- 54,000 women trafficked in Nepal
- 200,000 Nepali women trafficked in India
- 300,000 Nepali women trafficked in the Middle East
- Growing by Hundreds in Sub-Saharan Africa
- Increasing by thousands in China, South Korea, Hong Kong, Malaysia, Myanmar, and Russia

- Ex-marines are getting involved to fight trafficking as governments are not doing much.
- Trafficking is increasing in the U.S. Girls are being sold off Indian reservations. Hunters are using girls when they go deer hunting, even parents are trafficking their kids.
- 200,000 women and girls have been trafficked from North Korea and 100,000 are trapped in rooms and used for online sex.

~~*~*

The following info can be found on the Vision Beyond Borders website at <u>visionbeyondborders.org</u>.

Vision Beyond Borders is committed to helping women and children that are enslaved in sex trafficking around the world. Our goal is always to bring hope and healing one life at a time by working with our contacts to spread awareness and prevent trafficking before it occurs, provide resources for those still trapped, offer safety and rehabilitation for those who have been rescued or have escaped, and, most importantly, show each person the love and redemption of Jesus Christ.

Vision Beyond Borders partners with several Safehouses, Gospel-centered Homes, and/or orphanages. A few of them are listed here.

~~*~*

<u>Romania Safe House</u>

This is a **Gospel-centered facility** designed to **rescue girls from the clutches of sex-trafficking** and integrate them from orphanages to local culture with Biblical understanding, life skills and an occupation.

Vision Beyond Borders (VBB) has set up a safe house in the small town of Lipova where girls are cared for in a Christian environment and taught the basics of building a life. Over the period of 1-1.5 years, girls are taught necessary life skills, given job opportunities and loved on by Christian staff. VBB's ultimate goal is to teach them the ways of Christ by demonstrating the Gospel of Jesus. The home serves orphaned girls who have aged out of the government system, girls who have been abused by family members, widows who have nowhere to go, and women who have escaped abusive relationships where their spouse or partner was likely to traffic them.

Join VBB to put an end to trafficking. This battle isn't defensive. We're taking the fight directly to the traffickers' backyards. For years, Romanian girls have been deceived into a lifestyle of sex-trafficking. In Romania, girls in the orphanages age out at 18. They are expected to start their lives with only $33 dollars, no trained skill sets, and no Biblical worldview. VBB offers you an opportunity to directly influence the lives of Romanian girls by joining this team to end trafficking before it even begins.

~~*~*

India – Day & Night Care Center
+ Brothel Ministry

Since February 2018, **India's Day & Night Care Center** has been a light in the midst of darkness. It provides a safe and Christ-filled atmosphere **where mothers in the red-light district can send their children** during times when they are unable to care for them. The children who attend have a safe place to play, receive basic lessons in reading and writing, and hear Christ-centered teaching. The goal for the center is ultimately that the Lord will use it to **help end the perpetual cycle of the children born into the red-light district being sold** into the red-light life or exploited by those who would do them harm by providing them with a safe place to go during the most dangerous times of the day, basic educational skills, and a solid Christian foundation. The staff at the Center also work to facilitate opportunities for the children attending the program to become enrolled in schools outside the red-light district. We partner to provide support for the needs of the care center, including well balanced meals and pay for the staff there.

The **Brothel Ministry** in India works to give hope to women in the red-light districts by providing resources, education, skills training, counselling, food aid, basic legal help, and medical care when possible. Through a variety of programs such as Salon Skills, Spoken English Class, Literacy Empowerment, and Livelihood Trainings, **women in the brothels are given crucial tools they will need for creating a new life outside the red-light district** and are introduced to the love and of Jesus.

~~*~*

United States

While our focus is mainly international work, Vision Beyond Borders is also seeking to fight human trafficking at home as **trafficking is increasing in the U.S**. By hosting conferences, visiting with community businesses that are likely to come into contact with trafficking situations, and sharing at churches, our goal is to spread awareness of the issue and unite the community in fighting trafficking in our own country. Our prayer is that we would be able to serve those who want to know more about how they can be involved in the United States by putting them in touch with a number of **Christian organizations that are actively doing anti-trafficking work in the United States**. We pray that many would join the fight against trafficking in our own country. Contact VBB to learn more.

~~*~*

Visit visionbeyondborders.org/women/ to download the
Women's Prayer Guide.
Visit visionbeyondborders.org/children/ to download the
Children's Prayer Guide.

~~*~*

Asha House of Rest (Nepal)

This **safehouse and orphanage** in Nepal is actively rescuing women and children out of brothels and red-light districts in India and Nepal. They provide them with a safe place to stay while they recover from the trauma and abuse they have endured over the years.

Due to the outbreak of COVID, this home has been having tough times. They couldn't receive some of their expected funds, donations, and support this past year, and are now in financial crisis.

Please join us in praying for **Asha Hetauda** and **Asha House of Rest**. VBB has been able to send some funding to assist them, but the hardships they are facing due to COVID could become an even larger problem. Pray for health to be restored in Nepal and pray that the Lord would help provide financial security for these homes.

Pray that the children would continue to learn and grow stronger in their faith during these hard times.

~~*~*

Ms. Emerald's Home (Mayanmar/Burma)

Located in a primarily Buddhist community, Ms. Emerald's is one of the largest homes VBB supports. It's **home to many children who have experienced traumatic situations**. In a war-torn nation these children have seen their families killed and homes destroyed. Yet, the love of God is shown to them in their new home.

You can learn more about this home and the **story of Ms. Emerald** in Pam Johnson's **new book, *Though I Run Through the Valley*.** All proceeds from the book directly support the home and the children living there. Find it at: visionbeyondborders.org/books-to-read/.

To **meet Ms. Emerald**, watch a **short trailer** as well as the new wonderful (25 min) **documentary called *"They Call Me Mother."*** Find these videos at visionbeyondborders.org/the-story-of-miss-emerald/.

~~*~*

Safe Haven Home (Pakistan)

This home was started when two of VBB's main partners in Bible distribution **felt God calling them to**

reach the 1.5 million street children in Pakistan. At Safe Haven they are provided with a loving, Christ-centered home to grow up in. The kids quickly grow to love their new brothers and sisters in the home, which strengthens the family dynamic for all of the kids. As the COVID pandemic arrived in Pakistan, the government ordered children's homes like Safe Haven to close.

Clara's update: "There are 15 kids in the home now. Our house is really **maxed out on space**, so we are praying the Lord will provide a bigger place so we can bring in more children. Azeem is always receiving calls about new kids. This is an urgent matter to pray about.

"We now have hired three professional teachers for the kids. They are doing a lot better in their schooling now. After I arrived back in Pakistan, I was reading the children's books with them in the evening and noticed their books were really lacking. They have to use state approved books in Pakistan, in order to graduate and get a diploma here. So, Azeem brought them very good books which were more expensive, but they will get a good education.

"We are **teaching them Answers in Genesis Sunday school lessons**. We want them to have a good foundation for their faith; so, they will not believe lies in the future which would destroy their faith in God's Word. A percussion teacher comes twice a week and teaches the kids authentic Pakistani music. I am also teaching them mandolin, guitar and ukulele. We can only live and exist by the daily protection of the Lord."

~~*~*

Find these and many other ministries, safehouses, orphanages, and homes at <u>VisionBeyondBorders.org</u>. And please be praying for them and for safety as they travel to deliver Bibles, medicines, and other needs.

ABOUT THE AUTHOR

D.I. (David) Telbat is a Christian author best known for his **clean, Suspenseful Fiction with a Faith Focus**. This includes his bestselling and award-winning *COIL Series*, *Steadfast Series*, *Last Dawn Series*, and other Christian Suspense and End Times novels. He wrote his first book at age 14, and he hasn't stopped since!

David studied writing in school and worked for a time in the newspaper field. Getting into serious trouble with the law as a young man became a turning point in his life. The Lord used that experience to draw David into a personal relationship with Him. Re-focusing his life for Christ, he now seeks to honor God with his life and writing by doing what he loves most—writing and Christian ministry.

Subscribe to receive David Telbat's FREE, bi-weekly **D.I. Telbat Newsletter** with one of his Christian short stories, or an Author Reflection, or his Novel News Update. You'll also receive **exclusive subscriber gifts**, such as his ***Three For Free***—three-novels-in-one eBook! You can join the adventure by visiting his site at books2read.com/DITelbat/ and click on the "**Follow this Author**" button.